THE JUST AND THE UNJUST

Books by James Gould Cozzens

S.S. SAN PEDRO (1931)
THE LAST ADAM (1933)
CASTAWAY (1934)
MEN AND BRETHREN (1936)
ASK ME TOMORROW (1940)
THE JUST AND THE UNJUST (1942)
GUARD OF HONOR (1948)
BY LOVE POSSESSED (1957)
CHILDREN AND OTHERS (1964)
MORNING NOON AND NIGHT (1968)

The Just
and
the Unjust

JAMES GOULD COZZENS

A HARVEST/HBJ BOOK
Harcourt Brace Jovanovich, Publishers
San Diego   New York   London

Library of Congress Catalog Card Number 42-17992

0-15-646578-7

To EDWARD G. BIESTER

Cuilibet in arte sua perito est credendum
COKE ON LITTLETON, 125

Certainty is the Mother of Repose;
therefore the Law aims at Certainty.

LORD HARDWICKE

THE JUST AND THE UNJUST

RECORD

DOCKET ENTRIES

May Thirty-First, 1939, Wednesday, Court called at 10:00 o'clock A.M. Honorable Horace Irwin, President Judge, and Honorable Thomas F. Vredenburgh, Judge, presiding.

Eo die, the District Attorney, Martin M. Bunting, Esq., moves the Court for leave to submit Bill of Indictment Number Nineteen, May Sessions, to the Grand Jury.

Eo die, Leave is granted the District Attorney to submit the above Bill of Indictment Number Nineteen, May Sessions, charging Stanley Howell, Robert Basso, and Roy Leming with Murder, to the Grand Jury.

Eo die, Affidavit that Robert Basso is an Indigent Person filed.

Eo die, Petition of Robert Basso, a destitute person, for Counsel, filed.

And now, to wit, May Thirty-First, 1939, upon consideration of the within Petition, it appearing to the Court that the Deponent, Robert Basso, is wholly destitute of means to employ Counsel and prepare for his defense, the Court hereby appoints George Henderson Stacey, Esq., a Member of the Bar of this County, to represent the said Robert Basso upon trial of the said cause, and to prepare his defense. By the Court. Horace Irwin, P.J.

Eo die, Court adjourned at 5:30 o'clock P.M.

June Twelfth, 1939, Monday, Court called at 10:00 o'clock A.M., Honorable Horace Irwin, President Judge, and Honorable Thomas F. Vredenburgh, Judge, presiding.

Eo die, the Defendants, Stanley Howell, Robert Basso, and Roy Leming, being present in Open Court, the Defend-

3

ant Stanley Howell being represented by his Counsel, Henry L. Wurts, Esq., and the Defendant Robert Basso being represented by his Counsel, George Henderson Stacey, Esq., the District Attorney, Martin M. Bunting, Esq., moves the Court for a severance of the trial of these cases and sever the trial of the case of Roy Leming, one of the Defendants in the Bill of Indictment, and proceed with the trial as against Stanley Howell and Robert Basso, the other Defendants.

Eo die, Henry L. Wurts, Esq., Counsel for the Defendant Stanley Howell, objects to the severance as far as the Defendant Roy Leming is concerned.

Eo die, Objection Overruled. By the Court.

Eo die, George Henderson Stacey, Esq., Counsel for the Defendant Robert Basso, objects to the severance as far as the Defendant Roy Leming is concerned.

Eo die, Objection Overruled. By the Court.

Eo die, A severance having been granted in this case, the Court directs that the trial proceed. The Cause being heard before Honorable Thomas F. Vredenburgh, Judge.

Eo die, the District Attorney, Martin M. Bunting, Esq., begs leave to arraign the Prisoners, whereupon the Court directs that the Prisoners Stanley Howell and Robert Basso be arraigned separately and that the Clerk read the Bill of Indictment.

Eo die, the Clerk reads the Bill, whereupon the Defendant Stanley Howell pleads Not Guilty and desires to be tried "by God and my Country."

Eo die, the Clerk reads the Bill, whereupon the Defendant Robert Basso answers not, by reason that he stands mute of his own will. The plea of Not Guilty is entered as the plea of Robert Basso. By the Court.

Eo die, the Defendants Stanley Howell and Robert Basso having been arraigned, the District Attorney, Martin M. Bunting, Esq., begs leave to enter upon the Bill of Indictment their pleas of Not Guilty.

4

Eo die, Motion Allowed and District Attorney replies Similiter, issue et trial.

Eo die, the Court directs that the trial proceed and that the Clerk call the Jury.

Eo die, the Prisoner Stanley Howell and the Prisoner Robert Basso are remanded into the custody of the Sheriff and returned to the County Prison.

June Thirteenth, 1939, Tuesday, the requisite number of Jurors being completed, the Court directs the Clerk to swear the Jury as a body, which is accordingly done.

Eo die, the Assistant District Attorney, Abner Coates, Esq., at 10:40 o'clock A.M. opens the Case for the Commonwealth.

One

THE CASE of the Commonwealth against Stanley Howell and Robert Basso was the county's first trial of men charged with murder in more than a decade, and the district attorney's office, which had a good record for convictions, was anxious to win. Moreover, it was the ~~D. A.~~ first murder case in which Abner Coates had participated, and though he took care to behave as usual, as the trial approached he felt, if not a nervousness, a nervous stimulation that keyed him up. Abner Coates had been practicing law for six years, four of them as assistant district attorney. With Martin Bunting, or by himself when the judges were sitting separately as they usually did to expedite the business of Quarter Sessions, Abner had prosecuted or helped to prosecute several hundred cases; but since the charges were all less serious, they were all less important. He had addressed dozens of juries, and as a rule thought nothing of it; but today, as well as a jury, he had a crowded courtroom before him.

Abner was not disturbed by the prospect of many people watching him while he spoke. He knew that he was no orator and never would be, but his experience proved that he could make an adequate speech if he took the trouble to prepare it. In the present case he began two weeks in advance. With Martin Bunting, he planned it in detail, diagraming the points to be made, and repeatedly revising, to make it simpler and clearer, the outline of what the Commonwealth intended to prove. Then, without telling Bunting, who might have thought he showed undue nervousness, Abner wrote it all

7

out and showed it to his father; and then, without telling anyone, he rehearsed it a number of times before a mirror in his bedroom—a thing he had not done since his first few months of practice.

The Commonwealth's case, though not entirely simple, was so plain that Abner, timing himself in his bedroom, found that it could be stated in very little over twenty minutes. However, speaking to himself in a mirror and speaking to the full courtroom were not the same. The Childerstown courthouse had been erected in 1880, and architects of the period either did not understand the principles of acoustics or held them secondary to that day's taste for rich stateliness and fancy grandeur. Abutting on the back side of the clock-towered stone structure which faced Court Street over steps, walks, and a small fountain, and which housed the record rooms and clerks' offices, the architects built as a main courtroom the recognizable dodecagonal chapter house of some monstrous Gothic cathedral whose incredible corporate body presumably numbered five hundred canons.

Inside this curious edifice with its pinnacled buttresses, vast hip roof, and stilted, ecclesiastical high windows, the shape of the courtroom was a semicircle. Nine concentric tiers of oak seats looked over the railed enclosure of the bar to the great bench, a massive and solid black-walnut pile. Behind the bench the tan, sand-finished wall rose thirty-five feet to a round spoked skylight of stained glass. The flat impressive wall was decorated with an American flag and an arrangement of large, gold-framed oil paintings of deceased judges.

Though impressive enough in appearance, the high wall served as a sounding board. Words addressed to the Court went echoing up, reverberated across the void until they hit the oiled and varnished matchboard of the ceiling, whose sloping panels were supported by hammer beams. Refracted six new ways, a medley of booming sounds came down on the tiered seats. A few minutes before Abner began his opening address Tuesday morning, Nick Dowdy, the crier,

8

counted four hundred and eighty-three spectators. Those in
the upper rows had little chance of hearing anything intel-
ligible; but seeing them lean forward, cup their ears, strain
to hear, Abner could not help straining in response, enunciat-
ing with tiresome care, speaking slowly.

It might be argued that so long as the jury heard, it did
not make much difference whether the spectators, whose only
business was their curiosity to see a spectacle rare in country
courts, heard or not. It might be argued that providing
spectacles was not now, or ever, the office of a court of law.
Good in theory, in practice these arguments overlooked the
fact that spectators made anything they watched a spectacle,
and those who performed public duties before an audience
became willingly or unwillingly actors, and what they did,
whether they wanted it that way or not, became drama. In-
voluntarily an actor, Abner could not be unconscious of his
audience's expectations, nor unaware that his audience was
finding the performance, of which he was part, a poor show
compared to what true drama, the art of the theater or the
motion picture, had taught them to expect.

Art would not take all day Monday to get a jury. Art
never dreamed of asking its patrons to sit hour after hour
over an impossible-to-hear lawyers' colloquy, with no action
but the self-conscious walking down of person after person
from the panel of petit jurors as the names were called. By
a cruel refinement of tiresomeness, those who walked down,
after long inaudible questioning and the amplest delay, usually walked back. Harry Wurts and George Stacey whispered
together at the defense's table and fumbled with their lists.
They pouted reflectively; finally they shook their heads.
If by any chance they accepted a juror, Martin Bunting was
fairly sure to exchange a word with Abner and shake his head.
That brought matters right back where they started; so Mat
Rhea, the clerk of Quarter Sessions, stood up under the
bench, looked at his list, and called a new name.

Monday's show had certainly been a complete flop; and

9

Abner doubted if his opening act in Tuesday's show had been any better. When he finished speaking he gave the filled seats a glance. The ranged faces remained intent for a moment, as though not sure whether he had finished or not. Then there was a turn of heads, glances questioning each other, and a movement of lips, whispering. Abner walked back to the Commonwealth's table, and the heads turned again, the eyes following him in vain speculation. Martin Bunting was studying the column of witnesses' names on the back of the bill of indictment. Without looking up, he said, "Good, Ab. That's fine."

Though preoccupied, he spoke with emphasis, and Abner felt both pleasure and surprise. Bunting was little given to praising people. If you ought to have done differently or better, he let you know at once; for, to Bunting's mind, that was the same as not doing what he asked you to do. If you did well, that was all right; that was what he expected.

Abner said, "I didn't know whether anyone could hear me."

"I could hear you all right," Bunting said. "If I could, they could." It was apparent that he meant the jury. Without further pause he got back to business. He said, "I'll call John now. We ought to have time to put William Zollicoffer on before lunch. I think you'd better take him. We won't want anything from him but identification."

"O.K.," Abner said, reaching for the file folder.

Bunting pushed his chair back and stood up, holding the folded bill of indictment and looking at Judge Vredenburgh.

The spectators, though they ought to be wary now and slow to hope, responded with a stir of relief. It occurred to Abner that even those who could not hear could at least see, and since they were local people, they might not suffer as a stranger sitting among them must suffer. They looked at the body of the court and the small happenings there as they looked at the *Childerstown Daily Examiner*. A stranger unfolding the paper would see nothing worth reading—"Local

Mill Workers Receive Pay Boost"; "Women Voters League Visits County Seat"; "Warwick Auxiliary Installs Officers"; "Bible Class Sponsors Saratoga Luncheon"; "Wed in Newmarket"; "Former Music Teacher Welcomed"; "Blaze on Farrell Farm"; "Hart Home Scene of Anniversary Party." But when you knew the mill and some of the workers, when you were a member of the Women Voters League, or the Warwick Auxiliary, or the Saratoga Bible Class; when the girl or the man married at Newmarket had been at school with you; when the former music teacher had taught you; or when the Farrell farm was right down the road, and you could remember the day twenty-five years ago of the Harts' wedding, each headline started up importuning the eye, absorbing the attention.

Scores of people who strained to hear and failed to hear what Abner Coates said to the jury knew Abner by sight, and his mere appearance had a meaning. Abner's bigger than average frame and slightly stooped big shoulders, his dark, harsh-textured, stubbornly waved hair, his sallow, long, intelligent face with large deep-set dark eyes under the moderate brows, declared that he was one of the "Lawyer Coateses." Abner's father, Judge Philander Coates, known as the Young Judge when he sat on the bench here before his elevation to the Superior Court, was not so dark as Abner and not so tall (that came from Abner's mother, who was Edith Lynch, and all the Lynches were tall); but Judge Coates had the same nose and eyebrows and the same slight strong stoop. Anyone would know whose son Abner was.

On the wall behind the bench, in still more arresting resemblance, the face of Judge Linus Coates, the Old Judge, hung among the gold-framed portraits. Abner was generally held to be the spit and image of his grandfather. When people from out of town, lawyers from other counties, came up on some case in which Abner happened to take part, almost every one of them, if he met Abner in the Attorneys Room, commented on it. At the first conversational opportunity, the visitor, excited by his own perspicacity, was fairly sure to observe, "Mr. Coates, I noticed one of those pictures in there. Aren't you some relation—?"

Childerstown residents who could remember the Old Judge were yearly fewer; but Judge Philander Coates, the Young Judge, had been, and still was, a figure of local note. Three months ago in March Abner's father suffered a stroke, and he had not left his house since; but every week or two the *Examiner* gave him a paragraph headed: "Judge Coates Doing Well," or "On Road to Recovery."

In the same way, with the same knowledgeableness, the spectators knew Martin Bunting, a short, neat, prematurely graying man, now near the end of his second term as district attorney. They knew Harry Wurts and George Stacey, sons of local people, Childerstown boys—George Stacey really looked like a boy, and there would be an interesting surprise for many people in seeing him there, a practicing attorney. They knew Judge Vredenburgh on the bench, and the clerks under him. They knew the tipstaffs in their blue jackets. Some of them probably knew one or more of the jurors. Even the state police, two officers at each of the doors to the back hall at the right and left of the bench, were young fellows from the Childerstown substation who had been kids in the school-yard, swimmers without bathing suits down in the old canal, summer evening loiterers at the corner of Court and Broad Streets a year or so ago. Their transformation by polished black leather and gray whipcord into armed men could be viewed with amazed indulgence.

The only people who were unknown, who had never been seen or heard of before, who had no history, nor even any names, since few spectators would be sure yet which was Howell and which was Basso, were the defendants and their confederates and the witnesses associated with them. They, and the man Frederick Zollicoffer alleged to have been murdered by them in this county, were what the rustic townships still called foreigners—the people from somewhere else.

12

The word, like one of those old men who still used it, and who still drove a shabby curtained carry-all to town, sparing a poor horse's hoofs by keeping to the shoulder of the concrete highways, was a homely joke; but Abner was not sure that it didn't fit the present case better than any other word. Stanley Howell and Robert Basso; their two former associates, Roy Leming and Dewey Smith; Susie Smalley, their shocking slut of a girl friend who sat next to Mrs. O'Hara, the Warden's wife, wearing a dress of thin green stuff which seemed pasted at all points to her jointless body; Mrs. Zollicoffer, the black-draped widow of the dead man; the dead man's gross brother, William Zollicoffer; the dead man's gross one-time partner, Walter Cohen—they did not belong here. They came not merely from some other county but from some other world.

Now that they were here, they were not welcome. Even the spectators who had them to thank for the show they hoped to see did not thank them. The encircling eyes were curious but all cold. They looked at Stanley Howell, pale, peaked, and furtive, and Robert Basso, dark, round-headed, stocky, and sullen, as they would look, gaping, with a shrug or a shudder, at that tight wire-netted box in which the owner of a local hardware store often kept for a few weeks a couple of rattlesnakes somebody had managed to catch alive. Next time, in the unlikely event that Howell and Basso were going to have any next times, Howell and Basso might do well to notice where they went when they drove out at night in search of a quiet place.

Bunting said, "If your Honor please, the Commonwealth will call John Costigan."

Nick Dowdy came infirmly to his feet. He gave his lapel a tug to settle his blue jacket, neatly embroidered on the left sleeve with the word *crier* in silver thread. He moved over behind the stenographer, lifted a small Bible, and laid it flat open on the rail of the witness stand.

Joe Jackman, the stenographer, snapped on his green-shaded light. He picked up successively and examined several stylos, chose one, and held it poised. Joe was a tall, spare man with a grave expression that would have become a minister of the gospel. In the course of the last six or seven years more than ten million words had been pronounced from the witness stand a yard or so above his left shoulder and bent head. To get every one down, it was necessary for him to form the habit of listening to the sound, not the sense. While others sat back, free to decide what was important and worth hearing and what was not, free to speculate on the speaker's meaning and motive, to recall what had been said before and to anticipate what might be said next, Joe Jackman, with an intent dedication of mind, simply wrote. It was not a job for a casual man, and Joe, though he smiled cheerfully and, meeting Abner's eye, even made a face, took serious views of life.

While John Costigan walked to the stand, there was another stir. At the long table to the right, the one used by members of the bar waiting to come before the Court, sat four men from city newspapers, Maynard Longstreet, editor and owner of the *Examiner*, and Adelaide Maurer, who was the local correspondent of a press association. They all shifted and stretched, rousing themselves, moving their folded copy paper, laying out their pencils. One of the city reporters, craning across two others, addressed Maynard Longstreet, probably asking him how to spell Costigan.

Judge Vredenburgh looked sharply down at this table. By the set of the Judge's mouth and the hard dimpling of his chin and cheeks, it could be seen that the presence of visiting reporters irked him. Maynard Longstreet had good reason to be there—it was right for the local paper to report proceedings. Adelaide Maurer was a nice girl, divorced from a worthless husband and doing what she could to earn a living.

The others were present with the intention to manufacture and print sensational rubbish prejudicial to the dignity of the law; and Judge Vredenburgh would have been glad to send them about their business. Since this could not very well be done, at least while they behaved themselves, he turned his gaze critically on the full courtroom.

The spectators, stirring, shifted feet, cleared throats, exchanged whispers in a swell of sound like the rote of surf. Judge Vredenburgh frowned and said loudly, "I want everyone's attention, please!"

Nick Dowdy, leaving his Bible on the rail, dodged back to his seat under the bench, lifted his mallet, and struck the block twice. A hush fell on the sloping tiers. John Costigan stood still at the steps to the witness stand. The newspaper writers became motionless, looking at their pencils.

Judge Vredenburgh said, "This is a case of importance, and a large public attendance is proper. However, it is not easy to hear in this courtroom; and with so many people present, it will be impossible unless everybody is perfectly quiet. There will be no whispering, and no moving around, please. The tipstaffs will have to see to this." He bent his formidable gaze on them for a moment, his mouth grumpy but his eyes not unpleasant, so that those who could not hear would understand anyway.

Martin Bunting stood silent with an easy, dry expression, his convex profile to the jury, his eyes sharp and level on John Costigan by the steps. Bunting lifted a hand and stroked the close-cropped gray hair at the back of his head, watching the Judge, who finally gave him a nod. John Costigan moved again, mounting the steps. He put his hand on the Bible, cocked an ear to Nick Dowdy, nodded, and sat down. Nick, sidling past Joe Jackman, blinked at the bench and said, "John Costigan sworn."

Bunting said, "Where do you live, Mr. Costigan?"

"Cherry Hill Road, Harfield Township, sir." Costigan's blunt-featured, ruddy face was composed and attentive. He

15

took care to talk into the microphone set in the rail of the stand; and, in mechanical reproduction, his voice dropped distinctly from the loudspeaker in the corner above the jury.

Bunting said, "What is your position?"

Bunting could not be in much doubt about that, since, as district attorney, he had appointed John to it; but they looked at each other formally, and Costigan said, "County detective, sir."

"Were you near Milltown in this county on the tenth of May of this year?"

"Yes, sir."

"Where?"

"At the Childerstown Pike bridge, the state road over Fosher's Creek."

"What were you doing at that place at that time?"

"I was grappling for a body."

Costigan's voice was level and his face impassive. Costigan's lips closed calmly after the word "body"; and a second's deep silence fell while the jury took it in.

The twelve jurors, and the spare sitting with them in case one of them became sick or died, had hardly given the case they were hearing a thought until now. They had all been busy affecting intelligent attention and easy dignity. Since not one of them, in so novel and prominent a position, actually felt either, their postures, though varied by their various ideas of intelligence and ease, were one in being stiff and self-conscious. Though different, as their ways of conveying attentiveness and dignity were different, their expressions were the same in being all solemnly silly.

Costigan's word jarred them; and, jarred, they let their affectations slip. In the front row, Genevieve Shute's middle-aged face quivered as she swallowed twice. Old man Daniels twitched his long upper lip and explored his ear suddenly with his finger. The foreman, Louis Blandy—a short, stout man who owned the Childerstown Bakery—stole a glance at the defendants seated with counsel at the second table. He then looked at Bunting, puffed out his lips, pulled in his chin. His look said that he had been prepared to hear something like this.

Bunting said to Costigan, "Did you succeed in raising a body from Fosher's Creek at that time and place?"

"We did, sir."

"At about what time of day, Mr. Costigan?"

"About noon, sir. That is, about eleven-fifty-five A.M."

"And you were in charge of the persons engaged in grappling for this body?"

"Yes, sir. I was."

"And you were present while it was being done?"

"I was present."

"And you saw a body raised from the creek?"

"I did, sir."

Abner, who had also seen the body raised, admired John Costigan's air of modest achievement. The state highway crossed Fosher's Creek above the mill dam where the water was eighteen or twenty feet deep. Because the county line was fixed at the middle of the creek, and it had not been certain just where the body would be found, the party included a city police captain from a suburban precinct and a couple of homicide squad men, who were glad to leave the dirty work to Costigan. It was raining hard and a steady patter of drops on the pond could be heard against the low rush of water pouring out the spillway under the old brick walls of the mill. Officers of the state motor police blew their whistles incessantly while they waved on cars that tried to stop on the bridge to see what was happening. The mill employees were more fortunate. Their faces crowded every window. That morning not much work could have been done in the mill.

Bunting had driven over with Abner in Abner's car, and they ran it down in a grove of trees whose buds were just breaking into a haze of light green foliage at the end of the dam across the water from the mill. In the parked car they sat and smoked while the rowboat went back and forth. First the grapplers brought up the frame of an old kerosene stove, and then an automobile tire. The city police on top of the dam included at least one humorist, who called out when the tire came into the boat, "Can't keep that, bud! Got to throw the little ones back!"

On the dam top, too, was Stanley Howell in the custody of a deputy warden of the state penitentiary. Howell had been given a policeman's raincoat, but he wore his own checked cap, limp with rain. He kept indicating further to the left. He made forlorn, awkward gestures, throwing his left hand out, for his right hand was not free. He was joined by his right wrist to the deputy warden, and the two of them, in identical black rubberized coats, formed a double monstrosity; Siamese twins, obliged to do everything together. Under the sodden cap, Howell's pale face was frail and wasted and marked like a martyr's with long-endured suffering. Bunting, Abner knew, had been displeased with Howell's appearance. Looking at Howell, a jury might feel some doubt about the confession that the Federal Bureau of Investigation agents got from him. Howell looked as though he had been having a bad time.

This was only the truth. Abner had pieced together most of the story of what happened to Frederick Zollicoffer's kidnappers after they killed him. You could say that they seemed to be out of luck; and as a matter of fact their luck was so fantastically bad that another age surely would have been awed by Retributive Justice's celerity and precision. The night of the killing they had all left the bungalow where Zollicoffer was held and returned to the house where Howell and Susie Smalley had been living before the enterprise was undertaken. They were there about a week, probably arguing about whether to lie low or to attempt some other job. There were some conversations during this period to be put in evidence, but the only definite action appeared to be an attempt to steal another car. They had already stolen one car, the car in which Zollicoffer had been murdered; and Abner supposed they thought it prudent to get rid of this. He could not do more than suppose, because their plans never seemed to follow any logical pattern. If they rose at times to a sort of shrewdness, without intermission they fell to the most staggering stupidities. Only they themselves could know what they thought they were doing.

The attempt to steal the second car was a failure; they were frightened off. Indeed, they seemed to have been frightened so badly that they must have decided to scatter. Robert Basso drove away the other car, the car in which Zollicoffer had been murdered, and abandoned it. That was when Robert Basso's luck ran out. He got rid of the car by leaving it in a country lane. It was long past midnight, and he could be sure nobody saw him. His next move was to walk back to the state highway and boldly try to thumb a ride. By a chance that could be only one in a hundred the first car he signaled, or at any rate, the first car that stopped, turned out to be the state police motor patrol. The two officers in the car asked Basso what he wanted.

Though armed police could never have been a welcome sight to Basso, he was probably able to tell himself that he was still all right. He did not happen to know that there was a state law against thumbing rides. It was rarely or never enforced because it was impractical to enforce it, but it existed, and the officers certainly didn't expect anyone to ask them to help violate it. Probably they did not realize that the dark and the glare of headlights had kept Basso from seeing that the car was the patrol car. They thought he must have stopped them because there had been a breakdown or accident and he needed help. They asked him where his car was.

The car, which had been on the teletype as stolen, was the last thing Basso wanted to show them; and, anyway, his story was that he was hitchhiking. If he had been a different sort of person, the police might have warned him that he was breaking the law, and driven on, or even given him a lift to the nearest town. On Basso they probably saw those indescribable little signs which mark, if not a criminal type, a man who has been in trouble with the law. Abner could imagine their expressions hardening as they listened to Basso trying to explain how he came to be hitchhiking there at that time of night, until one of them jerked his head and said, "Get in, Joe! Down to the clubhouse!" They had a charge they could hold him on until the next day. The next day the stolen car was found, so they sent in Basso's fingerprints and continued to hold him.

Meanwhile Bailey, who had undoubtedly directed the kidnapping and managed the killing of Frederick Zollicoffer, ran into bad luck, too. Bailey went to New York and several days after his arrival he heard a knock on the door of the Bronx apartment in which he was hiding out. When he asked who was there, the answer was, "Police." If Bailey had waited a moment, he would have found out that the patrolman had come to tell the people in the next apartment that a dog, by its license number belonging to them, had been found running loose and taken to the police station. He had knocked on the wrong door.

Bailey did not wait. He jumped to the conclusion, perhaps not without justification, since Howell and Basso and possibly Roy Leming were the only people in the world who knew where he was, that one of them had betrayed him. He tiptoed through the apartment, got out a back window onto a fire escape, and, presumably, slipped, for he fell three stories to the paving of the areaway. He was taken, fatally injured, to a hospital. What had happened was plain to the police. They did not know who Bailey was, or why he wanted to get away; but they thought it worth while to try and find out. Two detectives waited by his bed in case he recovered consciousness. When Bailey did recover consciousness, he recognized his attendants for what they were and told them, befuddled by pain and drugs, and also by his idea that one of his friends had, as he said, split on him, that he knew why they were after him.

It then became merely a matter of keeping Bailey alive, and at least semiconscious, and making him think that they already knew all about it. What the detectives took down was rambling, incoherent, and as evidence dubious; but they got places and names. Before Bailey died that night, it was all on the wires; Roy Leming had been arrested; Basso had been located, still in custody on the stolen car charge; and the Federal Bureau of Investigation which was persuaded that Howell had been mixed up several years before in a mail robbery, either by an informal arrangement with the local police or by getting there first, picked Howell out of hiding and took him to headquarters to have a talk with him.

This was where Howell's luck ran out. From the professional standpoint the F.B.I. agents cared very little whether Howell had killed Zollicoffer—whoever killed him saved the authorities trouble. But an F.B.I. agent was shot in the investigation of that mail robbery and they meant to get everyone who might have been involved. They wanted to turn over to state authorities a case that would take care of Howell. They knew what the case was, but they needed a few details to clinch it. It was no good Howell's saying he didn't know anything. They knew he knew. Neither Bunting nor Abner would be likely to imagine that under such circumstances agents experienced with men like Howell would rely altogether on friendly chats, reproachful appeals, or the pangs of Howell's conscience to make him admit his guilt. Howell, once he was out of the hands of the F.B.I., had his own story to tell about that; but, whether extorted from him or not, there was good reason to believe that he told his questioners, or tormenters, as the case might be, the truth. Roy Leming gave the good reason after he had read a copy of Howell's confession.

Up to that point Leming made the routine denial of everything. After Leming read the confession, his counsel, a city

THE JUST AND THE UNJUST

lawyer named Servadei of a notorious shyster firm, told Bunting that his client had concluded to make a clean breast of it, plead guilty, and offer to testify for the Commonwealth against Howell and Basso.

This was the best possible news; but Bunting distrusted Servadei. The reputation of Servadei's law firm and the respect criminals felt for it did not come from advising clients to plead guilty or turn state's evidence. Abner, present at the conference, was impressed and, in a way—for Servadei probably considered them just hicks—proud, to see Bunting handle it. Bunting said drily that the indictment he sought would be murder. The Commonwealth expected to have no trouble in showing that it was first-degree murder. Since the law presumed second-degree murder, that was all Leming could plead guilty to. The Commonwealth already had all the evidence it needed. Why should Leming be let off? In short, no.

Servadei said it was just in a way of speaking. Leming was not asking to be let off. If a severance could be granted, Leming would throw himself on the mercy of the Court and testify in the interests of justice. Servadei said that, frankly, he was persuaded that his client was guilty. He, Servadei, did not make a practice of defending guilty men; it was better for everyone if they pleaded guilty. All Servadei wanted to see done was justice; and moreover, he believed that it had been held that where a defendant pleaded guilty to an indictment for murder, the presumption was that the crime was murder in the first degree.

Bunting answered that such a presumption might have been held to exist once. He would let them know about the possibility of a severance. He would have to talk to the Judge. Leming, on his oath, was naturally expected to testify to the truth. If he wanted to testify as Commonwealth's witness, the Court usually considered that a point to be taken into consideration. He, Bunting, did not know what the Court would do in this case. Servadei and his client would have to take their chances. Servadei said that he understood perfectly; but he did not feel able to advise his client to adopt such a course if there was no severance. A man on trial was not, if Mr. Bunting would excuse him, expected to testify to the truth where the truth incriminated him. He could refuse to answer without prejudice.

This delicate exchange of threats and promises naturally ended in Leming being granted a severance and accepted as a witness for the Commonwealth. With Leming testifying, Howell's confession lost much of its importance—it had, in fact, without ever coming in evidence at all, served its purpose when it scared Leming—and whatever the F.B.I. might have done to get it no longer mattered much, except perhaps to Howell.

Even for Howell it could only amount to just one thing more. What Federal agents might have done to him would be nothing compared to the things he had done to himself, and the consequences of those things, during most of his twenty-eight years. His record showed that Howell had been at war with the law since he was a child; and of all wars, that is the one in which there really is no discharge. From the misery and poverty and, probably, hunger of his youth Howell graduated to prison life and prison food; and when he was let go, it was to a still worse regimen. Crime was his trade; so, to live, he had to tax his limited brain, strain his broken-down body, rack his ruined nerves, devising new crimes, new risks, new narrow escapes, new vigils of lying in wait or hiding-out. He had no idea of recreation outside depressing debaucheries for which he had no energy and from which he probably could get no pleasure—bad liquor; girls like Susie Smalley; adulterated cocaine borrowed from those who used it—and much of the time he must have been too tired and too sick. The liquor would knock him out, the cocaine nauseate him, that horrible young hag be no good to him. In the ceaseless rain, dragging along the concrete dam top chained to the deputy warden, Howell looked sick to death. Abner tried not to watch him.

The grapplers brought up the body then.

From the car window Abner could see it; a stir in the water a dozen yards behind the boat as the lines tightened. Something swam from the depths and was visible an instant, still under water; an indistinct shape in loose floating clothes, like a huge, tattered, long-dead fish. The corpse broke surface; but, being weighted, immediately it sank from sight as the grapplers rushed in the slack. Howell, who got a close look, doubled up, his right arm lifted a little by the chain of the handcuff. Heaving and retching, he vomited on his own shoes.

Abner raised his cigarette to his mouth and filled his lungs with smoke. In the hundred windows of the mill, hands and faces crowded and danced with animated movement. The city police captain, who had joined them in the car to get out of the rain a while, said, "Caught something that time! Look at the bastard!" He nodded toward Howell. "He don't like it! They ought to make him pull it out himself!"

To John Costigan, Bunting said, "How was that body clothed at that time?"

Costigan considered the question a moment, passing his eyes over the paper in his hand. "It was clothed in, well, a coat, a shirt, and gray, like-flannel trousers; and with a bag, a burlap, where the wire on the weights had been put, sir."

"And where was that?"

"The feet. By the ankles, sir."

Bunting walked over to the folding table set up by Joe Jackman's desk. He said, "At the time the body was raised, was the man alive or dead, Mr. Costigan?"

"Dead, sir."

"Did you know the dead man?"

"No, sir. I couldn't say that I did."

Bunting said, "Mr. Costigan, I show you four pieces of iron that have been marked for identification as Commonwealth's exhibits one, two, three, and four, and ask you whether you have ever seen them before."

"Yes, sir. I have."

"Where?"

"I saw those by the dam there, Fosher's Creek. They were tied around the body's feet—around the ankles of Frederick Zollicoffer, Zollicoffer's body."

In his seat beside Howell, Harry Wurts jerked his head up. Harry's fuzz of short reddish hair and cropped fragment of reddish mustache seemed both to bristle. His oval face shone, his somewhat slanting eyes slanted more. "I move that be stricken!" he said.

Judge Vredenburgh said, "Yes. This body has not been identified."

Bunting said to Costigan, "Around the ankles of this body which you saw raised from Fosher's Creek. Is that correct?"

"Yes, sir," Costigan said, blushing. "We took them off this body."

"And what did you do with them?"

"Why," said Costigan, "we put them in the undertaker's truck of Philip Westbrook, of Twenty-seven North Court Street, of Childerstown."

"And what did you do with this body that you had just raised?"

"That was likewise placed in that truck."

"In the same truck with the irons?"

"Same truck. Yes, sir."

"And where in Fosher's Creek, as nearly as you can fix it, was this body found?"

"Well," Costigan said, "I would say it was very near the center below the bridge and very near the dam."

Bunting looked over and said, "Mr. Wurts?"

25

"Yes," said Harry Wurts, arising. "I have a question or two."

Walking down toward the stand, Harry Wurts smiled with an air of unassuming blandness, of youthful ingenuousness. Since Harry was the same age as Abner, thirty-one, he could not and did not actually pretend to so much youth and ingenuousness; he put that on sardonically, with the plain, and astonishingly effective, intention of pointing up and somehow by the contrast exaggerating Bunting's dry exactness. There was not much Harry Wurts could do with Bunting's examination—as usual, a model. Dry and exact, except for Costigan's little slip, which was no fault of Bunting's, the whole thing was laid down precisely—just when, just where; the raised body, the identified weights wired to its ankles. There could be no fooling around about the corpus delicti. Harry would not do much with any of that; so Abner supposed that Harry was going to see what he could do with Bunting himself, or Bunting's witness.

Coming up close to the witness stand, Harry said, "Just what do you mean by 'very near,' Mr. Costigan?"

"I mean, not far, sir," Costigan said. Someone in the jury gave a snicker, and Harry Wurts smiled indulgently toward the sound. Harry said, "An inch, a foot, a yard, a mile?"

"Five or six feet."

"Five or six feet. From the dam?"

"From the dam."

"And how far is this bridge from the dam?"

"Oh, not far. Say, a hundred feet above."

"Then you would say this body, weighted with these irons here, had somehow floated or drifted a distance perhaps a little bit farther than from where you sit to the main door up there?"

Costigan said, "I wouldn't positively know just how far that door is from where I sit, sir. The bridge is farther from the dam than that."

Bunting said, "We don't mind Mr. Wurts establishing the

26

distance of the bridge from the dam, if he cares to; but I will offer an objection to the 'floated or drifted.' The Commonwealth will show in due course how the body came to be where it was, your Honor."

"Very well," Harry Wurts said. "I will withdraw it. Let me ask instead, Mr. Costigan, if you have had much experience in the art or profession of body-grappling?"

"Objection," said Bunting. "He has shown that he had enough experience to grapple for this one. What is Mr. Wurts trying to get at, anyway?"

"Mr. Wurts," said Harry, "is vainly trying to fix the exact location of the body Mr. Costigan says he found somewhere, by something we can really check on, like the dam or the bridge."

Judge Vredenburgh said, "I think the district attorney's questions brought out the location, Mr. Wurts."

"Then I have no other questions, sir." He turned and walked back to his seat.

Bunting said to Abner, "All right." He looked over his shoulder and called, "William Zollicoffer."

While he was asking Mr. Zollicoffer his name and his occupation—William Zollicoffer made and sold what he called beauty and barber supplies; hair tonics and so on, Abner supposed—Abner reminded himself that his purpose here was to identify the body—though it might be worth getting Zollicoffer, if he could, to identify the weights again. Abner did not like William Zollicoffer, a man of that particularly piglike German type, who, though they are often honest, kind, generous, and good family men, look brutal when they are serious and insincere when they are smiling. In the district attorney's office William Zollicoffer had, moreover, annoyed everyone by his airs of importance, and of being in a special position to do the Commonwealth a favor; and, at the same time, of being owed special consideration and a final say on what would or would not be done. He had, of course, found out that his view was a mistaken one; but he took the stand now with offensive alacrity. He looked around, pleased with the full courtroom.

Abner made an effort to regard his witness impartially. He said, "Did you know Frederick Zollicoffer during his lifetime?"

William Zollicoffer expanded. He sat back, clasping the lapels of his coat, one in each hand, and crossed his legs. "Why, yes," he said, "naturally, naturally. I—"

"Were you related to him?"

"Sure. Sure. I was just telling you—"

Zollicoffer was going to be a handful, Abner saw. It would be necessary to make him realize who was running this. Abner said sternly, "Answer the questions I put to you, please."

William Zollicoffer paused, his mouth open, staggered by the sudden rebuff and crestfallen. To Abner's surprise he then said, "I beg your pardon if I did anything wrong."

Abner found himself reddening. He had discovered before this that when he assumed sternness, a quality not natural to him, he was likely to put on a good deal more of it than he intended or the occasion needed. He said, "I don't mean to stop you from answering as fully as necessary, Mr. Zollicoffer. We just don't want to take up more of the Court's time than we have to. Will you state whether or not you were at the point near Milltown where the highway crosses Fosher's Creek on the tenth of May, last."

"Yes, sir. That is where I was."

"Did you see a body raised from Fosher's Creek at that time?"

"Yes, sir."

"Did you recognize that body?"

"Body of Frederick Zollicoffer."

"Your brother?"

"Yes, sir."

It had been apparent from the office talks that the Zolli-coffer brothers had not, in recent years, seen much of each other—a circumstance to William's credit, if anything. They had not been on affectionate and probably not even on good terms. For himself, Abner approved William's tone. He would prefer a man not to pretend to feelings he did not have; but, on the other hand, it was up to Abner to take care of his witness. The jury might dislike a man who viewed the body of his murdered brother with complete indifference. William Zollicoffer ought to be kept in as good a light as possible. Abner said, "Mr. Zollicoffer, I know these questions must be painful to you; but will you tell the jury whether you noticed any weights attached to the body at that time?"

William Zollicoffer was quicker than he looked; or at least, when it was put to him, he quickly saw the chance to cut a figure. His face fell. He hung his head and shook it with coarse, and to Abner not particularly convincing, distress. He said, "I might not have observed every detail. I was too shocked. I was—"

Abner cut in quickly, "I think we all understand your feelings. We'll try not to prolong this. Will you tell me if the body was clothed at that time?"

"Yes, sir; coat and pants."

"And it was in a fair state of preservation?"

"Well, it didn't look too good."

"What I mean, Mr. Zollicoffer, is that you had no difficulty in recognizing the body?"

William Zollicoffer said, "Oh, no. It was Fred. No doubt about that at all."

"And did you see the body later at the undertaking establishment of Mr. Westbrook here in Childerstown?"

"Yes, sir."

Judge Vredenburgh stirred and said, "Did you accompany it to Childerstown?"

"Yes, sir," said William Zollicoffer, turning to him. "You see, I—"

"Yes, I see," Judge Vredenburgh nodded. "Answer Mr. Coates."

Judge Vredenburgh's precise, almost photographic sense of the record was something you had to learn to accept; and Abner could, in fact, accept it with appreciation—a lesson, usually administered with tact, in clearer or simpler ways of handling simple material. There was no reason to leave to implication or inference the simple point that a body, shown to have been raised from Fosher's Creek and identified as the body of Frederick Zollicoffer, was the same body that the coroner would be called to testify about. Abner said, "Did you see where the body was placed after it was raised from the creek?"

William Zollicoffer said, "Well, to tell you the truth, they started before I got there, see? It was a bad day and I couldn't make such good time. When I first saw the body it was in a rowboat. I never seen it actually raised from the creek. They had it in the boat already." The virtuous look of great honesty and exactness did not become him; and Abner saw that it would be wise to get William Zollicoffer off the stand as soon as possible, without giving Harry Wurts any more points on which to cross-examine. Abner said, "But after the body had been taken from the rowboat, did you see it put in a conveyance of any kind?"

"Yes, in the undertaker's hearse, the dead wagon. That was there."

"In the undertaker's hearse; and you came with that hearse to Childerstown?"

"No. Followed it."

"You followed the hearse to Childerstown, and saw the body brought in to Mr. Westbrook's?" Abner turned so that he could see Bunting. Bunting nodded.

"Yes, sir," said William Zollicoffer.

"Thank you," Abner said. He looked at the defense's table and said to Harry Wurts, "Cross-examine?"

Harry Wurts pushed his chair back and stood up without moving from his place. He said, "Mr. Zollicoffer, I understood you to say that you never actually saw any body raised from the creek. You don't then, of your own knowledge, know where it came from?"

"Well, it was all wet. It was—"

"That's all," Harry said.

Abner said to William Zollicoffer, "That will be all." Apparently unable to believe that the great moment had come and already gone, William Zollicoffer sat still, his heavy face dazed or disappointed. Malcolm Levering, the tipstaff seated behind the jury, left his chair, approaching the steps to the witness stand. "Step down," he said. "You can go back now."

Abner went around and took his seat by Bunting at the Commonwealth's table. Bunting looked at the clock and said, "Five of twelve. We haven't got much done, but the Judge will be getting hungry pretty soon. Hill's going to take some time." He piled his papers together and stood up. He said, "The Commonwealth intends to call the coroner, Doctor Hill, next, sir. Do you wish—"

"Yes. Better break now. The Court will recess to one fifteen." Judge Vredenburgh arose, went along the bench and down the steps to the door of his chambers. Hugh Erskine, the sheriff, left his chair by the center aisle, signaling his deputy and the jail guards. To Howell and Basso he said, "All right, boys." Malcolm Levering propped open the hall door and stood with Albert Unruh, the other tipstaff in charge of the jury, while the jurors filed past. Bunting went across to speak to Doctor Hill. Standing, Abner looked at the courtroom, the tiers of seats emptying slowly toward the aisles and the high door.

Hermann Mapes, the clerk of the Orphans Court, came by the table. "Looking for someone?" he said.

"Hello, Hermann," Abner said. "No."

Hermann smiled at him and rolled his eyes, but he only said, "Good speech," and passed on to the aisle. Abner put a cigarette in his mouth and went over to the Attorneys Room.

Joe Jackman, the stenographer, who had preceded him, was strapping up his brief case on the window ledge. "Nice going, Ab," he said. "Thing I always like about opening addresses is, I don't have to take them down. Say, that William Zollicoffer is a louse, isn't he?"

The door opened and Bunting, lighting a cigarette, came in. "Ask Marty," Abner said.

"Ask me what?" Bunting said. He let himself down in a chair by the table.

"William Zollicoffer," Jackman said. "There's something about him."

"There was something about brother Frederick, too," Bunting said, yawning.

"Did he sell dope?"

"Sure. The Bureau of Narcotics was getting ready to grab him. Harry's going to make a big song and dance about—"

The door opened and Harry Wurts came in. "Well, gentlemen, and district attorneys," he said, "I heard that, I heard that! You're damned right he's going to! He will answer song with song and dance with dance, and you have a nerve even to mention it after the waltzing around Ab gave them. Ab, that was quite an oration! Boy, you're blossoming out at last! The part I liked was the moving passage about those nasty men. And those gestures! Only, you ought to use more of those, Ab. You ought to do your practicing in front of a mirror—oh, you do, eh? Well, next time, let yourself go. When you speak of the poor widow, you want to let a tremor break into your manly voice. A tear should tremble at your eloquent eye. You dash it away—" Harry quartered off, illustrating in absurd mimicry, and yet he did manage to put into it a turn of head and tone of voice that Abner realized was at least a little like himself—not himself as he was or had been, but as he would be if he were to do what Harry was doing. Harry said, "When you speak of that good and great man, Frederick Zollicoffer, don't just say he had a right to live. He was your only friend! Now he's dead and gone! You have no other friends, except me—"

"As long as I have you," Abner said, stemming the tide as well as he could, "why do I need any other friends?"

Harry had, in fact, been his best friend both when they were at college and when they went together to law school at Cambridge afterward. Like most redheaded people, Harry was given to extremes of mood, and the friendship was not always easy. One of his moods was playful and exuberant, and when this was on him Harry enjoyed making himself a nuisance to people trying to work; he was inspired to play practical jokes; he embarked on tirades of teasing or jeering, fairly sure to end with a quarrel. In another mood, Harry turned sensitive and suspicious, alert to take offense, discovering slights and neglects in a failure to hear what he said; or, when he wanted you to go somewhere or do something, seeing an insult in your having another engagement. Wounded, Harry would retire and sulk for several days. At Cambridge he and Abner grew a little tired of each other. They had never stopped being friends, because, strangely (or naturally) enough, once their intimacy diminished they got on better. Now, across the table in the Attorneys Room, they were able to look at each other with what Abner realized was a patronizing amusement, each having his own reasons for not taking the other too seriously.

The hall door opened and Mark Irwin came in with a rush. Mark was the son of the President Judge. Some years younger than Abner and Harry, he was a good lawyer, but erratic. His pale lymphatic face showed that he had much of his father's temperament without his father's control. "Where's Jackman?" he said. Seeing Jackman by the window, he pulled up breathless. "Look, Joe. I have a Master's hearing. Rogers divorce. How about this week sometime?"

"Clear case of nepotism," Harry Wurts said. "Mark, how do you think your father feels when you keep pestering him for handouts? It isn't decent."

"Nuts!" said Mark Irwin. "I just got it from Vredenburgh. And it was damn well time I got one, too. I'd like to look at that list! After every two or three names comes Wurts again."

Joe Jackman took out his notebook. "Afraid not this week," he said. "We'll have this trial most of it, won't we, Marty?"

"Well, how about some night?"

Harry Wurts said, "You certainly must need that seventy-five dollars. What do you do with your money? Last thing I heard, you were grabbing off the Schling audit. Boy, I wish I could have got my teeth into that! Estate was more than a hundred thousand!"

Joe Jackman said, "No, I'm not going to work nights this week, Mark. You try taking two hundred and twenty or thirty pages a day sometime. How about next Friday; I mean, a week from this Friday?"

"Make it Thursday."

"Thursday afternoon, maybe; if we don't have court. Is it going to be long?"

"Evan Washburn is Mrs. Rogers' counsel. What do you think?"

Jackman groaned. "Two o'clock," he said.

"Rogers?" said Harry Wurts. "Say, that ought to be a picnic! Do you know what he did? He laid her sister."

"Who told you?" said Jackman. "Or were you helping?"

"Don't think I wouldn't help!" said Harry. "Ever see that kid, that Louise? Is that choice stuff!" He sighed.

The door opened and Nick Dowdy, the crier, came in. He stood still and lit the stub of a cigar. "Now, you fellows!" he said. Blinking, he moved along the high wall lined with the volumes of red-and-black-labeled reports.

Abner said, "Looking for something, Nick?"

34

"Judge wants one eighty-five, *Atlantic Reporter*. Aren't they in this room?"

Harry said, "Why don't you buy a new cigar some day, Nick? That one smells worse every year." Abner went over beside Nick and reaching up along a high row, pulled out a volume. Nick said, "Not so tall as you are, Ab. Thanks."

Bunting said, "When Nick brings it back, there's a case there that might interest you and your client, Wurts. Three fifty-one."

"What about?"

"I'm not clerking for you," Bunting said. "Look it up yourself."

"Ah," said Harry, "I know the one you mean. It was a fellow who stole a car and shot a policeman who stopped him."

"Yes," said Bunting, "and that happened to be the next day, and in another state; and the murder was held to be in perpetration of the felony. And that's just exactly what's going to be held in this case. We have all our evidence."

"Your evidence!" said Harry. "What is it? That Kinsolving, that F.B.I. man of yours, beats hell out of my client and I can prove it, and where's your damn confession? Roy Leming! Why I can prove he took dope for years. You think anybody's going to believe anything he says? Don't make me laugh!"

"I don't know about making you laugh," Bunting said. "You can laugh your head off, if you want. But I don't think Howell's going to do much laughing. All he and Basso will get out of this is one of those currents of electricity they have at the penitentiary, of intensity sufficient to cause death, and the application of such current to be continued until they are dead, and may God have mercy on their souls! They are just as guilty as hell."

Harry Wurts looked over his shoulder. "Sure," he said, "they're guilty. George Stacey and I don't discuss it, but I even have a good idea Basso fired one of those shots—"

35

"Oh," said Bunting. "That's your good idea, is it?"

"Yes, it is. But let me see you prove it. A man has a right to make the Commonwealth prove it! Where do you think this is? Russia? Germany? Say, what are you trying to do? Sap the foundations of equal justice under law? Destroy my means of livelihood? Now, be off with you! Who's eating?"

Abner shook his head. "I told Father I'd be home today."

"How is he?" said Bunting. "Meant to ask you."

"Pretty good."

"Give him my best."

"Give him mine," said Harry, "and, say, tell him I sent him this. Hear the one about the dwarf in the sideshow who married the girl in the next booth, the tallest woman in the world? Yeah, his friends put him up to it. See you in church."

There was a burst of laughter, and they went through the door into the hall, still laughing. Down at the end, by the grill to the passage to the jail, Abner was surprised to see the defendant, Stanley Howell, leaning against the wall. Max Eich, one of the jail guards, was next to him. Max clasped casually in his left hand an empty manacle whose mate was around Howell's wrist. Howell's ghastly, putty colored face was turned toward them; his intense sunken eyes fixed on them. Between his pale lips a wet fragment of cigarette was burning.

Everybody stopped laughing suddenly; and Abner went out the side door to his parked car.

The big old house was just out of town. Abner turned his car through the stone gate posts, up the neglected curves of the drive through the overgrown masses of shrubbery, and halted it by the porch steps. In the hanging gloom of the long brick-arched veranda, Lucius, his father's Negro man, was polishing the brass handle of the door. "Look, Lucius," Abner said as patiently as he could, "what are you doing that for? If you want to do something, why don't you get some of those weeds out of the drive?"

"This needed shining up. This needed it bad."

"It's needed it bad for the last five years."

"Well, Honey said why didn't I." His wife had actually been christened Honey. He intended no endearment. "I told her I had twenty other things to do. Judge is down. He's on the side porch."

"Well, stop now; and tell Honey I have to have lunch right away. I have to get back to court."

"They try that murder today?"

"Yes. Hurry up."

"Mister Abner," Lucius said, "I certainly like to see those gangsters. Kill a man as soon as look at him." Lucius turned his mild, faintly cretinous gape on Abner. "I don't guess I can."

"You needn't ask me," Abner said. "The trial's open to the public. But I'm not going to ask Mrs. Boorse to let you off this afternoon, if that's what you mean. Anyway, there isn't anything to see. They aren't gangsters, Lucius; they—"

But they were gangsters, all right. They were the very thing. Abner thought of Howell, sick and white, standing with Max Eich in the hall by the bars of the passage to the jail. He thought of Basso's dark surly face, the empty and feeble looks of menace as Basso bitterly kept whatever absurd pact Basso had made with Basso to get back at something—his invulnerable prosecutors, his own bad luck, fate, the indifferent world; it hardly mattered, for against none of them was any recourse possible—by refusing to answer. Abner thought of Roy Leming, meek, placatory, harrowingly beyond shame or pride, on the degrading anxious seat as state's evidence.

It was no fiction to say that they were killers. They furtively carried guns, and very little was enough to panic or confuse them into shooting, and then they were liable to hit some one. Because they were perpetually nerve-racked and

37

lived always in danger, they were cruel. Abner had come slowly, through a lengthening experience, to understand that side of it. Criminals might be victims of circumstance in the sense that few of them ever had a fair chance; but it was a mistake to forget that the only "fair chance" they ever wanted was a chance for easy money. When they remembered all that their own dumbness and greed and desperation had made them go through, and yet how little of the thing they were trying to get their suffering and effort had brought them, some of them—specifically, a man like Bailey, who had the cunning to contrive, with only such poor material as Howell and Basso and Leming, the kidnapping of Frederick Zollicoffer, and the cold nerve to shoot Zollicoffer afterwards; and yet who also jumped at a knock, ran at a word, and entertained hysterical fancies about being betrayed—would indeed, what with the one and the other, kill a man in a paroxysm of malignity and terror as soon as look at him.

Abner did not see how any of this could be explained to Lucius. He left his sentence unfinished and went in through the high dark hall, around the little open-work elevator that had been installed by the stairs for his father, and out onto the screened side porch.

Judge Coates sat in a wheelchair, a light blanket wrapped around his legs, a newspaper propped on a metal frame on the table. Beyond the frame were several leather-bound law books and some paper-covered printed records. He had insisted on sending in his resignation as a Judge of the Superior Court; but it had, at least temporarily, been refused, and the records of cases he would normally have been hearing this term helped to occupy some of his time. Beyond the books was an earthenware jug full of fresh rose buds; and beyond the table sat Mrs. Boorse, who, as well as being a so-called "practical nurse" (and a good one), was the Judge's second cousin. Abner said, "Hello, Father. Morning, Aunt Myrt."

"Well, son," Judge Coates said. He turned from the paper

and looked over the top of his spectacles. His high broad forehead shone a little. His gray hair, longer now than he would have worn it if he had been well, was in some disorder. The good side of his face worked, dragging the other with it, and he said thickly, "You home?"

"There, now," Mrs. Boorse said, "I told you he'd be along directly."

Judge Coates' expression changed, and Abner could see that he didn't like the remark, which might mean (though Mrs. Boorse would never mean it) that he had been silly or childish to say whatever he had said. Mrs. Boorse went on, "Abner, your father's had his lunch. I'll have Lucius bring yours out here, why don't I? You can have a good talk. Philander, have you got everything you want? Well, I expect Abner could get anything for you. Honey's waiting to start the jam. You just give me a call when you go, Ab." She swept her glance around, professionally, checking up. She said, "Aren't those roses pretty? Janet Drummond brought them." She folded up her knitting and went into the house.

"Talk, talk, talk," Judge Coates said. Though hushed, he spoke explosively, as though he had contained what he could not or would not say to Mrs. Boorse's solid, good-natured face as long as it was physically possible. "Talk your ear off! Yes, Bonnie brought the roses." He looked at Abner again over the glasses, turning the sagging side of his face away a little.

"How are you feeling?" said Abner.

"All right, I suppose." He brought up a handkerchief and touched the side of his mouth. "Mosher was in. It's hard on a doctor. There isn't much he can do. He's very patient with me. I talk to him as if he could help it."

"What's he say?"

"Oh, what they always say. Getting on very well. Little things annoy you. Astereognosis."

"I can imagine," Abner said.

39

"You don't know what that is!"

Abner, who had taken it for some unintelligible enunciation, smiled and shook his head.

"You ought to know Greek. How can you have any education if you don't know Greek?" He spoke censoriously, fixing Abner with a sharp look of impatience and reproof; but Abner doubted if his father had found the Greek he had been obliged to learn by switchings and boxings of the ears at Mr. Sutphen's long-gone Academy useful enough for him to remember much of it. The Judge was repeating something he must have heard often from the "Old Judge"—not, in his harsh age, a man to neglect the duty of admonishing that young son of his who now with his dragging face and half-paralyzed body sat there, indescribably old, admonishing in turn his son. Picking up a match box from the table, Judge Coates said, "You can't tell what shape it is. Not by the sense of touch. Things like that. You don't like it."

On Judge Coates' face appeared what he meant. His face displayed the realities behind that fretful understatement. He rebelled, still incredulous and angry, against the humiliation of being nearly helpless. Incredulity and anger were part of the means he used to hold up under those burdens of the mind, the hopeless and melancholy thoughts, the deadly moments of insight that showed him his state, the qualms of fear that must be met with repeated short efforts of control. Abner put a hand on his father's shoulder. He said with what heartiness he could, "Want to hear a story Harry Wurts said to tell you?"

"No," said Judge Coates, "certainly not. That young man. Mind like a cesspool."

"This one isn't so bad," Abner said. He repeated it slowly. His father laughed, the paralyzed cheek shaking, the tears coming into his eyes. "I'm a bad old man," he said with difficulty. "Like to know who thinks those things up." He held his handkerchief to his mouth. "There's your lunch," he said. He called out, "Bring it here, Lucius! Put it down. Don't hang around out there!"

"Yes, Judge. I was coming as fast as I could. You want some milk, Mister Abner?"

"Yes," said Abner. "What's your case there?" he asked his father.

"Oh, stupid affair. It's before the court on a stipulated set of facts—insurance contract. Waste of time. The test has always been whether there's a risk against which indemnity's given. Plaintiff's brief is practically illiterate, into the bargain. How are you getting on?"

"Not far this morning. We got the jury. Opened. Costigan and one witness have been on."

"How did your opening go?"

"So-so, I guess. Marty said it was all right." Abner paused, cutting at a lamb chop. "We have a pretty clear case. I'd have been bothering you about it quick enough if—"

Judge Coates grunted. "You don't have to tell me everything you're doing," he said. "Was Bonnie in court?"

"I didn't see her."

"She said something about it. She might have liked to hear you."

Abner said, "In that courtroom, nobody can hear anything. The defendants are a bad lot. I don't think we'll have much trouble disposing of them."

"Who's sitting? Tom? Yes. You told me. I suppose Horace didn't want to sentence anyone to death."

"Judge Irwin might not like it, but from what I've seen of him, he wouldn't try to get out of it. I think the real reason is, he was busy. I know he has three or four opinions to write."

Judge Coates said, "That's one thing I never had to do. It just happened, all the time I was on the bench here, we never had a capital case. Well, we did have one; but the defendant hanged himself in jail. We just had a county lockup in those days without proper arrangements. There

41

was quite a lot of agitation—" He broke off, as though pulling himself back to his subject. "Well, your grandfather used to say, 'I hanged 'em; and when my dinner was ready, I ate it, too.' He'd say you were soft about other people because you were soft about yourself. I used to think he was very wise—he wasn't any fool, either; but he spoke and acted a good deal on impulse—well, I suppose you think I'm foolish a lot of the time, too."

"No," said Abner. "I've thought you were darn stubborn on occasion."

"I'm afraid as you get older you'll find I've said a lot of foolish things." Judge Coates made a restless movement. "Yes. Bonnie was in. I only saw her a moment. Takes so long to get me fixed in the morning. I don't think those exercises do any good." He picked up his left arm by the wrist and let it drop. "I don't know why she bothers to bring me flowers." A suggestion of tears appeared behind his glasses, but he winked his eyes and drawing up his lower lip one-sidedly, bit it.

Abner said, "She does it because she likes you."

"Sorry for me!" said Judge Coates. "Aren't you two ever going to get married?"

"I don't know," Abner said, somewhat embarrassed. "You'll have to ask her."

"I wish you'd get settled. It's time you did." He hesitated. He then said quickly, "Great mistake for a lawyer to marry too early. Always hard to get established. But you aren't still a boy, and you ought to have something more than good prospects. Is Marty going to run for another term this fall?"

"I haven't the faintest idea," Abner said. He filled his mouth with apple pie; but since his father waited, saying nothing, until he had finished chewing, he added, "I know he had a talk with Jesse Gearhart. I don't know what about."

"The Attorney General sent for a number of county chairmen a month or so ago. I was told Jesse was one of them. They badly need some special deputies. It's an eight thousand dollar job."

"I don't know that Marty would want it. And if he did, I don't know whether Jesse would want me to run for district attorney." Abner finished the pie. "I could use the salary, if that's sufficient recommendation. Then perhaps I could afford to get married."

Judge Coates said, "Have a row with Bonnie?"

"No," said Abner. "The situation is the same, however. She thinks she has to keep her job. So—" He shrugged.

"Yes, I know," Judge Coates said. "Somebody's got to support her mother and the children. Could you do it?"

Abner said, "I'm sure I don't know, Father. I haven't figured it out. She says she won't have it that way. I don't think she even knows what you're giving Cousin Mary now."

Judge Coates said, "Her father was like that about money. Straight as a die." He paused. "I don't know a better thing you can say of a man. There have been cases where a girl got married and went on working."

"I'm afraid this won't be one of them," Abner said. He looked at his watch. "I'll have to run. We're starting in ten minutes. Could I get you anything?"

"No, no. I have everything. You aren't going to be here for dinner, are you?"

"I was planning to go on the Calumet Club party. I'll be back first."

"If you go by the office on your way home, you might bring me up Corpus Juris on Limitations. Doesn't matter much, though. Arlene very busy?"

"I haven't seen her since nine. She oughtn't to be. She only had the Blessington will thing, I think."

"Well, I may send down for her. I have a couple of letters."

"All right, Father," Abner said. "See you about five." Going through the living room into the dark hall, he called, "Aunt Myrt! I'm leaving now."

43

Two

THIS WAS THE HOUR when time stood still. The well of the court was sunk in tepid shadow. Above the slanting half circle of shadowed seats the courtroom windows were free from the sun now, but bright with light; and Abner, leaning back in his chair, could see the northeastern sky, a hazed hot blue behind the sunny treetops. The heavy quiet in the court was not broken so much as mildly stirred by Bunting's voice. Bunting's questions, even and dry, spoken slowly, rose in the silence and shadow, caromed off wall and ceiling, and the multiple echoes died. From .the witness stand, Doctor Hill, the coroner, returned his answers with professional deliberation, the ripple of sound beginning again, widening out, echoing, dying.

On the bench Judge Vredenburgh moved his head, his double-chinned but strong and firm plethoric face turning in sharp advertence, his blue eyes glinting, from Bunting to the witness and occasionally to the jury. His right hand under the desk lamp before him could not be seen, but the light winked now and then on the metal end of a pencil as he wrote. Under the bench Joe Jackman, in the glow of his lamp, wrote too, and paused and wrote and paused, his expression bemused, his thoughts apparently far away. Next to Joe sat Nick Dowdy, gray head bowed, fat chin sunk on his chest, placidly asleep. Next to Nick, Mat Rhea, the clerk of Quarter Sessions, looked at his clasped hands, slowly and patiently twiddling his thumbs. Farther down the line, Gifford Hughes, the prothonotary, sat back, his mustache sadly drooping, his eyes dreamily fixed in space. Beyond Gifford,

44

Hermann Mapes, the clerk of the Orphans Court, bent forward, plainly busy with some of his office work. In their elevated chairs around the circle of the rail, the tipstaffs were drowsing. Now one, now another, now two or three at once nodded slowly. Then one or another woke, lifting his head with a light practiced jerk, affecting to have been awake all the time. Down by the lower doors the state police officers yawned.

At the defense's table Harry Wurts slouched debonairely, easy and smiling. He wore a suit of thin tan material a good deal wrinkled. His coat hung open. His dark blue necktie was loosened and the collar undone around his sunburned neck. Across his fleshy chest his limp white shirt strained at the buttons. Sometimes Harry tapped his teeth with a pencil, or rolled it against the reddish bristles of his little cropped mustache. Sometimes he murmured something to Stanley Howell beside him, or inclined an ear to listen.

George Stacey, between Howell and Basso, wrote industriously. George was one of the youngest members of the bar, and he was probably glad of the Court's appointment. Starting a law practice in a country town was hard. Older people hesitated to give a boy like George important and profitable legal business; and George's contemporaries, to whom George might not look so hopelessly young and inexperienced, were not yet in a position to have important or profitable legal business. George had good sense, and he was a steady worker; but the opportunities that happened to be available for going in with an older man looked so poor that George was trying it the hard way—opening his own office. Abner, though he had enjoyed several advantages George did not have, knew all about those first years, and he was sure that George hardly earned expenses. This trial, putting George in the public eye, would do him good; and no doubt the judges chose him with that benevolent idea. Sitting there, slight, blond, and worried, George, it could be seen, was leaving no stones unturned. George could not have any

45

serious hope of getting Basso off, which would make his job discouraging enough; and Basso, by standing mute and refusing to help himself or his counsel, made it difficult to the point of impossibility to do anything for him. George, writing so hard, must be taking most of the testimony, scrutinizing every bit of it for possible technical points, and Abner had to admire such resolute if probably futile industry.

On George's right, Basso, playing his dogged part, glowered straight in front of him, his round little face hard and contemptuous. He did not look at anything. He did not seem to hear anything. Howell, on the other hand, shifting in his seat, hitching closer to Harry, letting himself drop back, whispering, nodding, his hands always in movement, heard everything and looked everywhere. He paid avid attention to Bunting and Doctor Hill. He bothered Harry constantly.

Bunting was winding up his examination. He said to Doctor Hill, "And did you see those irons also at Mr. Westbrook's undertaking establishment the night you performed the postmortem examination?"

Remote and sonorous, Doctor Hill said, "I did."

Bunting looked at the card in his hand on which he had jotted his notes, turned it over, and put it in his pocket. "Now, Doctor," he said, "referring to these wounds, would either of the wounds you have described for us as found upon this body have proved fatal to the man receiving them?"

"Indubitably both or either would, Mr. Bunting."

"And could you tell, from your examination, how soon death must have ensued following such gunshot wounds?"

"I have no hesitation in saying, within a very few minutes."

"Doctor," said Bunting, "did you make any tests to ascertain whether the body of the man you examined was dead when it was placed in the water?"

"I did, sir."

"And what conclusion did you come to, if any?"

"That body was dead when it was placed in the water."

46

"Thank you, Doctor," Bunting said. "Cross-examine."

He came around the table and sat down by Abner. He drew a deep breath and relaxed, tilting back a little. "That's work," he said. "Damned stuffed shirt. You can't tone him down any. Harry will have a field-day." He reached out and took a paper cup of water in a plastic holder beside the little vacuum carafe on the table and swallowed some.

Harry Wurts came casually down past the jury, shrugging his wrinkled coat into place. He put his hands in his trouser pockets, tilted his head back, and looked at Doctor Hill. "By the way, Doctor," he said, "just how did you ascertain whether the body was dead before it was put in the water?"

"Quite simple," said Doctor Hill. "I removed the lungs and found air in them. Therefore he did not drown."

"We are quite simple people," Harry Wurts said amicably. "Just how do you apply this test of yours? Describe it, if you will."

"The test is not mine, Mr. Wurts," Doctor Hill said sharply. "It is a standard test. You can determine whether there is air in a lung by feeling it with your hands. Put the lungs in a bucket of water, and they will float."

"Then you opened the chest cavity, removed the lungs, and placed them in a bucket of water?"

"Quite so."

"And because the lungs floated after you put them in water, you concluded that their former owner was dead before he was put in water. What date was this?"

"The eleventh of May."

"Who was present beside yourself?"

"Oh, a lot of people. You can't expect me to list them all."

"If there were too many for you to remember all, can you remember any?"

"Well, the district attorney and his assistant, Abner Coates, there; and Westbrook; and John Costigan, and the sheriff, Hugh was there, I remember—I suppose there were fifty people there."

"You were holding a public postmortem?"

"I didn't have a public one, no."

"Fifty people," Harry Wurts said. "Do you generally make a spectacle out of it when you post a body?"

Annoyed, his dignity given an obvious cut, Doctor Hill said, "I made no spectacle. I have no control over the morgue. I was doing the posting."

"You have no control over it. I see." By a motion of his head Harry managed to suggest that such an admission destroyed any possible value the coroner's testimony might have. He said, showing patience, "Well, Doctor, you testified to these supposed bullet wounds. You mentioned what you described as points of entrance. How do you distinguish a point of entrance from a point of exit, or can't you?"

"I can distinguish them readily," Doctor Hill said. "It is very simple. At the point of entrance the skin will go inward with the bullet. At a point of exit, the skin breaks open, driven out."

Bunting said to Abner, "We might get Mrs. Zollicoffer on. I don't think she'll take more than an hour." He looked over toward Frederick Zollicoffer's widow. "Don't know whether she's going to act up or not—" He snapped his attention back to Harry. "What was that?" he said to Abner.

Abner said, "He asked whether the bullet wounds were of the same size and Hill said yes."

"Without the other bullet, I don't think he can get anywhere," Bunting said, "but we'll have to watch that."

Abner nodded. He was still looking at Mrs. Zollicoffer, surprised again to notice that she was not altogether unattractive. Not young, though she must have been younger than Frederick Zollicoffer, and not pretty in any ordinary meaning of the word, she was thin and graceful, her legs and arms narrow but round and flexible. Frederick Zollicoffer had been, in life, of much the same general appearance and build as his brother William, now sitting beside her, and it was impossible to see such physical disparity without wondering how on earth she came to marry a Zollicoffer.

Bunting would have been glad to emphasize the query, for Frederick Zollicoffer was a weak point. The truth was, and Harry would certainly bring the truth out, that Frederick Zollicoffer had been a drug peddler, an addict himself, and a man with a criminal record of a particularly low and despicable sort. Though killing him was, of course, a crime, his death was no loss—even a gain—to society at large. Thinking along this line, a jury might do something silly, like deciding the defendants were not so bad after all.

This was where Mrs. Zollicoffer could come in. To counter with law or logic was hard, for in adopting such a line of thought, a jury already had declared the intention to abandon both. Collective entities—a jury, a team, an army, a mob—often showed a collective apprehension and a collective way of reasoning that transcended the individual's reasoning and disregarded the individual's logic. The jury, not embarrassed by that need of one person arguing alone to explain and justify what he thought, could override any irrelevancy with its intuitive conviction that, irrelevant or not, the point was cogent. To this there could be no assuredly right answer; but answering that Frederick Zollicoffer's bad character did not extenuate his murder was assuredly wrong, beside the cogent point. Bunting had hoped, if the need arose, to answer with the piteous spectacle of Mrs. Zollicoffer, to let her appearance demand the punishment of the defendants, and by her appearance to suggest that, anyway, whatever Frederick Zollicoffer might have been, she was nothing like him, and was thus doubly to be pitied—for the pain caused her by his sudden death; for the pain caused her by his criminal life. That would about fill the bill, and even go Harry one better, since it not only answered irrelevancy with irrelevancy, but had the added valuable feature of a contradiction; that is, two chances, on more or less opposing grounds, to evoke another intuitive conviction, this time favoring the Commonwealth.

Unfortunately Mrs. Zollicoffer had a mind of her own, and it was a poor one. She also had her own feelings. Bunting, annoyed, regarded her feelings with incredulity; but Abner, noticing her once or twice yesterday and today, was prepared to believe that her feelings fell in the limited class of things that might be incredible but were, even so, real. Mrs. Meade, the tipstaff sitting with her, had sat near and observed distressed women for years and could probably distinguish, as well as such things could be distinguished, degrees of genuineness in feeling. Mrs. Meade considered this distress the real thing and felt distressed too. Though, for everyone else, Frederick Zollicoffer was an impersonal object known as "that body" with skin that a bullet pushed inward on entering and outward on leaving, he could not have been that for Mrs. Zollicoffer. She sat there trembling while on the stand Doctor Hill, bumbling on, said, "I have testified that it went downward, the second bullet. I removed it from between the fifth and sixth ribs on the right side in a mid-axillary line."

"In your opinion," said Harry Wurts casually, "was the bullet of the same size as the one you found, the one that made the head wound?"

Mrs. Zollicoffer flinched, and Doctor Hill said, "Similar, I should say." Bunting touched Abner with his elbow and said, "Pay attention. I'll want you to ask him a few questions. I don't want that to stand."

Seeing them whisper, Harry Wurts smiled. He said to Doctor Hill, "What bones would that bullet strike in passing through the body?"

"It would not strike any. It did not pass through any. It passed posterior to the clavicle and anterior to the scapula."

"Now, just say that in English, if you will."

Abner glanced again at Mrs. Zollicoffer. She had taken out a handkerchief; unfortunately, a gesture also possible to those whose anguish was neither irrepressible nor even real. The show of real feeling was, of course, all right for Bunting's purpose; but thanks to that feeble mind of hers, Mrs. Zollicoffer might not get the benefit of it. On the stand Harry would certainly show that she was a liar, and so false in everything. She had told Bunting the absurd lie that she did not know what her husband's business was; and when you thought of all the trouble that willful piece of stupidity was going to make, it was difficult to feel much sympathy for her.

Clasping his shoulder, Harry Wurts said, "I don't know whether I'm any different from that body, but when I feel my shoulder, I feel a bone wherever I feel. What I am trying to find out is how this bullet could pass through here and not strike any bone."

"I tried to explain to you, Mr. Wurts."

"You said a shot through the shoulder could not strike any bone?"

Bunting, who was drawing a face on the pad before him, left it with one eye and said, "Oh, no. He didn't say that."

Doctor Hill said, "Mr. Wurts, the bullet entered the flesh and passed through the fleshy part of the lungs and lodged in the flesh again between the fifth and sixth ribs."

"That bullet did," said Harry. "That bullet, though it encountered nothing but flesh, lodged. The other bullet, the one you did not recover, was obliged to pass through the hard bony skull, the brain, and came out below the angle of the jaw." He stood delicately poised, balanced on his toes. His voice had a sudden, cocky, assertive note, and Abner looked at him, astounded. He looked at Bunting, but Bunting was biting his lip; and, jolted, Abner had to admit his own slow-wittedness in only then grasping the bold maneuver. Harry said coolly, "How do you try to account for one bullet having so much more force than the other? I suppose you admit it must have had?"

The play on Doctor Hill's conceit of knowledge and

touchiness about his dignity was perfect. Unable to help his witness, Bunting winced; and Doctor Hill said with asperity, "I do not 'try' to account for it, Mr. Wurts. I account for it without difficulty. There is no reason to suppose that one bullet had more force than the other. The longer passage through the tissues of the body would add up to offer more resistance than the relatively short passage through the head. The skull is only relatively hard, Mr. Wurts. A bullet fired at it point blank, at close range, would be retarded very little."

Harry Wurts said, "Do you mean to tell me that bullets of identically the same caliber, from identically the same gun, could behave so differently?"

"I do, indeed," said Doctor Hill.

"Then in your opinion both bullets came from the same gun?"

"No, Mr. Wurts, I did not say that. I—"

"You said both could have come from the same gun."

"Why, yes. I see no reason why not—"

"You see no reason why not. That is all."

Bunting said, "Just a moment, Doctor." To Abner he said, "We'll have to show he doesn't know anything about it."

"Have trouble without crossing him," Abner said. He saw Harry, back in his seat, looking at them with amusement.

"Yes," said Bunting. "You're the goat. When Harry kicks, I'll cover you with the Judge as well as I can. It's better that way, because you couldn't cover me. See?"

"Yes," said Abner. "Want me to barge right in?"

"Might as well."

Abner got up and walked around to the witness stand. He paused a moment, wishing he could find a way to do it cleverly; like Harry Wurts, to make Doctor Hill out of his own self-importance, apparently of his own accord, declare now, with the same pompous insistence, that though one shot came from one gun (Bailey's), the other probably came from another (presumably Basso's). However, if you tried being clever and failed, you were worse off for being caught at it than if you never tried. Abner said as disarmingly as he could, "I believe that you said that the wounds made by these separate bullets were somewhat similar. Did you reach that conclusion from the diameter of the bullet holes?"

"Diameter," said Doctor Hill, "yes."

"Did you judge just by eye?" Abner said, and caught himself up, waiting in apprehension. Bunting would see that it was a dumb question. You should know the answers when you questioned your own witness; and, for all Abner knew, Doctor Hill had some scientific form of measurement which might show that they were not merely similar but exactly the same. To his relief, Doctor Hill said, "Just by eye. But—"

Abner cut in, speaking quietly, trying to offer along with the question, a sort of encouragement or reassurance that Doctor Hill might take as a sign that he should assent, "You are not, of course, an expert in bullet wounds, Doctor?"

"Oh, now!" said Harry. He laughed out loud. "I object! He can't cross-examine his own witness! I never heard of such a thing!"

"Your Honor," said Bunting, "the Commonwealth simply is clearing up a line of questioning Mr. Wurts opened and then, having established a very misleading impression, tried to drop."

"He can't continue my cross-examination!" Harry said. "What is your witness? Ignorant? Unwilling? Perjuring himself? I don't know any other grounds."

Bunting said, "I think it is the province of the Court, and not of Mr. Wurts, to decide what questions may be put. We respectfully ask his Honor to rule."

"He may answer," Judge Vredenburgh said. "There is no prejudice to the defendants if the witness states whether or not he is an expert on gunshot wounds."

"I ask an exception," said Harry Wurts.

"Exception granted," said Judge Vredenburgh. "Proceed, Mr. Coates."

Abner said, "Are you an expert in bullet wounds, Doctor Hill?"

"I never said I was," said Doctor Hill. He gave Abner an offended look.

"Or in the caliber of bullets?"

"I don't pretend to be, Mr. Coates."

"That's all, thank you."

"If you please!" said Harry Wurts, starting up. "You have had experience in examining bullet wounds, have you not, Doctor?"

"I have examined them, yes." Doctor Hill plainly viewed this deferential approach with suspicion. He felt that the Commonwealth was now against him, and Harry for him; and he had no idea what was going on. Resentful, he suspected that a plot to impair his dignity had been joined.

"More than once?" said Harry Wurts.

"More than once. Certainly."

"You were a doctor in the army, were you not?"

"During the last war. Yes."

"You saw gunshot wounds then?"

"Yes. I have also seen a certain number during the hunting season." The jury laughed.

Judge Vredenburgh said, "That is no laughing matter," but he smiled.

Harry Wurts smiled too. "In short, Doctor," he said, "when you answered the question of the learned assistant district attorney you meant that while you did not pretend to know it all—"

Bunting said, "I object to counsel's telling the witness what the witness means."

"Correction," Harry Wurts said. "In short, Doctor, your experience has familiarized you perfectly with bullet wounds?"

"I think I may say that I am familiar with them."

"When you stated that, in your opinion, the wounds, bullet wounds, in Frederick Zollicoffer's body were the same size, that was a conclusion you formed on examining and comparing the wounds at the time of the postmortem?"

"Quite so."

"And you are still of the same opinion?"

"I am."

"I have no more questions," Harry Wurts said.

Bunting said, "That is all, Doctor Hill." He looked at the clock above the door to the Attorneys Room. He said to Abner, "Quarter of four." He looked at his list of witnesses. "I think we could get through with Mrs. Z. if she behaves herself. If she makes a mess of it, it would be all to the good if Harry can't cross-examine until tomorrow morning. We'll let Cholendenko wait." Ida Cholendenko, the Zollicoffers' servant, had presented a little problem. Though, in one sense, her testimony corroborated Mrs. Zollicoffer's, she could testify to events preceding by a few minutes on that night of the kidnapping anything Mrs. Zollicoffer could testify to.

Abner said, "There's this about it, Marty. If Harry wrecks Mrs. Z., it would be handy to have Cholendenko. She could straighten some of it up; and I don't think Harry could do a thing with her."

"We'll need her," Bunting said. He turned and looked sharply at Mrs. Zollicoffer, pushed his chair back, and arising, called out her name. To Abner, he said, "Look through that folder and get what she said about the telephone calls. Just lay it open so I can look at it if I need to."

Mrs. Zollicoffer sat first in the row of the Commonwealth's witnesses, with Mrs. Meade in the tipstaff's chair beside her. Mrs. Zollicoffer hesitated, dazed and quailing; and Mrs. Meade confirmed Abner's guess. Mrs. Meade, with gentle solicitude, arose and helped Mrs. Zollicoffer to arise. Though she did no more than her duty, her duty now served the Commonwealth in a way the record would not show. The jurors all looked at Mrs. Meade, who made a good figure.

Her white hair was tidily waved. Mrs. Meade wore a blue skirt, and a blue jacket which did not differ from the jacket the men wore, with the word *tipstaff* embroidered on the sleeve, and the silver badge pinned to the breast; but Mrs. Meade wore with it a white blouse with a lace-edged open collar, pretty and neat. She was the widow of a former clerk of the Orphans Court, and came of good people, and looked it. Sympathetically showing Mrs. Zollicoffer how to go, even giving Mrs. Zollicoffer's arm a reassuring pat, Mrs. Meade offered in evidence her opinion that Mrs. Zollicoffer was an unfortunate, unhappy woman who should be treated considerately. Because of Mrs. Meade's official position, her ladylike appearance, and the fact that she was well known to all or most of the jurors, her evidence was at once accepted as excellent. Though, subsequently, the jury might themselves observe, or hear other people say, things to change the picture, a general prepossession in Mrs. Zollicoffer's favor would remain, mysteriously breaking the force of good arguments against her, persistently suggesting that, even so, how could you be sure?

Mrs. Zollicoffer passed behind the jury; and Malcolm Levering, from the tipstaff's seat at the end by the door of the Attorneys Room, came to meet her. The two state police officers drew back to make more room, and Malcolm gave her an encouraging smile, bobbing his mostly bald head politely, half offering his arm, which she did not take, half shooing her along to the steps of the witness stand. He remained a moment while she dragged herself up them. Nick Dowdy had come in behind Joe Jackman's desk and proffered his Bible. Mrs. Zollicoffer stood dazed; so Nick indicated, with a gesture, that she should put her hand on the open page. He reeled off the oath and looked at her inquiringly, nodded himself, to show her that she should nod, and said, "Your name, please?" She whispered something, and Nick turned away, saying loudly, "Marguerite Zollicoffer."

Joe Jackman twisted in his chair, looking up from the light on his ruled paper, and said, "-g-u-e-r-i-t-e?"

Starting at the unexpected voice from an unexpected direction, she nodded, continuing to stand; and Judge Vredenburgh said, "You may sit down."

Bunting, who had been looking at her closely, his sharp nose up, his eyes narrowed, came down before the jury and said to her, "Mrs. Zollicoffer, where do you live?"

Running through the piled folders of notes and stenographic transcripts, Abner had found the conversations about the telephone calls. He twitched the open folder around and pushed it up to the edge of the table behind Bunting.

Bunting said evenly, in a mild clear voice with the slight stiffness of good control that betrayed to Abner, who knew of it, but probably to no one else, the annoyance and contempt he felt, "You are the widow of the late Frederick Zollicoffer?"

Mrs. Zollicoffer's appearance, the black clothes, the gaunt but regular features, the faded blonde (and not, as you would have expected, in any way retouched) hair that showed under a simple, and even becoming, hat, spoke for her, just as Bunting hoped; but now, speaking against her, was something else, like her appearance, like Mrs. Meade's solicitude, not part of the record, yet incontestably part of the evidence. In the office it had not seemed so apparent; but here, set off by silence, her speaking voice was bad. Abner saw the change in one or two members of the jury as they recognized, surprised and then displeased, strong traces of a tough and uneducated accent.

The jurors were plain or homely speakers themselves, indifferent to grammar and disdainful of elegant pronunciations; but that particular accent of Mrs. Zollicoffer's served as a reminder that she, like all the rest of these people, came from the city. With irritation the jury heard the foreigners, the people from somewhere else, having their presumptuous say. Justice for all was a principle they understood and believed in; but by "all" they did not perhaps really mean persons low-down and no good. They meant that any accused person should be given a fair, open hearing, so that a man might explain, if he could, the appearances that seemed to be against him. If his reputation and presence were good, he was presumed to be innocent; if they were bad, he was presumed to be guilty. If the law presumed differently, the law presumed alone.

Bunting said, "And did you see your husband, Frederick Zollicoffer, on the night of the sixth of April?"

"No, sir."

"Do you know of your own observation whether your husband returned to your home that night?"

Bunting had been at pains to go over this part of it with her, explaining to her what the question meant, and what the Court would and would not allow her to answer. She hesitated, and Abner knew that there was a good chance she would either forget or deliberately answer as she pleased.

She said finally, "No, sir."

"You don't know, of your own observation," Bunting said, probably with inward relief. "Did you hear anything at or near your home in the course of the evening?"

Mrs. Zollicoffer hesitated again. "Why," she said, "do you mean his horn? He blew his horn about twenty minutes after ten."

Bunting bit his lip. "If you do not understand any of my questions, Mrs. Zollicoffer, just ask me to repeat them. Who blew what horn?"

"My husband did. He blew it like he did—always when he came in he blew it so I would know who it was."

"Objected to," said Harry Wurts.

"Sustained," Judge Vredenburgh said. He gazed intently at Mrs. Zollicoffer, as though trying to make up his mind about her.

"Just how did he blow this horn?" Bunting asked.

George Stacey, half arising beside Basso, said, "I also

object to it, implying this 'he' was her husband, and whether he blew his horn or not, unless it is shown he was in his car." The effort made him turn red, but Harry gave him a cordial nod and George sat down.

Bunting said, "Mrs. Zollicoffer, you say you heard a horn blown. Is that correct?"

"Yes. My husband's horn."

"I object to that!" Harry Wurts said. "That is what we object to!"

"Yes," said Judge Vredenburgh. "That part of the answer is stricken."

Bunting said, "Now, please answer only what I ask. You say you heard a horn that night?"

"Yes."

"How was that horn blown?"

Mrs. Zollicoffer shook her head distractedly. "I don't know how you mean did he blow it. Just about twice. Like a little tune on it."

"Exactly," said Bunting, "that is just what I mean—"

Everitt Weitzel, the tipstaff who usually acted as doorman, came down the sloping aisle from the main door and limped carefully, as though making himself invisible, across the well of the court. Coming up beside the Commonwealth's table, he bent low past Abner's shoulder and spread out a half sheet of printed stationery. It was headed "Earl P. Foulke, Justice of the Peace." In Earl's fancy, but now senile, curlicue script was written: "Mr. Bunting or Coates. Like to have you get touch with me at once. Important. E. P. F."

"Where did you get this?" Abner murmured.

"Kid up there brought it in. One of Mr. Foulke's grandsons, I think."

"He didn't say what the trouble was?"

"Just said Mr. Foulke said to see you got it right away."

"Well, tell him we did get it. Tell him to say we'll call him when court adjourns."

Bunting, his left arm doubled behind his back where he

clasped and unclasped his fingers, took a turn past the end of the table. "After you heard this horn blown," he said to Mrs. Zollicoffer, "did you hear anything else?"

George Stacey got to his feet and said, "I object again to this witness testifying in relation to the blowing of any horn unless she can some way identify it. All cars of the same make have the same horn. This is on a traveled thoroughfare."

Judge Vredenburgh took off his glasses. "That objection was sustained as to the identification at this particular time." George Stacey's father had been a close friend of his, and the glint of his eye was affable, the light of amusement over seeing the children grow up. "There is no objection, however, to her stating that she heard a horn. That she can testify to. Objection overruled." He shook his head, smiled faintly, and put his glasses on.

Bunting said to Joe Jackman, "Will you repeat the question?"

Jackman drew a breath, stared at his notes, and read it. "No, I did not," said Mrs. Zollicoffer.

"Did your husband return to your home that night?"

"I heard him down as far as the garage."

"That I object to," Harry Wurts said with an accent of long-suffering.

"Objection sustained," said Judge Vredenburgh. "She has not shown how she knew it was her husband."

Looking at Abner, Bunting rolled his eyes up, though he took care to keep his face turned away from the jury. Pushing out the sheet of paper with Foulke's message on it, Abner tapped it; and Bunting gave it a quick look. "Old fool!" he said softly. He faced the witness stand and said, "Madam, you stated that you heard sounds down as far as the garage, after you heard this horn. Did you see anything?"

"No, sir."

"When was the last time that you saw your husband?"

"In the morning. That morning. The sixth of April."

"That was the last time you saw him alive."

Mrs. Zollicoffer brought up a handkerchief from the wadded ball she had made of her gloves and put it to her nose. "Yes."

"When did you next see him?"

"When they found him, brought him up to the—" She began to cry.

"You were present when he was brought to the undertaking establishment of Mr. Westbrook in Childerstown?"

She nodded, the handkerchief in the palm of her hand pressed over her mouth. Judge Vredenburgh said to Malcolm Levering, "Bring her a glass of water."

"You saw the body and you were able to identify it?"

Mrs. Zollicoffer took the paper cup Malcolm Levering held up to her, swallowed a little water, coughed, and nodded.

"Whose body was it?"

"My husband's."

"Take a little more water," Bunting said. "The jury can't hear you. It was the body of Frederick Zollicoffer?"

"Yes."

"Mrs. Zollicoffer," said Judge Vredenburgh, "you must try to control yourself."

Mrs. Zollicoffer began to sob aloud, catching her breath with wailing gasps, letting it out in lamentable broken groans that carried clearly to the statuelike rows of spectators in the gloom. The shadows of the latening afternoon filled the great wood-paneled vault, but now a little slanting sunlight was reaching the inside edges of the northwestern windows. Reflected from black walnut, the radiance was melancholy; less than the light now falling from the thousand watt bulbs behind the stained glass wheel of the skylight.

Bunting said, "Do you wish me to stop, sir?"

"Well, does she go on like this? She'll have to be examined. She must know that—" Judge Vredenburgh looked at

Harry Wurts, and jerked his chin, beckoning him up. "What about this, Harry?" he said.

Harry Wurts said, "We don't like it, naturally, your Honor. I don't think the district attorney ought to provoke such a display—"

Judge Vredenburgh said, "I think it is beyond the district attorney or anyone else's control."

"Well, sir," said Harry, "if Mr. Bunting stops harping on the body, there might be some other line he could take, I suppose. I'm perfectly willing to waive cross-examination today, if the Commonwealth will recall her tomorrow morning."

Judge Vredenburgh said, "We will recess for ten minutes. Mrs. Meade, will you come and take the witness out, please? Very well, Mr. Wurts. Make whatever agreement you like. Perhaps we can have another witness."

Bunting turned from the sidebar and, looking at Abner, formed with his lips the word, Foulke.

Nodding, Abner got up and crossed over to the door of the Attorneys Room. Inside he leaned against the wall by the telephone, waiting while the number was rung. Above the fireplace, empty, unused for forty years, hung a big framed photograph, faded and a little blurred, taken in 1866 of the county bench and bar gathered in the old courthouse. Abner's grandfather, who was then, like George Stacey now, one of the youngest members, peered over a couple of heads at one side. Despite fading, and the handicaps that the photographer, using a wet plate indoors, had to overcome, the faces were mostly clear, and Linus Coates, despite his youth, carried an air that you didn't find in George Stacey.

Linus Coates had, in fact, been to the wars. He served in a nine months' regiment and got a bullet through his hip at Chancellorsville. In those days it was not the fashion to be embittered or disillusioned by such an experience, so what Linus Coates looked was simply grown-up, self-possessed, ready for responsibilities. When, years later, the duty confronted him as a judge, you could understand how he sentenced men to hang, just as he said, without loss of appetite.

As though to emphasize the point, George Stacey came in then, headed for the lavatory. Seeing Abner at the telephone, he said, "Well, how's the assistant superintendent of the waterworks?"

"You're a hard man, George," Abner said. "Shut up, will you? Yes. Mr. Foulke. Mr. Foulke, this is Abner Coates. Mr. Bunting is in court. Can I help you?"

Earl Foulke's voice was high and rapid, and hearing it, Abner could see Earl's face, his prominent pale eyes magnified by his silver-rimmed glasses, his lips tucked in over his toothless gums—he put in his teeth only when he held what he took care to call, not a hearing, but Court; or when he performed marriage ceremonies under a portable white-painted wood arbor covered with artificial roses which stood ready in the corner of his parlor. When his teeth were not in, the ends of his scanty, scraggly long mustache hung well below his chin. Earl owned and wore a black frock coat—one of the only two such garments remaining in the county (the other belonged to a Baptist minister who wore it at rustic funerals). He was a preposterous figure, and even the farmers of Kingstown Township could see that he was; but Earl had been Squire for twenty-five years, and Abner supposed that the voters kept re-electing him because they felt that he now had a vested interest in the office; and, moreover, was too old and incompetent to go back to farming for a livelihood.

As well as preposterous in appearance, Earl was stupid and officious; and Marty, who had been obliged to straighten out several senseless legal snarls in which Earl had involved both himself and the district attorney's office, no longer regarded Earl as merely pathetic or comic. Earl Foulke was a damned old nuisance who ought to be forcibly retired. It was an opinion that Abner was obliged, in common sense, to share.

"Yes, Mr. Foulke," Abner said when Earl seemed to have finished. "We know about the Williams case. That was assault and battery. Marty has your transcript, I know. He'll want to see Mrs. Williams—"

"Now, just a minute, just a minute, Ab," Earl Foulke said. An annoying habit of Earl's was his trick of beginning in the middle. He would describe a situation and ask what he should do; and when he was told, he began at once to scruple or object; and in support of his objections, he trotted out new, not-before-mentioned circumstances leading up to or ensuing from the situation described, which, Earl was quite right in maintaining, certainly did change the picture.

"Oh, Lord!" said Abner to himself. "Well, Mr. Foulke," he said, "I'm afraid you couldn't do that. You accepted bail for Williams' appearance here in court, you know. That exhausts your jurisdiction."

Earl Foulke's voice went squeak, squeak, squeak; and Abner said, "No, Mr. Foulke. It's impossible. You wouldn't be competent; a justice of the peace isn't allowed—no, I can't off-hand cite the act, or whatever it is. You must have one of those handbooks. Your powers are defined there. Marty wouldn't have any authority to do it. Even Judge Irwin or Judge Vredenburgh couldn't authorize you to re-open the case, because it is out of your hands. If Williams decides to plead guilty, he'll have to come in and tell Marty. He can't just go to you—" Sudden suspicion seized Abner, and he said, "You haven't done anything about it, have you?"

"Course I did something about it!" shrilled Earl Foulke. "Tell you exactly what I did. I want to amend the record, my record—" With each new phrase his voice got higher and higher; a nervous, obviously alarmed, gabbling.

"Mr. Foulke," Abner said, "do you mean that what you

have done is accept Williams' plea of guilty and fine him ten dollars, and discharge him?"

Earl Foulke said defiantly, "Certainly did!" But he faltered, his voice quavering. "Now, Ab," he said placatingly, "those Williamses, I know about them. He's a drinking man, but he's a good provider. Amy Williams don't want him to go to jail. Be much better this way. You tell Marty I know what I'm doing."

Abner said, "Mr. Foulke, that isn't the point. You have no authority to do what you've done. When you do it, it's no more valid than if Mrs. Williams herself fined Mr. Williams ten dollars and discharged him. It's not she, it's not you, it's the Commonwealth that's prosecuting Williams. Don't you see that?"

"Prosecuting him for what?" said Earl Foulke.

"For assault and battery, of course. For beating his wife up."

"What evidence you got?"

"His wife's evidence. What else? What did you swear the warrant out on?"

"That was then," Earl Foulke said. "Now, why, she isn't going to give evidence against him. Changed her mind. No case against him. That's why I—"

Such a change of mind was common, even customary, in these cases. In exasperation, Abner said, "Why should he plead guilty, then?"

"Now, Ab," Earl Foulke said, "he beat her up. Blacked her eye; everything. He hadn't any right to do that. I told him he'd have to plead guilty. I wasn't going to let him off, like nothing happened. They stopped in to see me after lunch today. Anyone could see she didn't want to go on with it. She'd have to testify in court, a lot of trouble, scandal, all that. See?"

"Well, of course we can't make her testify," Abner said, "She can withdraw her complaint—"

"Of course," Earl Foulke said with alacrity. "What I

told her myself. She just didn't think it out. So what I said, I said, 'Look it here, Amy. He beat you up bad and he can't do that. So I'm going to fine him for that. If,' I said, 'you agree not to testify against him, we'll settle this right now.' So I said to Williams, 'You got to plead guilty, so I can fine you. That's only fair to Amy, if she says she won't testify. Now, you make up your minds.' So I left them in my office awhile; and they said they agreed."

"You mean," said Abner, flabbergasted, "that Mrs. Williams was ready to testify, and you told her that if she wouldn't, you'd fine him ten dollars, discharge the case, and save her a lot of trouble?"

"She was still kind of mad, Ab," Earl Foulke said defensively. "You got to look at it from her standpoint. She got a pretty good beating. But if she goes up to court, testifies, and maybe he has a jail term, why, what about her? First she gets beat up; then she has all that embarrassment; then maybe for a couple of months, or however much, she gets no support. Punishes her more than it punishes him."

This sudden deviation into sense astonished Abner; but Marty was right; something clearly ought to be done about Earl Foulke. He said, "Mr. Foulke, that may be all true; but do you know what misprision of felony is? Well, one thing it is, is a criminal neglect to bring to justice a man who commits a felony. Williams commits a felony, and you step in and persuade the only witness, for a consideration, not to testify against him, with the idea of preventing the case from coming to trial. Now, it doesn't matter why you did it. I'm pretty sure Marty could prosecute you for that—"

In law, of course, it was true that it didn't matter why Foulke did it. Foulke had probably told plenty of people in his time that ignorance of the law was no excuse; and just plain ignorance was no excuse either; and why should Earl Foulke be excused? Abner said vainly, "Mr. Foulke, you had no business to do that—"

To rebuke a man who had been older than Abner was

66

now when Abner was born was awkward; and, anyway, not Abner's business. What he had to do was report Foulke's action to Marty, and Marty would take care of it, all right; and without any such qualms. That Foulke, the old fool, meant well, that he had effected a probably just disposal of the Williams case, with no real harm to anyone, and much trouble saved the Commonwealth as well as Mr. and Mrs. Williams, would not weigh with Marty. Marty would say— and it was true; it was the truth that all experience confirmed; it was, in little, the exemplar of the greatest and hardest truth in the world: the good end never has justified, and never will justify, the wrong, bad, or merely expedient means—that the law, whatever it might be in this case, would have to take its course, and Foulke would have to take the consequences.

The long thought filled only part of a second. Abner leaned against the wall in the shadowed room, his eyes on the old photograph above the fireplace—the quaint stiff throng of dead attorneys, the dead bewhiskered judge, the gas fixtures on the bench, the tall spittoons conveniently placed, all the plain outmoded furnishings of the little courthouse pulled down more than half a century ago. George Stacey came out the lavatory door, saluted Abner ironically, and left the room. Abner said, "Mr. Foulke, you understand that I haven't any authority to deal with this. But I'll tell you what I think you'd better do. Get hold of Williams and give him back his ten dollars. Tell him he's not discharged; he's still out on bail. I'll have to tell Marty why you called; so you'd better come up to his office about five this afternoon. You'll have to explain that you misunderstood your position and thought Williams was under your jurisdiction until the case came to trial. Don't say anything about what you told Mrs. Williams. Just say they came to you today and wanted to settle the matter."

Abner paused, aware that if what Earl Foulke had done was misprision of felony, what he himself was doing might very well be called misprision of misdemeanor, at least. He said, "This conversation is not in any way official. If you put a case to me, I can tell you what I think this office's attitude will probably be; but that's all. Then it's up to you. Do you understand that, Mr. Foulke?"

Earl Foulke said, "I know Marty's got a grudge against me. Don't have to tell me that. He always has had. Well, if that's what you want me to do—"

Anticipating with some discomfort the old man's thanks, the well-intended but necessarily offensive thanks for his humanitarian gesture, but also for his not-wholly-straight-forward decision to keep a counsel that was not his to keep, but Marty's; and which he could keep only because Marty trusted him, Abner had been ready to cut Foulke short. He did not want any thanks; but when he did not get any, that too was offensive; and more offensive still, was the crowning effrontery with which Foulke consented to oblige Abner by letting Abner save him. About to set Mr. Foulke right on that last point, about to say that Mr. Foulke was wrong if he thought Abner wanted him to do anything, or cared what he did, Abner could see suddenly that old Foulke, the old fool, was not in fact wrong at all. Who else but Abner volunteered to get Foulke out of his predicament? Abner himself was the only one who could make Abner suppress those worse than asinine, those definitely illegal, acts of telling Williams he had to plead guilty and telling Mrs. Williams that she must not give evidence; and if Abner did not do it because he wanted to, why did he do it?

Abner could find no satisfactory answer. He said curtly, "Be there at five o'clock, Mr. Foulke." He hung up and went into the courtroom.

Judge Vredenburgh sat back in his tall carved chair, holding his glasses patiently. His face looked tired in the reflected light of his reading lamp. Mrs. Meade had just brought Mrs. Zollicoffer in. The only available washroom was upstairs, off the women jurors' room, and getting there and back took some time. Mrs. Zollicoffer was still pale and red-eyed, and the trip did not appear to have done her any good.

Bunting stood by the Commonwealth's table. He said to Abner, "What did he want?"

Abner said, "He's coming up to see you at five. It's that Williams A and B case. He thought he could discharge him if Williams pleaded guilty. I told him he couldn't."

Bunting nodded. Preoccupied, he said without intensity, "I wish he'd go drop dead! Yes, your Honor. If Mrs. Zollicoffer feels able, we are ready."

Abner sat down and Bunting went over to the witness stand. "Now, Madam," he said, "after April sixth, the night of the kidnapping, did you receive any communications from your husband?"

The jurors shifted and settled, taking up again the burden of listening. There was a slight movement in the high ranges of spectators—three women making exaggerated efforts to be quiet while they gained the aisle. Judge Vredenburgh glanced toward them and they slunk quickly to the door.

Mrs. Zollicoffer said, "Yes, sir. Two or three letters."

"In your husband's handwriting?"

"Yes."

"And after that date did you receive any telephone calls?"

Harry Wurts stood up wearily. "I'm sorry, your Honor," he said, "I don't want to interfere unnecessarily; but I will have to ask for an offer of proof from the Commonwealth. I want to know what they purpose to show by these letters and telephone calls."

"I will say to Mr. Wurts," said Bunting, "that I don't intend to go into the subject matter of these letters and calls at the moment."

"All right," said Harry.

"Mrs. Zollicoffer, do you recall whether you received a telephone call on the night of April eleventh?"

"I don't recall the date; but I got calls."

"Did the person who called you on the telephone give any identifying symbol or name?"

"Some man said I have got Fred—"

"No. Please listen to the question—"

Harry Wurts lifted his hand and said, "I move that be stricken."

Judge Vredenburgh said, "That may be stricken as not responsive."

"Did any of the persons who talked to you give any names?"

Mrs. Zollicoffer gazed at him, distraught, probably throwing her mind back in search of what she had said before, either in the office or to the grand jury. "Just asking whether it was me, Marguerite," she said.

"Just a moment," Judge Vredenburgh said. "You should answer yes or no."

"No. I didn't know who that was."

Bunting came back to the Commonwealth's table. To Abner, he said, "I'll drop it. She isn't making any sense."

"Want to ask her about Walter Cohen?"

"Well—" Bunting faced about and said, "Mrs. Zollicoffer, do you know a man named Walter Cohen?"

Since Walter Cohen, her husband's partner or associate, had been sitting two seats away from her all day, she looked bewildered. Then she said, "Yes, sir."

"That's all," Bunting said. "Mr. Wurts?"

"No questions," said Harry.

Howell, apparently not understanding the arrangement, put a hand on Harry's arm, his sickly face stricken; for he doubtless felt that in the important matter of his life everything ought to be gainsaid, every inch of the Commonwealth's course contested. Harry took the hand between two fingers, lifted it, and returned it to Howell's lap. George Stacey said something to Basso, who scowled and shrugged.

Judge Vredenburgh said to Mrs. Zollicoffer, "That is all

for now. You may return to your seat." In answer, Mrs. Zollicoffer took out her handkerchief and began again to cry. "Mrs. Meade," said Judge Vredenburgh, "come and get her, please."

Back at the table, Bunting took up the bill of indictment and put it down again. He said to Abner, "I don't want Cholendenko until I see what Harry does tomorrow. If the cross-examination is bad, we'd be more or less stuck with it—" He said to the bench, "I don't know exactly what your Honor would like. The Commonwealth has no witness that could be briefly disposed of. It's quarter of five, and—"

Judge Vredenburgh looked at the clock. "Yes," he said, "I think that's enough. I think we will adjourn." Nick Dowdy had turned his face up and the Judge nodded to him. Nick struck the block with his mallet. "All persons take notice that this Court now stands adjourned until tomorrow morning, June the fifteenth, Wednesday—"

Judge Vredenburgh came down from the bench, going toward the door of his chambers. In the well of the court, he stopped, faced the jury getting to its feet, and said, "You will bear in mind what was told you about discussion of the case. You understand what is meant by separation. You will now go to the hotel. You are in the bailiffs' charge, in the charge of Mr. Levering and Mr. Unruh, the tipstaffs who have been with you. In short, no one of you can go home until the trial is concluded. Somebody sometimes thinks he can, and so makes us a great deal of trouble. Good night." Unhooking his robe, he went into his chambers.

Piling papers together, Bunting said to Abner, "Now, what about Foulke?"

"He ought to be over at your office."

"I suppose I'll have to give him hell. Going on the barge party?"

"I thought I was," Abner said.

"Well, go ahead. It's all right."

"We've got plenty of time, Marty. I'll go over with you."

"I have to speak to the Judge. Do you want to go right over?"

"Not me," said Abner. "I'll wait for you." He took up his brief case and went into the Attorneys Room.

Joe Jackman was seated in the old leather chair by the window reading the afternoon's copy of the *Examiner*. Looking at Abner over the top of it, he said, "I see where Mr. Coates, the assistant district attorney, in a clear and forceful opening speech for the Commonwealth, said that it was a long time between drinks—"

The door opened and Harry Wurts, preceded by his loud voice chanting, "Loyal and true, Calumet Club, to you—" came in. He added, "Drinks! That's the word I was trying to think of! Now, for the barge party, and the drinks that cheer, and thank God, inebriate! Go put your white pants on, Ab. Court's over."

"It may be for you," Abner said. "We've got a date with Mr. Foulke."

"Not old Lawless; not my old pal, Squire Necessity?" said Harry. "Say, did I tell you about the time he had in Zeb Smith—you remember him—for a certain offense; scilicet, a crime against nature; scilicet, sodomy with a goat—"

"You did," said Jackman, "about twelve times."

"Just for that, I won't tell you," Harry said. "Well, teach him some law, if you can. And don't worry about the party, if you can't make it. I'll take care of Bonnie for you. I'll tell you what she said tomorrow."

"That will be swell," said Abner. "About eleven o'clock, don't forget to fall overboard."

"I don't like your inference!" said Harry. "Say, do you know the legal distinction there? It's time you did. A witness who swears that he saw a woman walking with a man pushing a baby carriage with a baby in it is stating an alleged fact. If he concludes that the baby belongs to the woman and the man doing the work is her husband, that is inference; but if he concludes further that the woman's husband is the father of the woman's baby, he soars into realms of pure conjecture. All for today, students." The door swung closed after him.

"Quite a card!" said Joe Jackman. "Really, aren't you going?"

"Sure. We may be a little late. We can catch the barge down the line somewhere."

"O.K. Be seeing you."

Three

IN THE YEAR 1825 certain leading citizens of Childerstown—the Judge of the Court of Common Pleas, several lawyers, the doctor, the master of the Childerstown Academy—joined together to form for their self-improvement a reading circle or society, which they called the Calumet Club. They accumulated a library and they kept it first in a rented room, and then in a house on East Court Street purchased with a bequest. Other bequests gave them a small endowment. Women were admitted in the '60s, and the female members devoted themselves to charitable enterprises, particularly the care of unmarried mothers.

Some of the charitable work was still carried on; but as time passed, the library was given to the Public Library, and the self-improvement part of it was limited to sponsoring an occasional lecture or concert, and the club's real function became the social one of giving two dances during the winter. These were called cotillions; and though the idea was found too pretentious to be put in plain terms, and anyone (a reporter for the *Examiner*, for instance) who did put it in plain terms caused a laugh, the cotillions were, in fact, coming-out parties. When the daughters of members were old enough to go to them, they were old enough to be married.

Of the four thousand odd inhabitants of Childerstown, about a hundred belonged to the Calumet Club. About thirty-eight hundred had not the least desire to belong, and if they thought about it at all, laughed not merely at the pretentious sound of calling the dances coming-out parties, but

74

at the idea itself, with its suggestion that the course of nature waited on formal Calumet Club recognition. That left a few people who did have a desire to belong, but had not been asked. Since they considered themselves plenty good enough in all basic or important qualifications they spoke bitterly of those hoity-toity snobs. Calumet Club members thought the accusation of snobbishness absurd. Qualifications for membership were ordinary respectability and education, and some interest in the avowed objects of the club. You did not have to have money, and your grandfather did not have to have been a member. It was not their fault that most of the members were in fact children or grandchildren of former members. It was not their fault that respectability and education so often went with an adequate income. If people with means but no grandparents were congenial they were invited to join; if people with grandparents unfortunately lost their means they would certainly not be invited to resign. Since giving parties was now the club's principal activity it would be silly to have members who did not fit in. That was all there was to it.

The Calumet Club had always held dances in the winter, meaning that the dances dated from the 1890s; and it had always held barge parties in the summer, meaning that the barge parties dated from the 1920s. At that time the canal, eighty-five years after its triumphal opening with speeches and the firing-off of cannon, was abandoned. The bankrupt operating company had at last been allowed to discharge its lock keepers and bridge tenders. From the shells of the stone warehouses and the barge basin at what was called Port Childerstown six miles of waterway, though silting up, remained navigable. An old deck barge had been recalked, painted white and green, and fitted with benches and bails for an awning. Teams of mules could tow it up and back in four or five hours while the passengers ate a picnic supper. It was a pleasant way to spend a summer evening.

The barge parties left at six o'clock. It was ten minutes

75

past six when Bunting finished with Mr. Foulke; and Abner went home then to change his clothes. They had arranged that Abner would drive by and pick Bunting up in half an hour. The Buntings lived in one of the new houses out near the golf course on the extension of the hill on which Childerstown was mostly built. From the road in front there was a good view of the lower country and the course of the canal, much of it tree-lined, bending away east through the fields and woods to the gathering horizon haze. The effect was spacious; a burst of calm and pleasant landscape filled with the evening sun, the summer foliage full but still fresh, the fields in a pattern of blocks of different greens. Through gaps in the trees the narrow water of the canal could be seen; and, studying it carefully, Abner was able at last to catch a glimpse of the barge hardly moving, a mile or two away. He pointed it out to Bunting. "We can pick it up at Waltons," he said.

Bunting called to the maid, "All right, Pauline!"

Hearing him, his two little girls came running down the lawn from where they had been playing croquet. "Daddy, could we—"

"Nope!" said Bunting.

Abner said, "Hello, Jenny. Hello, Sarah."

They said, "Hello, Mr. Coates. Daddy—"

"No, sir!" said Bunting. "Not on your life! I have to go. Mother's going to be plenty mad, already." He got into the car while they climbed on the gate, their serious faces and dark heads swaying above the white pickets. "Good-by, Daddy! Good-by, Mr. Coates!" they yelled.

Abner let his clutch in and slid away down the hill. In court, or in the office, it was hard to think of Marty playing with children, or of children being so attached to him—or, for that matter, of Marty bowing meekly to Muriel Bunting's efficient and sensible direction of his household, his children, and himself. The children looked like Muriel, a handsome dark girl, a little taller than Marty. She had sharp ironic ways of checking and correcting Marty; of complaining about the hours he was often obliged to keep; even, of jeering gently at his position and powers. While she did it, she gazed at her husband with an intent, intense devotion that made nonsense of everything she had just said of his unreasonableness or his other failings. Like his daughters, Muriel was, in a word, crazy about him. Thinking of the simple pleasant house, the devoted wife, the agreeable children, Abner said, "Nice kids. You must have lots of fun with them."

Bunting said, "They have their moments. And then they have their other moments. You know, I've been thinking about Earl Foulke. It's definitely second childhood. He can't keep anything in his head. That Williams thing is just an example. Did I tell you, it was last month, I guess, he issued another one of his suspicious character warrants? He's been told half a dozen times there's no such offense! Why do you think they go on electing him?"

"They think this is a free country," Abner said, not quite easy. "Nobody in Childerstown is going to tell them their business. He's been good enough for Kingstown Township for twenty years; and so he's good enough for us."

"Well, sooner or later," Bunting said, "he's going to do something we can get him for—I don't mean prosecute him, though he's as likely as not to do something he could be prosecuted for, but something we could use to make him resign."

Abner said, "I don't know how much harm he does down there. I sort of feel sorry for him."

"I feel sorry for him myself," Bunting said, "but that isn't the point. It's not fair to the people who come before him. There are lots of them, and there's only one of him—thank God! It isn't right to let him off."

"Speaking of that," Abner said, "did John Costigan tell you that he thought he was going to get some evidence this week to show that McCook has been buying junk from minors again? There's a man that never should have been let off."

"Been Vredenburgh, he never would have been let off. If it comes up again, we'll try and see if we can't make sure Vredenburgh hears it. Judge Irwin's trouble is, he always thinks maybe the defendant didn't really mean to do what he did."

"Unless it has liquor in it," Abner said.

"I'm not even sure of that any more," Bunting said. "You didn't hear that Eustis non-support case. I guess you were upstairs. Eustis admitted what the trouble was—he'd go on these bats and spend all his money, or at least forget to make the weekly payments for his wife to Bill's office. Irwin said, 'Well, if that's the only reason—' and I would have bet Eustis was going right to jail; but Irwin goes on, 'it is plain that a simple change in your habits will enable you to make your remittances to the probation officer regularly. Now, we can't close all the saloons; and the saloons can't, or won't, stop you at the door, or refuse to sell you a drink. And then one drink leads to another. You know that.' Irwin looks at him and smiles and says, 'Now I know of a system that works very well if you care to apply it. I've seen it work successfully for more than sixty years because I use it myself. I make sure that I will not take that second drink, or those successive drinks, by not taking the first drink; and I make sure that I will not take the first drink by walking right on by every saloon I see. You might like to try that.' So Eustis is out on his own recognizance. Only thing is, in about three months or less he'll be in again."

Abner said, "Irwin's a good man."

"I don't think anyone would ever argue with you about that," Bunting said, "and he knows more law than anybody in the county, except maybe your father. But he shouldn't have let Eustis off. I was afraid for a while he was going to sit in this Zollicoffer case. I know Harry was praying that he would. I think we have that pretty well in hand. Mrs. Z.

wasn't too bad; and I think Leming is going to be all right. Doctor Janvier says he's much better. You never know what will happen when these dopers lay off. The jury won't like him because of his turning state's evidence; but they don't like Basso standing mute, either. Probably about cancels out—" He fell silent, absorbed and reflective.

Warm air sang by. The new gray concrete road rolled smoothly in long gradients, bent gently right and left between its cable-strung fences. At the white church and stone store at Waltons Corners, Abner put out a hand and swept into the dirt lane that went down through an orchard of rotting apple trees to cross the canal. He parked the car below the old fan-trussed bridge, and they got out.

The barge was approaching on a mile-long straightaway of tranquil water. Between the low green banks, beneath the green arch of overhanging trees, it moved at a snail's pace, fanning out slow smooth ripples from its bow. Hoots and cheers came from it to show that Bunting and Abner had been observed. Ben Wister cried to his mules and aimlessly cracked his whip. On board somebody had a portable radio, and the beat of music grew louder, approaching. Thickets of underbrush shadowed most of the canal, but level sun here and there broke across the tow path. Suddenly the mules would amble into shafts of splendor. Immaculate and glowing, the barge's new paint lit up; on deck, the dazzling gold light gilded women's dresses and men's white flannels. Waiting where the tow path, revetted with stone, passed under the hump of the little bridge, Abner could hear ice clatter in a cocktail shaker; and, regardless of the radio, Harry Wurts' unmistakable voice, loudly lifted, singing: "I wish I was single! Oh, then, oh, then . . ."

The mules came up, ducking their stubborn heads, twitching their big ears. Bunting said, "Hello, Ben. Don't you get tired walking?"

Ben winked. "Slipped me a little that snakes' milk they got there. Some of that, and you can walk to China."

The long tow line went by, the barge drew abreast. Mark Irwin, who had evidently been at the snakes' milk, too, said, "Stand by to repel boarders, men!"

Muriel Bunting called out, "Marty, where on earth have you been? Honestly, you might have—"

Abner stepped onto the moving deck. He nodded to Doctor Mosher, who said, "Want to speak to you later, Ab." Abner made his way through the crowd along the board table where hampers were being unpacked and supper laid out. Harry Wurts, filling cocktail glasses from a huge silver shaker with two crossed calumets on it, said, "I admit the law, but deny its applicability to the case in hand. Wake up, Bonnie! Here's the boy friend."

Abner took the glass held out to him and looked at Bonnie and laughed. She had both hands full of knives and forks. Pushing him gently with her elbow, she said, "Get out of my way. I have to—"

"Let them grab their own," Abner said. He took a swallow of the mixed whiskey and vermouth. Bonnie pushed on by him. "Hello," she said. "Don't you get tight."

"The thing I like about her," said Harry, "is that she looks so damn Scotch— Oh, wad," he said, with dramatic expression, "some power the giftie gie us—" He laughed and laughed, pouring himself another drink.

Abner was obliged to laugh, too; for though he wished that a way could be found to make Harry mind his own business, Abner knew what Harry meant. Bonnie was well-made, but long in the leg, with narrow hips and square thin shoulders. Her hair was a light curly brown. The shape of her face was delicate, thin-skinned, with a fresh but faint coloring; yet it was the same shape that, seen in a man with a man's coarse complexion and heavier features, is generally called raw-boned—the wide forehead; the spaced brown eyes; the outstanding cheekbones and the cheeks sloping to the straight jaw and neat, expressive but controlled mouth. It was attractive rather than pretty. More noticeable than the features was her candid mien, her spirited carriage of the head, her air of knowing her own mind. The resulting expression was an odd, and to Abner, appealing blend of the light-heartedness that came from physical well-being with the sobriety that came from her thoughts, which must have been anxious during most of her twenty-five years.

Abner knew a good deal about it. He and Bonnie were relatives in one of those involved patterns of consanguinity that have no actual meaning and could hardly have been kept straight except in a small town. Her mother, Mary Coates, was Cousin Mary to Abner's father; but she was actually the Judge's great-grand-uncle's son's daughter; which meant, as nearly as Abner could figure it out, that Bonnie and he had a great-great-grandfather in common, and so were either third or fourth (he was never quite sure which) cousins. Mary Coates was, however, a closer connection of the Judge's by affinity than by blood. Her mother's sister was the wife of Judge Coates' Uncle Nate, who thus became also Cousin Mary's Uncle Nate. Furthermore, Mary had married Robert Drummond, for years Philander Coates' most intimate friend. There were thus three grounds on which Cousin Mary's affairs concerned the Judge.

When Mary and Robert Drummond had been married nine or ten years—the summer that Bonnie (she had been christened Janet, but nobody who knew her ever called her that) was seven—a grotesque and unforeseeable accident occurred. It was the sort of thing that often gets a paragraph in the papers, but for practical purposes may be said never to happen. Robert Drummond, recently making a good deal of money out of the Childerstown Building & Loan Society, decided to buy a farm on which he thought he would breed Aberdeen Angus cattle. Late one July afternoon he went out to the farm he had bought to look at the work in progress. While he stood talking to the builder in the uncompleted barn, a thunderstorm came up. He had left the windows open in his car, and seeing what was coming, he ran to close them. It had not yet begun to rain, so Robert Drummond turned to walk back to shelter. The builder, half blinded by the flash, saw him struck down in the barnyard and instantly killed by a lightning bolt.

Though it would be hard to devise a better way to die, everyone found it appalling. The loss had not been made easier by those thoughts, consolation of long preparatory illness, or senile decline, that all was for the best, that the dead now suffered no more, that a term was put to the uncertainty and expense of the living.

Judge Coates was very much upset. He regarded Cousin Mary with the tenderest sympathy. He felt deep compassion for a woman, still young, who had lost so suddenly and tragically one of the finest men who ever lived. He knew that she suffered a grief time could not cure. She must never be expected to take much further interest in life; and Judge Coates, though he did all he could to cheer her, and even reminded her of what she owed her child, never seriously expected her to get over it, and could not blame her if she wished that she were dead, too. Therefore it was a great surprise to Judge Coates when, about two years later, Cousin Mary told him, saying that she wanted him to be the first to know, that she had gone to a town in the next state with Jared Wacker and married him.

It was not in itself an objectionable match. The Wackers were good Childerstown people, as good as the Coateses. Moreover, Jared was a lawyer, which, in a legal family, was a point in his favor. It was true that Jared was not popular with the rest of the bar; but sometimes this could be expected when a man won, as Jared did, most of his cases. It might or might not be true that Jared was sarcastic, secretive, oversmart, and disobliging to his colleagues. It was certainly true that for one reason or another plenty of local lawyers would say that, if you wanted their private opinion, they didn't trust Wacker any farther than they could throw the jail.

Here was reasonable doubt; and Judge Coates had little personal knowledge of Jared. Before Jared was admitted to the bar, Judge Coates had gone to the Superior Court, and so he lacked the basis of appraisal he got, or thought he got, from hearing a man plead. He gave Jared the benefit of that particular doubt. Judge Coates never listened to such talk until something tangible was brought before the Bar Association. Judge Coates objected to the match on other grounds. An injury had been done to his idea of the fitness of things by Cousin Mary's unaccountable resumption of interest in mundane, and even (the idea was highly distasteful, but elopement hinted impatience, a posting-with-dexterity) in carnal matters. This he could not mention; but another thing Judge Coates didn't like was the difference in the newlyweds' ages. Jared Wacker was five or six years younger than Mary. Judge Coates wondered—in fact, he wondered out loud, and to Mary—just how anxious Jared would have been to marry a woman older than himself, a widow with a daughter almost ten years old, if she hadn't been, at least by Childerstown standards, very well-off.

After that Mary did not speak to Cousin Philander for three years. In the course of them she became, with a dispatch many people thought indelicate, the mother of a son, and then of twins. Though nobody knew it, nor even (for Jared's business seemed good) thought of suspecting it, Jared had been applying himself to her fortune with similar dispatch. That came out when, in a scandal unexampled locally, Jared Wacker walked one morning across the courthouse square to his office and was never seen again. He took along whatever remained of his wife's money, and several trust funds to which he had access. Presumably he also took along his stenographer, a girl of bad reputation; for she, too, was seen no more.

Judge Coates forced Mary to abandon the not-speaking nonsense and devoted his considerable influence and experience to having Jared tracked down. While this went on, and

it went on several years without the least success before the
Judge was willing to drop it, Mary and Bonnie, and Jared
junior, and the six months old twins, Philip and Harold,
lived at the Judge's. That was before Abner's mother died;
and there was increasing friction. It finally reached such a
point that Mary, in the heat of a quarrel with her hostess,
blamed Cousin Philander for the loss of her money, or at
least, for the failure to recover it. The row, though about
the Judge, was strictly between Mary and Mrs. Coates.
Abner, away at college at the time, was told very little of
what happened. Perhaps Cousin Mary had not been entirely
to blame, for Mrs. Coates was a sick woman and died before the next spring.

Moved, no doubt genuinely, by this sad circumstance,
Cousin Mary faced about again. She took to herself all the
blame. She was filled with despair to think of her inexcusable
conduct toward Edith Coates, whom she had always loved,
and who had done everything for her. She did not know
what to say to Cousin Philander, who had also done everything for her; and this was no more than the truth. When
his wife ordered Cousin Mary out of her house, the Judge
necessarily arranged for another house for them to go to,
and since Cousin Mary had none of her own, he provided
her with money. This he continued to do; and later he also
supplied the money for Bonnie to take a secretarial course,
so that she could get a job; and then, by speaking to appropriate people, got Bonnie a job as secretary to the principal
of the high school.

Abner could see Cousin Mary busily unpacking hampers.
Cousin Mary sometimes said that what she had been through
was more than mortal woman could bear; but the truth was,
she looked considerably less than her fifty years, and her
manner, at least in public, was unsubdued, almost gay. A
person who knew her history met her for the first time with
surprise and admiration. Most people did admire her; and,
in a way, Abner admired her, too; but with a good many

reservations. Her gaiety, her habit of not troubling about her troubles, was all right up to a point. After that it was better described as willful and exasperating irresponsibility. The job of managing her affairs was not easy, and when she had done as much as she felt like doing, Cousin Mary lay down on it with a shrug. She implied that the whole business bored her; and, anyway, she was above niggling economies and petty calculations. You got the impression that she was improvident on purpose and careless by design because she liked the air of pretty negligence she thought it gave her. Abner had sometimes wanted to ask her why, when she didn't care herself, anyone else should be expected to care. He had sometimes wanted to ask how she had the cheek to expect Bonnie to spend her life supporting her mother and Jared Wacker's children.

Abner stood aside, still watching Cousin Mary, while people, mostly men, came up to get a drink. Mr. Schaeffer, the Burgess, said to him, "Quite a case, Ab. What do you think about those fellows?"

Abner said, "Personally, I think they ought to be convicted." He found himself awkward; not because of Mr. Schaeffer, who was a harmless and agreeable old man; but because, behind Mr. Schaeffer, was Jesse Gearhart. Jesse would not be coming up to get a drink, for Jesse did not drink; so he was probably coming to speak to Abner.

Mr. Schaeffer said, "Well, I guess you're right. Don't like their looks much."

Jesse stood calm and grave, waiting without impatience, without choosing to intrude himself, for the exchange to end. Abner said, "We don't like them much."

"No," said Mr. Schaeffer. "That fellow they killed wasn't any good, either, I hear. Dope dealer or something, wasn't he?"

"We think so."

"That's what I heard," Mr. Schaeffer said. He put his

glass down. "No, no," he said to Harry Wurts. "One's my limit."

Abner said, "Hello, Jesse."

Jesse Gearhart's thin gray hair lay flat and damp on his wide head. Jesse nodded in reply. His large, tired-looking gray eyes, pensive in his somewhat gray face, brightened a little as he left whatever his thoughts were and gave his attention to Abner. Abner had never liked Jesse, but he had not always disliked him. As Republican county chairman, Jesse was for years accustomed to consult with Judge Coates; and Abner had early taken Jesse, and Jesse's relative or local importance, for granted. The county had been Republican for almost a generation. This meant that the Republicans were entrenched in power; they had all the jobs. Having all the jobs meant having also an increasing monopoly of the ambitious, able and experienced men. Ambitious men could see the situation; able men could not expect to get anywhere with the Democrats; and as for experience, a Democrat could never be elected, and so could never get any experience.

Abner had seen how this worked. He had done a good deal of speaking for the party ticket at elections since he had been in office on Marty's appointment. The Republican candidates for whom he spoke, though no great shakes perhaps, were invariably and obviously better fitted for the office they sought than their Democratic opponents. It was simple enough to say so; and to point out why; and Abner was glad to do it, when some lodge, or Loyal Republican Club, wanted a speaker. Few of these gatherings were so small or so insignificant that Jesse Gearhart did not manage to be on hand, if only briefly; and when Jesse was there, he was at pains afterward to thank Abner and to congratulate him.

It seemed an odd thing to dislike a man for; but Abner knew that was how and when he had begun to dislike Jesse. At college, where he had done some debating, and at law school, Abner had learned that he was not a gifted speaker, just as he had learned that he did not have to be gifted in order to make a sensible and adequate speech. When Jesse told him he was wonderful, Abner did not know what to reply. If Jesse really thought so, Jesse was a fool; if Jesse did not really think so, he must imagine Abner was a fool. Furthermore, Abner did not like Jesse's—well, the word was presumption, in acting as though Abner worked for Jesse, when in fact, Abner did what he did because Marty asked him to; and because he himself believed that the public interest would be better served by the Republican candidates.

These grounds for disliking Jesse were not good nor reasonable; and Abner made every effort to conceal his feelings. To conceal them was not, however, to be rid of them. Abner supposed that his mental process was the ordinary one; but, just as concealing dislike did not cure dislike, recognizing a shifty piece of rationalization did not end the process of rationalizing. If a man felt hostility and aversion, but saw that he had poor or no grounds for his feeling, the remedy was to look for good or at least better grounds—a search his predisposing thoughts would help him in. Abner could say that he did not like politics; nor Jesse's function in them, a function clearly at variance with avowed principles. In theory, the people could, and surely ought to, enounce the nominations at the primaries; but in practice what they did at the primaries was accept the men Jesse designated. At the election, which the Republicans were sure to win, the people then elected those men to office. If this did not mean that Jesse had the whole say about who was to fill every elective public office, what did it mean? If it meant that, Abner, in spite of his speeches, and notwithstanding Jesse's men were the better men, did not like it.

Jesse said, "Have a hard day, Ab?"

"So-so," said Abner. "It gets pretty long."

"Such a crowd, I didn't come over."

With an effort of will, Abner said, "If you want to hear any of it, Marty could get you a seat all right. I don't know that it's very interesting."

"Have a lot of newspaper men?"

"Quite a few, this morning. I noticed most of them weren't there this afternoon."

"One of their editors, a friend of mine—Ed Robertson, as a matter of fact, maybe you know him—called me up. He was trying to find out when the defendants were going to be on the stand."

"I couldn't tell you that," Abner said. "Basso refused to plead, so I don't suppose he's likely to testify. I guess Harry will put Howell on, all right. I think the Commonwealth ought to finish tomorrow. So, maybe Thursday. There's no reason why your friend shouldn't ask Harry, if he wants to."

"Marty's not going to call them?"

"How could he?" Abner asked, taken aback. Jesse Gearhart often showed a good knowledge of law as it applied to county and municipal business; but presumably his knowledge stopped short where it ceased to have practical value. Abner said, "That's up to the defense. You can be pretty sure it won't be tomorrow. We have this Leming fellow—well, of course he's technically one of the defendants, but we can call him because he's turning state's evidence."

"Are you going to have him tomorrow?"

"I think so, sometime tomorrow," Abner said, "but I can't really say, Jesse. Marty decides. You'd better ask him." Abner spoke earnestly and as cordially as he could—perhaps too cordially; and he was aware that he did not like Jesse any better for causing him this discomfort; for making Abner sound artificial and feel insincere; maybe for thinking (and why shouldn't Jesse think it?) that Abner was awkwardly making up to him with the ignoble hope (what other?) that some day, when Marty resigned, Jesse might condescend to pick him as the candidate for district attorney.

Jesse nodded and moved on. Like most of Jesse's acts and gestures, and, for that matter, many of his remarks, the nod and the moving-on were not informative. There was no way of knowing whether Jesse resented Abner's exclamation at what Abner considered Jesse's amazing ignorance; whether Jesse thought Abner was currying favor at the last there, and if he thought so, whether he was delighted or disgusted. The nod could be either thanks or dismissal, the walking-away could be either because he was satisfied, or because he had wasted enough time. Abner moved, too; and with some discomfort of mind, sat down at the long, disordered supper table.

He had seated himself, saving a place next to him for Bonnie, but she did not immediately come to take it. Abner could see her talking to her mother while they were busy with the coffee over an oil stove. About thirty-five people were at the table under the awning, and there was not much room, so when Annette Vredenburgh, the Judge's daughter, appeared at his elbow and said, "Can I sit here, Ab?" he was obliged to say, "Sure."

Annette was not more than eighteen. Privately, Abner was surprised that her parents let her come on these parties; and also that she wanted to come, since everybody else was older. She was a plain girl, but popular with her contemporaries. Because she did not have a pretty face, her confident, presuming air of a sought-after woman must almost inevitably be due to liberties she was ready to allow when boys took her out. Annette was one of the kids who went to the Black Cat, a road house Bunting kept his eye on. Abner did not think she was aware that the district attorney's office had obtained her name, along with several others, as a frequent patron; and it made him impatient with her—silly little fool!—to know that she probably imagined her father could never find out. She said to him, "Father didn't think it was suitable for him to come. Because of the trial. It didn't stop you, I see."

"Why should it stop me?" said Abner. Her manner of a fascinating woman—the glances through her eyelashes, the little capricious jerks of her chin, the tone, which perhaps she considered coolly ironic—was so patently supposititious, so plainly an imitation of something she had seen, or read, that Abner could not help smiling.

Annette said, "Oh, you know! Father's so solemn. He told mother he thought it would be very improper, when he was sitting in a capital case, for him to attend parties or entertainments. I suppose he has to be that way. Would you like to be a judge?"

She was a fresh brat; but she was also a young woman, and it was awkward to tell her off, so Abner said, "Don't you think I'd make a good one?"

"Maybe you would," she said. She gave him the look she probably thought of as enigmatic; veiled but searching. "It depends upon what you're really like, I suppose. It's hard to tell about people, isn't it?"

"I generally don't find it hard," Abner said indifferently.

"That's because you have an analytical mind," Annette said. "I wish I had. It isn't easy to be a woman in a man's world. You think I'm just a silly little fool—"

Since that was exactly, to the word, his thought of a few minutes ago, Abner nearly laughed, and so nearly choked. He swallowed and said, "But, you mean, you aren't."

"Oh!" said Annette. She had her father's blue eyes, and bridling, they took that same glinting cast that Abner had seen a hundred times directed from the bench on counsel or a witness. "Men are all alike!" she said. "You don't think I could possibly be serious, do you? It's so tiresome! That's what I mean. I keep hoping that maybe the reason boys are so boring is that they aren't grown-up—you can't imagine how tired I get of them. All they want to do is go dancing in stupid dives, or drink too much, or paw you—"

"You don't mean out at the Black Cat, do you?" Abner said.

She looked at him, surprised, very wide eyed (her tragic look, no doubt). "Yes," she said, lowering her voice. "I don't know how you knew. I went once or twice because I thought it might be amusing." She lifted her shoulders and looked away past him toward the canal bank in the twilight. "Well, what can you do? Don't imagine I like it."

"Then you ought not to do it," Abner said.

She said reproachfully, "Don't you ever do anything you shouldn't?" She managed to imply that, beset with temptations, her sensual nature often betrayed her; and so, if you wanted to tempt her, too, you would not necessarily be wasting your time.

Abner said, "It wouldn't be very nice for your father if something happened out there and you got subpoenaed."

She was disconcerted; but she said lightly, "Oh, surely father would fix that! What's the use of being the Judge's daughter if you can't get away with anything?"

Abner was inclined to answer, "You don't know your father very well." But, of course, she was right; except that it wouldn't be her father. The use of being the Judge's daughter was that the district attorney's office would make sure before any officers were sent to the Black Cat, that Annette was not there; or if she were, that she got out first.

Annette said, "Anyway, how thrilling! Think of the scandal! Is Mr. Bunting going to raid it—like the movies? If I were Mrs. Bunting, I'd go, too. I wouldn't let him get that Dagmar, that fan dancer, alone for a good grilling. I mean that as a joke. She is the most revolting creature, in case you haven't seen her."

From across the board table, Dorothy Nyce said, "What are you two so absorbed in?"

Abner said, "Miss Vredenburgh is discussing local conditions with me." Dorothy Nyce, known then as Dotty Wellman, had been at school with him; and, now Abner thought about it, had enjoyed a popularity probably not unlike Annette's. That had been, say, fifteen years ago, when Annette was an infant. Now that Abner thought further about it, he could remember, excited by what other boys told him, himself pursuing Dotty. He had .ot got much for his pains; but he wondered if Dotty ever thought of things like that; and whether it embarrassed her to be able to guess—she must be able to, by now—what her "admirers" had really thought of her; in short, whether she despised herself, or just despised them. Abner guessed it was the latter. She had had several drinks, and she said with an intentional leer, "And how are conditions, fair and warmer? Dick's having a birthday party tomorrow night. Come?"

"Try to," said Abner, who had no such intention. He saw Dick Nyce, her husband, down at the table's end where he and Harry Wurts and Mark Irwin had their heads together over the littered table singing softly against the babble of voices and the continuing radio music: ". . . but his mind was weak and low; he was wild and woolly and full of fleas—"

Adelaide Maurer brought up a chocolate layer cake. Annette took a piece; but Abner shook his head. "How'd your story go?" he said.

"Oh, they only wanted half a column! I think they're mean! I tried to give them your speech; but they didn't want it."

"They've got a nerve!" Abner said.

He heard Cousin Mary's raised voice crying, "Why don't some of you men light the lanterns? Harry Wurts, why don't you stop singing that disgusting song and—where's Ab? I saw him just sitting there stuffing himself."

"I'll do it," Abner called back, getting up with relief.

Farther down the table, Joe Jackman got up, too. While Abner lifted down the colored paper lanterns and held them collapsed, Joe struck matches and lit the candles inside. He said, "What are you trying to do, rob the cradle?"

Abner said, "Robbery is the felonious and forcible taking from the person of another, goods or money to any value, by violence or putting in fear. It won't stick."

"Somebody ought to put her in fear," Joe said. "If I were her father, I'd warm her little bottom."

The Chinese lanterns, replaced one after another along

the frame of the awning support, brightened softly as the candle flames increased and steadied. The fragile shapes glowed pink and yellow and green in the dusk under the dark masses of the canal-side elms. Surrounded, half overhung and canopied by these tree shadows, the gliding barge, its colored lanterns, its sounds of music and voices, seemed to float in pure twilight, midway between the water and the sky.

Doctor Mosher had been sitting near the bow with Mr. Schaeffer, their red cigar ends burning together. He got up and came over to Abner as the last lantern was lighted. Doctor Mosher's stocky figure with its firm little belly was clothed in a white linen suit. His short gray hair was mussed up, his square pugnacious face down in the mouth. "Ab," he said, drawing him aside, "why the devil don't you do something about your father? Can't you see what he needs? He says you don't tell him things."

"Well," said Abner, surprised, "there's nothing much to tell him."

"It doesn't have to be much," Doctor Mosher said. "God Almighty, boy, what do you suppose a man thinks of, sitting there all day? Well, maybe you aren't old enough to know."

"I can see he'd naturally get pretty low in his mind," Abner said, "but—"

"Pretty low in his mind!" said Doctor Mosher. He shook overboard ashes from the cigar between his blunt fingers, "Well, that'll do, that'll do; until you find out for yourself. Get after him, Ab! Don't do it so any fool can see what you're doing; but tell him about what's going on in court, ask him things, make him talk. When you see him sitting there, not saying anything, do you know what he's thinking about half the time? He's thinking about dying. The human mind doesn't like that. Pitch in and break it up!" He put a hand against Abner's shoulder, half patting him, half pushing him away, turned and went back to the camp stool next to Mr. Schaeffer.

Silently rounding a long bend, the barge rounded a rise of ground, too; and there, just on the treetops, above the humped frame of an approaching wagon bridge, the vast dusky full moon floated clear, floated mirrored in the unstirred lane of silent water. "Hurray!" shouted Harry Wurts. "Soft o'er the fountain—" He swept out an arm, clasping the first female within reach, who happened to be Bonnie, and seated her on his knee. "What beauty!" he said, "what romance! What—"

Bonnie said, "Unhand me, you souse!" and got up.

Abner walked down and said, "You don't need protection, do you?"

"A lot I'd get from you!" Bonnie said. She undid a flowered apron she had been wearing and tossed it folded into a hamper. "Now, maybe I can eat," she said. "Ab, get some coffee for me, will you? Mother has a pot over there."

Abner brought the cup down to her and sat at the corner of the table. "Haven't you had anything to eat?" he said. "I tried to save a place for you—"

"I saw you trying."

"You mean my new girl-friend?" Abner murmured. "Don't you like her?"

"She isn't such a fool as you think," Bonnie said. "She isn't after you."

"Well, who is she after? You wound me."

"I could tell you that, too. If you weren't so wrapped up in yourself, you could see."

"Say, are you mad?" said Abner, advancing his elbow to slouch across the corner of the table. "Say, who made that chicken salad? It's good."

"I made it," said Bonnie.

"I knew you did. That's why I said it. You mustn't be mad because all the girls like me. I can't help it."

Bonnie's clear race had clouded, and she looked at her plate, entirely engaged in eating. Abner took a drinking straw from the package beside the iced tea pitcher and poked her cheek with it. "Don't be such a clown, Ab," she said; "it doesn't suit you."

"Now, wait a minute," Abner said, "you were all right before supper. What don't you like? My elbow on the table?"

"You thought I was all right. You always think I am."

"No, I don't," said Abner. "I'll tell you how I tell. There is your all-right voice, and your not-all-right voice, if you follow me—O.K. I'm sorry. But tell me sometime, will you?"

He stood up. Harry Wurts dropped an arm over his shoulder and affected to hang on him. "Let her eat!" he said. "Never argue with women on an empty stomach. You need exercise. I see someone tapping a beer keg. I must prepare. I mean, there is a little tapping—er, excuse me, m'am! It's time we stretched our legs, Counselor. Carry me ashore!"

At Locktown, in the basin below the old locks, Ben Wister turned the barge around. The whitewashed fieldstone walls of the Locktown Inn, a big place with long sheds and stables built when traffic on the canal was heavy, still stood above the basin. Most of the building had now fallen into disrepair. Nobody had stopped or eaten there for years; but the Inn bar still did business, and it had other accommodations, not all that could be desired, but, by arrangement of the Club's secretary with the proprietor's wife, prepared as well as possible, and better than nothing.

While Ben swore at his mules and worked with a pole, a number of women went up for a minute, and a number of men visited the taproom to see whether the beer there was as bad as what they had on board, or worse. Abner, who had stayed with Joe Jackman to give Ben a hand with the boat, thought that he couldn't remember a more beautiful night. The beauty, helped perhaps by beer, seemed to swell the heart and stretch the nerves until they rang with pleasure. Abner sat with Joe Jackman against the low stern bulwark by the tiller while moonlight bright enough to read by fell on them. The tops of the great trees above the locks were frosted gray. On the tow path the waiting mules cast exact black shadows. The Inn's moonlit stone walls were intensely white, a chalky candescence brighter than the yellow squares of the taproom windows. Under the deep shade of the awning Abner could hear the quiet voices, see the moving cigarette ends, of the people still on board. Over the water a delicious breeze stirred. "Pretty nice," he said to Joe.

"Yeah," said Joe, "and not even any mosquitoes." He got up. "Want some beer?" he said.

"If you get it."

Sitting alone, Abner looked at the moon. Up in the awning shadow someone picked the strings of a musical instrument—Adelaide Maurer, since the instrument was a mandolin—and the thin, tinkling notes began to arrange themselves, trying for a tune, while one or two voices helped, singing tentatively: "Every time my honey leaves me, I get the blues—" Then, dissatisfied, they broke off, arguing about how it really went.

Abner listened, surprised, not sure how old that song was, but remembering it perfectly. During his childhood there had been a phonograph record of it, among a number of records which, with pleasure in the noise but little interest, he often played, trying to kill some of the endless time of those days—vacant hours of a rainy morning or a winter afternoon, or the too long pause after supper on a summer evening before it finally got dark. From the corner of the living-room the mahogany veneer victrola, almost as tall as, and bigger than, Abner, poured out the rapid tinny music, against which a voice, rapid and tinny, too, suddenly sang; while Abner fidgeted, looking around the room in the grayness of the rainy day, or watching the light reflected on the ceiling from the snowy lawn, or staring through the screened windows at the June dusk. Adelaide, who was older, might remember the tune as one they played at the first dances she went to; and, recalling it, she thought of—what?

Bill Maurer, if he had been Adelaide's honey, left her, all right; but, by then, Bill's leaving was a relief and even a joy; and Adelaide wanted nothing so much as the divorce that would finally rid her of him. As counsel Abner had handled one or two divorces; and sat as Master in one or two more, so patterns of the change from wanting to not wanting, from attraction to revulsion, and the budget of sorrows—first quarrels, disappointments, humiliations, idle tears, bitter speeches—implicit in the change, were known to him. The primary trouble was the same. Differences were only in detail. When Adelaide married Bill Maurer, when Cousin Mary married Jared Wacker, when what was to be the petitioner in any action sub sur divorce married what was to be the respondent, someone had married someone that he or she (usually she) did not really know. Ruling out occasional cool moves to get money or deliberate resolves to take a last or only chance, it would seem that those about to marry avoided rather than sought real knowledge; and were content to investigate nothing but their own feelings; and were satisfied if, among their feelings, they discovered some truth, such as: every time my honey leaves me, I get the blues.

Abner did not mean to make fun of such truths. He had experienced their impact. Long ago at law school when he tried—how callowly, how fervently!—to work into the hard schedule of his last year time enough for a Boston girl named Eunice Stockton, the incontinent force of those truths had surprised and tormented him; and their irremediable ache had filled him with despair when he began to realize that it was all coming to nothing.

Of course, all having come to nothing, and a nothing so absolute, and reached so long ago that Eunice Stockton's name, out of mind since he did not know when, made him start, Abner could be sure now that those forces would spend themselves and that those aches could be remedied. This was wisdom, the eschatology of what is true in the long run, and better than rubies; but things Abner knew now could not affect what Abner had felt then, and the feeling made it no thanks to him, nor to his prudence, nor to his common sense, that he was not today married to Eunice Stockton.

The thought of Eunice dismissed itself, being without present interest for him; but a melancholy remained. From the thought of Eunice—though no more than from the disinterested thought of Adelaide Maurer's unhappy marriage; perhaps, no more than from the tune on the mandolin with its same assurance that everything could be counted on to die—the moonlight took a superinduced sadness. Abner found himself thinking, still at random, of Howell and Basso and Leming in their cells at the jail, with the same moonlight through the bars. It was no night to be in jail. Probably it was no night, either, to sit, like his father, alone trying to read, or, little better, playing cribbage with Aunt Myrt. Abner thought of Earl Foulke, and of how he had not been entirely above board with Marty; and how it would have been better if he had been. He thought of the talk with Jesse Gearhart; and he did not actually care what Jesse thought, or whether Jesse was pleased or displeased, or liked him or didn't like him; yet he could see the difficulty or misunder standing waiting there in plain view, a sort of ox in the road, which Abner on his way to the future would have to deal with—and perhaps deal with very soon, if Marty were really getting ready to go to the Attorney General's office.

From the barge-side a couple of planks had been laid to the bank. Hearing steps, Abner turned his head and saw Bonnie. She was just coming down from the Inn. She walked with easy light erectness, not looking at him; but something, he did not know what, told him that she had been looking at him until a moment ago, and his spirits lifted. The end of the plank was hardly a yard away, and when she reached it, he said, "Feel better?"

"Don't be coarse!" she answered.

He patted the deck beside him, and she poised a moment, hesitating. Then she stepped off the bulwark and came up. Holding her skirt in under her pretty knees she seated herself, not too close to him. Joe Jackman, by the beer keg, saw her, and called, "Have some suds, Mis' Drummond?"

"No, thanks, Joe," she said. "Yes. I will."

Abner said, "I have to get off at Waltons to pick my car up. Suppose you get off, too; and I'll take you home."

"No. I have to take mother home."

"She could hitch-hike, couldn't she?" Abner said. "Not, of course, that I object to her company; but—"

"No. I can't. I drove the Ormsbees' station wagon down."

"You mean you're still mad?" said Abner contentedly.

"Yes," she said. She gazed at him with defiance, her lips pressed tight together. "Oh!" she said. She gave way and laughed. "How can anyone stay mad at you, you dope!"

"What you need," said Abner, picking up her left hand and inspecting it, "is a ring. You know. Not too expensive. Then when you felt mad, you'd have something to give back to me."

"No. And I'm not engaged to you. Did you tell Cousin Philander I was?"

"On the contrary," Abner said, "he told me. He asked me if we'd had a row. He said it was high time I got married. Wait!" She tried to pull her hand away; but he held it. "Is that what you're—you *were* mad about?"

"No. Not that. I don't mind what Cousin Philander thinks. He's sweet. I mind what you think." With a quick motion she got her hand away.

"And what do I think?" said Abner.

"You think you can just—"

"Do I intrude?" said Joe Jackman. He stood over them,

99

holding the beer mugs. His shadow fell on Bonnie's linen skirt.

"Yes," said Abner.

"No, you don't!" Bonnie said. "Thanks, Joe."

She took the mug in both hands and brought it to her lips. It was not a gesture that might be expected to stir the heart; but, like the ordinary tones of Bonnie's voice, her ordinary gestures were moving to Abner. Perpetually fresh, they were familiar, too. They were the tones and gestures of the thin quiet child who had lived several years in the same house with him, long ago. Bonnie had been too young—almost six years younger—to deserve actual notice; and he had little occasion to notice her, for she was shy and retiring and never bothered him. He saw her at meals, and sometimes, distantly, playing with her dolls in the summer house, or pedaling a bicycle on the curved paths through the shrubbery. He had not needed to be told (though he was told) never to do or say anything that would make Bonnie feel that he wasn't glad to have her there, or that it wasn't just as much her home as his.

When Abner returned on a vacation from college and found Bonnie gone, after that last row of Cousin Mary's, it would be too much to say that he missed her; but, on the other hand, he had noticed her more than he realized. He remembered her in the press and hush of his mother's funeral, looking like a child with her child's dark blue hat and curls on her coat collar, coming up to him. In an agony of constraint, her lifted face scarlet, her voice insecure, she said how sorry she was.

When Abner returned on vacations from law school he found that Bonnie had unexpectedly grown up. He took her to a couple of dances; because he liked her, and because she did not seem to have much fun; and most of all because it was easier to take her than any other girl. Any other girl might think he meant something that he did not mean, since, during that last year when he was home for the holidays, and during the year or so following when he was home all the time, he was busy being true to Eunice Stockton in Boston. When all was over with Eunice, Abner felt less inclined than ever to start anything serious with local girls his own age; and the simplest way to avoid it was to continue taking Bonnie around. As time went on, and he heard indirectly that Bonnie had more than once turned down boys who asked her to parties because he always took her, Abner saw that, however easy and agreeable for him, it was very unfair to her; and finally he spoke to her about it, driving her home early one morning after the spring cotillion at the Calumet Club. She said, "I like going with you." After a moment, she added, "Are you getting tired of taking me?"

"No," he said, "but I thought—"

"No," she said, her voice suddenly strangled, "no, you're wrong. You don't think. You don't use your head at all. Why do you think I'm here? Do you think it's because nobody else ever asked me? Do you think—"

"I thought," he said, "that you thought I was the next thing to your grandfather."

It was not however possible to do anything about it immediately. Abner had just been appointed assistant district attorney, and it meant, while he learned his job, that he had less time for his own practice and temporarily earned less money. Bonnie had her position at the school and because of her mother, needed it. Their relationship, though fundamentally changed, did not change very much outwardly. It was simply recognized that, in the local usage, they were going together; a status that could subsist, if necessary, a long time without prejudice to the general assumption that they would be married. They took it for granted, and everyone who knew them, like Joe Jackman, took it for granted.

It was what Joe meant when, still standing, he said, "I suppose I can sit somewhere else if you have a private fight you want to finish."

"It's finished," Abner said. "I won."

"Did he?" said Joe to Bonnie.

"He has the hide of a rhinoceros," Bonnie said. "He just goes lumbering along without a care in the world—" She set down her beer mug, looked vainly about, and then wiped her mouth on the back of her hand. Laughing, Abner brought a handkerchief from his breast pocket, took the hand, and wiped it. "You blow it off," he said. "What would you do without me?"

Ben Wister yelled at his mules, and the barge began to move.

In immediate response came other yells, wilder and louder. Down the slope from the Inn, gamboling in the moonlight, rushed Harry Wurts, his head decorated with maple leaves. He had somehow possessed himself of a harmonica, which he blew rather than played. Reaching the tow path, he jumped on board safely.

After him, pell-mell, hallooing and whooping, came Dick Nyce and Mark Irwin. Mark flung himself, plainly with intention, short of the stern and struck the water with a prodigious splash.

"Throw him the anchor!" shouted Harry. "Blow the man down!"

Mark came to the surface, gave a roar and struck out, swimming after the barge; but he made little progress and soon he touched bottom and clambered streaming up the bank. Dick Nyce, on the tow path, was doubled up helplessly, convulsed with laughter, so Mark rushed at him and pushed him in.

"The damn fools!" said Joe Jackman. "Boy, are they going to feel good tomorrow!"

It could be seen that his sentiment was generally shared; but Harry Wurts, throwing his maple leaves overboard, said, "That's what I say! Only, why wait till tomorrow? Sit near Joe, and feel bad right now!"

By way of dismissing these monkey-shines, the mandolin sounded under the awning and several voices began to sing:

"Last night I was dreaming of thee, Love, was dreaming . . ."

Harry Wurts, hearing it, groaned and covered his ears; but the older people liked it, and the volume increased. The barge glided on, the bow ripples running silver, the moon behind lifting higher above the narrow water. At farm houses across the fields the aroused dogs barked and barked as the singing floated to them faintly, moving back toward Childerstown.

On its hill Childerstown extended indistinctly, a dull shine of moonlight on the ranges of slate roofs, the few towers and many treetops bathed in pale radiance. Abner, driving up the Broad Street pike, cut off by the great shaded park of Beulah Cemetery to go home a shorter way. In Beulah were graves whose denizens had been laid there in the seventeenth century; but about 1850 the bounds were much enlarged by avenues extended across the neighboring fields and planted with hard maples. These trees now made a fine show, serenely quartering the jumble of plinths and monoliths, of mean little temple-shaped mausoleums, or crosses and urns and angels, that seemed to show how all the dead had been in life vain and pretentious, and in death left a memory cherished by imbeciles and vulgarians. Abner thought that he would rather be buried, if he had any say about it, down in the yard of the old Friends Meeting House; but since the Coateses were Presbyterians this was unlikely; and furthermore he was amply provided for in Beulah, where the Coates plots, purchased with economical foresight at the time of the enlargement, had room for a dozen more ready— even, as in the case of the four ton granite block over Abner's mother, waiting. Balancing her name, the Judge's was cut, and when Abner's father died all they had to do was fill in the second date.

Abner drove by the silent, mostly dark brick houses of North Court Street. The square stone façade of the court-house lifted above the street lights and the dark trees. At the corner before the county administration building Abner saw the uniformed figure of Bill Ortt, the chief of the three Childerstown policemen, crossing toward the obelisk of the Civil War monument on which moonlight fell so bright that the names of battles, raised in relief on the surfaces of the shaft, could be read—Spottsylvania, Brandy Station, Cold Harbor. Bill Ortt recognized the car and lifted a hand to Abner. Moonlight glinted on the big slate roof of the court-room and a few lights burned in the jail behind.

Abner drove out West Court Street, past the less frequent houses, with not a car on the road nor a person in sight. Turning between the stone gateposts he could see one light at home, in the lower hall; but the house, big, blocky in the shadows, was dark everywhere else. He tiptoed up into the cavern of the veranda and slid his key into the lock.

As he opened the door, the telephone rang suddenly, like a signal; and he jumped to catch it before it woke everyone up. In the dark corner under the stairs he bent and said "Hello."

"That you, Ab? Hope I didn't wake you up."

"I was out. I just got in. Who is it?"

"Pete Wiener. Look, Ab; there's just been a honey of an accident on route sixteen. One driver killed, and the other one I have here, charged with manslaughter. I don't really think it was so much his fault, what they say—"

As justices of the peace went, Pete Wiener at Newmarket was a good one, and when he didn't know what to do you could depend on him to find out before he proceeded. Abner said, "But the other fellow's dead?"

"Cut his head right clean off," Wiener said. "You never saw such a mess. Now, what I want to know is, I have to hold my man for the coroner, don't I? He thinks he can put up bail. He's got an auto club card—"

"No. You can't take recognizance in manslaughter, Pete."

"Well, what'll he have to do to get out? He wants to know, naturally."

"There's nothing he can do tonight. He'll have to go to jail. If he wants to get out before the inquest, what he'll have to do is petition for a writ of habeas corpus in order to be admitted to bail. Understand? You can draw one up for him and send it over to Judge Irwin tomorrow."

"About what I figured. What'll I do with him meanwhile? I got the state police here, now. Should I give him to them?"

"Better tell them to bring him right up here to jail," Abner said. "The Judge doesn't like them holding people at the sub-station; and he'll direct the writ to the sheriff in the morning, so the sheriff'd better have him. Make sure he isn't hurt, Pete. Sometimes they are, but don't know."

"Yes, I will, Ab. Thanks very much."

Abner hung up, switched out the hall light, and began quietly to climb the long stairs. The door of his father's bedroom was ajar, and as he turned at the top, Abner heard the low, thickened voice, "That you, son?"

Abner stepped to the door. "Yes, sir," he said. "Telephone wake you up? Sorry."

"No. I was awake. Who was it?"

"Pete Wiener. Wanted to know about bail for a fellow."

"You're home pretty early. Sober?"

"Afraid so."

"Who was there? Come in; don't stand there or Myrt'll hear you."

The high bedroom was duskily lighted by slats of bright moonlight on the floor under the shaded south windows, which formed a bay. Abner sat down by the bed.

"Sleepy?" his father said.

"No," Abner said. "Schaeffer was there, and Doc Mosher, and Jesse Gearhart—"

About to make a comment on Jesse, he checked it; for that problem was his own. On most subjects it was possible to be open with the Judge; but Abner found himself disinclined always to discuss plans or hopes—very likely, Abner admitted, because they sometimes changed; and his father, who never forgot what you told him, would remark on the change. Judge Coates thought that courses of action ought to be planned slowly and carefully, and then not swerved from. Abner said, "Cousin Mary was there. By the way, Father, did you say something to Bonnie this morning about us getting married?"

"Why, I don't think so," the Judge said. He stirred against the pillows. "Well, I may have said something. Sometimes I think you don't show much sense about women. That foolishness with that girl in Boston! If you could have seen yourself all that time—"

Altogether without malice, indeed with the kindliest anxiety, older people often seemed to feel that, just so long as they implied that you were today improved, you would not mind hearing, and might profit by the reminder, that once when you were younger you were everyone's laughing stock. Abner said, "Bonnie was feeling a little snappy about it. I think she thinks you and I take too much on ourselves."

"I think all she wants is for you to ask her a little harder. This business has been going on long enough. A girl likes to see some ardor, sometimes. You can overdo this common sense attitude. Did I offend you, speaking about Boston?"

"I don't know about you, sir," Abner said, "but when somebody tells me I am, or was, an ass, I may grant the truth of the matter alleged; but nobody can stop me wanting to interpose a demurrer to the evidence."

The Judge grunted and gave his difficult laugh. "I think in this case the evidence may be prima facie insufficient," he said. "I'll sustain you. Don't mind what I say, Ab. Your Boston girl wasn't any of my business. I just never liked her. I don't know why. How did you get on in court this afternoon?"

"All right." But Abner remembered what Doctor Mosher

had said, and continued, "Actually, it isn't much of a case. Harry and George are out for technicalities, so we have to be careful; but I always remember your saying once that there was never any trouble about the law if you just kept the facts straight. Ex facto oritur jus! How's that. You ought to hear Vredenburgh on maxims, sometime."

"I have heard him. Tom's not very patient with abstractions. He's got a literal mind; and it's a good thing to have; but he hasn't Horace Irwin's feeling for the law. When you come to the bench, I hope you'll have a feeling for it."

"When I come to the bench, they'll start a revolution, probably," Abner said. "About this case, I know one thing Harry's going to appeal on is the severance—whether this Leming may testify for the Commonwealth while he still stands as a defendant. Do you think Harry has anything?"

In the dusk of the moonlight, Judge Coates rested silent a moment.

"No," he said finally, "that's a matter of competency. The act takes care of it, I think. All persons are competent, except the stated exceptions. A convicted perjurer. Husband and wife, except in certain cases—they are not competent on confidential communications. There is a point there, by the way. It has been held in a bastardy case that a married woman is not competent to rebut the presumption of access by testifying that she did not have intercourse with her husband. Well; and counsel is incompetent on confidential matters."

He took a tissue from the pile on the bedside table and wiped his mouth. "Now," he said, more energetically, "your man either is, or he is not, one of those exceptions. If he is not, he's competent, and that's the end of it—as far as you're concerned. The other sections of the act aren't relevant. One case I remember in this state of a codefendant being disqualified was under section five, clause E—Burke versus Burke, if you want to look it up." He closed his eyes a moment. "Two forty; three seventy-nine. It was the case of an interested party to a contract. Well, I guess you don't want me to write your brief."

"Don't we, though!" Abner said.

"Well, when Harry gets his together, I'll look at it, if you and Marty Bunting want." He moved his mouth, biting at the lip. "I wrote an opinion several years ago that involved the competency point. But the basic theory is put about as well as it can be in Benson versus U. S., one forty-six; three twenty-five."

Abner shook his head; there was no doubt about it, the old boy knew his stuff. "I don't know how you do it, sir," he said sincerely. "When a case is over, I can never remember any citations."

"Well, I don't remember much any more," Judge Coates said. "I don't know whether you want to hear this or not. Wouldn't blame you if you didn't. I think slowly. Hard to get it out."

"I want to hear it," Abner said, "but I don't know whether I ought to keep you up."

"Better worry about yourself. You don't sleep much when you lie around all day."

Abner found and lit a cigarette. "Want one, sir?" he said.

"All right."

The light of the match Abner held for him fell golden on the hanging side of the paralyzed face, and the Judge moved his head a little to shadow it. "Well, the general idea," he said, holding the cigarette up to the corner of his mouth, "is that the defendant actually on trial is certainly not excluded by his interest, and his being party to the record. How, then, can you reason that a codefendant is? He's only technically a party to the record. He—"

Smoking, Abner listened, locking his jaw against the little impulses to yawn. "Seems reasonable," he said.

Judge Coates jabbed out the cigarette end. "You can rely on the common law," he said. "They say the Catholic Church is like that—I mean, aside from the supernatural side of it.

If you do what they tell you, you won't make many mistakes.
I never could. There's something about their organization
that seems to me to debase a man." He raised his good hand
and yawned behind it.

"My life's about over," he said. "I don't know whether I
really grasp that when I say it, or not; whether it's a thing
you ever can really grasp. Grasp it near enough, I guess. So
I can say that I'm glad I spent my life in the law. I don't
know how you feel about it—there are disappointments; there
are things that seem stupid, or not right. But they don't matter much. It's the stronghold of what reason men ever get
around to using. You ought to be proud to hold it. A man
can defend himself there. It gives you a groundwork of
good sense; you'll never be far wrong—" His voice, getting
slower between the spoken sentences, made Abner look
sharply at him.

"I don't know anything," Judge Coates said. "You can't
think everything out for yourself. Lay hold on something—"

With a faint peaceful snoring, it was apparent that Judge
Coates had drifted off to sleep. Abner stood up softly. The
cigarette smoke had dissipated, the moonlight had moved
on the floor. Passing the screen before the open windows
Abner could smell the perfume of flowering shrubs scenting
the warm silent night, drifting through the silent house.

Four

IN THE MORNING a cool wind blew over the hill of Childerstown, but the cloudless sky and the splendor of the sunlight meant that it was going to be hot soon. When Abner walked up with Bunting from Bunting's office to the courthouse the wind was dying. He could feel the blaze of sun on his cheek and bare head as they crossed by the county administration building from the shade on the east side of Broad Street to the shade of the trees around the courthouse steps. When court opened, the cavernous chamber seemed a little warmer than what had been the fresh morning outside. Now, an hour later, the air inside began to be cooler than the air outside. On the southeast windows the folding walnut shutters were drawn together, shadowing the round of benches, today only partly filled. The windows on the other side had been open, the colored glass top-sashes drawn down, the lower sashes drawn up. Judge Vredenburgh sent the tipstaffs to close them. He said that those jurors who wished to do so might remove their coats. From the way the black silk of his robe clung to his shoulders it was plain that the Judge himself wore nothing under it but a shirt.

Mrs. Zollicoffer, recalled, was on the stand; and this was a wearisome business. Last night Mrs. Zollicoffer must have taken something to make her sleep, and taken so much of it that she was still numb. After half a dozen questions Bunting abandoned his examination abruptly and handed her over to Harry Wurts. He said to Abner, "She doesn't know whether she's coming or going." Abner supposed that Marty had made one of his quick and usually correct decisions, and was ready to write her off, figuring that she could do his case no good answering that way, and though she might answer Harry unguardedly, her stupid stubbornness about what she pretended she didn't know would be increased if anything by the feeling she probably had that everything around her was remote and unreal.

Harry, cross-examining, was not quite himself, either. He was alert enough, and aggressive enough; but his manner was jerky and it could be seen that Mrs. Zollicoffer's sluggishness worked, as perhaps Bunting hoped it would, on his nerves, while the efforts he made to work on hers, because of the sluggishness, got nowhere. He kept moving around. He fired his questions at her from all directions. He asked her whether she wore glasses to read with; and when she said she did, he asked her whether she had received any communication from her husband during the day preceding the alleged kidnapping. When she said no, he walked away toward the Commonwealth's table, turned and snapped suddenly, "Did you ever see a can of opium?"

Mrs. Zollicoffer said dazedly, "I beg your pardon?"

"You heard my question!" Harry said.

Mrs. Zollicoffer looked distractedly at Bunting who said, "Did you hear Mr. Wurts' question?"

Mrs. Zollicoffer said, "I don't know what the gentleman means. I didn't hear it."

Harry said, "Simply tell the jury what a can of opium looks like. Describe it. How big is it? Has it a label?"

"I don't know the meaning of it. I'm sorry."

Harry looked at her with every sign of amazement. "You don't know the meaning? You can't describe the way opium is packed?"

"No," said Mrs. Zollicoffer. "I wouldn't know what that was."

Nearly shouting, Harry said, "You never heard of opium? You don't know what it is?"

"No, sir."

"Ah—!" said Harry. "Madam, you are under oath?"

"Yes, sir."

Harry pressed a hand across his no doubt painful forehead and closed his eyes a moment. "Where were you living when you first married Frederick Zollicoffer?"

"Several places," Mrs. Zollicoffer said woodenly.

"Where?"

Bunting half lifted his hand and said, "Objected to as immaterial."

Judge Vredenburgh nodded. "It is immaterial."

Looking to the bench, Harry said, "It goes to the credibility of the witness, your Honor."

"What does?" said Judge Vredenburgh. "Where she lived?"

"Or when she was married?" Bunting asked, standing up. Judge Vredenburgh moved his head from side to side. "No," he said.

"That is my ground, sir," said Harry Wurts, "for asking my question, subject, to be sure, to your Honor's infallible ruling."

Judge Vredenburgh, his hand over his mouth, thumb against one cheek, forefinger against the other, gave him a short dangerous stare. Harry must be feeling terrible if he were going to try being funny with Vredenburgh. "I will sustain the Commonwealth's objection," Judge Vredenburgh said. "You may except if you want to."

To Mrs. Zollicoffer Harry said, "Well, what was your late husband's business?"

"Salesman, I guess," said Mrs. Zollicoffer.

"You guess!" said Harry contemptuously. "You would! Where did he have his office?"

"Somewheres in town."

"Where in town?"

"I don't exactly know that."

Harry lifted his shoulders and threw up his hands. "What was he selling?"

"Some kind of a brand of whiskey, or something like that." Harry was at last succeeding to the point of annoying her. The woman scorned was reacting.

"Something like that!" said Harry with increased contempt. "Was he working for a distillery?"

"Perhaps."

"Perhaps! You mean he was bootlegging?"

"No, I don't!" said Mrs. Zollicoffer.

Bunting drew a breath and came to his feet. "Just a minute, now!" he said. "I object to that as not being cross-examination. We have been very patient with Mr. Wurts. This witness was recalled on matters which we went into in chief."

"I think this may be material," Judge Vredenburgh said. "Overruled."

Harry said, "Well, did he ever bring any samples of this some kind of brand of whiskey home?"

"No, he didn't."

"Just a simple 'no' will do, Madam. Wasn't your husband also engaged in selling opium and narcotics?"

Bunting said, "I don't know how far your Honor wants to permit this to go. I object to it as not being cross-examination, or if it is, as an immaterial line."

Judge Vredenburgh said, "We will continue to overrule you."

"Again," said Harry, "I must direct your attention, Madam, to the fact that you are under oath."

"You don't need to do that all the time," said Bunting. "She knows it."

"I don't know whether she does or not," Harry said. "Will you answer the question?"

"No. He wasn't."

"He wasn't engaged in the sale of narcotics, if you know what the term means?"

"Not that I know of."

"You mean, not that you want to know of! Your husband

was in a low and criminal business, which you had to pretend to yourself you didn't know about. Wasn't he? Wasn't he?"

"Your Honor," said Bunting, "that I do object to. He—"

"Mr. Wurts is within his rights in asking if that were the case. There can be no objection to describing dope peddling as low and criminal. I think you'd better let your witness stand on her own feet, Mr. District Attorney."

Whatever Mrs. Zollicoffer might, a moment ago, have been stung or goaded into saying, she was able to say now, "Not that I know of."

Harry had wandered back to the defense's table. He spoke to George Stacey and looked at a memorandum. He made a gesture as though to dismiss the witness, and Mrs. Zollicoffer visibly relaxed. "In short," said Harry, looking at her with a smile, "you want the jury to believe that your late husband was a salesman, or something like that—" He mimicked her voice genially. "Only a cheap whiskey salesman, and nothing else. Not that we know of." His tone was now the very opposite of that harsh or brutal tone which he had risked for a moment, and which a jury so resents when it is used to a woman; but Harry nonetheless managed to insinuate derision, to invite her and everyone else to join him in contempt for the deceased. Harry had seen where and how to wound her without doing himself any damage; and, caught unguarded, Mrs. Zollicoffer burst out, "That doesn't say those people ought to kill him, regardless what he did! That—"

"That's all, Madam," Harry Wurts said. He bent his head to listen to something Howell was saying.

"Cheap but good," Bunting said to Abner. "Shall we—oh, let her go!" He stood up and said, "You may step down, Mrs. Zollicoffer."

Harry left the defense's table and went up to the bench. Sitting back, the Judge said, "There will be a five minute recess. The defendant Howell may be taken out."

Everitt Weitzel came limping across to the Commonwealth's table and said, "Your office called, Mr. Bunting. When you had time."

"All right," Bunting said.

Harry Wurts went into the Attorneys Room, and Joe Jackman stood up and followed him. Abner took out a package of cigarettes and went after Joe.

"Not much of a house, this morning," Joe said, yawning. He held a match for Abner and they stood together by the screened windows. Below them sounded a splash of water in the little cast iron fountain under the trees. Occasionally figures, coatless men, girls in thin dresses, moved slowly on the diagonal cement walks under the trees. "Going to be a hot day," Joe said. "I'll bet it's ninety right now."

"What happened to Harry?"

"In there," Joe said, indicating the lavatory. "He is taking a little something for that miserable morning-after feeling, or over-indulgence in stimulants. You missed it, last night. Dick Nyce made a pass at Annette; and there was quite a row down at the landing. Dotty didn't like it. I think everybody's had about enough of those barge parties."

The lavatory door opened and Harry came out. "A much-needed pause!" he said. "Well, Ab, what did you think of your witness? She don't know nothing no time."

"I don't think she had anything to do with his dope business. She doesn't have to tell you what she thinks."

Joe said, "What's the trouble with that little boy blue of yours, Wurts? Got the trots?"

"Jackman," said Harry, "if you had ever been spread over a table and given a good kidney massage, an idea not wholly repugnant to me, you would suffer from certain disorders for some time afterward."

"Did he forget to suffer from them yesterday, or did you forget to remind him?"

"I don't blame you," Harry said, "you see the Commonwealth putting on these tear-jerking acts, that poor dear little widow-woman and all; and so you think everything's like that—"

The courtroom door opened and Nick Dowdy came in. "About ready," he said. "Judge Irwin's just come on the bench, too."

"Well, what the hell does he want?" said Harry. "Why didn't you tell him that it isn't the function of this court to gratify the vulgar curiosity of typical sensation-mongers?" Harry was reviving. "Just let me ask you," he said, backing Nick against the wall of buckram-bound reports, "has his Honor, the President Judge, read Mr. Wurts' concise and brilliant three thousand page brief submitted in the matter of Mat Moot, Max Moot, Manny Moot Junior, Mary Moot Moot, Mike Moot, Maurice Moot, and Muriel Moot by her next friend and brother Moe Moot, versus Moot and Moot, a corporation, action in assumpsit? I doubt it! I sincerely doubt it! Well, what's he idling around here for?"

Joe Jackman said to Abner, "He's certainly feeling smart this morning. I don't know why the Judge didn't slap his ears down in there—"

"Now, you fellows," Nick said, escaping from Harry. "Defendant's back, I think. Judge Vredenburgh was looking around—"

Joe Jackman went out, and Harry said, "What's he riding me for? Not that I wouldn't ride him, if I could; but it's hard riding only half a horse."

The answer, Abner thought, was that Harry still held, just as he had years ago on the occasion of their difference at law school, that one of the perquisites of being Harry Wurts was making fun of people, so no reasonable person ought to object; while, of course, Harry had every right to resent the manifest usurpation when one of his ordinary victims took to answering affront with affront. Harry would have to content himself with the fact that one of his affronts was usually equal in effectiveness to several of most other people's.

In the courtroom, Bunting stood at the bar, his elbow on

the edge of Judge Vredenburgh's desk, while they talked.
Abner stepped up beside him, and Judge Irwin nodded.
Abner said, "Good morning, sir."

Bunting had already called Walter Cohen, who waited
awkwardly in the witness stand, the swart skin of his round,
big-nosed face shining, his right hand with a diamond ring
on it, suspended, while Nick Dowdy withheld the Bible on
which he was to swear, pending the outcome of Bunting's discussion. Judge Irwin whispered to Abner, "How's your
father?"

"Pretty well this morning, sir," Abner said.

Judge Irwin nodded with a little nervous, smiling grimace.
His nature was reserved and aloof—unless, perhaps, you
were a member of his own generation—and it was difficult
to imagine being familiar with him. Judge Irwin's attitude
was strict; but, by the simple if uncommon practice of dis-
ciplining himself just as strictly as he disciplined other people,
he aroused, even in a heavily sentenced prisoner, no special
resentment. His air of virtue, instead of being hateful, had in
it an austere sweetness. Judge Vredenburgh sat calm, full-
blooded, the intelligent sensual man, irascible about what
struck him as wrong or unfair, astute about the failings of
human beings, dealing with facts and things as they were,
with no special interest in why. Judge Irwin thought constantly of why.

They were about the same age, in their early sixties; but
Judge Irwin looked a good deal older than Judge Vredenburgh. He had little flesh on his face, and his finely formed,
entirely bare skull was fringed with an inch or two of gray
hair along the base from ear to ear. On the bench, he sat
intense and earnest, tightening and relaxing his lips, clearing
his throat, sometimes plucking with his thin long hand at
his chin. To see him and Judge Vredenburgh sitting together
when, for instance, they both doubted a witness, marked the
contrast. Judge Vredenburgh cocked a hard, incredulous eye,
pouting slightly, sometimes even giving his head faint an-

noyed shakes; Judge Irwin bent his angular, anxious gaze on the witness as though he hoped, because he wished so hard that men would not deliberately perjure themselves, to make this man stop.

It would not be fair to say that Judge Irwin was less attentive to the facts than Judge Vredenburgh, for he ended by acting on them with precision, abstractly balancing the offense against what the statutes provided; but in a way he hated the facts. He hated them as symptoms of a disease of folly and unreason pandemic in the world, and constantly infecting and reinfecting his fellow men. A good example was Judge Irwin's notorious antipathy to liquor. He understood no better than Cassio why men should put an enemy in their mouths to steal away their brains; but it was that pandemic folly and unreason that he blamed, rather than the individual. He did not even favor trying to abolish liquor by law, since that proposed the absurdity of blaming the liquor and enhanced the principle, false among free men, of preventing a choice instead of punishing an abuse.

What Judge Irwin knew was what everyone with his experience knew: that if there were no such thing as liquor, half or even three quarters of the work in each term of court would be eliminated. He was not fanatical about it; he did not suppose that a man who took a drink now and then, or even one who got drunk now and then, was a criminal. Undoubtedly he knew that his son liked a drink; and though he probably hoped that Mark never got as drunk as Mark had been last night, Judge Irwin would not be enraged if he found out—only, discouraged by the imprudence, the shortsightedness that defied common sense and invited danger in seeking so brief and miserable a pleasure.

Judge Vredenburgh sat back, and Bunting said to Nick Dowdy, "All right, swear him."

As they turned, Harry Wurts stood up and called out, "Just a moment, please, your Honor! I'm going to ask for an offer of proof here with Cohen."

"I thought so!" Bunting said to Abner. "All right, Mr. Wurts. At side bar?"

"I don't care," Harry said.

"Well, certainly I don't, either," said Bunting. "We expect to prove by this witness that on the night of April seventeenth he met a person outside a saloon near Milltown and talked with him. That he turned over to this person the sum of eight thousand dollars in bills of various denominations."

Judge Vredenburgh said, "Mr. Wurts, you stated that you did not care whether the offer was made in the presence of the jury or not. Do you want the whole offer to be made?"

"Well, no." Harry scratched his head. "If he's going to make a complete offer, I would ask that it be made at side bar. What I want is for the Commonwealth to show how this man Cohen's testimony can be material. Of course, if to show that, he has to trot out all the—"

"I can't be expected to guess what you mean," Bunting said. "I supposed you wanted—"

Judge Vredenburgh said, "Yes; the offer should be sufficient to show the relation. Come up, Mr. Wurts. Come up, Mr. Stacey. This concerns you, too."

Abner came up with Bunting and they stood close together under the bench. Bunting continued, "This money was brought for the purpose of securing the release of Frederick Zollicoffer. To be followed by further evidence that on that same night Robert Basso, one of these defendants, brought into the presence of Roy Leming, the defendant not now on trial, but to be called as Commonwealth's witness, the sum of eight thousand dollars; which money Basso, at that time and later, stated to Commonwealth's witness was obtained by him and Howell from Cohen, now on the stand, who was paying it for the release of his associate and business partner, Fred Zollicoffer. To be followed by further testimony corroborative in admissions by the defendant, Stanley Howell."

"Yes," said Harry. "Well, for the defendant, Howell, I

119

object to the offer." He turned to the bench. "Your Honors will understand—"

Judge Irwin said with his thin, pleasant smile, "I'm not sitting, Mr. Wurts. I am present, but I am not participating."

"Nonetheless," said Harry, inclining his head, "I think the point will be as apparent to your Honor, as to his Honor, Judge Vredenburgh. The offer is immaterial and irrelevant as to the offense charged here; namely, that of murder. All this is evidence of a separate and distinct offense; namely kidnapping, holding for ransom."

Judge Vredenburgh said, "Is this evidence to show that the money had anything to do with the kidnapping?"

"Yes," said Bunting, "naturally, your Honor. The Commonwealth offers to prove that this identical money was divided among the kidnappers."

Judge Vredenburgh said, "Mr. Wurts seems to want to know whether your offer relates the kidnapping to the murder for which the defendants are on trial."

"Oh, yes," Bunting said. "We intend to prove that the killing was carried out as an integral part of the kidnapping, in the course of the perpetration of it."

"Well," said George Stacey, "in that respect there's no averment in the indictment."

George had made the discovery—Abner remembered making it himself—that a natural impulse to defer to the impressive, seemingly never-to-be-equaled experience of his elders, like Bunting and Harry Wurts, while often politic in a younger man, was not always necessary. George said, "The indictment merely charges an unlawful and felonious killing amounting to murder in the first degree. It does not set forth that the killing was in perpetration of any other felony."

"It doesn't need to," Abner said, smiling. "Any killing in perpetration of the felony of kidnapping is unlawful and felonious and amounts to murder in the first degree."

Bunting said, "I think you'd better give his Honor some authority for your statement, Mr. Stacey."

With all eyes on him, George said, "I am familiar with the law that holds an indictment sufficient that simply charges a defendant with first degree murder." Abner could see that George had still to learn not to be afraid that, if he did not say everything, people would think that he did not know everything. The measure of his inexperience was in his error of anticipating objections. George said, "It is true that such indictments need not set forth as to the manner, or means, or instrumentality with which the crime was committed; but the law can certainly not be so elastic as to include other crimes, other felonies; and if these defendants are going to be charged with committing a different felony—" He threw out a hand. "Well, I don't think Mr. Bunting can do that."

"That's the whole point, your Honor," said Harry Wurts. "We object to this offer because the kidnapping was over, completed, finished, with the payment of the ransom money. As Mr. Stacey so well said, this isn't the crime these defendants are on trial for. It was not in perpetration of a felony that this killing was done. That was all over."

Judge Vredenburgh turned his head and spoke to Judge Irwin. "No," he said, turning back. "We will overrule you. You may have your exceptions. Let's get on with it."

Abner went back to his seat. Walter Cohen ought not to take very long; and Abner doubted if Harry would cross-examine, when Harry discovered (as he was bound to, if he didn't know already) that Cohen was going to lie out of helping the Commonwealth. Cohen was very willing to testify about handing over the sum of money for Frederick Zollicoffer's release; and he expressed himself as eager to see Fred's assassins pay for their crime, but he was full of nice scruples. He explained in Bunting's office, and again (to Bunting's helpless annoyance) before the grand jury, that he meant, of course, the actual assassins. He could not positively identify the person to whom he handed the money.

This was as ridiculous as Mrs. Zollicoffer's claim that she did not know her husband's business; and, in fact, both lies were probably Walter Cohen's. Probably he had told Marguerite to say nothing about Fred's business, no matter what happened. From Leming, and from Howell's confession, Bunting knew that it was Basso who received the money, and Basso himself had told Leming that he knew Walter Cohen recognized him. Walter Cohen would know that Bunting knew; but he had doubtless also made sure that Bunting could not or would not do anything about it. Probably Cohen judged accurately the importance to the Commonwealth's case of his identifying Basso. Bunting could show that money, to the same amount as Cohen paid a mysterious stranger, had been brought on the same evening to the bungalow and divided by the kidnappers. Bunting had all he really needed. No jury was going to suppose that by a coincidence other people had gone out that night carrying bundles of bills to pay ransoms at the same spot; and there, by a mistake, met one or more other kidnappers coming to get it, with the result that Cohen gave his money to the wrong person, not Basso; while Basso took his money from the wrong person, not Cohen. All the circumstances identified Basso; and Cohen could rightly conclude that Bunting would not bother to make any determined or dangerous attack on his own witness—compelling Cohen to identify Basso was not worth it. Cohen was left free to play his own game, moved by who-knew-what anfractuosities of honor among thieves, or fears of a man who could never call the police, or hopes of keeping the confidence of his business associates. Since Harry and George did not want the identification made, either, Harry had no reason to ask questions.

The Commonwealth's next witness would be Roy Leming, and Abner laid out the folders. This was important; and Abner would have liked it better if Bunting were going to handle Leming. Probably Bunting would have liked it better, too; but Leming, a nervous man, was more afraid of Bunting than Abner. Perhaps because Abner was younger than Leming, Leming shook and stammered less when he could address himself to Abner. Though Bunting seemed to feel no misgivings about leaving the most important witness to his assistant, and this both pleased and (as it might have been meant to) heartened Abner, Abner could not say that he felt no misgivings of his own.

For one thing, Mr. Servadei was present. Servadei was an insignificant little gray-haired man, and his part in the proceedings appeared only that of an interested observer. Nevertheless, Abner wished that when the matter of Leming's turning state's evidence was settled, Servadei had seen fit to withdraw and go about his business. From his firm's standpoint Servadei's time must be valuable; and Abner could not help wondering just what figure went down in Servadei's day book for each hour spent here doing absolutely nothing.

Of course, Servadei's waiting might be innocently explained. Servadei might want to see Harry handle this tough case so as to get a line, for his firm's information and possible future need, on a criminal lawyer in this county. The chances of such a need arising were not likely to be great, or not great enough to make such a purpose certain and shut out entirely the possibility that Servadei was there to preside over the pulling of a fast one. Once started in that direction, disquieting thoughts multiplied. The business of Servadei's firm was getting criminals off. Why should they advise a client of theirs to give testimony that would probably get two criminals electrocuted?

Without Leming's testimony the Commonwealth could hardly hope to convict Basso, and might not convict Howell; and there sat Servadei; and how easily he could slip Leming a word, a threat from those hidden parts of Leming's criminal past, a promise to help him in ways that the Commonwealth could not anticipate. Such a plan might even tie up with Basso's standing mute; and though Abner did not see how, it was always possible that he and Bunting would find out how in good time. Abner shrank to imagine the upset— Bunting's sudden angry realization as he arose to interrupt Abner and request permission to cross-examine; Bunting's biting, but if Leming lied firmly, vain attack; the eventual ignominious entry of a nolle prosequi, or the Court's necessary charge that there was no evidence against Basso. Servadei, finding Abner's eye on him, bowed civilly; and Abner, obliged to nod back, looked away in confusion and gave his attention to the witness on the stand.

Bunting said to Walter Cohen, "Does either of them look like the man you saw?"

"I object to the cross-examination of this witness," Harry Wurts said.

The tactic of constant obstruction was a boring one to Harry, whose type of mind was the type that demurs, that admits all you claim, and in a flash, taking a new direction where you are entirely unprepared, shows that for one reason or another there is no case. He tilted back in his chair, smiling at Bunting, and added, "The witness has said with the utmost positiveness that they don't look like the man he saw."

Judge Vredenburgh shook his head. "Exception noted," he said.

Bunting said, "Does either of them look like the man you saw that night?" Abner saw that he was venting his annoyance—a thing Bunting sometimes did when it could not make much difference to his case. Bunting was grimly going to force Cohen to anatomize his lie.

"I can't say they do," Cohen answered. He was probably not altogether easy. The careful way in which he was being obliged to perjure himself might make him wonder if, all unknowing, he was putting his foot in it. He gave Bunting a placatory, almost entreating look. He tried a rueful smile, as though to say that he only wished he could help.

Bunting said, dry and grim, "I ask you to look particularly at the defendant, Robert Basso."

Crossing and uncrossing his legs, joining his fleshy hands together, Cohen said, "I don't know that particular gentleman, sir."

"Just a moment!" Abner could see Bunting's silent ejaculation: *You damned liar!* "Did you ever know him?"

"No, sir."

"I ask you whether or not—" Bunting turned to the defense's table. "Do you mind having Basso stand up?"

George Stacey looked at Harry, and Harry said, "No. Stand up, Basso!"

For a moment it seemed doubtful if Basso would obey. Maybe he saw then that he could do the Commonwealth more despite by agreeing than by refusing. He got slowly to his feet and turned his black, rarely blinking eyes on Cohen in the stand.

Bunting said, "I ask you whether or not the man that you saw was about the size and weight—height and weight, of Robert Basso, this defendant."

Cohen went through his excruciating dumb-show of anxiety to please. He tilted his head. He looked critically at Basso. He narrowed his eyes to weigh and measure him. Then he shook his head and said regretfully to Bunting, "To the best of my recollection, you understand, he may have been a slight bit taller and a slight bit heavier. I say about one hundred seventy-five pounds—"

Abner let his eyes go around. Beyond Servadei and Leming, Hugh Erskine sat in the raised chair at the end of the row. His slight elevation let him overlook his charges and Hugh from time to time gave them a glance. He then subsided, his solid slab-cheeked face in dignified repose, his long lipped big mouth shut in a firm line. Brown hair was thinning on the crown of his big head. Hugh's deep-set mild brown eyes encountered Abner's gaze, and he closed one in a slow amiable wink. On Hugh's broad chest, pinned to the left suspender strap, Abner could see, shining in the shadow of the coat hanging open, the silver, eagle-crowned high sheriff's badge.

Right under Hugh sat Dewey Smith. Dewey had been a sort of hanger-on and general handyman around the Rock Creek Road bungalow where Frederick Zollicoffer had been held prisoner. Dewey was frail, and sensitive-faced, with an alert manner that concealed from a casual glance the fact that he was a low grade moron. Abner had seen his record, which covered eight states and included over forty arrests, though always for minor offenses. Dewey would not have the nerve to plan anything serious on his own; and those who did have the nerve to plan something serious would not be likely to risk giving Dewey a real part in it. Bunting did not much care what disposal was made of him; but meanwhile Dewey might have a use. It depended on whether or not Susie Smalley decided to plead guilty to the charge of being an accessory.

For the purpose of defense, Susie was represented as Howell's so-called common law wife. Old John Clark from Watertown was her lawyer; and nothing could have been more surprising than his appearance for her. Mr. Clark would not have taken the case to get a fee—he had plenty of money; and, anyway, Susie had none. Leaving out Susie's person and character, it was not likely to be for love, since Mr. Clark was considerably over seventy. Abner, himself, guessed that Mr. Clark was appearing for no reason at all but an old man's vagarious impulse to show somebody or other that he could and would decide for himself what he was going to do; and if it were something unexpected, all the better. The position Mr. Clark had found for Susie was that a common law wife could not be prosecuted as an accessory; and this had been upheld more than once. The Commonwealth's only apparent chance was to destroy Susie's status. This ought to be possible, for Bunting believed it a factitious one; but unfortunately for Bunting, there was no evidence of the kind he wanted except Dewey Smith's.

Put baldly (though not so baldly as Dewey himself put it) Dewey's story was that Susie Smalley had relations with Bailey often and with Basso and Leming occasionally. If this were true, and could be shown, Bunting thought he might be able to explode Mr. Clark's common law wife theory—it would be a nice point, and would take some looking-up. The hitch, of course, was Dewey as a witness. Dewey had told his story with good circumstantial detail, and probably he would be able to repeat it on the stand; but, cross-examined, Dewey must soon show that he was a moron; and cross-examination would be bound to bring out, too, many things about him that were better kept in the district attorney's office than presented to a jury. It was simplest to describe Dewey as not normal; and investigating in open court the intricacies of his abnormality did not seem to Bunting in the public interest.

Bunting, though perhaps he would not have put it that way, meant to use Dewey (if he could) as a threat to persuade Susie or Mr. Clark to plead guilty. The complicating truth was that, good circumstantial detail or not, Bunting rejected Dewey's story, or at least the extension of it (Basso and Leming as well as Bailey) that would be most useful for his purpose. The district attorney's office had reason to know that a group of men might patronize the same prostitute, all friends together; a group of men might take a girl out and successively rape her; but they did not do things like this—have one of them bring his girl, and then all live together, all having coitus with her. It was not impossible; and looking at Susie, a jury might very well believe it. They might find her guilty of having a wide, smudged-looking, dissolute face, dead and shabby hair with streaks of fake blonde, and a debauched body under the tight green dress—doubly guilty because of the disproportionate, grotesquely

127

prominent breasts. In Bunting's place, Abner did not know
what he would do.

He saw Harry Wurts shake his head, and realized that
Bunting had finished with Walter Cohen. Cohen came down,
directing little bows to everyone—the Judges, the jury, Bunting, Abner, Harry, George, and the defendants. Bunting,
approaching the table, shot Cohen a look, and said to Abner,
"If you ever want any nice fresh narcotics, give him a ring.
Deliveries at all hours."

Abner laughed. "Leming?" he said.

Bunting looked at the clock. "Yes," he said. "We can
get some done before lunch. All set?"

"Sure," said Abner, "but look, Marty. I think Harry's
going to kick about the severance right away, and I'd better
leave that to you, hadn't I? And of course, if Leming starts
to balk, you'd better take it over, because I won't know what
you want to do."

"Let him try!" said Bunting. "I don't know what Servadei may think he's going to do; but just remember we can
always bring Leming to trial for murder. If that wasn't what
he was more afraid of than anything else, he wouldn't be
testifying for us. Don't worry about it. Keep his story moving, and we'll be all right. Ready?"

"O.K.," said Abner, palming the card on which he had
his notes written.

"Roy Leming," said Bunting, "take the stand, please!"

While asking Leming where he lived and how long he
had lived there, and how old he was—Leming said he was
thirty-eight: a significant admission, for in crime, as in ath-
letics and war, youth counted; and Leming was past his
prime, fit only for jobs of secondary importance—Abner, by
his tone and manner, made what play he could for Leming's
good will. It was not an effort that Abner enjoyed making,

nor one that seemed on the face of it likely to succeed. Just
the same, as Bunting said, if Leming had the idea that the
assistant district attorney, as contrasted with his boss, was
friendly or a nice fellow, it was clearly worth encouraging
him. Abner knew that it was a mistake to assume that everything that seemed false or unreal to you, offending your
sensibilities and insulting your intelligence, must necessarily
seem so to everyone else.

Leming was nervous. He smoothed his thin blonde hair,
shifted the knot of his necktie, tried, by shrugging his shoulders and pulling his sleeves to make his worn blue serge
suit sit better. However, his voice was clear and pleasant.
He was humble and obliging and the jury looked at him
with glances that made their surprise plain. Leming was
not their idea of a case-hardened criminal and dope addict.
His air of being their humble servant was just right—they
did not want him to fawn on them, only to look up to them,
and this Leming seemed to do.

Abner said, "You are one of the defendants named in
this bill of indictment, are you not?"

"Yes, sir."

Abner looked at Harry, who was busily scribbling on
a slip of paper. Abner said to Leming, "Do you know one
of these other defendants, Robert Basso?"

"All right," said Harry, holding up his hand. "If your
Honor please, we object to this witness. We submit that
under the law a joint defendant cannot be a witness either
for or against those indicted with him until his own indictment is disposed of by trial, and, as the case may be, acquittal, conviction, or a nolle prosequi. That is not the condition of this record in this case."

Abner went back to the Commonwealth's table and Bunting stood up; but Judge Vredenburgh said, "Do you have
any authority for that, Mr. Wurts?"

"Yes, sir," said Harry, holding up his slip. "I cite Whar-
ton's *Criminal Evidence*, volume one, paragraph four thirty·

nine; and Bishop's *Criminal Procedure*, sections ten twenty, eleven thirty-six, and the cases thereunder, which I would like to submit to your Honor." He turned, lifted the open books from the table beside him and brought them up to the bar. Nick Dowdy took them and laid them before the Judge. Judge Irwin, approaching his bald head to Vredenburgh's ear, said something. Judge Vredenburgh nodded, stared briefly first at one volume and then at the other. "Objection overruled," he said, delivering the books back to Nick Dowdy. "You may have your exceptions."

Leming looked politely at the Judge, and then at Harry, and then at Abner. Bunting said, "That puts the cork in there." He crumpled up the paper on which he had noted his opposing authorities. Abner went back to face the jury; and Leming said, "Yes, sir. I do."

"And do you know the other defendant, Stanley Howell?"

"Yes, sir."

"How long have you known Robert Basso?"

Leming had known him for some time. The story of how they met was naturally not relevant, and anyway Abner had no wish to remind the jury that Leming was not so harmless as he looked. Leming, an old hand, had met Basso in jail. Basso was relatively new, just out of reform school, and Leming, by being older, by his boasting, by showing, as he surely could, that he knew the ropes, probably induced Basso to work with him after they got out. Basso, young, vicious, and without the experience to see danger, was just what an older man like Leming wanted. Basso could do the risky and strenuous dirty work in schemes that Leming could think up.

Leming was guarded about speaking of such matters. He freely admitted as much of his criminal record as he knew would be forwarded as soon as Bunting broadcast a request for it; but the list of Leming's arrests and convictions were his failures. He had not always failed. In telling his story Leming picked his way from fact to established fact. He did not want to let out anything that Bunting might recognize as likely to interest the police in certain cities. His fear and dislike of Bunting were partly due to his early realization that Bunting was no fool and would catch any slips.

Though some of Leming's track was thus covered by silence and omission, it could be followed—a sort of tour of that everyday, routine world of professional crime. It did not differ as much as the imagination might suggest from the everyday world of those who were not professional criminals. In one, as in the other, the principal problem was how to make a living; and criminals who made good ones were as rare as millionaires. The rank and file could count on little but drudgery and economic insecurity; and for the same reason that most men in lawful pursuits could count on little else. They had no natural abilities, and lacked the will and intelligence to develop any.

Leming spent most of his time job hunting. He did not mean quite what the law-abiding incompetent meant by the dreary phrase; but the results, in their high proportion of disappointment and dissatisfaction, were almost identical; and in fact Leming's motions were those of the ordinary shiftless man looking for work. If you asked him what work, he answered with exemplary earnestness, any work at all. In search of employment, he would appear briefly taking a train here or there, getting a lift in somebody's car, disappearing into the poorer streets of the eastern cities. Often he could name jobs that he had obtained. Probably he could have named others, but thought it better not to, because, either while he held them, or directly afterward, there were pilferings, or even payroll robberies, not yet cleared up.

Several years before Leming met Robert Basso he had got to know Stanley Howell. Very likely it was an acquaintanceship resulting from the habit Leming had contracted of taking drugs, which Stanley Howell distributed. This was just a guess; plausible, because it would explain Howell's knowing so much about Frederick Zollicoffer—his habits, where he lived, the likelihood of being able to extort money from him. Perhaps Howell was once part of a little sales organization Zollicoffer had worked up; and Zollicoffer might have, for one reason or another, got rid of Howell, refused to use him any more. At any rate, Leming, coming and going on those searches for work of his, treated Howell's place as a base. When he and Basso got out of jail, Leming took Basso there, no doubt with the hope of making him useful.

It was unlikely that being useful to Leming had ever been part of Basso's idea. He meant to use Leming; and when he met Howell, Howell. Since they were two to one, he probably disguised his intention for a week or so, listening to their talk, sizing up the prospects—poor, he probably concluded, as long as a doper like Leming and a gutless wonder like Howell had charge. Perhaps the Zollicoffer idea looked good to him; and so one day he brought around a friend of his who also brought a friend.

Basso's friend was Mike Bailey, and Bailey's friend was Dewey Smith. In neither case was the word "friend" exact. Basso feared and respected Bailey; Dewey Smith was less than nothing, a half-wit who did what Bailey said; but now there were three against two, and one of the three, Bailey, was formidable. Abner had seen the rogue's gallery pictures of Bailey—a pop-eyed young man with a prominent Adam's apple and large irregular features. He did not look formidable; but few men do with a number hung around their necks, floodlights on the face, and the head against a wall-scale showing in feet and inches the subject's height. Formidable looking or not, Bailey proceeded to take over. Within a week they were all doing what Bailey told them to do. He had Basso steal a car; he had Leming plan out a route to Zollicoffer's house; he had Howell rent a bungalow out on the Rock Creek Road; and, if Dewey Smith were to be believed, he had Susie, whether through love or fear, sharing his bed.

While he continued with his questions, Abner tried to keep in mind as much of this knowledge of the general situation as he could. He needed it to check against Leming's replies. He was watching sharply, half expecting the first contradictions, a hesitancy, a little sticking or resistance, that might mean funny business; but Leming, though he avoided looking in the direction of Basso and Howell, was answering properly. He said that it was about a week after Bailey came that he heard the plan.

"What did you hear?" Abner asked.

"This about snatching Zolly, that we would do it."

"Kidnapping Zollicoffer," Abner said. "And what exactly did they say?"

George Stacey said, "If your Honor please, I think this witness should be pinned down to which of these men made the statement."

"Or, at least," Judge Vredenburgh nodded, "which ones were present when the statement was made. Yes."

Abner said, "Were Basso, Bailey, and Howell all present?"

"Yes, sir. All of them."

"Now, just state what you heard these three men say."

"Why, they were talking about the best time at night to go out and get hold of him. I just can't tell you exactly word by word what they said."

"Well, give the substance," said Abner.

"They decided the best time to get out to his house was about eleven at night, I believe, so they asked me would I show them the way; and I told them, no." Leming paused; but only for the reason that he doubtless needed an instant to consider implications; and, if necessary, not to invent or falsify the facts, but to edit them. "I had told them I was going over to New York, and they told me not to go to New York; and I told them I had to go; and so they asked me when I would be back. And I told them the following afternoon, late; so I got over to New York, and I was stuck there a couple of days."

The trip, Abner knew, had been to get dope. The trouble with asking a witness to give the substance was that the pressure of your questions, if not leading, certainly directing, was removed. There was no reason to help Harry put emphasis on Leming's former habits. Ignoring the concerted gaze of the jury, whose innocent instinct would be, regardless of relevancy, to ask: Why did you go to New York? Why did you have to? What do you mean, you got stuck there? Abner said, "Well, when you returned, did you have any further conversations?"

"Yes," said Leming. "So when I go up there, they were pretty sore about it, about me staying over; so they bawled me out pretty good about it; and I told them I had to stay over, the occasion called for it."

"After that, what, if anything, did they say to you?"

"So, finally," Leming said, "Bailey came to me and he said, 'Listen . . .'"

"Were the other two there?"

"Yes, sir. Right there."

"All right. What did he say?"

"He told me, he said, 'We were out there to grab Zolly the other night, and we got lost, and we want you to take us tonight.' I said, 'No, I am not going to take you. I told you before I would not take you.' And Bailey said, 'If you know what is healthy for you, you will take us out there tonight.'"

The formal, artificial-sounding phrasing served Leming's purpose—to show that he was threatened and felt fear— very well. Bailey might or might not have expressed himself so stiltedly; but the sinister quality of the conversation, by an unconscious onomatopoeia that picked words to fit the serious sense, was increased if anything when reported this way. "All right," said Abner. "Then what was said?"

"So, finally, I told them, I says, 'I will take you as far as

Parkside'—that is the name where the road goes out to Zolly's. So we come to an agreement. They said, 'That is all right. Parkside is all right.' So I asked them what they are sore about. Well, it appears the night I left, there was this machine pulled down the street with the lights out, with two men in it, and they got out."

"Now, this is what they told you, is it?" Abner said. It was a curious little story, both for the light shed on relations between the kidnappers; and for the possibility, not to be ruled out, that Leming did, in fact, know more about "this machine" than he admitted. "Yes," said Leming, "so Bailey spoke up; and he said, 'It looks pretty funny as soon as you leave, this car comes right down. It didn't look so good to us.' And they claimed the whole three of them went out to see what these men were looking for; and they followed them, while these men were striking matches, looking at the different houses; and finally after fifteen or twenty minutes they went away. So I spoke up, and I says, 'It looks like you trust me pretty good, then.' And Basso says, 'What would it look like to you?' As much as to say—"

"Well, I object!" said Harry Wurts.

"All right," Abner said. "Never mind the 'as much as to say.' Basso said, 'What would it look like to you?' Now, will you state whether, on this night of your return, you did go to Parkside?"

"Yes, sir."

"Well, just tell us what you did, and what happened."

While Leming explained about the trip—he in one car, leading the way; the other three in another, Abner could not help wondering whether the real reason that Bailey assented to an "agreement" which gave Leming no active part, wasn't that Bailey had decided that Leming, with his drugs, would be worthless or worse. It would be interesting to know why Bailey trusted him at all, in that event—and the answer probably was that, in spite of all appearances of planning and strategy, Bailey acted mostly on impulse, and so never could think far ahead.

"Very well," said Abner. "And when you saw the other car come back, what?"

"Well, I saw they stopped; so Howell got out of the car, and I got out, and I came over."

"What, if anything, did Stanley Howell say to you?"

"He was laughing," Leming said. "He says, 'We got Zolly in here.'"

"Did Stanley Howell say anything else?"

"He told me they had to bust his head open pretty good, and said he was bleeding like a pig."

"Yes. Anything else?"

"Well, he told me they snatched Zolly, and had to bust his head, and he put up a pretty good fight with them. He said when they first grabbed him, Zolly thought they were the cops. He pulled out a can with some opium, and about fifty or sixty dollars, and said, 'Here is the money,' as much as to say, leave him go for it—"

The jury stirred. They were ready to go off the track again; for, of course, into every mind jumped the meaning. Down there, policemen could be bribed. This man thought it was the police—and why; unless the police did come sometimes; and then for fifty or sixty dollars, let him go. They sat up sharply. Left to themselves, the jurors would have dropped everything and haled in those corrupt policemen, and dealt with them. Abner felt like telling them that the detail, for what it was worth, had been brought to the attention of the district attorney's office in that county; and this was all they could do; and all that would be done, too. It was one thing to learn of irregularities on third-hand evidence; it was another to prove that they ever took place.

"This is what Stanley Howell told you?" Abner said.

"Yes."

The jury looked almost mutinous, and perhaps Harry Wurts thought it would do no harm to give them a little time to mull over the wickedness and hypocrisy of those who enforced the law. He said, "If your Honor please—" He got up and came to the bar.

"All right," Judge Vredenburgh said, "if it is necessary." Max Eich marched over to Howell and they went out the door together. "This is a five minute recess," Judge Vredenburgh said, "but I don't want everyone going out. Too long getting back."

Abner sat down beside Bunting, who said, "What's this about Pete Wiener and some accident last night?"

"Gosh!" said Abner. "Forgot about it! Pete called after I got home. One driver was killed. Pete had the other for manslaughter. He ought to be up in jail here. I told Pete to help him get a habeas from Judge Irwin this morning."

"I sent for the police report. It may be over at the office, but I haven't seen it. Was this fellow drunk or anything?"

"I don't believe so," Abner said. "Pete seemed to think it wasn't his fault. He called up because he wanted to know if he could take bail. All I know is, the other driver was killed. Pete could give you the details. He said it happened right out there on route sixteen."

"Jesse Gearhart called the office about it," Bunting said. "He told Theda he wanted to find out about it. It's the son of a friend of his, or someone he knows, who called him from New York. Name's Mason."

"Well, that's too bad," Abner said. "Maybe somebody ought to tell Jesse his friend's son isn't back in New York now."

"Look, Ab," Bunting said. He paused. "If you don't mind, I'll give you a little advice. You seem to be afraid someone won't know that you don't like Jesse. Don't worry! Everybody knows; and that includes Jesse. Now, just ask yourself sometime what you're trying to do. I can tell you Jesse is wondering. You haven't quite done it yet; but keep on, and you can make yourself a pretty serious enemy there."

"Well!" said Abner. "How long since Jesse's been your

dear old pal? As for what I'm trying to do, I don't happen to like the way Jesse horns in on things. I think he has a hell of a nerve to call you up and—"

"Yes; and what?" said Bunting. "What do you think he's going to do? Slip me a hundred dollars to let this fellow off? Has he ever made you a proposition?"

"If you mean, did he ever try to give me a can of opium and fifty or sixty dollars, no," Abner said. He laughed a little uncomfortably.

Bunting—he was angry in his controlled way; and that was understandable. Abner wouldn't have liked his own attitude in someone else—said, "Did he ever make you any kind of a proposition? Did he ever offer to do anything for you if you'd—to influence your official action? If you have any evidence we'll slap an indictment on him for corrupt solicitation of a public officer and ask Irwin to recall the grand jury this evening. Now, how about it?"

"Ah, be yourself, Marty!" Abner said, smiling. In other walks of life a man who showed signs of temper was often about to go off the handle; but in the law, with its special training in altercation, signs of temper usually meant that a man was prepared to make peace. When you noticed them, he was himself apprised; and his instinct set him to get hold of it, to avoid at all costs that fatal error. Abner said, "If you think Jesse would ever give anyone any evidence, you think he's more of a sap than I do. But you know what I mean; and that's what makes you sore. If you can honestly say that isn't what makes you sore, I apologize."

"You're what makes me sore, Ab," Bunting said. He was already over his annoyance. He turned his pointed nose and sharp dry gaze on Abner, his tight lips shadowed with a smile. "You don't do it often; but when you get high and mighty it gripes me. I'm older than you are, and I know a damned sight more about these things than you do. There's no reason why you can't get on with Jesse if you stop acting like a young squirt."

"I don't mind whether I get on with him or not. I'm not just saying that, Marty."

"I know you're not," Bunting said. "And that's the squirt in you! The reason you're in office is because I appointed you; and the reason I'm in office is because for twenty years Jesse has been seeing that our ticket was better; and then doing the hard work of getting people out to vote for it. You may not like the way he wears his hair; but I think most people, because he's shown sense and had experience, would rather take Jesse's advice than yours. So, don't forget it. Here's Howell."

"You still haven't told me what you want to do about the boy in jail," Abner said, getting up.

"We'll see," Bunting said.

Patient on the stand, Leming straightened himself with a look of relief at Abner's approach. Abner said, "Now, if you'll just continue, please. After the conversation with Howell, did you get back in the cars?"

"Yes, sir. We went to Rock Creek Road, and they brought Zolly in the house, and put him in this room upstairs. That's where they kept him all week—"

Abner thought to himself: I'll bet Marty's resigning! That would explain a good deal—why Marty was sore. Jesse had probably told him within the past week or so about the new jobs Judge Coates had mentioned in the Attorney General's office, and that one of them was his if Marty wanted it. In that event, they would need to decide soon who would run for district attorney here in the fall. This, then, was the moment; and though Abner had taken care never to show that he expected the job, or that he saw what everyone could see—that he was the logical choice; it would be idle to pretend to himself that he did not expect the nomination. Since he had been consciously preparing for it, and as far as it was modest or prudent, counting on it, for the last three years, it would be absurd to tell himself now that he did not want it. He tried to control, and he hoped, succeeded in concealing, that moderate yet essentially jealous ambition, that egotism of confidence in one's ability and one's resulting right, which can never be shown safely, since it intrenches on every other man's ego. This could be damped down by a sense of proportion, by the ludicrousness of great passions directed at small ends—to be district attorney of a county whose importance was well declared when the legislature put it in class five—but when he finished such exercises, the job was not any less what Abner wanted. In fact, Abner could see that his dislike of Jesse was not so frivolous —annoyance at some blundering compliments, or various unprovable suspicions about Jesse's integrity—as he might want to believe; but, short and simple, resentment at a power, without regular authority or justification in law, that allowed Jesse to interpose between Abner and Abner's long standing aims and (he might as well say it) deserts, the impertinency of Jesse's pleasure or displeasure. Abner brought himself up short, and said, "All right. Now who was there at the bungalow during the time Frederick Zollicoffer was held prisoner?"

"All of us. Bailey and Basso and Howell."

"How about Dewey Smith?"

"No, he didn't live there. He came in to bring the groceries and things."

"And Susie Smalley?"

"They had her there one day, a couple of nights, only. Not regular."

Abner hesitated, wondering if a sudden question might help Bunting by putting on the record something useful about how Susie employed her nights; but Bunting did not expect him to open that up, so he'd better let it lie. He said, "And Frederick Zollicoffer was there. Did you see him every day?"

"Not every day, I didn't. He was upstairs and they didn't leave me go there. I heard him. I knew he was there. But

I think only once I actually saw him. On the fourth or fifth day."

"What was he doing on that occasion?"

"Well, Bailey was dictating, Zolly was writing a letter, and Bailey was dictating what he is to put in that letter. One of the letters of Walter Cohen."

"Now, do you recall hearing any reference in conversation between the three men about what was to be done with Frederick Zollicoffer?"

"Oh, yes," said Leming. "I came in one night and heard them discussing about it—"

"Who was 'them'?"

"Howell and Bailey and Basso. They had been out, and they crossed this creek—"

"Fosher's Creek?"

"Yes, sir. They come across that bridge, and they got out and looked at it—"

"I object to this," Harry Wurts said wearily.

"All right, Mr. Wurts," Abner said. "Leming, is this what somebody told you?"

"Well, I heard them saying it."

"Who?"

"Bailey and Basso."

"They were in your presence?"

"Yes, sir. They said they found a good place to throw him."

"Anything else?"

"They said they looked at this bridge, and the water looked pretty deep to them; and this is where they were going to throw him."

Harry Wurts said, "I want to know whether that's a conversation or a conclusion."

"Isn't it clear, Mr. Wurts?" said Abner. "All right, all right! Is that what they said in your presence, Leming?"

"Yes."

"That that was where they were going to throw him in?"

"Yes, sir."

"Do you remember which one said that: Bailey, or Basso, or Howell?"

"Well, all of them said it."

George Stacey arose and said, "We want to get this clear, if we may, your Honor. Now, is that a conversation between these men, Leming, or a conversation with you?"

"Well," said Leming, spreading his hands, "they were talking amongst themselves; and I was in their presence then. Did I answer what you mean, sir?"

"Did he?" said Abner, facing George.

Abner's eye took in the shadowed ranges of seats rising in semi-circles behind the defense's table, the sloping aisle and Everitt Weitzel's bent, blue-coated figure at the top. Just beyond Everitt, he was astonished to see Bonnie and Inez Ormsbee. No doubt they had been downtown shopping together, and one of them had said: Have you been to the trial? Let's go in a minute, if it isn't too crowded. Abner unexpectedly found that he would like to think the suggestion had been Bonnie's—perhaps because she generally showed little interest (no more than she, or most people, felt) in what went on in court. In slight ways, mortifyingly silly, not-to-be-given-into, Abner had often felt this disappointment. He was not so unreasonable as to require everyone to find the routine of the law interesting— just unreasonable enough to be aware of the wish that Bonnie would, or would pretend to, take an interest; not because it was interesting, but because it was what he did.

Abner looked up at them a moment, his eyes narrowed against the high light of the pointed windows. He could see Bonnie's bare graceful arms, her face clear against the big brim of a straw hat. She was wearing a blue checked frock, and Inez (they must have got them from the same shop) was wearing a red checked one. They looked cool and pretty. Abner could not tell at this distance whether they

142

were looking at him, too, or not. He smiled, in case they were, and turned back to Leming.

The evening of April seventeenth had been busy. At Bailey's direction, Basso arranged, in Leming's phrase, "to make a meet" for ten o'clock with Walter Cohen. Howell was to drive him over, but not to show himself; pretty clearly indicating that Howell could identify Walter Cohen for Basso, but must keep under cover because Cohen would know him if he saw him. However, something went wrong; and an hour later Howell called back to Bailey at the bungalow and said that Walter Cohen—they called him Buck— had not showed up. Bailey thereon ordered Leming to telephone Mrs. Zollicoffer.

"And did you?" said Abner.

"Yes. Bailey tells me ask for Buck when I called up, in case he was there. So when I called, Mrs. Zollicoffer got on the phone. I says, 'Is Buck around?' She said, 'No.' So I said, 'What is the matter with Buck wasn't there?' She said, 'He just called up a few minutes ago, and he has been waiting there.'"

"You reported this to Bailey, did you?"

"Yes, sir. When I came back, I said, 'That man is still over there.' They was waiting in this pay booth; so Bailey calls back; and they wanted to talk to me. It appears something don't look right to Howell; and he got scared, so he balks. He wouldn't stop the car. He said it looked like cops or somebody there. Bailey is beside me and he could hear this, so he takes the phone and says, 'Well, if you are afraid—' and he bawled him out pretty good. He says, 'You are not worth the sweat off my—'" Leming paused in embarrassment, and coughed. "He says, 'You aren't worth anything—' To Howell. He says, 'Maybe I am coming over there; and Bob and I will get it; and maybe we will give you something.'"

Judge Vredenburgh said, "I take it that was a threat."

"Yes, sir," said Leming. "Well, then Basso says, 'Aw,

the hell!' You could hear him. So they went and made the meet, and in about an hour, they are back, and Basso has this package."

"What did the package contain, if you know?"

"Money. It counted to eight thousand dollars. Bailey counted it in the kitchen there."

"And then what happened?"

"Well, after they checked up the money, they seen they were four thousand dollars short—it was agreed this Buck was to give twelve thousand. So they counted it two or three times to make no mistake. Then Bailey took Basso and Howell in the other room, the dining room, and they held a conversation. So Howell came out after a couple of minutes. He says to me, 'You and Dewey go down to the delicatessen and get some beer and sandwiches for later. We are hungry.' "

"Yes?"

"I said, 'How about Zolly?' Howell says, 'I will be frank with you—' He did not look so good and I could see he had been having a drink. He says, 'Frankly, we are going to see Zolly home.' I says to him, 'I hope that you are.' I hoped that they had changed their minds. He begins to laugh and says, 'Yes, Zolly doesn't live here any more'— like in the song. I did not like the sound. So Dewey and I, we go for the sandwiches."

"And how long were you gone?"

"I should say an hour, hour and a half. We didn't hurry none. They were not gone so long; and when we came back, they were there."

"What were they doing?"

"They had out this money, piling it out in piles on the dining room table."

"Did you receive any of this money?"

"Yes, sir."

"How much did you receive?"

"They wanted to give me five hundred dollars. I told them I did not want it."

"But you took it?"

"I didn't want no trouble." From the way Leming looked at him, Abner could see that he was wondering if the admission might, in law, mean something he didn't know, and expose him in some fatal way. It was the answer to any doubts he or Bunting might have felt about Leming's intentions. Far from planning to double-cross the Commonwealth, Leming wilted secretly with a recurrent fear that the Commonwealth had it in mind to double-cross him. To Abner it seemed natural that, looking at Leming, one should not trust him; it might be worth remembering that Leming, returning the look, saw nothing a man would want to trust, either.

"How about the rest of the money?" said Abner. "Was it divided; and do you know how?"

"It was divided. I don't know for sure how. There is three piles, about the same. Oh, yes. Then Bailey sees Dewey look at them; so he reaches and takes this hundred dollar bill off of Howell's, and shoves it to Dewey."

"Now, it is your belief that while you and Dewey Smith were absent, getting the sandwiches, the other three, Bailey, Basso, and Howell, also went out, taking Frederick Zollicoffer with them?"

"I know they did. They are talking about it—"

"And the conversation was in your presence?"

"Yes, sir."

"What, if anything, did you hear them say in reference to Frederick Zollicoffer?"

"Well, one thing I heard them say; after they shot him, they tried to hitch the irons on him in the car; so they said they finally had to take him out of the car and lay him on the ground and tie the irons on him; and then they put him back in the car; and take him up to the bridge, and throw him over."

Harry Wurts stood up. "I object because this witness is testifying to conversations with the ridiculous implication that all three men are all saying the same things all together, all the time. I submit that this witness should be required to answer specifically, and identify the particular individual who made each particular statement."

Judge Vredenburgh shook his head. "No. Not if they were all present and heard it. Who made each particular statement is a matter for cross-examination."

"Continue," said Abner.

"Well, I heard them say—"

George Stacey said, "Now, is this supposed to be a conversation this man heard?"

"Yes, it is," said Bunting from his seat. "His Honor has been over all that, Mr. Stacey."

"Well, I think he ought to name the speaker."

Bunting said, "Where have you been for the last five minutes?"

Judge Vredenburgh said, "He may if he can. He does not have to. It is a matter for cross-examination."

"Well, should I go on?" said Leming.

"Yes," said Abner. "Do you remember who was speaking? If so, name him."

"Basso. Basso said they are there, driving down this road, and Bailey fires a shot. The first shot Bailey fired. And Basso said he fired the second shot."

Abner said slowly, "The defendant, Robert Basso, there—" With a startling simultaneous movement like men drilling, or a ballet, every juror's head turned "—told you that Bailey fired the first shot; and he, Robert Basso, then fired a second shot?"

Basso, looking at the table, lifted a hand and yawned. The simultaneously turned faces of the jury simultaneously quivered with shock and outrage at such calm callousness; but Abner guessed that the calm was assumed. Basso had been hit. The bald truth jarred him, because Basso's defense

146

against truth was every man's defense; a sort of story of his
life in which he, the ill-treated hero, understood all, explained all, excused all. It took care of everything—his
shooting of Zollicoffer, his trapping by the police, his helplessness here on trial for his life; but it did not take care
of that sudden turn of faces. In them, the world suddenly
looked him to shame. Given time, that too might be taken
care of; but at the moment, in anguish, he lost his grip; he
weakly tried to outrage those who had outraged him.

Leming said, "That is right."

Abner said, "And do you recall any further conversation
with the defendant, Robert Basso, that night about that
time? A conversation about a gun?"

"That is objected to!" George Stacey said in some excitement. "It is decidedly leading!"

Judge Vredenburgh said, "Objection overruled."

"Well," said Leming, "not exactly a conversation. Basso
give me a gun. He says, 'Chuck it away somewheres.'"

"And did you?"

"Yes, sir."

"Did you throw it out of the car; or—"

"Objected to!" said Harry.

"Correction," Abner said. "Where did you throw it?"

"I threw it in a little creek, like."

"Do you know where the creek was?"

"Well, it was by the road. I think, what is called the
Paper Mill Road."

"Do you know where the Black Cat Inn is?"

"Objected to!" said Harry. He got to his feet again. "I
submit that the Commonwealth has no right to ask leading
questions. Mr. Coates knows better than that; and I think
these defendants are entitled to have the questions asked in
the proper way. I object to that question."

"Objection sustained," Judge Vredenburgh said. "You
must take care of the location, Mr. Coates."

Abner said, "Well, you did throw this gun into a creek?"

"Yes, sir."

"Would you recognize that gun again?"

"Yes, sir."

Abner lifted the paper laid over it on the table before Joe Jackman, and said, "I show you a gun that has been marked for identification as Commonwealth's Exhibit number—" He paused, and Joe, marking the tag, said, "Eight."

"Commonwealth's Exhibit number eight; and ask you to look at it." He picked the gun up and gave it to Leming. "Did you ever see that before?"

"This is the one that Basso had and give me the night Zolly was killed."

"At any time subsequent to the night when you threw a gun into a creek—" (that ought to hold Harry!) "—did you point out to Mr. Costigan, the county detective, the creek into which you had thrown it?"

"Yes, sir."

"And this is that gun?"

"Yes, sir."

With Frederick Zollicoffer disposed of, and the money divided, everyone left the Rock Creek bungalow. It was a fairly workmanlike job, and in engineering it Bailey showed the qualities that make a man a leader. Bailey might not have great intelligence or abilities, but his whole aim, thought and study was that of the born leader—to look out for himself; and he did it with that born-leader's confidence and intensity that draws along the ordinary uncertain man, who soon confuses his own interest and his own safety with that of the leader. The others did all the work—found Bailey a victim, arranged a hideout, collected the money. Bailey simply put a period to it with a revolver shot, and disposed of the body where nobody would ever find it. The bones of Frederick Zollicoffer with the wires and the iron weights could have lain in the bottom of Fosher's Creek until Judgment Day. That they didn't, that they lay there only a day or so over three weeks, was no one's fault but

Bailey's. This was where the lack of abilities and lack of intelligence came in. The lack was apparent when Bailey took up crime, for the first test of ability and intelligence is to find a field of endeavor in which profits are large and risks small. A week or so after the murder, Bailey left the others, having got what he could out of them, and went to New York. He left his fairly workmanlike job behind; but he carried his fatal lacks with him; and if not this time, then the next, or the next, they must surely finish him.

Abner said, "How long did you and Basso remain at this house?"

"Around about ten days," Leming said. "I think ten days. Howell wanted we should get rid of this car; and after about a week, they were arguing about that. So finally Basso said he would take care of it—"

"Yes," said Abner. "He was arrested the twenty-sixth, according to our records. That would be a week. Now, during this period, from Sunday, April eighteenth, to Sunday, April twenty-fifth, did you have any conversations with Robert Basso?"

"Yes, sir," said Leming, recognizing what he wanted. "Yes. I had a conversation with him."

Harry Wurts, recognizing it just as well, said, "If this is going to be a particular conversation on some particular subject, I must ask that you distinguish it as to time and place, Mr. Coates, if you will."

"I am about to do that," Abner said. "You mentioned a conversation that you had with Basso," he said to Leming. "Was there something about it that fixed this conversation in your mind?"

"What conversation?" said Harry. "Did he have only one all the time they were there?"

"Yes," said Leming, "this particular one was in the bedroom, I remember—"

"Which particular one?" said Harry. "Mr. Coates asked

149

you if you had any conversations. Did the Commonwealth prepare you carefully on one particular conversation?"

Bunting said, "Your Honor, who is conducting this examination in chief? The assistant district attorney, or Mr. Wurts? I must protest—"

Judge Vredenburgh tightened his lips, his cheeks dimpling with the repressed smile. "The witness says that he remembers a conversation in his bedroom with the defendant Basso. He may repeat this conversation, if Mr. Coates wishes him to. If the substance of it is not material, that will be what you may and should object to, Mr. Wurts."

Abner said, "Now, if you will just describe that conversation."

"Well," said Leming, "we are lying down in the bedroom, and we are talking about different things; so Zolly's name happened to be mentioned; and Basso spoke up and said he hated to have to kill any man in cold blood; so he told me about Bailey fired the first shot, that he fired the second."

"By 'he' you mean?"

"Bob Basso."

"Basso fired the second shot, and Bailey fired the first shot?"

"Yes," said Leming. He spoke with understanding regret. You could see that he thought Basso's expressed sentiment did Basso credit; and though he was obliged by his own interests to testify against Basso, he would not do Basso the injustice of denying him right feeling. "He said he never liked to kill a man that way; especially after he got to know the man so good while he was watching him; and he hated to do it. He watched him, and they played cards, and all; so he got to know him good. He hated to do it. He says if a man puts up a fight with him, he would not have minded it so much."

"Was anybody else there during this conversation?"

"In the house there was; not in the room."

"All right. Now, did you ever have any conversation with the defendant Stanley Howell in reference to Frederick Zollicoffer?"

"Yes, I had one. I was out driving with him, and we happened to come to that bridge."

"That bridge?" said Harry Wurts. Howell, beside Harry, was gazing at Leming with an intensity of mortal malice or fear. What the increased sickness and passion in his face proved—that he feared Leming would now tell some truth about him? That Leming, because he had lied about Basso, would now lie about him?—Abner found it hard to decide. He said to Harry, "The Fosher's Creek bridge, Mr. Wurts."

Leming said, "We are near that bridge. I asked Howell, I says, 'Did you really kill Zolly on the road, or did you kill him in the house?' There had been some talk about killing him in the house. He says, 'No, we killed him on the road.' I says, 'He is in there?' and he says, 'I guess it won't do no harm to tell you now. Yes, he is.' He never knew Basso told me."

"And where did you indicate when you said, 'he is in there'?"

"On the bridge. I pointed like to the deep water."

"The deep water of Fosher's Creek?"

"Yes."

"And that was where Stanley Howell said that he had helped Bailey and Basso put Frederick Zollicoffer's body after the shooting in the car?"

"Yes, sir."

Abner looked at Bunting, and Bunting nodded. To Harry, Abner said, "Cross-examine, Mr. Wurts."

Judge Vredenburgh said, "It is five minutes of twelve. I think it would be convenient to break now. Until one-fifteen."

He and Judge Irwin arose. Nick Dowdy tapped his block. With a shuffle and stir of people standing, stretching, beginning to speak, movement spread over the courtroom;

the benches emptying, the jury going out the side door. Rocked back in his chair, Bunting produced and lit a cigarette. Leming, leaving the witness stand, stood motionless a moment and Hugh Erskine crooked a finger at him. Mrs. O'Hara went out the door with Susie Smalley. Adelaide Maurer came up to Abner. "Ab," she said, searching in her folded sheets of copy paper, "how much money was the ransom what's his name paid? I thought I heard someone say ten thousand; but your man said when they counted it, it was eight; and I gathered that what they had been expecting was twelve."

"Eight was what they got," Abner said. "Know what they asked for first? A hundred thousand. If they'd be any use to you, I think Marty would show you the notes. He has them right there. Ask him."

John Clark approached, tucking his glasses, which were attached to a chain that reeled into a little round metal case on his lapel, into his pocket. He shook his long scanty locks of white hair. His noble, large-nosed face was tilted up. His eyelids drooped over his blue eyes. "Abner," he said, "how's the Judge? All right for me to go around and see him? Or had I better not?"

"Why, yes, he'd be glad to see you, Mr. Clark," Abner said. "He's getting on fine." Abner did not know whether his father would thank him for that.

"Good," said Mr. Clark. "I may go up this afternoon, if it's all right. This woman of mine. I think she'd better plead guilty, Ab."

"We think she'd better, too," Abner said. He saw Bonnie and Inez Ormsbee standing up, getting ready to leave. "If she decides to, tell Marty, will you?"

"Well, now, of course, if I advise her to, she'll kind of expect, you know—"

Abner had observed before this, though every time it surprised him, that older men, lawyers like John Clark who had been in practice thirty or forty years, felt a sort of privilege, really, assumed a sort of prerogative, to ignore arbitrary canons of ethics; as though the law were something that applied to the lay public, and rules were for the record. They understood each other; not in a cynical or dishonest way, but just as a matter of common sense. You went through the forms in court, just as you addressed young Horace Irwin or Tom Vredenburgh as your Honor; but, for heaven sakes, John Clark could remember them when—

Abner said, "Mr. Clark, you know all we can tell her is that it's up to the Judge. She mustn't expect anything—"

"Stuff and nonsense, son!" said Mr. Clark. "How many guilty pleas would you get if nobody expected anything? And just where would you be if everyone stood pat and demanded that trial to which he has a constitutional right? I'll tell you. You'd be up the creek without a paddle."

"I guess we would," Abner said, "but I'm not district attorney. You explain it to Marty and see what he says. Would you excuse me a moment, sir? I have to speak to someone—"

The get-away, desperate rather than smooth, carried him to the aisle. Mat Rhea, the clerk of Quarter Sessions, met him there, holding up the printed pamphlet of the Criminal Trial List. "Look, Ab," he said, folding it open, "about number forty-six, here; Commonwealth versus Giuseppe, or however you say it, Bacchilega—God, what a name! First count, assault and battery with intent to kill; second count, aggravated assault and battery; third count, assault and battery. Have you got the papers on that? Judge Irwin wants to see them."

Maynard Longstreet, hurrying on his way back to his office (the *Examiner* went to press at one o'clock), brushed his hand across Abner's shoulder, saying, "What you say, Ab?" and went on.

"Hello, Maynard," Abner said. "No, I haven't," he said to Mat Rhea, "I don't know anything about it. Ask Marty—"

"Hey, well—"

"See you later!" He overtook Bonnie and Inez Ormsbee just past the swinging doors in the hall by the prothonotary's office. Inez said, "My, Ab, you were wonderful. I couldn't hear a thing you said."

"I'll talk to you about that afterwards," Abner said. "I want to make a date with your friend, here."

"See if I care!" Inez said, walking on. Bonnie said, "What do you want?"

"Not like that!" said Abner. "What are you doing tonight?"

"I don't know yet."

"Good," said Abner. "Want to go to the movies?"

"No. Anyway, I said I might go to the Nyces'."

The lofty hall, paved with worn, often cracked, squares of black and white marble, was thronged by the people leaving. Nick Dowdy, who had replaced his blue crier's jacket with a faded gray one of washable material, set on his head a limp, grimy straw hat, and relighted his stub of cigar, paused at Abner's elbow. His big, homely face, rounding in fat amiable curves under his chin, warmed as he looked at Bonnie. He grasped his hat at random and lifted it a little from his head. Around the cigar end clenched in his teeth he said, "Morning, Miss Drummond." He studied her face and arms calmly, with frank satisfaction. "You hear that fellow say when they jumped on him, this Zollicoffer, he thought it was the police? What do you think of that! Being a policeman must be a good business down there. Wish they'd give me a job." He poked Abner's arm with his forefinger. "Harry Wurts wants to see you, Ab. He's down in the Attorneys Room." He lifted his hat a little higher, smiled, nodded several times at Bonnie, and dropping the hat back on his head, went waddling contentedly toward the door and his dinner.

"As we were saying," Abner said. "Come in here—" He pointed into the prothonotary's office, "before somebody else joins us. You don't want to go to the Nyces', do you?

It will just be one of those brawls. Why don't we go out to the quarry and go swimming?"

For a moment Abner, concerned, thought that she was going to refuse. "All right," she said, "maybe Inez and Johnny would like to go."

"If they would, let them go by themselves. I'll take you somewhere and we'll have supper."

"What time?"

"Well, suppose I come around about six, or six-thirty. Do you like our trial?"

"Inez wanted to see it. Who was that awful little man on the stand?"

"He's not awful, he's wonderful," Abner said. "He's the Commonwealth's prize witness—"

In the door, Arlene Starbuck, Abner's secretary, had appeared. She was a small, dark, energetic girl; snub-nosed, cheerful, and intelligent. She had her hands full of papers. "Oh, Mr. Coates!" she said. "Thank goodness! Nobody knew where you were! You didn't come in this morning and—" Stepping in, she saw Bonnie, then. "Oh, hello," she said. "Oh, I'm sorry. I thought—"

"O.K.," said Abner. He smiled. "I had to go over to Mr. Bunting's office. Just couldn't make it."

"Well, there isn't so much, really. Excuse me just a minute, will you," she said to Bonnie. "I didn't know what to do about the praecipe in Overland Mutual. Did you want me to file it? Well, anyway, I guess you don't want to look at it now." Holding the sheaf of papers against her breast, she thumbed over the corners. "In the Steele estate," she said, "there's that petition for citation on the trustee business—there's a note from Mr. Leusden with a copy of the reply the Auditor General's office sent him. He wants to know whether, in view of it—they say no, we can't exempt the interest—you want to answer, to show cause why the tax shouldn't be paid."

"Call him up and say I'm studying it. Anything else?"

"That Mr. Willis, I think his name is, from Warwick, came in with Mr. Van Zant. I told them they'd better see Mr. Bunting."

"I don't place it. What did they want?"

"That was that F and B case last Wednesday." Arlene colored, apparently because of Bonnie's presence. In the office, fornication and bastardy were words in the day's work; but before another woman they offended modesty. "Mr. Van Zant said they were going to move to quash; he just wanted to show you some new evidence."

"Very kind of him," said Abner.

"That's all. I can take care of the rest."

"Thanks," Abner said. "That's fine, Arlene. I know it's hard on you when I don't get in. Look; this is a hot day. Why don't you just shut up this afternoon? Let it all go. I'll try to be there by eight tomorrow for a while."

"Well, I'll just finish typing the Blessington stuff. We have to file that appeal tomorrow, you know. There's the security—that's taken care of; it's entered. And I'm going to have the Register certify the record of proceedings had before him, now. Then we'll be all ready."

"Fine. Do you want another girl in for a few days?"

"Oh, Mr. Coates, I don't need any help! I would have had it done yesterday, except the Judge gave me some letters." She nodded to Bonnie and left.

"She's a good kid," Abner said. "You know who her father was? Old Dan Starbuck, who used to drive the ice wagon. Remember the ice wagon? I guess that's before your time. Arlene is smart; and she never had any help, either."

"Well, a girl always likes to be appreciated," Bonnie said. "I'll bet she's very happy working for you."

"Who wouldn't be?" said Abner. "Where are you going?"

"I have to go. I have to get home to lunch. Are you coming this evening?"

"You know I am," said Abner. "Look, Bonnie—"

"Well, all right. I'll see you then."

Gifford Hughes, the prothonotary, came in, his gray mustache drooping. He sighed with the heat. "Marty's looking for you, Ab," he said. "Hello, Bonnie! My, don't you look pretty in all those checks! Nice and cool! Isn't this a scorcher of a day! Wish I were down at the shore!"

"Wish I were, too," said Bonnie.

"There, now," Gifford Hughes said, winking at Abner. "If I were your age, Ab, I'd know what to say to that."

"What you say now is pretty nice," Bonnie said. "Goodby, Mr. Hughes." She went out and passed quickly down the hall to the sunlight in the big door.

Abner turned and went back to the empty courtroom. A burst of muffled laughter sounded from the closed door of the Attorneys Room, and Abner went in. Bunting sat in the corner looking at a copy of a New York paper someone had left there. George Stacey was leaning against the mantel of the disused fireplace. Sitting on the old leather settee near the lavatory door was Jacob Riordan, generally allowed to be the best lawyer in Childerstown; and, to Abner's surprise, Jesse Gearhart.

"Gentlemen," Abner said, bowing. Harry was sitting on the oval table, facing John Clark who occupied the principal armchair. Over his shoulder, Mr. Clark said, "What do you think of a question like that, Jake? Impertinent, I call it."

"All I want to know, Mr. Clark," Harry said, "is whose woman she was. Didn't she confess to you? Didn't you conduct an examination in your office—I mean, verbal, of course? I need hardly say that my interest is purely scientific. And then, besides that, I have a dirty mind."

John Clark was heh-hehing, regarding Harry under his drooping eyelids with that old man's this-boy-isn't-such-a-damned-fool-after-all look. "What a client tells me or doesn't tell me is locked forever in this bosom," he said.

Jacob Riordan said, "What d'you want to mix up in it for, Johnny? It just makes everything longer. Wish they'd get through with these foreigners—going to have Miscellaneous Court next Monday, Marty?"

"We'll have court," Bunting said, throwing the paper aside. "But we won't be through the list."

"Well, when are you going to finish this thing, this murder?"

"Tomorrow, I hope. If Stacey and Wurts don't obstruct matters any better than they're obstructing them now."

"I never saw anybody so damned bloodthirsty as the district attorney," Harry said. "Due process for him is a kind of legal bum's-rush. It isn't decent."

"You want to see me?" Abner said, tapping his knee.

"Not any more. I have arranged matters with Mr. Bunting. Come on. Let's eat! My God, the time wasted around here! Enough to feed a French family for a year—"

"Ab," said Jacob Riordan, "I'm going to represent this Hamilton Mason, the boy in the accident last night. Marty said you talked to Pete Wiener about it. I'm going in to see him now. Anything I ought to know?"

"Not that I can tell you," Abner said. "The state police's charge is manslaughter, I understand. If it's the way Pete seemed to think it was, I guess we'll"—he looked at Bunting inquiringly—"be glad to do what we can to get it through as quickly as possible. I suppose it may develop at the coroner's inquest that there's no reason to hold him, that he can be discharged without returning the case to court."

"Judge Irwin is admitting him to bail," Riordan said.

"Well, we'll get him out. I guess the boy'd like to go home."

Jesse Gearhart was looking at him; and Abner supposed that it was a moment to show his good will. He cast about in his mind for something to say; but a stubborn resistance of instinct frustrated him. He found himself shrugging. "That's certainly all right as far as I'm concerned," he said. "Did you want to speak to me, Marty?"

"Just about this," Bunting said, getting up.

Jesse, getting up, too, said, "Ab, are you going to be busy after court?"

"I don't think so," Abner said.

"Had something I wanted to talk to you about. Could you come over to my place when you finish?"

"Sure," said Abner.

It was useless for him to try to like the way Jesse put it. The request was natural, and naturally phrased; but since, for a dozen reasons, it could not be answered no, what was it but a command? Abner couldn't say: No, I haven't anything to see you about; and so he would go, obedient to a practical order; and stand, hat in hand, while Jesse instructed him. A man ought not to want anything in the world enough to do that.

Abner reminded himself that there was only his own guess to make him think that Jesse planned to instruct him, to offer him anything, to sound him out about running for district attorney. "Going to eat, Marty?" he said.

It was embarrassment speaking; but Abner was able to realize that he had acted straight against any good, though half-hearted, intention he might have had to please Jesse. Jesse, if he wanted to be sensitive, too, must read into the short answer and the turning away to speak to Bunting an indifference or contempt that he would have the right to resent far more than anything Abner resented in Jesse.

"Come on, come on," Harry said. "We have to be back here at one-fifteen. Want to eat, Mr. Clark?"

"No, no. Never eat lunch," John Clark said. Getting up, he went and extended himself on the leather couch, laying a handkerchief behind his head. He took the paper Bunting had discarded and set it like a tent over his face. "Let's have a little quiet around here," he said from under it.

They went out the back door, beneath the stone arch of the passage to the jail. In the parking space under the trees,

Judge Vredenburgh was just getting into his car, which Annette was driving. "Ah," said Harry, gazing after her. "There's the little siren! Did you hear how Dick Nyce thought he was Ulysses? Dotty had to tie him to the mast."

They came down the diagonal walk and out of the shade to cross the blazing pavement of Court Street by the monument. Bill Ortt, his cap on the back of his head, his badge pinned to his sweat-soaked gray shirt whose sleeves were rolled as far as they would go up his tanned, tattooed arms, stood at the box from which the traffic lights were manually controlled. "Hi, Mr. Bunting," he said. He stopped the traffic two ways to let them go over.

"Thank you, my good man!" said Harry. "You know," he said, "in my subconscious mind, if any, that must be what I'm always hankering for. Traffic should halt when I appear; and then a breathless hush falls, broken perhaps by a few cries of 'Wurts for President!' " Lifting his panama, Harry held it at an angle, and bowed right and left to the halted traffic. They reached the sidewalk in front of the Childerstown House and pushed through the shadowed screen doors.

The dining room was crowded; but the round table in the corner where they usually sat had somehow been saved for them. "Want a drink?" said Harry. "No. You two pillars of public temperance have to sneak your drinks. And not you, George. The district attorney's watching, so they can't serve minors. Well, I will drink alone, and be damned to you! Hello, Marie. Get me a dry martini; and some cold cuts."

When they had ordered, Harry said, "Ab, see the paper, that *Times* up there? Well, remember your friend Paul Bonbright at Cambridge? I happened to see a note in back in the business section. They just made him a partner. Frazier Graham, and Rogers. Pretty nice, I'd say, at his age."

Abner heard Paul Bonbright's almost forgotten name with surprise. With surprise, too, he saw that Harry, reporting the item, looked disconsolate; as though he were thinking of his own prospects, compared with Paul Bonbright's; or of what a partner in a firm like that made, compared to what he made. Harry stared a moment, his face discontented, down the crowded dining room. He met the eye of someone he knew, nodded mechanically, and looked back.

"Well, Paul can have it," Abner said. "How'd you like to be with Frazier, Graham, and Rogers, Marty?"

"No," said Bunting. "Not on a bet. Life isn't long enough."

"Huh!" said Harry, "a little bird, must have been a buzzard, told me that even you had simple aspirations or ambitions, one of which might be about to be realized. So never mind that exalted tone."

"If you go around talking to birds," Bunting said, "you know what happens to you? They put you in the booby hatch."

"At least I wouldn't have any expenses there," Harry said. "But that twirp Bonbright! That's what gets you down! Right upon the scaffold, wrong upon the throne! Why—"

Abner said, "He was no twirp. I think he won the Ames Competition one year. I know he was on the Board of the *Review*—" Reminded of Paul Bonbright, Abner could recall him very well—a thin faced, long jawed boy with wiry black hair, of which he had already lost enough to make his high forehead higher. He and Abner had never been close friends; but they were cordial, casual acquaintances, borrowing cigarettes and books from each other. It was an acquaintanceship begun by accident, a throwing-together in sections and lecture seatings during the early days of first year, before the class sorted itself out. Bonbright was one of the people who brought Abner to realize, with dismay and some chagrin, that there are definite levels of intelligence, brains of differing strengths and capacities. The innocent supposition, entertained by most people, that even if they are not brilliant, they are not dumb, is correct only in a very relative sense.

Abner had never been anything but modest about his own

accomplishments. He knew that he didn't know much; and he had at least an inkling of how much there was to know. At Childerstown High School and at college he had never led his class nor taken prizes; but, without being aware that he did, he really blamed this on his failure to work hard, or any harder than he needed to. He knew that he was often inattentive, that he loafed a good deal, that at college he had been more interested in baseball and in the debating society than in his courses. What he did not know, what Paul Bonbright, among others, showed him, was that those abilities of his that got him, without distinction but also without much exertion, through all previous lessons and examinations, were not first rate abilities handicapped by laziness, but second rate, by no degree of effort or assiduity to be made the equal of abilities like Bonbright's.

The important truth was borne in on Abner, for he started with advantages that made him feel superior, able to help Bonbright. Many young men, confronted with the case system, have to admit that for their first term at least they literally do not understand anything. Abner had been born and bred in a family three generations old in the law. At home, spare rooms were lined with old reports and piled with back numbers of law journals. Engravings of Judge Story and Chancellor Kent hung in the hall. At table, the jargon of the courts, the law Latin, the principles of jurisprudence were ordinary conversation—what Father, sitting in Common Pleas, had been doing today. Abner knew the language. Of course, the assignments, the amount of stuff they expected him to read and memorize, staggered him; but he worked as hard as he could, harder than he ever had in his life, and he imagined that he was doing about as well as the rest of them. He found out that he was mistaken when Bonbright gradually stopped consulting Abner, the oracle, and began to correct and advise him; and then inevitably they saw less of each other, and Paul took up with his mental peers. Abner said to Harry, "Is it Bonbright's fault that he has more brains than you have?"

"Few if any people have more brains than I have," Harry said. "The Ames Competition! A petty triumph of grinds and pedants! Why, it seems to me you were in that one year. No, no; a Wurts would never sink so low."

"Well, I only sank low enough to come out last," Abner said. "They gave the Scott Club an old *Bouvier* for a booby prize. If you think the man who wins doesn't have to be good—"

George Stacey had been attending closely. He said, "I guess it must be pretty tough up there." He was ready in his diffidence (untinctured, because they were older, not his rivals, with ill-feeling) to admit that his own degree was not quite in the same class.

"Tough!" said Harry, now reminded that after all it was his school. "Why, you come up there with an A.B. from some hick college and they eat you alive. You know what the first thing they say to you is? They say, 'Gentlemen, look well at the man on your right and on your left, because next year one of you will not be here.'"

The classic exhortation was impressive, Abner must admit, when you first heard it. Harry might like it still; but Abner found that he himself definitely didn't. It rang with that unpleasant, really childish, cocky quality which went with the rigor and the exacting standards. It reminded you of certain professors, men of great learning and wisdom; but they none the less sought and enjoyed the poor and mean sport of traducing the stupid. Along with torts or contracts you learned in their lectures a lot of things like that; things you would have to unlearn afterward, or be the worse for all your life.

Bunting, who had prepared for his bar examinations at night school, and in Judge Irwin's office, and who had often found that he knew as much as (and sometimes more than)

163

graduates of the best universities, was listening with the look that answered all these pretensions. He was amused to see Harry (the more fatuously, because it was unconscious) pluming himself to George, not on what he knew, which would be absurd enough, but with an ultimate, almost indescribable absurdity, on where he had learned it. Watching Bunting's face, Abner was jolted to guess that Bunting in the dry and cool privacy of his own mind might very well consider him, Abner, touched with the same ridiculous presumption, ready with the same vauntings and vaporings; so dear to those who had them, so laughable to everyone else.

Mat Rhea, picking his teeth thoughtfully, walked by, headed for the door. Over Harry's head, he said, "Thick as thieves, you look. Who's doing who?" After him came Mr. Wells, who ran a jewelry and watch-repairing shop. "Got that clock fixed for you, Marty," he said. "Any time you want it. Going to cost you a little. I had to replace a lot of bushings. It's a dandy, though. You could get your money out of it, any time you wanted to sell it."

"What's that?" said Abner.

"Old clock I bought at an auction," Bunting said. "I like clocks. If I had some money, I'd collect them."

"Indeed?" said Harry Wurts, arising. "Well, if you gentlemen will now excuse George and me, I have a certain stenographic transcript I wish to pick up—"

"I wouldn't bother, if I were you," Bunting said.

"Of course you wouldn't," Harry said, taking his check. "The secret of my success is that I leave no stone unturned. Do you know what Fisher Ames said of Alexander Hamilton? I often think of it in connection with myself. He said: 'It is rare that a man who owes so much to nature descends to depend on industry as if nature had done nothing for him. His habits of investigation were very remarkable; his mind seemed to cling to his subject until he had exhausted it—' Let it be a lesson to you. Come on, George."

When they were alone, while Bunting was swallowing the last of his coffee, Abner said, "What's Jesse want to see me about?"

Putting down his cup, Bunting said, "You'll have to ask him."

"Don't you know?"

"I might have thought I knew last week," Bunting said. "But for all I know now, he may be going to tell you where to head in."

"And for all he knows," Abner said, "that may be what I'm going to tell him."

"That's right," Bunting said. "I've said my say, Ab. Maybe, like Harry, you think all this is beneath you and you ought to be in New York at Frazier, Graham, and Rogers, or somewhere, getting your twenty-five thousand and your stomach ulcers. I thought you had better sense."

He pushed back his chair, lit a cigarette, and, bending forward, put both elbows on the table. "We didn't mean to tell everyone, because it upsets things; but it seems to be getting out anyway, and you certainly have a right to know, if you care. I'm going into the Attorney General's office in the fall. It's some special trial work I'd like to do. If you want my job here, I'd like you to have it, because you're the best man for the job. You know the ropes now, and you could handle it. Both Judge Irwin and Judge Vredenburgh would like to have you. I always thought it was what you wanted; but I may be wrong. You know about that."

Bunting narrowed his eyes and looked at the smoke rising from his cigarette. "I've done what I could for you, naturally. I've been making you do all I could in this trial, because I wanted it to be as much your work as mine, getting these birds convicted." He shrugged. "I thought your idea was—I mean, that you had it pretty well settled in your mind that you'd go on being a hick lawyer, if Harry wants to call it that. I mean, marry and settle down, and maybe in the end get a judgeship—they seem to run in your family. I don't say it amounts to a lot. You won't get rich and you won't get famous; but you have a good life; one that's some use, and makes some sense."

"I agree," Abner said.

"Well, I wonder if you do," Bunting said. "Maybe you just think you do. Look at Harry! That business about your friend was eating him up—"

"Look, Marty," Abner said, "I don't know about Harry, but I know about me. I haven't any use for that kind of a job, and I doubt if it would have any use for me. I'm not good enough. I don't know enough law—"

Bunting said, "I was in a big office for a couple of years after I was admitted to the bar. You know, twelve dollars a week, while you're learning the flourishes. It really isn't law at all. It has nothing to do with justice or equity. What it really is, is the theory and practice of fraud, of finding ways to outsmart people who're trying to outsmart you. Sure, it takes brains! Sure; they'll pay you anything if you can do it for them. But you only have one life."

"I know that," Abner said. Bunting was not much given to speeches; and to hear him making one, and making it so earnestly, not only surprised Abner, but, by the concern or regard it showed, touched him. "And thanks, Marty. I see your point, and I'm going to bear it in mind."

"Bearing it in mind doesn't do any good," Bunting said. "You ought to get yourself organized. Why don't you get married?"

"Well," said Abner, "anyway, I don't see the connection. And if you don't mind my saying so, I don't think I could do it, just on someone else's advice."

"All the same, and I know it's none of my business, there is a connection."

"Gosh," said Abner, "that's a romantic idea!" He stood up. "Say, was that the bell? My watch is wrong."

Coming into the lobby to pay their checks at the cashier's desk, they could hear the heavy tolling from the courthouse tower signaling five minutes to go.

In the shadows and heat of the afternoon Harry Wurts grew warmer as he worked on Leming. Harry's face was red; his cheeks shone with moisture, and little beads of sweat caught in the quarter inch hairs of his sandy mustache; but he worked without distress. Like an athlete warmed to the game, the more he sweated, the better he felt. He tackled his hard problem with all his might, elatedly bucking the odds against him.

The books tell you that the object of cross-examination is to sift the evidence and to try the credibility of the witness. This may be done by showing that the witness has little or no means of knowing what he is talking about, or that his memory for facts is poor anyway, or that his motives are crooked and self-interested, or that his character is such that nothing he says should be believed. Harry had no wish to sift strong evidence—a fool's trick, in which you bring out, and with telling effect because you do it, any points in your opponent's favor that he might have overlooked. Harry could hardly hope to show that Leming had no means of knowing the facts, or that his memory was at fault. As for Leming's motive, that was conceded. He was testifying to save his skin. Harry's best hope, and a poor one, was to show that Leming ought not to be believed. There, as in the matter of motive, he was unfortunately anticipated. Harry could not make impressive the point about Leming being a criminal or a drug addict, because the jury already knew. Harry, questioning Leming on his criminal record, only bored the jury. The long series of arrests and trials and short prison terms fell, if anything, short of the mark set by the jurors' imaginations. At this stage they asked themselves not: Can such things be? but: Is that all he did?

When regular approaches, felt out carefully, proved all to be blocked, there remained for the man with the temerity to use them, irregular ones; and Harry was that man. The cardinal principle, never cross-examine at random, posited a working hypothesis that would be good enough to convince a jury if the opposition allowed it to stand. It stood or fell in so far as the facts, or most of them, fitted in. Anybody could see the folly of deliberately asking for more facts on the off-chance that they would prove to be facts for which there was a place. The measure of Harry's resource was the bold admission to himself that the only hypothesis the facts would fit was the Commonwealth's own. The measure of his hardihood was his decision to admit his client's guilt, to abandon the strong position prepared for him by the law in its presumption of his client's innocence. The measure of his acumen was his cool grasp of the fundamentally changed position. The shoe was on the other foot. Bunting would have to find a place for every random fact Harry turned up, so the more the merrier. The only plan Harry had or needed was to go in wherever the Commonwealth paused or backed off, and lug out whatever was there.

Harry said, "Now during this period, you mentioned a trip to New York on which you were gone several days. Was that something you just made up?"

Leming said, "I went to New York."

"And what did you go to New York for?"

"Well," said Leming, "I went over to get something for myself."

"Ah?" said Harry. "What?"

"Some narcotic," Leming said. His manner was deeply distressed. Perhaps he really was ashamed to have to confess his vice; but it was also possible—Leming exhibited curious little flashes of shrewdness—that he knew very well that shamefaced testimony always passed as credible testimony;

and a man who confessed what he seemed to want to conceal often gained more from the apparent triumph of honesty over dishonest inclination than he could lose from the substance of the confession.

"Narcotics?" Harry said.

"Yes, sir."

"Opium?"

"Yes."

"Are you a—" Harry hesitated while he selected his term —"a yen hawk?"

"I was," said Leming. He looked apologetically at the jury.

"You smoke opium, do you?"

"I did."

"How long have you been doing that?"

"I did it a couple of years."

"Quite a steady user, eh?"

"Well," said Leming, "I had a habit; yes."

"That means you smoke how often?"

"Twice a day."

"So you went to New York on an opium jag?"

"No, sir. I went to get some."

"You—" Harry stopped. He must have seen or sensed Leming's success with the jury. They felt sorry for him, sitting meek and sad there, while Harry lashed sarcastically at him. Harry said, "Correction. Now, Leming, you testified about a car that came into the street the night you left—"

"No," said Leming. "I never saw that car. It was they told me. Basso says it looks funny, me going, and that car right after. They were sore."

"And what did their soreness signify to you, if anything?"

Leming spread out his hands. "It looked like to me what I told them; they didn't trust me good; like they felt I was selling them out."

"That must have been a shock," Harry said sympathetically, "I mean, to find they had you sized up so well."

"I don't get you, sir."

"You say they thought you were going to sell them out!" Raising his voice harshly, Harry said, "Well, were they right or wrong? That's what you're doing now, aren't you?"

Leming tightened his mouth and color came into his cheeks. He looked at the carpeted floor before the bench and said, "You think so." He nodded several times as though to show that both the question and the lack of understanding that prompted it were what he had expected.

"Yes, I think so," Harry said, watching intently these small maneuvers and plays of expression.

"I don't think so," Leming said. He screwed his mouth up further, wagging his head in silent conference with his conscience. He let it be seen that he had an inner knowledge of one or more circumstances that changed everything.

"Well, you're certainly selling out Howell and Basso, aren't you?"

"No," said Leming.

"No? Why, of course you are! Selling them all out. Trying to save your own skin! Aren't you?"

"No." Leming shook his head. Lifting his eyes, he looked sadly at Harry; but, unable to maintain a gaze to equal Harry's, he looked away.

"What?" said Harry. "How about the promises they made you, if you'd testify for the Commonwealth? You knew they were making a bargain with you, didn't you?"

"Nobody give me promises."

"No promises? Didn't they tell you you'd get off with a short jail term if you sold out Howell and Basso?"

"No."

Seeing Bunting and Abner smiling, Harry was obliged to smile, too. "I am glad to hear it," he said. "Now, you've talked to the district attorney, Mr. Bunting, the man sitting there smiling, haven't you?"

"Never about promises or anything."

"But you've talked to him?"

"Oh, yes."

"Down in your cell in jail here in Childerstown?"

"It was nothing pertaining—"

"I am asking you," said Harry, "haven't you had talks with the district attorney in your cell?"

"Yes."

"And in his office, haven't you?"

"Yes. To him and the other; to Mr. Coates."

"And you have your attorney, Mr. Servadei, watching this case, helping you, haven't you?" -

"Yes," said Leming. "My attorney is here." He sat tense in the stand, straining to meet this beating about of questions. He added, "But he don't help me at all."

The strain of Leming's harassment, conveying itself to the court and jury, was broken by laughter. Judge Vredenburgh drew down the corners of his lips, looking at Servadei, who bowed and smiled. "No," said Harry, smiling too, "I didn't really think Mr. Servadei was responsible for these yarns of yours. You just made them up yourself, didn't you?"

"No, sir."

"You didn't make anything up. I see. They told you, then, that all they wanted from you was the truth, that that was all you had to tell to be let off?"

"Yes—no, sir. They never—"

"Well, which? Yes? No? A little of each?"

"No, sir."

"All right. We'll leave that for the moment. Now, who was at this bungalow the night you left to snatch Zolly? Bailey? Basso? Howell?"

"Yes, them."

"And Smalley, of course?"

"Susie? No. She went back to the other house. She wasn't there."

"Sure she wasn't in the bungalow that night?" Harry's deliberate lack of plan made it hard to follow his intention; but Abner supposed that Harry was willing, if he could, to involve as many of them as possible, to show that the defendants had been arbitrarily selected for some sinister reason of the Commonwealth's.

Leming said, "I am positive. Bailey said she was to go. He didn't want she should know about it."

"I see. But some of the time she was there living with you. Why? Why didn't she stay at the other house?"

"Well," said Leming. He spread his hands out again and shifted in his seat. "Well, after we moved up to Rock Creek, she didn't right away know where we went. We would stop and see her, Howell and me; but we did not tell her where the bungalow was. Then Bailey, after a few days,—you see, there was this jail break thing. He did not want to go out."

To Abner, Bunting said, "Get that, will you? Clark said he'd plead her guilty, but you never know until he does."

Leming said, "So Bailey says, after awhile, he would like to see Susie. He asks Howell is Howell sure she is all right? And Howell says, 'She is all right, you don't have to be afraid of her, isn't she, Bob?' he says to Basso. And Basso says, 'Yes, she has proved all right to us.' So Howell and I, we bring her up."

Abner glanced over at Susie Smalley. The seat John Clark had occupied was empty and she sat isolated with Mrs. O'Hara. She was chewing gum slowly, her face sullen and resigned in the afternoon shadows. Whatever her allure was, it had gone out of her. The symbols of it, the dye-spoiled hair and the tight green dress, were set on her like the hair and clothes of a dummy. Perhaps she was thinking of the prison days ahead, which she knew all about, and which she might have promised herself last time she would never risk again. Yet here she was; and she might be mutely arguing why—or, even, seeing why; but what else could she have done? They—the boys—were going to make a lot of money, and she left it to them. She proved all right to them; keeping her mouth shut, doing what she was told, giving Bailey what he wanted; until the whole thing blew up in their hands. What she herself wanted out of it all only she could know; but it was certain that she never wanted to be here, a prisoner, waiting her turn to hear what her acquiescence had cost her this time. Of course it was a mistake to think that Susie deserved sympathy. If she were the victim of misfortune, it was mostly the misfortune of being herself; but Abner knew from the records that she was just Bonnie's age; and the circumstance affected him. It was one of the ordinary horrors of life.

Harry Wurts said, "You brought her up. To do the cooking and light cleaning, I suppose?"

"Yes. She cooked," Leming said.

"And after she had done enough cooking to hold you all for a while, she left," Harry nodded. "And didn't come back until the night Zolly was killed?"

"I never said that," Leming answered.

"Then I am mistaken?"

"Very much."

"When did she come back?"

"She never come back. We went back, after, to where she was."

Harry said, "Now, Dewey Smith was there, too, wasn't he?"

"Well, he come in."

"He heard the discussions there in the bungalow, didn't he?"

"Never at no time."

"Never at no time!" repeated Harry with pleasure. "Quoth the raven; never at no time!"

"Your Honor," said Bunting, "does the witness have to submit to Mr. Wurts' feeble witticisms? He is here to be questioned on a serious matter."

Harry said, "Strike out the raven. Now, you know Dewey was there with you, and he took part in planning the kidnapping, didn't he?"

"I will tell you why not," Leming said. "In the first place, they never put that much confidence in him."

"It's too bad for them that they didn't feel the same way about you, isn't it? You mean to say he never came there while Zolly was in the bungalow?"

"He come; but he didn't know about Zolly. I will tell you why he came. He had been like a steamfitter, an assistant. The pipes there is muddy, and he went down and cleaned the tank. He used to do something for Susie when she was there; fix the heater in the cellar, and drained the tank, the hot water tank. About six or seven times to my knowledge."

"You mean, while he was there he was always doing odd jobs like that, so he couldn't have heard what was being discussed?"

"He would never put himself in their way when they had any conversation; and they will tell you that themselves."

"But you put yourself in their way?"

"Oh, yes. They discussed with me."

"You were just as much involved in all of it as they were, weren't you?"

Bunting said, "I object to that as a conclusion."

Harry waved his hand. "You knew as much about what went on as Bailey or Basso or Howell did?"

Abner admired Harry. The cards were stacked, and he had not been dealt a single good one, yet Harry held those he had with confidence. Playing them close to his chest, Harry exhausted every resource of bluff or finesse to make them count. Would Leming want to say that there was no difference between himself and the others? He might not. He might think it better to say that he had not shared fully in their wickedness. If he said that, his competence was going to be open to attack.

Leming, however, was no novice. He had been in traps before; and even when he could not see them, he sensed them. He said warily, "I didn't know all that business, no."

"You did not?" said Harry.

"No."

"You've told all of it here on this witness stand, haven't you?"

"What I heard them say, yes."

"As a matter of fact, you're the one who planned this kidnapping of Frederick Zollicoffer, aren't you?"

Leming said, "It is pretty hard to plan something when you don't even know them."

"You knew Zollicoffer?"

"I never knew him."

"You knew Mrs. Zollicoffer well enough to sit on that stand and call her Marguerite."

Under the steady pelting of accusation, Leming had the look of a man caught in a cloudburst. He hunched himself up; he glanced about for shelter. If he had been able to, he would certainly have scurried away as fast as he could. He was not nervous in the desperate, distracted sense that Howell was nervous, full of twitches and fidgetings; he was simply shaken and pulled-about so that he could hardly think. Taking hold of the rail in front of him, Leming said, "If I ever saw his wife before, I hope God never lets me get off this stand!"

"If I were you," Harry said, "I would be careful how I invited divine intervention in my affairs. You knew her well enough to call her Marguerite."

"When the phone call was made, they tell me, ask for Marguerite."

"You used to buy opium from Zollicoffer, didn't you?"

"Never," Leming said.

"You knew he was a dealer in opium?"

"I never knew the man."

"You were a salesman for him yourself, weren't you?"

"You are wrong there. I—"

"You peddled dope all around this part of the country for Zollicoffer, didn't you?"

"I never peddled it. I used it, but I never peddled it."

"You are an addict, an opium user?"

Bunting said, "He has already answered that!"

"If you don't mind, Mr. Bunting," Harry said, "I will cross-examine without your assistance. You were an addict, and to get the stuff, you handled it for Zollicoffer, delivering it to customers, or bringing them around, didn't you?"

"Never."

"And the only explanation you have as to why you so easily and naturally spoke of Mrs. Zollicoffer as Marguerite is that it was a name somebody told you to use in a phone call two months ago?"

"That is right," Leming said.

Shaking his head softly, rolling up his eyes, Harry turned and paced toward the Commonwealth's table; halted; and started back. From the bench, Judge Vredenburgh said, "The Court will now recess for five minutes." He stood up, passed along behind the bench, down the steps, and through the door to his chambers.

George Stacey had signaled Max Eich, who came over to Howell; and Bunting said to Harry, still close to the Commonwealth's table, "Putting on the act again, eh?"

Harry smiled. He shoved aside Bunting's file folders and sat on the table. "Bunting," he said, "let me look at you. You must be pure intellect, mind untrammeled! Your airy dance of ideas bewilders us earth-bound creatures. I don't want to drag you down to our brute level—"

"Mr. Coates," Everitt Weitzel said.

"Yes," said Abner, turning to look up at him.

"Mr. Riordan asked me when there was a break to ask you could you see him just one minute. He's in the other room, there."

"Better see him later, hadn't I, Marty?"

"No," said Bunting. "Go ahead. He probably wants to know what to tell the Mason kid about the inquest. Say we'll have it the day after tomorrow. I'll fix it with Doctor Hill."

Abner arose and went over to the door. Moving along with him, Everitt said, "Boy's there too."

"Mr. Gearhart there?"

"I didn't see him."

Like the Attorneys Room, the room next to it was lined with the books of the law library. Jake Riordan, smoking a cigar, was sitting across the table from a young man with short curly hair and a piece of adhesive tape diagonally down his forehead. They both got up, and Jake said, "Ab, this is Mr. Mason. I wanted him to meet you before he went home."

"How do you do?" Abner said, holding out his hand. He had been—for no reason at all, when he thought about it—expecting some snotty little brat with the marks of too much money on him, and the cock-sure, even contemptuous, assurance that his father would take care of him. Mason looked as though he thought nobody would take care of him; and while his clothes were good and expensive, they had necessarily been slept in; and on the sleeve of his coat was a large, partly removed stain—blood. He gave Abner a damp hand. "Have a cigarette," Abner said, offering the package he had taken out. "Were you hurt?"

"No, sir. Just cut my face a little." He took the cigarette and after several tries, got it lit from the match Abner was holding.

"Well, it's a nasty thing to have happen," Abner said. "We hear it wasn't your fault. That true?"

"I don't see how it could have been, sir. It happened pretty quick. But I was on my side. The state police said the tire marks showed that."

"Did they say why they held you?"

"Well, one of them said it was the law. He had to, sir."

"He didn't have to charge you with manslaughter. You hadn't been drinking, had you? I don't mean, were you drunk. I mean, had you had a drink any time that evening?"

"Absolutely not, sir."

Jake Riordan said, "Some of these motor police, Ab, don't

show very good sense. The officer should have charged him with being involved in a fatal accident, and the J.P. could have taken bail, and that would be that."

"Yes," said Abner, "that's the only thing." He looked at the boy, and it did not seem likely that Mason was lying; but the first principle in matters like this was not to jump to conclusions. It was true that the police sometimes didn't show good sense; but, in general, the police, particularly the state police, knew and performed their routine business with intelligence and precision—in motor vehicle cases they were almost always right. If the driver disagreed about the speed or circumstances, he might make a case for himself when it was his word against the officer's; but if corroborative evidence appeared, inevitably it showed that the driver was mistaken. As Mason said, those things happened quickly; and alarm, self-interest, and shaken nerves obfuscated the moment's impressions. The crisis past, very few people failed to tamper with their recollections—just a touch here and there to details which, with only a second or fraction of a second to fix them, could easily be altered, or even wiped out, leaving the conscience clear for any practical purpose of meeting a man's eye or swearing a solemn oath.

Abner said, "I don't mean to doubt Mr. Mason; but we haven't had a police report yet. And, of course, we'll want to see the arresting officer. If he has no specific grounds for the charge, we'll have to take that up with his superiors. Well, Jake, Marty's fixing the inquest for the day after tomorrow. Mr. Mason understands what bail means, doesn't he?"

"Yes, sir," Mason said.

"All right, then," said Abner. "See you both Friday." The boy's anxious, uncertain face led him to add, "Don't worry about it. You go home and get a good night's sleep and you'll feel better."

In the courtroom they had already resumed.

Harry, his arms folded, his head tipped up as though he

were admiring the shadowed, gold-framed portraits on the high wall behind Judge Vredenburgh, said, "And during that time, were you given any opium?"

"Never."

"No," said Harry. "It was taken away from you down there, wasn't it?"

"I had none on me," Leming said.

"You had to go without it, didn't you?"

"Yes, sir."

"And prior to that you had been smoking regularly?"

"That is right."

"And when they took it away from you, you wanted it, didn't you?"

"Yes, if you got a habit, you want it."

"And to get it, you knew you'd have to testify, didn't you?"

Leming said, "That is a lie."

"You mean, a misapprehension on my part, I hope. It was taken away from you, and you needed it?"

"I needed it," Leming said doggedly, "but I didn't get it."

"They cured you, cold turkey, didn't they?"

"I cured myself. They help me."

"Now," said Harry, "isn't it a fact that since you've been in jail here in Childerstown you've been getting narcotics?"

"Never."

"You weren't given some last night after you got back from this court?"

"No."

"You deny that?"

"I positively deny it. I was given sleeping pills, but no narcotic."

"Oh!" said Harry. "You call it sleeping pills!"

"It isn't opium."

"How often does the doctor come to see you down at jail?"

"Well, he stops sometimes every night or so. He asks me how I am feeling, something like that."

"But he always gives you something, doesn't he?"

"He left a pill for me last night. He says, 'If you cannot sleep, ask the guard for it.' And I didn't take it last night."

"I see," said Harry. "He leaves enough pills for you to go over one night to the next?"

"He leaves pills; but they don't do me no good; so he might just as well not leave me them."

"You'd much rather have it to smoke in a pipe, wouldn't you?"

"Well, not now."

"You wish us to believe you are all cured. How long have you been a doper?"

"How long have I been what?"

"A doper; a user of morphine."

"I never used morphine in my life."

"Just opium, eh? How long have you used that?"

"I told you a couple of years. Around about that."

Abner had been listening abstractedly. He looked at Bunting, who sat relaxed, following the questions and answers with a sort of invisible pointing of the ears, in the habit of court practice that hears, you might almost say, without listening; though paying little outward attention, missing nothing. Bunting held in his hand an inverted pencil, tapping the eraser at measured intervals on the yellow pad before him. He had written: *Doctor Janvier*, the name of the jail physician; so probably he intended a memorandum to answer Harry's insinuations. Next to it he had idly sketched a forlorn, lop-eared dog; with, on second thought, a large bone in its mouth.

Bunting's face, bent down, tipped to the side, caught light from the high windows on the fine textured skin where, around the lips and eyes, the first wrinkles were forming. His flat firm line of cheek and jaw was a good one. Starting, when young, with no claim at all to handsomeness, Bunting's face could be seen to have gained, as the years passed, a fineness of finish. His pointed, convex profile and long neat-lipped mouth took on character. The use of good sense, the habits of control and judgment, informed every feature with strength. Abner was aware of a mild envy, a discontent with his own looser, younger look.

Across the floor at the defense's table Abner could see George Stacey, who was giving good enough examples of what discontented Abner with himself. George's expression showed great but uncertain effort. A look at him told you that George did not know what might happen next, nor what he would do then, if for any reason he were expected to do something. George's fresh, nicely formed face was tense. He was watching Harry closely and calculatingly; he wanted to learn the secret of that assurance. He would like to imitate that ease, that ready command that sent the witness here and there. Knowing his own failings of self-consciousness, the vigor and variety of Harry's attack on Leming probably discouraged George. George had a hand up to his chin, the end of his thumb at his lips, rubbing his teeth with the nail. Beyond George, Basso sat slumped down. He seemed to be asleep. Abner touched Bunting, to point it out to him; but at that moment, Basso moved his eyelids.

On the other side, next to Harry's empty chair, Howell sat huddled, as though, in spite of the oppressive warmth of the shadowed, unmoved air, he felt cold. Howell kept his chin down, half hiding his pale sick face; but his small baleful eyes shifted constantly in furtive arcs. Perhaps in thought he was acting out dramas of escape—perhaps he saw himself starting up, with a blow disposing of one or more of those old men, the tipstaffs; by his speed, making the upper door before the state police at the lower doors woke up. Out the doors and down the hall, he would probably meet no one. Before the courthouse (he was the author of this and could have in it anything that suited him) would be a car at the curb, with the ignition key carelessly left in. Then, with the speed of thought, the engine roaring up, the flashing dartaway down the sun-filled street; off, at seventy miles an hour, while the police whistles died behind him across the summer countryside—only, Howell never made the first move; and he never would. The galvanic fear of death, applied too often and too long, wore out the body's responses. Howell did not stop fearing; but he remained paralyzed, and only his mind hit and ran and got away.

Abner studied him thoughtfully; not himself insensible to that distracting fear; and well enough able to imagine himself in Howell's place. In a month or two Stanley Howell would be dead. They would pronounce him dead, unstrap his body, and carry it out and bury it. Horrible and inconceivable as the idea might be to Howell, that was what was going to happen, not some day, but within a few weeks; as soon as his appeal was turned down with the direction to carry into execution the sentence of the law that you, Stanley Howell, be taken hence by the sheriff—

The words, hard for a man to hear without trembling for himself as well as for Stanley Howell, made Abner recoil. Along with Howell they took hence something in himself— the pleasures of living, the confidence of days to come, the succession of the seasons, the events of the years; and though, of course, in the end it was all one (Beulah cemetery lay there in the moonlight and tree shadows last night)—better later than now! Abner remembered reading in some book, some school book probably, about Greek history or something, of Socrates having been supposed to say, when they told him that the thirty tyrants had condemned him to death: "And Nature, them." The come-back, though noble and even snappy, did not make much sense. Abner shook his head.

Beside him Bunting drew a weary breath. To Abner he murmured, "Don't know whether this wears down the witness; but it certainly wears me down."

Harry said to Leming, "When you speak of these little cans, little packages of opium, they cost about how much?"

"Oh," said Leming, "there's different sizes. You get small ones; five dollars."

"How long do they last?"

"Well, a small one, about three days."

"Then your use of opium costs you about ten dollars a week. Is that correct?"

This testimony might be wearing to Bunting; but Abner could see that the jury found it full of interest; as good as a conducted tour through opium dens or haunts of vice. In simultaneous movement all eyes went to Harry; and then to Leming, as Leming answered, lingered a moment, fascinated; and then back to Harry; and then quickly back to Leming again. "Now, I think you said you smoked twice a day?" Harry said. "At what hours?"

"Well, generally before I got to bed at night, late at night; and when I first get up."

"First thing in the morning?" (A touch of collective nausea appeared on the jurors' faces. Most men wouldn't even smoke a cigar before breakfast.)

"Whenever I get up first."

"And after you smoke the opium, what happens then?"

"Well, I get up and eat."

"I thought an opium user had no appetite after he smoked."

"Oh, no," Leming smiled and shook his head. "I see you don't understand anything about opium," he said mildly.

"I probably don't know quite as much as you do," Harry said. "That is why I ask."

"You wouldn't ask that question if you understood it."

"Well, can you answer?"

"Yes, I can. Anybody that has the habit can eat after they smoke; but you can't eat before you smoke."

"You smoke; and go right on about your business?"

"That is right."

"I suppose this opium has no effect on your memory?"

"No."

"Well, what effect, if any, does it have?"

"No effect," Leming said, smiling and shaking his head again. "If you was to smoke cigarettes, and I was to ask you what effect they had, what would you say? You have the habit; you keep smoking them. If you see you are out of cigarettes, you have to go get some right away. It is when you don't have them, they have effect. In narcotic, you got to take it to keep yourself from being sick, that is all."

"You mean, as long as you keep taking it, you feel all right?"

"That is correct," Leming said. He smiled encouragingly at Harry. "Now, you are getting it!"

"I should say I am," said Harry. "How long do you stay sick if you don't have your stuff?"

"Oh, well, five or six days. I mean, if you break your habit, after five or six days you don't crave it."

"Now, these pills they gave you in jail; they have the same effect as opium?"

Bunting said, "He has already answered that."

Leming answered, "I should say not!" He was eager, glad to have the advantage of Harry, and aware of the jury's attentiveness. He smiled again; he gave his head a sadder-but-wiser shake.

"You mean they are not a good substitute?"

"They just give them to try to make me get some sleep; but they don't do no good."

"And what keeps you from sleeping?"

"Well, I told you that before," Leming said. "When you get off the stuff, you can't sleep for a couple of months."

"It isn't your conscience that's bothering you?"

Taken by surprise, and plainly wounded or deflated by the jab, Leming said, "Oh, no. Nothing on my conscience bothering me. It should be on the men you are representing!"

Harry said, "I move that be stricken!"

Judge Vredenburgh jerked his chin up and down. "It may be stricken out."

"Now, Leming," Harry said, "if I understand you rightly, you claim that you were not offered any inducements of any kind to testify. But you must have had some reason. What was it?"

"Well," said Leming, "when Howell told his statement, well, then I figured it was time for me to tell the truth; after Howell had opened up himself."

"Who told you to do that?"

"I told myself to do it."

"Had you been advised by your lawyer, Mr. Servadei, or any member of his firm, of any appeal to be made for you if you took the stand for the Commonwealth?"

"Positively not."

"Did the county detective, Mr. Costigan, offer you anything in the way of a promise of leniency?"

Bunting said, "If he did, I would like to know it."

"Never," said Leming.

To Abner, Bunting said, "Mr. Wurts is about washed up, I think." He straightened himself in his seat and began to assemble the papers and file folders on the table. "Ten of five," he said. "I guess his Honor's had enough, too. I was going to put Smalley on and get it over. But she won't take long. We'll have her first, tomorrow. I want Dunglison and Kinsolving; and we'd better read Howell's confession into the record. With luck, we can rest by noon."

Harry said, "Now, Leming, you admitted the police records of your arrests during the last ten years—"

Bunting said, "Do we have to have all that again?"

"The Commonwealth's anxiety to get its witness off the stand is readily understandable," Harry began, but without much spirit.

"I object!" Bunting said. "Mr. Wurts is now testifying himself, your Honor."

"On the contrary, I am trying to conduct a cross-examination, and the district attorney has no business to interrupt it constantly!"

Judge Vredenburgh said, "I must ask both of you to come to order. No more by-play, please! If you have further questions for this witness, Mr. Wurts, put them promptly. The jurors have had a very hot and uncomfortable afternoon, and ought not to be kept here unnecessarily."

Harry said, "My only endeavor is to get through, your Honor. Leming, did you ever conduct any sort of business during these years—I mean, apart from crime; or did crime take all your time?"

"I manufactured dice," Leming, who saw that Harry knew all about it, said.

"Loaded ones, I presume."

"Well, if they wanted loaded ones, and they pay the price for them, I can make them, too."

"You mean you supplied big gambling operators with loaded dice?"

"Big operators don't need no loaded dice," Leming said, smiling indulgently. "They only watch nobody playing with them brings any. With straight dice, by like the law of averages, they got to win."

"I hope we will all bear that in mind," said Harry to the jury. "In short, when not engaged in any definite crime, you made dice."

"I had other jobs," Leming said. "I told you some of them. I was an iron worker, cement finisher—well, numerous things—"

"Yes, numerous things is right," Harry said. "That will be all, thank you."

"Mr. District Attorney," Judge Vredenburgh said, "have you any questions? Or is there anyone else you want to put on whose examination could be disposed of very briefly?"

Bunting shook his head, and Judge Vredenburgh continued: "I think, then, we will suspend at this point. The jury may be withdrawn until tomorrow morning."

While the courtroom emptied, Abner sat watching Bunting pack his brief case. "Want to see me about anything before court tomorrow?" he said. "I told Arlene I'd try to get down."

"I'll ring you there if anything comes up. What did you make of the Mason boy?"

"He's all right, I think. He looked like a decent kid."

"Well, maybe his father's a perfectly decent person, too. If you're seeing Jesse, you might bear that in mind."

"I'm not going to have any row with Jesse."

"If you do, you're a damned fool," Bunting said. "So don't be. Good night." He crossed the empty well of the court and went into the Judge's chambers.

In the Attorneys Room Harry Wurts had taken off his coat and necktie. He lolled on the window ledge in his limp shirt. "And then I said to him," said Harry, " 'My son,' I said, 'the world is full of sin and sorrow, of trial and tribulation; and the heart of man is heavy, and we know not what to believe—' "

Joe Jackman said, "This is still you talking?"

Paying no attention, Harry leveled his finger at George Stacey and Nick Dowdy, whose mouth hung open as he watched. " 'Receive this truth!' " said Harry, " 'Remember it! Mark it! Write it in letters of purest gold! Amid the storms of adversity, in the heyday of triumph, at the hour of decision, in the article of death, say to yourself, as now I say to you: *The wheel that squeaks the loudest gets the grease!*' I thank you!" Carrying his coat and tie, Harry marched out the other door.

"He ought to be on the radio," Joe Jackman said bitterly. The closing door reopened, and Mark Irwin came in. "Hello, toss-pot!" Joe said. "Here it is. That's the whole thing." He lifted one section from a stack of sheets bound in blue paper, glanced at the title page, and handed it over.

"Thanks a lot," Mark said. "Hello, Ab. Going to the Nyces'?"

"No," said Abner. "So long, Joe."

He went out into the hall and down to the back entrance. The windows of Mrs. O'Hara's sitting room in the jail were open and boxes of petunias grew between the bars. There was no breeze, but the sun, declining at last, made everything look cooler. There were shadows across the paving of Court Street. Abner walked down to the gaping Romanesque arch of the door to the three-story, shabbily stone-faced Gearhart Building. He went into the hall, and up the wide, much worn wooden stairs. At the head of them was a window with a drawn yellow shade against which the sun blazed full. Abner passed the open office doors of the Childerstown Building & Loan Association. Next to them was a closed door marked *Childerstown Water Company*. At the end, giving access to the rooms at the front of the building, were double doors of ground glass with black lettering half faded and flaked off: *Michael Gearhart's Sons. Real Estate & Insurance*; and, lower down, *walk in*.

Abner walked in.

Five

THE DOUBLE DOORS opened into an anteroom, from which, on the far side, other doors opened. The anteroom was lumbered up with golden oak furniture—desks for a couple of stenographers; filing cases; straight chairs around a circular table. On the walls hung a bird's-eye view of Childerstown in 1890, a stuffed salmon, and the color print of a painting by Frederick Remington. Between the windows stood a rubber plant, almost eight feet tall and famous in Childerstown offices—most of the girls grew or tried to grow something; but Hazel Finch (not exactly a girl, since her hair was white. She had been thirty years in the Gearhart office) and her rubber plant had never been matched.

Neither Hazel Finch nor anyone else was there now; but a moment after Abner closed the door, Jesse's voice sounded from the corner room. "Who's that?" he said.

"Hello," said Abner, stepping to the door.

Jesse Gearhart sat at his desk opposite an old-fashioned safe whose front was decorated with dim gold banderoles and a murky pastoral scene. The desk top was heaped with papers and letters piled around a miscellaneous collection of gadgets; bronze ink stands and pencil racks; two telephone instruments; an onyx ash tray with the gilt figure of a naked girl dancing on the edge; a brass clock mounted in a miniature ship's wheel; two volumes of the state *Manual* and one of *Who's Who in America* between book ends that were replicas of the sphinx; a bronze elephant with a howdah lettered G.O.P. on its back; all half-buried. In the center,

189

before him, Jesse had cleared a space in which he was writing a letter.

He said, "Come on in, Ab. Let me finish this, will you." He nodded at the chair to his left in the corner formed by the corner of the building, a five-sided bay window. Seating himself, Abner could look down Broad Street to the north; the building fronts giving way to tree tops; and, far away, to the lower fields and woods; and farther still, backing the narrow vista, to the blue hills—light blue where the slopes were gentle; darker blue where they were steep.

Jesse's pen scratched rapidly. Above Jesse's head hung the photograph of some political dinner, the long white tables lined with guests, all sitting back and turning their faces so they could be seen. On the wall beyond was a big framed photograph of former President Harding with a personal inscription to Jesse. Abner let his eyes rest a moment on Jesse himself, then. Jesse's wide head was tipped forward, but not far enough to hide the tired-looking eyes as they moved from word to word with the moving pen. Abner supposed that Jesse was about fifty-five; and it could be seen that politics was hard on a man. It was a waiting game, with all that meant in delays and postponements, in negotiations never quite finished, in nursing plans, in working things little by little. There was never any rest; and the rewards, as far as Abner knew, were neither very great nor very certain. In state politics the party chairman of a safe county had some importance, for safe counties were never too numerous; but Jesse probably had enemies among his nominal friends, and these must have succeeded in keeping him down. Though not old enough to pay attention to it at the time, Abner knew now that Jesse had little, and perhaps nothing, to do with his father's appointment to the Superior Court. That, and Judge Coates' subsequent nomination on the state ticket, was all done over Jesse's head, presumably through Judge Coates' friendship with the Chief Justice, and the Chief Justice's advice to the Governor. Abner supposed that the size of it was that Jesse was gladly allowed to manage the county and get out the vote; but in larger affairs he carried no special weight.

Jesse folded the sheet and put it in an envelope. Licking the flap, he said, "How's your dad, Abner?"

"Pretty well," Abner said.

Jesse sealed the envelope and put a stamp on it. He said, "Good. Glad to hear it. You know, my father had a stroke. He got over it, almost entirely. If the Judge is better now, he'll go on getting better, ten to one."

"I hope so," Abner said.

Jesse pushed his chair away from the desk and tilted it back. "See that Mason boy?"

"Yes. Jake brought him around."

"What did you think of him, Ab?"

Abner said, "He looks like a nice kid."

"He's a son of George Guthrie Mason, the National Committeeman, you know. He's a fine man. He was certainly upset when he called me. The boy just sent him this telegram saying he'd been in an accident and was in jail—he was coming home from college. The boy's mother was frantic, of course. Mr. Mason called me up at seven this morning."

This was all understandable and could be viewed with sympathy. In such circumstances, anyone would and ought to do what he could for anyone he knew. Abner nodded. He swallowed down the unreasonable discomfort Jesse's words caused him—Jesse's unphrased but present and detectable alacrity to serve, and real pleasure at the chance, must be the irritant. This George Guthrie Mason, this National Committeeman, this fine man (and doubtless this rich man, this man of influence, this man worth pleasing) could be imagined looking at the date line of the disturbing telegram, finding out right away what county that was, racking his brain for someone from there he might have met sometime. Suddenly Mr. Mason (all men in his position had phenomenal memories) would place the inconsequential country politician. It

191

just showed you! You should always be genial to such small
fry; it was little trouble and took little time and they appreciated it. So here was what's-his-name, Gearhart or something, by George Guthrie Mason himself brought to the telephone at seven o'clock in the morning; and tickled pink to
find that Mr. Mason remembered him perfectly, and when
he thought of Childerstown, thought of Jesse at once; and of
course Jesse would find out about it, of course he'd see the
boy had the best lawyer, of course he'd speak to the district
attorney—

Abner made himself say, "I think there may be a good
chance we won't have to hold him. Marty's arranged the
coroner's inquest for the day after tomorrow. He probably
told you. He's probably seen the police report by now."

"How's Pete working out as a J.P.?"

"As far as I know, we've always got along with him fine."

"You've had some trouble with Earl Foulke, though,
haven't you?"

"I think Foulke's made Marty pretty mad once or twice.
He goes off half-cocked, and then we have to straighten it
out. But they seem to like him, down there; so I guess we'll
just have to put up with it."

"Not necessarily," Jesse said. "A younger man who was
popular would have a good chance, I think. Do you know
Albert Greer?"

"I think I've met him," Abner said. "Isn't he the one who
has the lumber yard at Jobstown? You see his coal trucks
around all the time."

"No, that's his brother, older brother," Jesse said. The
ready, encyclopedic information was part of Jesse's business.
"Bert's at Middlebrook. Real estate. He's been handling that
development out by Candy's quarry—" Reminded that he
had thought of going there with Bonnie to swim tonight, and
that it was getting later, Abner inclined his head a little so
that he could see the clock on a column before the *Examiner*
office. Maynard Longstreet, a straw hat on the back of his

head, his coat over one arm, and under the other a batch of copies of his newspaper which he was not above delivering himself to the newsstand by the Childerstown House on his way home, let the screen door to the office slam and came down the three steps to the sidewalk.

Jesse said, "Bert's as smart as a whip. I think he'd run. I hoped you knew him. Anyone down around there, Jobstown, Middlebrook, Saratoga, you think would be good?"

To find himself gravely consulted by Jesse on such a matter made Abner want to laugh, and yet at the same time there was a sort of annoyance in it—what kind of a damned fool did Jesse take him for? If this Bert Greer wanted for some reason (generally it was a curious little vanity, a perverted self-importance that sought gratification. The trifling perquisites and fees would not pay a busy or able man for the time required) to be a J.P., it was nothing to Abner. Abner said, "I don't know anyone who'd want to bother with the job, Jesse."

As soon as he had said it, Abner saw that it was a lapse in tact or judgment. Simulating cordiality or friendship toward a person you did not like was taxing. However tough on the surface, however cynical and designing (Jesse surely filled that bill), at heart the parties to the make-believe were as sensitive as young girls, suspiciously looking for affronts and expecting rebuffs. Unless you were a good natural deceiver and could throw yourself into a part with the sincerity of being pleased to play it well, you were out of luck. Abner knew that he had no talent for that kind of thing.

But at that kind of thing Jesse was past master. The anger in Jesse's eyes, when he jumped, by taking what Abner said the wrong way, to·the right conclusion that Abner had no use for him, was scarcely disclosed before it was gone. Fruit of a lifetime of dickering, Jesse's control was as good as a saint's. Jesse was slow to wrath. If you let yourself be angered when somebody, whether clumsily or with intention, said something to anger you, what was that but letting him tell you what to do? He called the tune, and at his word, you like a fool danced.

From a coign of vantage, unreachable, withdrawn behind his pale wise opaque eyes, Jesse inquired suddenly, "Want to run for district attorney in the fall, Ab?"

It was not that Abner couldn't answer; but, exactly like Leming on the stand this afternoon when Harry hounded him, the answer was demanded before there was time to get it ready. Here was a trick of Abner's own trade, the calm but sudden devastating question. Abner knew all its dangers and he also knew the defense. Judge Coates often said, and indeed it was not only his saying, but the wisdom of the ages, that when you were not sure what to answer, then keep your mouth shut. This was advice so simple and clear that nobody could doubt or mistake it. What anybody could do, and what most people did do, was forget to remember it. The impact of surprise and embarrassment opened Abner's mouth, and before he could stop, he had said, "Well, that depends—"

"What's it depend on?" said Jesse, sitting back farther in his chair.

Jesse's tone, the tone of the much-tried man who asked a plain question and could not get a plain answer, suggested that Jesse was resigned to beating about the bush (but did not see why he had to), and Jesse's movement, which was that of settling himself as comfortably as possible to wait out the explanations, made Abner say sharply, "Well, for one thing, it depends on Marty, of course."

Abner saw at once that this was another mistake. Either Marty had told him of his plans, or Marty hadn't. If Marty had; what was Abner's idea in pretending he didn't know them? If Marty hadn't; did the answer mean that Abner was ready to be sounded out behind his boss's back? Abner repaired it as well as he could. "Marty told me he was thinking of resigning," Abner said, "but until he does—"

"Look, Ab," Jesse said patiently, "every now and then you say funny things. Marty's one of the best district attorneys in the state. You know what his record is. He could keep the job just as long as he wanted it. You don't have to worry about that. When he quits, you're naturally in line for it. If you want to run, that is."

"Frankly—" said Abner. He paused; for, frankly, what he wanted was to get out of this, to end the discussion (how, hardly mattered). After all, he had one advantage over a hapless defendant on the stand. If he wanted to get down, he didn't have to wait until Jesse said he might. Abner said, "As a matter of fact, I don't know how good a candidate I'd make."

"Well," said Jesse dispassionately, "your name's worth something. A lot of people know you; but everybody in the county practically knows your family. You've had this experience working with Marty. He thinks you're the man. The Judges would be satisfied. From what I hear, we'll have Art Wenn running against us again. He won't be hard to beat."

Art Wenn was a lawyer from Warwick, a big cheerful back-slapper. Most people liked Art, and he was widely acquainted. His politics were loud and vigorous—at the last election, when he ran against Bunting, half the fence posts and telephone poles in the county had come out with red, white and blue cardboard squares bearing simply the words: SAY WENN. This quip was much appreciated; but, on counting the votes, three quarters of them, more than the normal majority, were for Bunting. It was safe to guess that Art's exuberance and hearty ways, while they made people like him, won him little support. He was not taken seriously.

Abner said, "Well, if Marty thinks I ought to run, I don't mind."

"You don't mind," said Jesse. "If you aren't any keener about it than that, do you know what I think? I think we'd better get somebody else, if we can. It's an important job, and the man who has it ought to feel that. He ought to be willing to give all he's got to it; not just say he doesn't mind if he has it."

Put thus entirely in the wrong, Abner searched for words. A resentment, all too impotent, but rising, at the idea of Jesse reading him a lesson in principles filled him with a certain heat. "I think it's an important job," Abner said slowly. The thought came to him that since he had made such a mess of it, a little more wouldn't hurt—would, in fact, be a relief. "That's why I wouldn't take it, if I found I was going to be—well, obligated to someone."

Jesse said, "I don't quite get you, Ab. Do you mean that you think Marty's obligated to someone?"

"No, I don't mean that," Abner said, "and you know damned well I don't!"

"Well, what do you mean?" Jesse said. "Say it. You can say anything you like."

"Thanks!" said Abner. "Well, I'll tell you this. If I were district attorney and anyone called me up about some friends of his—" He necessarily paused.

"Sure," said Jesse. "Go on, go on."

"No," said Abner. "I won't. I guess what I mean is this. I don't like politi—politics, so I guess you're right; you'd better get somebody who does."

"Well," said Jesse, "we can do that."

"O.K.," said Abner, "good night." He got up and walked over to the open door.

"Just a minute, Ab," Jesse said.

Abner turned, and Jesse went on, "You're a young man and I'm an old one, so suppose I give you some advice. I don't know who said it first, but it's been a lot of use to me. Old Senator Perkins said it to me once. He said, 'You wouldn't worry so much about what people were thinking of you, if you'd just remember that most of the time they're not.'"

"What is that supposed to prove?" said Abner.

"Well, go along, Ab," Jesse said, "I can't explain it to you."

Abner went through the shadowed anteroom and closed

196

the ground glass doors after him. The Childerstown Building & Loan office was shut now and in dead air and echoing silence he went downstairs and out onto the shadowed street. His mind felt sore all over. He had not exactly had a row with Jesse—what he said didn't amount to a row. *So I told him he'd better get someone else; I simply said to him, I don't like politics*—in short, he rejected the proposals; only, as it happened, no proposals were made him. If he rejected anything, he rejected the possibility of proposals. Jesse had asked his "advice" about who would be a good justice of the peace; and then asked him if he wanted to run in the fall; and Abner answered that he didn't like politics; and that if he were district attorney and anyone asked for favors he would—he implied—refuse them. A connection did exist; but it wasn't strong or cogent. Could he say that confronted by a certain situation he had taken on principle certain steps? He had in fact acted on impulse, in a mood or state of mind in which instead of doing what he meant to do, he did what he meant to avoid, refused what he really wanted, and with unprovoked pique, out of hand, in a minute, came to new and definite decisions that might—more than might, must!— affect his whole life.

Walking up to where his car was parked behind the court-house, Abner did what he could to adjust himself to such a great change of plan. It would certainly be a load off his mind. When you were in the district attorney's office they kept you on a sort of treadmill. Quarter Sessions were sure as death and taxes. You cleaned up the term's trial list, and as soon as you were through, indeed, before you were through, it began all over again. Night and day, people (and often old familiar ones) were busy with projects considered or un-considered, which would suddenly collide with the law and become public. In advance you could count on case after case —always fifteen or twenty—of operating a motor vehicle while under the influence of intoxicating liquor. Boys were swiping things because they had no money; and some of them were going to be caught and held for burglary, larceny, and receiving stolen goods. There would be forcible entries here and felonious assaults there. Somebody would wantonly point a firearm; and somebody else would sell malt beverages on premises without license. Fornication had duly resulted in bastardy, and the Commonwealth was charged with seeing that the disgruntled father supported his little bastard. Heretofore respectable, an old man would feel indescribable urges to expose himself to women, and this was open lewdness. Forged instruments would be uttered, fraudulent conversions attempted; and, in passion or liquor, somebody might seek to kill a man or rape a woman.

And so the indictments piled up. The district attorney's office saw the prisoners, and talked to witnesses and listened to complaints. They arraigned the guilty pleas in Miscellaneous Court; and prepared the others for the grand jury. The county officers brought in to them the non-support and desertion cases; prisoners became eligible for parole, and the parole violators were picked up. Keeping step with it all (or sometimes a little behind) the papers to be signed and the forms to be filled kept accumulating—recognizances; petitions for appointment of counsel, for approval of bills of expense, for attachment, for condemnation and destruction of contraband, for support and to vacate support, for writs of habeas corpus ad prosequendum and ad testificandum; the criminal transcripts; the warrants; the waivers of jury trial —anyone ought to be glad to get rid of all that. Not to mention the endless hours in court while you asked formal tedious questions to foregone conclusions, while you waited for juries to make up their rambling minds, for his Honor to get through in chambers, for absent witnesses to be found and produced, for court to open and court to adjourn—"My God!" thought Abner. "What a way to spend your life!"

Abner drove home. As he left the car at the front steps he

heard Lucius, calling from the stables, "Say, Mr. Abner, you come here just a minute?"

"No, I can't!" Abner said. "What do you want?"

"See this mower, see here?"

"Do you think I have telescopic sights?" Abner called. "What did you do, break it?"

"No, sir!" said Lucius. "It wasn't getting enough spark. I just—"

"I'll bet you did!" Abner said. He walked down the path through the clumps of overgrown spirea. Lucius had the old lawn mower, powered with a gasoline engine, out on the flagstones before the stable doors. He lifted one greasy hand and scratched the tight fuzz on his head. "Go on; turn it over," Abner said.

"It don't do no good," Lucius said. "I been working on it all afternoon. They electrocuted those men yet?"

"Not quite," Abner said.

"I see in the paper yesterday where you said—"

"Go on; turn it over!"

Lucius gave the lanyard a jerk. The flywheel went around; the exhaust coughed.

"Got any gas in it?" Abner said. "If you have, the feed line's choked."

"Yes, sir—" said Lucius. He paused and said, "Perhaps I don't have quite enough in. It goes better, you don't fill it too full." Turning, he went toward the stable door. "Get a little bit more," he said.

Abner bent down and unscrewed the cap of the fuel tank. It was empty. To Lucius, coming with a gallon glass jug of gasoline, he said, "So hot today, it must have all evaporated. Go on. Fill it up, and it'll go all right. But you won't have time to cut any grass now."

"Well, that beats all!" Lucius said. "I put some in there the first thing I did. Mr. Abner, that man those gangsters kill, I guess he struggled some?"

"He never knew what hit him," Abner said. He crossed

over and went in the back door and through the kitchen. Honey said, "You be here for supper?"

"Not tonight," Abner said. "Did you get my shirts done?"

"No, today I didn't. I'll do them this evening. We're doing downstairs today."

"I've got to have one right now."

"There!" said Honey. "I knew you would! I seen this morning you hadn't no shirts left in your chest of drawers! Then Miz' Boorse wanted I should—"

"Well, just do one now, will you? I've got to get away. I've got to get a bath—"

"If I can I will," Honey said. "Lucius hammered something with my new electric iron. I think he broke it. I have to use that old one. It's a long time heating; but I guess I can use it—"

"Well, will you please hurry up?" Abner went through the pantry into the back hall.

A radio voice, in the middle of a news broadcast, came from the side porch. It was five minutes of six, and if he were going to pick up Bonnie at six-thirty he hadn't much time. Speaking louder than the radio, Mrs. Boorse said, "I'm sure I heard a car, Philander. It must have been Ab."

With a feeling of compunction or guilt—he had not come home to luncheon, and now he was going out again—Abner, who had planned to dress first, hesitated. There was no reason why he shouldn't go out; and there was nothing he could do; and if he stayed, his father would soon fret, preferring to be left alone rather than to feel that Abner or anyone else was obliging himself to sit there. Just the same, the thought of the old man waiting all day; and, it was plain from Mrs. Boorse's remark, asking if Ab hadn't come home yet, was—his father would have hated the word and hated the fact; but it was touching. In his present turmoil of mind, Abner would as soon have avoided his father; but he went through the living room and out the doors to the porch.

"Now! There he is!" said Mrs. Boorse. She arose with

her customary blunt obtrusive tact. "I'd better see what Honey's doing about supper—"

"See what she's doing about ironing a shirt of mine, will you, Aunt Myrt?" Abner said. "I've got to go out."

"Oh," said Mrs. Boorse. "You won't be here?"

"I've got a date," Abner said. To his father, he added, "I told Bonnie I'd take her out." Since this was something the Judge would presumably approve of, Abner tried to feel less inconsiderate. "How do you feel?" he said.

"All right," Judge Coates said. He snapped off the radio. "Hot, today. Must have been hot in the courtroom. Getting on?"

"We had Leming. He did all right. Harry climbed all over him, but he couldn't shake him any. It's pretty much in the bag, I think."

"Never know about a jury," Judge Coates said.

"That's right," Abner agreed. "We'll keep our fingers crossed; but I wouldn't give a great deal for their chances." With his own problems at the front of his mind it was hard to find things to speak casually about. He said, "John Clark wanted to know if he could come to see you, by the way—"

"I know. He came. What's this about Marty resigning? What I thought?"

"Yes," said Abner. "He told me at lunch." He added quickly, "I'll have to get a move on."

"He could do worse," Judge Coates said. "Yes. Mustn't keep a lady waiting. Give Bonnie my love. Where are you going?"

"Out to Candy's, maybe."

"The quarry? Jesse Gearhart's brother, Mike, with some friends about your age, went swimming there one night thirty years ago; and Mike hit his head on a rock, and that was the last thing he ever did."

"You wouldn't know the place now," Abner said. "A fellow named Walsh bought it and put a fence around it and built some bath houses, and has it all full of flood lights at night. It was better before."

"Well, don't go in too soon after dinner," Judge Coates said. "You'll get cramps."

Bathed and dressed—his shirt still smelling of the iron, and a little damp—Abner was only five minutes late. Cousin Mary lived in one of the dozen small houses on what was called Hillside Crescent, a new street laid out in an arc across a pasture behind the old Ormsbee place. The development had occasioned a lot of legal fuss; first, over the title; and then between the borough and the promoters about sewers and street paving. For Childerstown lawyers it was a picnic; and even Harry Wurts had joined in the general barratry long enough to name the project Cowflop Gardens. An aftermath of mechanics' liens still occupied Mark Irwin and George Stacey in Common Pleas. Jesse Gearhart was interested originally; but was supposed to have dropped out when the trouble began.

As far as Abner could tell, nobody made any money; for though the Ormsbees got a good price, they took notes instead of cash for the land. The houses, all new, all different —that is, different from each other—were built to prize-winning plans for low cost housing in a variety of materials. They were necessarily small, almost miniature—small areas cased with brick or field stone, cramped wings and gables of stucco or white clapboarding. Most of them had foundation plantings of miscellaneous mean evergreens, and the new curved street was set out with sycamore saplings, several of them now dead.

Abner halted his car at the clean new cement curb along which grew a little grass and many weeds. Jared, junior, was in the front yard trying to coax his brothers, the twins, within range of a revolving lawn sprinkler. He sang out,

"Hello, Ab! Bonnie's taking a bath." He was an obstreperous brat at an unattractive age, and made short work of any sympathy you might feel for him because of his father's misbehavior.

Cousin Mary showed herself at the screen door in the shadow. "Want to come in, Ab?" she called. "Bonnie will be right down. She was helping me get the kids' supper. Junior, don't do that! Now, just turn the hose off! It's simply wasting water. Harold, why don't you and Philip play in the swing? You'll have to go to bed pretty soon." She held the door open, so Abner, though he did not want to come in, was obliged to.

Putting down on the nearest table the dish and dishtowel she had been holding, Cousin Mary found and lit a cigarette. The little living room was in great disorder, partly the natural work of three small boys in crowded quarters, partly Cousin Mary's own lackadaisical neglect—a way of letting it be seen that it was all more than she could face. There were one or two pieces of good furniture, though much battered and too large for the room; things salvaged from the wreck Jared had made of his affairs and hers. These were supplemented with painted and poorly upholstered junk from Wister's, the cheap Childerstown "home furnishings" store. Abner did not claim to have much taste himself; but it seemed to him that Cousin Mary had none at all—unless, of course (and when you knew her it was not impossible), she deliberately let her surroundings be ugly and depressing, so that, while always brave and silent about it herself, her setting would protest her hard life.

Abner sat down with constraint. On a heap of old magazines on the table lay a copy of the afternoon's *Examiner* and Abner could see the two-column headlines: "Leming Called to Stand by Commonwealth." "Coates Questions Zollicoffer Defendant. Witness Says Basso Fired 2nd Shot." The story began: "Continued this morning before Judge Thomas Vredenburgh in Oyer and Terminer, the Zollicoffer murder trial was high-lighted by the examination, conducted by Assistant District Attorney Abner Coates, of Roy Leming, one of the . . ."

Abner, reading at an angle, read no further. The recount could be of no interest to him now, since this was the last criminal case he would ever help to prosecute. The thought represented, he realized, a new decision, arrived at while he was thinking of other things; but if he were going to quit, he might as well quit at once, as soon as May Sessions ended. That would give Marty more time to break in someone else, someone Jesse wanted. Casting his mind about, trying to think of someone Jesse might want, no name occurred to him; and Abner was aware of a certain grim pleasure at Jesse's predicament. Jesse might find getting someone on short notice harder than he thought; not because the work required rare abilities, but because it did require experience; and, like the post of justice of the peace, most men with the experience and judgment to make them desirable in the office used that experience and judgment to say no. Let some sap with political ambitions take the work and the worry and the responsibility! With Marty resigning, Jesse might find himself in a tough spot, and that was all right with Abner.

The little reverie of revenge held him only a moment; for he saw then with a jolt what was wrong with that picture of Jesse at his wit's end, and Jesse properly sorry that he didn't have Abner. It might be all right with Abner, sulky and disgruntled; but one thing you could be sure of was that Marty, who never had, never would let anyone down. To imagine that Marty, because of his own interest or ambition, would throw up a job for which he had assumed responsibility, that he would resign without being sure that he had left his office in competent hands, was impossible for anyone who ever knew Marty. If Abner were there, Marty might have planned to resign after September Sessions, leaving Abner, without too much work on hand, to fill the office to which, in November, barring a practically impossible upset, he would be elected.

Abner colored. That he had come so close to doing, that he had actually been deciding to do, a thing like that was a fact; and yet it was the kind of dirty trick he himself would not excuse a man for doing. He had never understood how a man could do such a thing; and if that mystery were now cleared up—the doer's own object engrossed him; he never saw what a louse he was—it did not make the things done any better. Abner's plan was to make Marty bear the brunt (to say he didn't mean it that way simply showed that, as well as a sorehead, he was a fool). Marty would have to abandon his plans for the moment, and perhaps for the next four years. He might think it was his job to solve Jesse's difficulties by running again; and if Marty thought it was his job, that was what Marty would at any cost do.

Cousin Mary said, "How's Cousin Philander? Does the heat bother him? I meant to go up there today. I didn't have a minute—" Not waiting for answers, she gabbled along quickly, shaking ashes from the cigarette onto the frayed and wrinkled chintz of the couch. "It was just too hot to do anything. I simply took the children this afternoon and went to the movies—it's the only cool place in town. Oh, Ab; look at this, will you? Do I have to do anything about it?"

She got up and went over to a flimsy little green-painted writing desk, emptied out several pigeon holes, and came back with a letter. "It's not legal, is it?"

Abner, unfolding it, saw the more or less expected words: "Dear Madam: We have repeatedly brought to your attention . . ." "No," said Abner, "it's just a letter. It's not legal, if you mean, is it a process; but, if you don't pay them they can—"

"Well, I can't pay them at present. What ought I to do?"

"If you tell them that, and offer to pay a little, they'll probably agree."

"Well, Ab," Cousin Mary said, "like a lamb, would you answer them? If they got a letter from a lawyer, they might stop bothering me."

"I don't know exactly what I could say to them," Abner said. "What they want is their money, I'm afraid—"

"Oh, Ab, write them anything! I mean, I'm sure if they saw your letterhead, they'd realize that they'd better be careful!"

Nothing would be served by telling Cousin Mary that she was the one who'd better be careful, so Abner said, "I could write them that you're unfortunately unable to settle in full; but—how much could you give them?"

"Ab, I don't see how I can give them anything now. You'd better just tell them they'll have to wait until September, or better say, October."

"Couldn't you give them a couple of dollars? You know, they don't pay much attention to what you say unless you do something, too."

"I don't see how," Cousin Mary said. Her face settled in hurt, resentful lines. "Bonnie has a little money; but I won't ask her for it. It isn't right. She hardly has anything for clothes and things—"

Abner did not like her air of virtuous abnegation. During nine months of the year Bonnie earned a fairly good salary in Mr. Rawle's office at the high school; and if she hardly had anything for clothes and things, there was a reason for that, and not a very good one. Abner didn't mean to minimize Cousin Mary's expenses; but what she did with her money was a puzzle—a feat of bad management. You could not blame her for taking the children to the movies on a hot afternoon, and doubtless stilling their subsequent clamors at Lloyds' soda fountain. Only in the meanest, most trifling sense could it be said to run to money; but that was where the money went, just the same. It was not possible to ask her to account for it—some of Bonnie's salary for last month, which she probably received when school ended Saturday, must be what Bonnie was mentioned as having; probably all Bonnie had been able to keep for her own use for six months or more; and keeping it might make her mother short. But how about the money, always fifty and often a hundred dollars, that Judge Coates provided for Cousin Mary every month?

Abner folded the letter and slipped it in his coat pocket. "I'll send them something," he said, "and tell them you'll take it up in September."

Cousin Mary said, "Oh, Ab! I don't want you to do that! There's no reason why you should—"

"Look, Mary," Abner said, "you've got to pay them sometime."

But the fact was, of course, that Cousin Mary didn't feel the obligation. By a not uncommon sleight of mind, time passing was made to eliminate the element of honesty or dishonesty. She would not steal from a shop counter (or, not to be arbitrary about a matter in which the district attorney's office had seen circumstances alter cases; she would not, unless the opportunity appeared ideal and her need very great); but if a shop wanted to let her have things, she would take them without considering too seriously how she was going to pay. When the bill was presented, it actually seemed to her unfair, the inconvenient reopening of a closed and half-forgotten transaction for which she now had nothing to show, anyway. Abner said, "They can make things pretty unpleasant for you."

Yes, they could! Nobody knew it better than Cousin Mary. They had the outrageous power; and that was now the point. Cousin Mary was furious with them; yet, in spite of the way they were acting, they had the effrontery to expect her to pay them! "Well, I wouldn't give them a thing!" Cousin Mary said. "Not one red cent! They were anxious enough to carry an account for me, heaven knows!" She crushed out her cigarette. "Now, don't give them much, Ab. They don't deserve it."

The quick click of heels upstairs sounded; and, lowering her voice, she added, "Don't say anything to Bonnie about it, will you? She'll just want to use her own money; and I don't want her to. Were you going out to the quarry swimming? I hope you'll both be careful. You know, it was out there, you wouldn't remember, I think it was the year you were born—yes, it was; I remember Edith couldn't go anywhere that summer—that Michael Gearhart broke his neck. It was the most shocking thing. He was such a good looking boy, and much nicer than Jesse—"

"Yes, Father told me," Abner said. "But I never heard of anyone else getting hurt."

The footsteps started downstairs; and, turning his head, he could see Bonnie—her white shoes and slender flesh colored legs; the short full skirt of a yellow frock sprigged with white flowers. She had a jacket of yellow linen over her arm and carried a loose bag into which she was tucking a bathing cap of white rubber. "Hello," she said, "I'm sorry."

She looked, Abner thought, very pretty; fresh and clean, remote from the shabby confusion of the living room into which she was descending; by youth or grace, by the candor of eye and manner, equally remote from her mother. Abner thought to himself, "I'd like to get her out of this damned place, this mess—" And that, the impulsive feeling, was perhaps the answer; and ought to resolve any uncertainty of mind.

Cousin Mary said, "You look sweet, darling."

"Yes, you do," said Abner; but he could not help seeing that he should have said it first. He took the bag with her bathing suit.

"Thanks, everyone," said Bonnie. "I don't think we'll be very late, Mother." Abner held the screen door open, and she went out and down the brick steps in front of him.

Jared, junior, lying on the grass, said, "Hi-yá, Toots?
Why don't you put your stockings on?"

"Because it's too hot," said Bonnie.

Jared got up, his small, insolent-looking tanned face coun-
terfeiting good will. Catching hold of Abner's arm he swung
into step with him as he reached the gate. Looking up, lowering his voice, Jared said, "Give 's a dime, will you?"

"No, don't!" said Bonnie, turning. "Jared, if I have to
speak to you again about—"

"Whyn't you go to hell, you crummy bitch?" said Jared.
His own dreadful words obviously shocked him; and back-
ing off with flustered defiance, he added in haste, "Now, tell
Mother! Go on, why don't you?"

"We won't have to bother her," said Abner, taking a step;
but Jared fled away through the gate and ran behind the
house as hard as he could.

"Isn't he nice?" said Bonnie, getting into the car. "Oh,
God, Ab; let's go somewhere and have a drink!"

"O.K.," said Abner. Starting the car, he said, "I don't
know how Cousin Mary's going to like it; but some day
fairly soon I'll lick the tar out of that brat."

"It wouldn't do any good."

"It would do me good," said Abner. "Mind the Black
Cat?"

"I don't mind anything," Bonnie said. She lay back in
the seat, her legs stretched tense and straight in front of
her; the warm air, rushed to a wind, catching at her hair.
"Or at least it takes a good deal. Something I minded happened this afternoon. I don't know why exactly; but I got
such a shock."

"What was it?"

"Do you mind my confiding in you?" she said. "Poor Ab!
You don't have much choice, do you?"

"I would be much offended if you didn't," Abner said.
He put out a hand and patted her arm. The affection he
felt for her made him suddenly awkward, and to cover it,

he added, "Don't forget I'm one of the county's public confidants. The things that have been confided in me! You'd be surprised. Interested, too, I daresay."

"Well, this will be another one you mustn't tell anyone; because I oughtn't to, really. It's not very nice of me; but it made me feel so funny. I couldn't even tell Inez."

"I see. Now, if you'll just sit down—it's Miss Drummond, isn't it?—and tell me in your own words what happened, I think we can—" But, imitating his own office voice, Abner disconcertingly remembered (at some point, it must have been during Cousin Mary's recital, he really had forgotten all about it) that he was through with the district attorney's work. "In short, go on," he said.

"Well, I don't know whether you've met him or not; this cousin of Inez's who's been staying up at the Ormsbees' for a couple of weeks. His name is Lawrence Harper. I suppose I've seen him half a dozen times—"

"I know," said Abner. "A little skinny fellow. He was playing tennis out at the club last week. Johnny introduced me to him. He's supposed to be a chemist. What is he really, a foreign agent?"

"He's a chemist, all right," Bonnie said. "He invented something, some process, and got an awful lot of money for it. He said it was really just an accident."

"Is that what shocked you?"

"No," said Bonnie. "I believed that." She laughed. "The truth is, I didn't pay much attention to him. He was such a mousey little man—or boy, I guess. He helped Inez a lot in the garden; and one day last week, the day it was raining, he spent practically the whole afternoon helping us sort out and copy about a thousand old recipes."

"You mean that in spite of his unexpectedly gained fortune, all his wealth and fame, he is just simple and natural?"

"Yes, he's simple, all right," Bonnie said. She drew a breath. "Well, I was home alone this afternoon. As a matter of fact, I was trying to get this dress finished. Mother and the kids had gone to the movies; and I heard someone knock, and it was this Larry—"

"Go on," said Abner, sobering. His pleasantry of a moment ago lost its pleasantness. Stories that began like that he had, indeed, heard several times, the office door closed, the strained and anxious faces fixed on him. The difference was that actors in them had always been strangers to him; and facts about strangers, however disagreeable, could be examined dispassionately.

Bonnie said, "This is a little embarrassing. I—"

"Go on," Abner said. His mind had set itself in a grimness that did not have much to do with equal justice under law. "What did he want?"

"He wanted to ask me to marry him," Bonnie said.

"Oh," said Abner. The reaction of relief left him without any words. To the first relief, that nothing had happened to her, the cooling and clearing of his mind added a second. To Abner in his anger, and to the law, too, it would have been simple enough—a man annoying her; but to Childerstown it would have been Inez Ormsbee's cousin. "Well, I hope you didn't say you would," Abner said.

"I simply didn't know what to say. I couldn't say anything for a moment. Then I told him—I was so stunned I must have sounded like an idiot—that I couldn't possibly do that; that I was very much complimented, of course—"

She paused, raising her hands and pressing them to her blowing hair. "But I can tell you I wasn't!" she said. "I was simply furious! I don't know why, except, I suppose, the idea that he must have thought I'd say yes, just like that. I mean, he'd have to think I was crazy! You know, I thought afterwards, that if he'd just tried to kiss me or something, I wouldn't have liked it; but I wouldn't have been nearly so mad. I think he must be insane."

"What did he say when you told him that you couldn't possibly?"

"Oh, he said he didn't suppose I could; but he thought

he'd ask me; and he hoped I wasn't offended. That he really meant it; and he was perfectly serious—I suppose that was what made me maddest of all! But I did hang onto myself somehow; and I told him I was sorry, but it was absolutely out of the question. I can't tell you what a fool I felt. So then he took his hat and left. He's going away tomorrow, thank God! Don't you think that's funny?"

"Yes," said Abner, "and no."

That anyone, even someone who must be insane, someone with no chance of being taken seriously, should presume to have designs on Bonnie created in Abner's mind not amusement but indignation. That this little squirt Harper should have the impudence in his imagination to make free with Bonnie, and to consider her as a girl he would like to have —but ordering and censoring other people's thoughts was clearly impractical, even for the jealous heart. Moreover, along with indignation, Abner could not help feeling a certain sympathy for Harper. You would not like to be the man who, misjudging so badly how he stood, brought down on himself a humiliation in which he was left not only bereft but ridiculous.

"I shouldn't have told you," Bonnie said. "I thought you'd think it was funny. I'm sorry."

Abner said, "What I meant was—"

He had been about to say that it was funny enough; only nobody else was going to marry her and people who attempted it failed to amuse him. The difficulty, coming up before, and always when it would do the most harm, was a sort of awkwardness; the difficulty of a change in attitude. Harper, because he knew Bonnie so little, could make her feel like a fool by attempting gallantries for which she wasn't ready; but Abner, knowing her all her life, was hardly any better off. His gallantries, too, must have something blundering in them. When he came to see her, or take her out to dinner, was it as her lover, or as her old and familiar acquaintance? And, if both, when and where did one become the other? The fact of the matter—that it was her old acquaintance to whom she told her story in confidence, but it was her lover who warmed with irritation and jealousy to think of another man in her life—meant that he must show her, by the change, that his ardor was intermittent, that he courted her in his spare time. This was, of course, the case; since neither Abner nor any male, unless he was a semi-professional lover or a schoolboy (in either event, with no other real work), could spend all, or even much, of his time thinking of his beloved. Every woman naturally knew it; but it was one of the numerous facts of life and love that she did not care to be reminded of. She did not feel, as a man felt, that any neglect was repaired by the vehemence of a man's feelings when he got around to them. Abner saw that he had better not explain what he meant.

"Look," said Abner, "when are you going to marry me?"

"Oh, Ab!" Bonnie said. Her voice rose in exasperation. She clenched her hands and said, "What's the use? You say something like that every now and then, as if you were doing something. And then, if I don't marry you tomorrow, it's my fault; so you can just—" To his consternation she began to cry; but with anger, grinding the knuckles of one clenched hand into her cheek.

The car had just gone through the crossroads—a store and a dozen houses called Saratoga—where they turned left to go down to the Black Cat. Drawing off the road Abner stopped the car under a group of big sycamores. He put an arm around her, and she said, "Oh, don't! I'm not going on like this. I just can't!"

"Now, what are we arguing about?" Abner said.

Sitting up, she worked loose, freeing her shoulder from his fingers and pushing his arm back. There was a shining line of tears down her cheek, but she had stopped crying. "Ab," she said, "what were you and Mother talking about before I came down?"

"A private matter," Abner said.

"I'll tell you how private it was. She was trying to get some money out of you, wasn't she?"

"Absolutely not," said Abner.

"Why do you say that? Mr. Stayman got tired of waiting and spoke to me about it. You don't have to do anything. It's paid. I paid it this morning. I didn't tell her because I just couldn't argue. She said she took care of it months ago. I gave her the money to, then."

"Nevertheless, it is a fact that she did not ask me for any money," Abner said. "And where did you get the money to pay it with now?"

"I had some saved. I had enough."

"And now you haven't any," Abner said.

"I don't need any. I'd rather not have any than—"

Abner supposed that she really would rather not have any money. It was a temperament or turn of mind that would strip itself of everything for the satisfaction of pride. Presumably there was no pleasure for her in new clothes if someone like Mr. Stayman could see her wearing them and be able to think that there went his bill. This was pride, of course; not any exalted principle; and the privation and sacrifice it entailed was accepted not for principle, but for Bonnie's satisfaction and self-gratulation—still, among the various expressions of pride, among the things people found satisfaction in doing, were so many worse ones, that Abner could not find much fault with it. When you thought of what it cost her—the yellow-sprigged dress looked nice to him and became her; but Abner dared say that any other female would know at a glance that she made it herself, and there could not be a woman born who enjoyed such glances.

"Ab, please," Bonnie said. "I'm sorry. Let's go on. I'm starved to death. It's probably what's wrong with me."

"There's nothing wrong with you," Abner said.

Touching her chin to turn her face, he kissed her mouth.

At the instant, the air was shattered by a horn blast. Jerking his head up, Abner was in time to see Harry Wurts, grinning from ear to ear. He was driving his new red convertible coupe, an expensive and flashy job. It went by with a glitter and rush. The top was down, and Harry held up and wagged an admonitory finger."

"Hell!" said Abner; for Harry's sense of humor might make it a long time before Abner heard the last of how he had been caught kissing his girl in a parked car—to Harry, a kiss was a kiss, and a girl was a girl, and if you tried to get highfalutin about it, Harry would really go to work on you; which you would either have to take, or be prepared like a couple of school kids to exchange punches in the nose. "Who was that with him?"

"Margaret Coulter, I think," Bonnie said with composure.

"Now, I will have to marry you, I guess," Abner said.

"Not as far as Margaret is concerned."

"What makes you think that?"

"Oh!" said Bonnie. "I wonder!" She began to laugh. "Ab, if you could see yourself," she said. "Is it injured innocence? Darling, did you think I never knew about her, or about Dotty Wellman, or about your girl in Boston?"

"Well, now, I don't remember mentioning them to you," Abner said. Though somewhat embarrassed, he was obliged to smile. "What do little pitchers have, big ears?"

"They have eyes," said Bonnie, "and I could name a couple more, too."

"No. Don't do that," Abner said. Her change in mood bewildered him; but even in his ill-ease, the implication was plain enough, and moving.

"Ab," she said, "I don't mind." Her voice, like the impulsive touch of a hand, was charged with meaning; at once pitying and placating.

"Don't you?"

"Not really. Not much." She stopped. "I don't mind now. But don't think I didn't mind! Oh, how I minded!"

Still more moved, Abner said, "Why, you weren't more than—"

"When Dotty nearly got her eyes scratched out, you mean. She'll never know how close she came. Now, you know something you didn't know before, don't you?"

Abner was not sure that he hadn't always known it; but in a vague general way, the idea deprecated, pushed back in his mind. If you had seen one or more of those fatuous boobs who believed that girls silently and secretly loved them, you took care to be more modest, or at least, to require irrefragable evidence. Given the irrefragable evidence —no doubt, in her life, Bonnie had said untrue things; but Abner had never happened to hear her say one—it was affecting to think back; to see again the slight, adolescently gawkish, yet always attractive young girl, silent in the background, her shy but clear brown eyes big in her undeveloped face.

"Well," he said, "I don't mind either. Not really. Not much."

"You'd better not! Now, hurry up and buy me a drink before I'm sorry I said it."

She had flushed; and feeling the impulse to kiss her again, Abner put his arm around her. Bonnie said, "No; don't maul me!" But she kissed him; short, direct, and vehement.

"And why did you say it?" said Abner.

"I said it because you're such an oaf, you might think I was one of your Dottys or Margarets, and you could ditch me when you got ready. So there!"

"Ah!" said Abner, "you think I thought that, do you?" He started the car. "Well, I'll get an application for a license from Hermann Mapes tomorrow; and he'll tell everyone; and that'll fix you." The car moved faster, the warm air stirring again. "And you might as well have a ring," he added. "For reasons of an official nature, you'll have to have it from Wells'. If the Chamber of Commerce saw one on you that came from the city—"

The thought in his mind had been that old Wells would
do him on the diamond—not that Mr. Wells was dishonest
or over-grasping; but for the reason, too familiar in towns
like Childerstown, that prices were higher than city prices
because there were not so many people to buy. Because Mr.
Wells sold less, he had to charge more; and because he
charged more, he sold less still. There could, of course, be
only one end for Mr. Wells; but until the end came those
who got money from the public payroll were well-advised
to support local enterprises, which, it would be claimed, provided the payroll. Recognizing the expediency, and resigned
to it, Abner abruptly remembered that to him it no longer
applied. If he did not plan to be a candidate for public office,
he was as free as other citizens to make purchases with an
eye to his money's worth, rather than to currying local favor.

"Or rather—" Abner said. But before he told anyone
else, he ought to tell Marty; and before he told Marty he
had still to work out a way of managing his withdrawal so
that it would not upset all Marty's plans. If Jesse picked
another candidate to run in November, Marty could—in fifth
class counties the district attorney had the power to appoint
"not more than two" assistants, if he needed or wanted them
—bring him into the office right away and teach him his
duties by letting him see how the Commonwealth prepared
for and conducted September Sessions. There would probably be a squawk from the county treasurer over having to
pay two assistants, so Abner, as a decent gesture, and to spare
Marty that almost certain wrangle, could offer to serve without pay. The gesture would not be likely to make Marty any
less mad; but it would at least make Abner feel better.

Bonnie said, "I don't think I want a ring, Ab. I mean it.
It's such a waste of money."

"Now, don't worry about that," Abner said, rousing himself. "If I don't—"

He was forced to stop again. If he didn't worry about
money, it was high time he started to! He must have lost

his mind! So he was going to make a splendid gesture and do without his salary, was he? Where, then, did he think money was coming from? He was going to get married; he was going to take over the support of Cousin Mary and her brats—

Abner could not answer. He bothered very little about money; but that was because his wants were simple and his expenses few. When Harry mentioned Paul Bonbright at noon, and what Paul was probably getting, Abner considered it with complete indifference. Perhaps he was even a little proud of his indifference, and a little contemptuous of Harry's uncovered envy. Abner's experience had been that if you applied yourself to your work, the money end of it would more or less take care of itself—unless, like Harry, you had to spend a couple of thousand dollars for a car to knock people's eyes out. Not having the desire for such a car, Abner had always found it easy not to buy one; but getting married was more expensive than any new car. Without going so far as definitely to plan it that way, Abner supposed that he had always assumed that when he came to get married he would have Marty's job, which meant enough more money to make it easy. He could plan not to marry until he could afford to; for it seemed to him that he was beyond the stage of infatuation, of the mental and physical excitements or impatiences that made for marrying in haste.

He hesitated. "We aren't going to be rich," he said. "Maybe you ought to reconsider Mr. Harper's offer." The joke, he saw, was not a success. His impulse, a natural forthrightness, was to tell her how things stood; but that was a job for somebody better with words than he was. He could not think of any way to explain his situation which would not amount to qualifying his proposal, now that she had accepted it.

"Don't tease me," Bonnie said. She spoke with constraint, and the insight of long acquaintance told Abner what the tone meant. She had felt the hesitation, and her spirits fell again. Her feeling for him was strong enough to survive, and even to encompass, what to her must seem his hopeless, his maddening ineptitude. She had made her choice; she had made it with the knowledge that he had none of those gifts of intuition by which her feelings would be conveyed to him and—how wonderful a pleasure, how enchanting a release! —her wish could hardly form before he was doing or saying the thing she longed for. She sadly accepted the fact that he would always manage to disappoint her a little; and could put against it only the poor consolation of knowing that when he did he probably wouldn't mean to.

Abner was so sure that these were her thoughts that he felt like telling her, describing them to her, giving her proof that he was not so dumb as he looked, that he understood perfectly. To comfort her, he would like her to know that he was not, with inept naïveté, showing alarm when he realized that he had committed himself ("Poor Ab!" she was probably thinking, "Poor Ab! But why does he have to let me see it?"). If she only knew, what he was trying not to show was his consternation, a sort of anger and dismay, that marrying her, now that he had made up his mind that he wanted to at once, not sometime in the future, was going to be, through his own act, difficult to manage. Instead of that vaguely counted on increase in salary, he had arranged to lose the too-little he already had.

No explanation offered any way out; and, this time, Abner did remember that when you don't know what to say, you'd better keep still. "I'm sorry," he said to Bonnie; and that was the truth.

Abner turned in at the end of the line of cars parked on the dreary stretch of cinders before the Black Cat, a sprawling frame building meant to simulate a Swiss chalet. Jutting up, a little brighter than the clear evening sky above the roof, a neon sign showed in vermilion outline the figure of a cat playing a violin. Through the tree trunks beyond, sunset colored the still water of the creek.

From the running board of the last car—there were about a dozen, including Harry Wurts' red one—a Negro boy got up. His old chauffeur's cap showed that he was allowed the office of harassing patrons as they left with intimations that he had somehow served them and should be rewarded; but he had other uses. He looked carefully at Abner; and then, with an unconvincing, casual walk, crossed to the side door under the electric sign: *Bar*.

Watching him go, Abner thought, amused, yet somewhat put-out, too, "The tip-off!" Howard Bessie was going to be warned to look out, the assistant district attorney had just arrived. Abner said, "Well, we'll spare Howard some anxiety. We can get you a drink out on the porch just as well."

"What's he anxious about?" Bonnie said.

"You'd have to ask him," Abner said. The pressure of his own anxieties made Howard Bessie's seem of little interest or importance. "Maybe, nothing. On the other hand, he may have something in the bar. I mean, what we describe as gambling devices."

"Those pin ball machines?" Bonnie was making a great effort. She could not feel much interest in the matter, either; but she was doing all she could to act as though nothing had happened.

Abner responded to the effort. He said, "It has been held that those aren't gambling devices, per se. But the customers might be using them to gamble. Then, there are several syndicates that distribute real slot machines. Marty's pretty well cleaned them out; but Fosher's Creek, there, is the county line; and they may have slipped one or two across." He shrugged. "If they have, I don't want to know it. Not to-night."

Bonnie looked at him curiously. "What would you have to do if you did know it?"

"Oh, well, I suppose I'd have to take steps." They went up on the long screened porch over the water and he drew out a chair for her at the table in the corner. "As a matter of fact," he said, "I get pretty tired of having to take steps. What do I care if people want to lose their money? Marty doesn't care either, really. He just doesn't like Howard—"

Through the big room, empty now and shadowed, where, later, they had dancing and the supposedly scandalous floor shows, Howard Bessie himself moved quickly, coming to the wide doors and stepping out on the porch. He nodded to some of the other guests—several couples at tables along the rail—and came right down toward Abner. He was a quiet, sober, round-headed little man neatly dressed in white linen.

"How you, Abner, Miss Drummond," he said, bowing. His full face was grave and polite, but he did not smile, nor speak with any false warmth of cordiality or conviction. Though he doubtless wished that Abner would not come around, a certain saving matter-of-factness, a sort of infinite disillusion about human motives and purposes, often seen in those who cater as a matter of business to the dissipations of the public, made him perfectly reconciled not only to the advisability of being civil, but to the inadvisability of trying to be friendly.

Abner nodded. He had known Howard for a number of years; and, in fact, Howard happened to be either the first, or very close to the first, person who came to consult Abner when Abner began practice. Appropriately enough, Howard's trouble was with the Liquor Control Board, which had discovered a misstatement in Howard's license application. To the question whether he was ever arrested, indicted, or convicted for violation of the Volstead Act when it was in effect, Howard had answered no. He had not realized that they meant, as well as convicted, indicted or arrested. Why

Howard did not understand that they meant what they said was hard to explain; but Abner thought it possible that Howard really didn't. The hitch was that the Board, checking up, had found a case in which Howard was arrested and indicted. It had been nolle prossed; and Howard seemed to think that his release canceled the whole proceeding. Abner explained to him what nolle prossed meant, and told him that even if he had been acquitted, he should have answered yes: a piece of legal advice Abner made no charge for. The next time they met over a matter of law, the Commonwealth was trying to have Quarter Sessions revoke Howard's license; and though they failed on a technicality, Howard could hardly have considered the attempt a friendly one.

Thinking perhaps of this, and of some subsequent brushes, Howard said remotely, his voice tired, "Your order taken yet?" He beckoned a waiter who had followed him through the doors. "Nice lobster? Nice steak? Nice young duckling? Something to drink first? Yes, sir. Dominic, you take good care of Mr. Coates and the lady." He dropped his chin, bowed faintly, and moved away.

When the waiter had gone, Bonnie said, "He's such a funny little man! I don't see what you have against him."

Abner said, "Oh, we call it keeping a disorderly house—"

Steps had been approaching from behind, and now a voice said over Abner's head, "But not, I hope, a bawdy house, Mr. Coates! Perish the thought!"

Abner did not have to turn to know who that was, and exasperation filled him. By not going into the bar he had hoped to avoid (as well as any sight of new slot machines) an encounter with Harry. It seemed to Abner that he had troubles enough.

Harry said, "Hello, Bonnie." He gave her a kindly smirk. He held Margaret Coulter informally by the arm, and Abner was obliged to rise. "Have tire trouble on the way down?" Harry said archly.

"Hello, Bonnie," Margaret said. "Hello, Ab. Don't pay

any attention to him. He's tight." From her tone and appearance it was plain that if anyone were tight, it was she and not Harry.

Harry said, beaming, "You weren't about to asseverate that this establishment is one that encourages idleness, gaming, and misbehavior by dissolute persons contrary to law and subversive of public morals? Well, why don't they start? I'm ready!" Lifting a hand above his head, he brought it down dramatically, pointing over the rail. "From that water there, my love," he said to Margaret Coulter, "was fished by Messrs. Coates, Bunting and their catchpoles the dilapidated cadaver of the late Frederick Zollicoffer. That ought to give your dinner a new taste thrill!"

"Oh, it was not!" said Margaret.

"Indeed, it was! A mere mile or two down. I call on Mr. Coates to bear me out. Zollicoffer is thicker than water."

"Look, Harry," said Abner. "I don't know whether you're tight or not. But don't come out here and talk to me about a case the Commonwealth's prosecuting. I don't care if you are kidding. Everyone can hear you—"

Harry, flushed already with liquor and good humor, flushed deeper, wounded in his own particular way, and tightened his lips. The look on Harry's face reminded Abner suddenly of a falling-out like this in Cambridge and for almost exactly the same reason. He and Harry were leaving Langdell late one spring night, their coats off, their arms full of those thick law school notebooks marked in colored inks. They were worn with work and anxiety; and Harry, by way of relaxation, was baiting Abner.

In the light that fell down from the reading room windows past the great Ionic columns, Abner, losing his temper, stopped short on the steps and answered back. Except for the armful of books, he would probably have punched Harry's jaw. He told Harry what he thought of him, and said it was an opinion everybody else shared; and Harry did not like it. Harry had been only fooling; he hadn't done a thing. Abner's stinging words caught him with his guard down, innocent and defenseless. His sensibilities smarting, the sulky color coming up his cheeks, Harry turned on his heel and left. He did not speak to Abner again for some time.

Though no longer the loud but sensitive boy of those days, Harry had feelings as tender as ever. The change was in his tactics and in the degree of his self-control. Staggering back in ludicrous caricature of a man mortally stricken, Harry clasped his hands to his breast. "Laws-a-mercy!" he cried, mingling a variety of low comedy accents, "I plumb disrecollected you for a spell, Mr. Commonwealth, boss! You all ain't a-going to let that old devil Ethics Committee sell this poor nigger south? I asks your pardon. I craves your grace—get along, gal!" he said to Margaret. "We-uns better make ourselves scarce!"

Abner had colored, too; for those tactics were effective. The imbecile phrases, the grotesque gestures, successfully implied that the grotesque imbecile was really Abner; and that Harry was getting, as best he could, down to Abner's mental level. The attention of everyone on the porch had been attracted; but to Abner, rather than Harry. Harry, openly and blatantly attracting the attention, showed that he did not mind it. The stares of surprise and amusement went to Abner, who offered the always interesting spectacle of a man embarrassed by attention and seeking to avoid it.

Left alone now, Bonnie looked at Abner a moment, about to say something, her expression generously indignant. Abner could guess the degree of confusion he must be showing by the tact with which she checked whatever she had thought of saying, and said instead, "Where do you suppose that waiter got to? I'm starved."

"There he is," said Abner.

His troubled mind, reverting to that long-ago row in front of Langdell hall—there had been others; but for some reason that was hardest to forget—showed him that then, as now, he had really been the one to blame. He misled Harry by his ordinary stolidity or evenness of temper. Harry was right, not wrong, in expecting Abner to take any amount of raillery in good part. Those times Abner lost his temper with Harry in Cambridge had always been times when everything seemed wrong, his efforts vain, his brain no good, his chance of getting through about on a par with the snowball's in hell. To pretend tonight that an improper reference to the Zollicoffer case—Harry had actually said nothing to which he could except. Harry was too good a lawyer to have been about to say anything exceptionable, either—had made him angry, was absurd.

His anger gone, his mind cooled, Abner ate his dinner; but with little appetite. Down at the far end of the porch Harry and Margaret were getting their dinner, too; and from Margaret's constant laughter, it could be guessed that Harry was in fine form. Abner certainly felt no remaining interest in Margaret; and that interest he had once felt he remembered now with discomfort. He winced to remember the bedraggled episodes of an affair in which his part seemed to have been that of an importunate, but scared, inexperienced, and rather nasty schoolboy. Margaret could not have a poorer opinion of him than he had of himself; yet he suffered a sort of chagrin to think that Margaret, if she made comparisons, could make them, as she laughed with Harry, at the expense of poor dull old Abner. Abner, even if he repented it, knew well enough what he had seen in Margaret; but Margaret would be utterly unable to imagine what she had ever seen in Abner.

To change his thought, Abner said, "You know, I like Harry; but he makes me sore sometimes. It's my own fault—"

"I don't like him," Bonnie said. "I never have. He's always showing off. He's a lot like Jared. He did that on purpose—I mean, speaking about the case. The only way he can be funny is by trying to show that anybody who is serious about anything is a fool. I was glad you said that to him! He wanted to show Margaret how smart he was; and he did."

Whether or not Bonnie would really believe that Abner came off best, the loyalty that made her act as if she believed it was grateful to him. He looked at her, feeling the pleasant surprise that comes with the recurring discovery that a woman, as well as always taking, can give; that you may expect to get, as well as a dependent, a confederate, or at least a devoted ally in your contest with the world.

The waiter said, "Mr. Coates, they want you on the telephone, please."

"Who is it?" Abner said, startled; for as far as he knew nobody could have known that he was going to be here; he hadn't even known that he was going to be here himself. If a search had been made, trying different places until he was found, the occasion must be urgent; and with a falling sense of alarm, Abner admitted that it was just what Aunt Myrt might do if something had happened at home.

"I'll have to see," he said, standing up. "Do you mind?"

"No. Of course not," Bonnie said.

There was only one thing that could happen at home. Walking quickly after the waiter, Abner thought of the morning when his father had his first stroke. Judge Coates had fallen in the bathroom, and Abner remembered the muffled sound—a peculiar jarring thud. It was not loud, yet it could not be mistaken for any ordinary or harmless sound. Abner, dressing in his own room, had rushed into the hall, saying loudly, "Father! Father! Was that you?"

It was he, all right.

Judge Coates lay on the tiled floor. His face was a ghastly pallid gray, his cheeks blown out by his slow loud breathing. His eyelids were not quite closed and through the slits he seemed to peer slyly but blindly to the side. His big, awkward, old man's bulk under a flannel nightshirt with faded stripes was limp in a twisted, somehow shrunken mound.

Apparently he had been on the point of shaving, for his pig-skin razor case lay beside him with half a dozen old-fashioned straight razors spilling out of it. Some had fallen open, and even in the shock of the moment Abner remembered think-ing how dangerous they were. It seemed a miracle that the Judge had fallen without cutting himself.

Though Abner had never seen a stroke before, the actuality was so close to what the word meant to the imagination that he recognized it instantly. It seemed to him that he had read somewhere that the head should be lowered—but im-mediately doubt assailed him; it would seem more sensible to raise it. Since he did not know which, he at least knew enough to do nothing. Automatically he gathered up the razors, dumping them with frantic haste into the washbasin. Even in that crowded moment he had time to start when he saw what he had done; for he could imagine his father roar-ing with indignation to see those razors, a pride and joy of his, the finest that could be obtained, and under no cir-cumstances was anybody to touch them, treated like that. Abner in shirt and shorts with one sock on and one off ran downstairs into the cold morning gloom of the hall and seized the telephone. Doctor Mosher answered at last, incredibly calm and mild; and, in spite of Abner's agitated stutterings, in spite of an intelligence he must have found grim (he and the Judge had grown up together and been friends for fifty years), still calm and mild, his voice graver as he went on, and more decisive, but unhasty, "All right, Ab. I'll be there. Now, take it easy. Just get a blanket—"

The horror of the moment—it seemed worse for being in the morning, before breakfast, with the whole day ahead—returned to Abner; but he could never again be so unpre-pared in heart and nerves. The waiter indicated a telephone booth in the hall, a modernistic cubby hole in scarlet enamel and stainless steel and glass to match the decoration, and Abner, bracing himself, stepped into it and took up the re-ceiver with little outward tremor. "Yes?" he said.

The answering voice, he heard with a shock of relief, was Marty's. Strained and irritable, Bunting said, "I had plenty of trouble finding you."

"I'm surprised you did find me," Abner said. "I didn't know you wanted me." In his relief he felt irritable himself. His instant anticipation was that Jesse had spoken to Marty, and Marty could not wait a minute to tell Abner what a fool he was. "What do you want?" he said. "I'm having dinner."

"Yes," said Bunting. "I know. I'm sorry; but this is important."

"Well, what is it?"

"I can't tell you on the phone. I want you to come up as soon as you can. I'm at the office."

"Oh, hell, Marty!" Abner said. "No, I can't come up! Is it something about Jesse?"

"No, it's not about Jesse," Bunting said. "I have some people outside. A constable came to see me at home with a story some people told him. I don't want to mention any names. It involves somebody I don't know much about; but you do, I think. I don't mean any particular friend. I want to try and see if there's any mistake, whether it's true or not, before I let it go to a justice's hearing. There's no warrant out yet, because I told the constable to bring the people to me first. So we've got to work fast—"

"O.K.," said Abner grudgingly. "I'll come."

There could be no arguing with the need to work fast; for, of course, Marty exceeded his powers when he held up a complaint that should go to a J.P. Marty would do such a thing only for the most compelling reasons and it was possible to guess that the business was bad and concerned someone of local importance—Abner tried to think who could come under that heading and yet be better known to him than to Marty. He went out on the porch and said to Bonnie, "I'm sorry, that was Marty. Something's up. I don't know what, but it must be pretty important. He wants to see me right away."

"Oh," said Bonnie. "Well, that's all right, Ab."

"I don't know how long it's going to take. It can't take very long. We can probably go swimming all right. Will you mind waiting? He's at the office, and I'll have to just leave you in the car."

"Well, I'd rather do that than go home," she said. "If you'll let me off at the school, Mr. Rawle left some things he wanted me to see about. I think I've got my key. Yes."

They were twenty minutes in reaching the dark oblong of the high school in the trees at the end of Academy Street. Abner swung up the loop of the drive. "I'd better see you get in," he said.

"Silly," she said, "I've got in plenty of times. I could find my way around there blindfolded."

Abner got out and went across to the side door with her. It was the door by which, thirteen or fourteen years ago, he used himself to enter every morning going to the boys' lockerroom. Through the glass covered with a strong crisscross iron netting a light could be seen burning down the hall. "Someone there?" Abner said.

"I don't know. It's Mr. Field's conference room."

She put the key in the lock and Abner pushed the heavy door open. "I'll see," she said.

Abner walked down the echoing cool passage with her. "The lights are right there by the stairs," she said.

Abner snapped them on. "Smells just the same," he said, sniffing. "What's Sam Field confer about?"

"Oh, mental aptitude, or something."

On the door beyond was a sign that said: *Department of Audio-Visual Education*, and Abner laughed. He said, "We never got any of that in my day."

The room, a small office with filing cases and a series of complicated charts posted on the walls, was empty. "That's funny," Bonnie said. "It looks as if somebody had been here. Maybe he's upstairs."

"Or maybe he's in the washroom. What's that?"

"It's a closet. I think he uses it for a dark room, to develop films."

"Well, maybe the corpse is in it," Abner said, opening the door. "Nope."

"I guess he just forgot to put the light out."

Abner said, "We'll go upstairs and look around, anyway."

"There's no need to, Ab. Mr. Field must have come in for something—"

"Or somebody else. Somebody might know that school was over Saturday, and think he'd just look around. There have been quite a few places broken into during the past month."

"I'm not timid," Bonnie said.

"Just the same, I'll have a look." He went upstairs with her to the principal's office and put the lights on. Bonnie went through to the little room beyond and sat down at her desk. "Ab, open the window for me, will you? It's stifling."

When he had pushed up the broad window, Abner went down the hall, snapping the lights on in the classrooms and in the big auditorium. When he came back he said, "All right. I don't see anyone. Not even Sammy."

"Ab, you've been hours! If they wanted to see you right away—"

"They can keep their shirts on. I'll be back pretty soon."

Outside, walking through the moonlight and tree shadows to his car, Abner remembered that this matter of her job was one thing they had not really settled. A great weariness came over him; for how could he settle that? If Bonnie knew his new circumstances she would certainly not give her job up, she really couldn't—that depressing, distinctive school smell seemed to be still in his nostrils. He drove down to the Childerstown National Bank building. The bank was locked and silent, a light burning behind the plate glass windows over the gleaming multiple knobs and dials of the vault doors. Street light fell on the bronze plaque: *Martin M. Bunting, District Attorney*, affixed to the jamb of the doorway on the left. Abner went through the narrow hall faced with polished stone and ran upstairs.

The door to the district attorney's office was open, and, to Abner's surprise, there was no one in the outer room but Marty. He sat with his coat off at his secretary's desk, by a shaded light, slowly typewriting with two fingers. He looked at Abner, for a moment abstracted or deep in thought. Then he drew a breath and leaned back.

Abner said, "Sorry, Marty. I couldn't get here any sooner." It occurred to him that if the affair had been settled so quickly it could not have been a very important one. "I got held up a minute," he said. "Bonnie wanted to stop at the high school. We thought somebody had been in there; and I thought I'd better look around."

"It's all right," Bunting said. "Got a cigarette?" Abner gave him one, and Bunting added, "I was at the school, among others."

"You were?" said Abner. "There was a light on down in some office Sam Field uses—"

"John must have forgotten it. That's where we went."

"Say, what goes on?" said Abner. He struck a match and held it out, cupped in his hand Bunting bent forward, bringing the cigarette end to it. "Yeah, Field," he said, exhaling smoke. Abner lit a cigarette himself and sat on the edge of the desk. Bunting said, "They left about fifteen minutes ago. I sent him over to Delp's with Bill and John Costigan. He's waiving hearing; but we have to have a J.P.'s transcript."

"What is it?"

Bunting gestured with the cigarette. "Two indictments there," he said. "I'm doing another. Reason I called you was —you knew him at school, or something, didn't you?"

"He was in my class," Abner said.

"I thought maybe you knew him well enough to have a talk with him. But he didn't stand up very long. About ten minutes after I called you he must have seen it wasn't any use."

Abner picked up the not yet folded sheet of the first bill of indictment, his eye skipping down the printed form and filled-in blanks. ". . . at the County aforesaid, and within the jurisdiction of this Court, with force and arms . . . then and there did to the great damage of the said Mary Beach . . ."

"For God's sake!" Abner said.

"There were at least eleven," Bunting said. "The Beach girl told her mother, and so her father went to Bill Ortt. He came around to see me about six o'clock. We've been rounding them up all evening."

"What did Sam say?"

"He said at first that they were making it up. It's true that the Beach girl, and some of the others, don't have a very good reputation. But I guess he picked the ones he thought wouldn't be likely to raise a row—" Bunting shrugged and began to typewrite again.

Taking up the second sheet, Abner read: ". . . did induce Nina Friedman—" "What Friedman? Leon Friedman?"

"Yes. Runs the auto supply store."

Abner read on: ". . . to enter his private office situate in the Childerstown High School, did engage in conversation with her as to sexual matters and did put his hands upon her person during such conversation. . . ."

"There's something else," Bunting said. The ash flew off his cigarette as he waved it and fell on a pile of photographs.

Brushing off the ash, Abner turned them over. "For God's sake!" he repeated. "These some of the school kids?"

"Uh-huh. The blonde one's Mary Beach. I don't think we need to identify them. It seems he told them he was entering photographs in a contest—you know, art; and if he won, they'd be given a screen test, or something. That's how he got them to pose."

"Well, if it got that far, are you sure it stopped?" Abner turned the photographs face down and put them back.

"Pretty sure. Miss Wheeler talked to the girls and she's satisfied that he never did any more than that." Bunting took

232

the sheet out of the typewriter. "Matter of fact, I think there's something wrong with him."

"Now you mention it, it does look a little that way," Abner said, taking up the new sheet. The terms were the same as the last.

"I mean, physically. I'm sending him up to jail tonight. I wanted Doctor Janvier to look him over. The way I think we'll handle it is, we'll arraign him before Irwin upstairs in number two tomorrow morning. He'll waive submission and plead guilty. The three girls will have to testify but no one else except Field. The Judge can sentence him, and we'll have it all polished off quick." He paused. "In a way, it's a break, the other trial. With that going on downstairs, it won't attract much attention. Do you know him so well you don't want to take it?"

"I know him, all right," Abner said. "But, no, not well enough to mind. I feel sorry for him—"

"Well, I would myself, except for those photographs. Or I might, because some of those little floozies aren't too young to ask for all they get. But a man in his position—"

Steps sounded in the hall downstairs. "That's probably Maynard Longstreet," Bunting said. "I asked him to come over so we could work out what the *Examiner* had better say. There's going to be an unholy stink. I think it will finish Rawle."

"I don't see how it's his fault."

"There's plenty of school board politics in it; but anyone would have a right to ask why, as principal, he never checked up on what was going on for six months or more down in Field's office. Hello, Maynard! Come on in. Did you get over to Delp's?"

"I got over," said Maynard Longstreet. His heavy black brows were drawn together, his eyes narrow. "Why, that dirty little son of a bitch!" he said. "Somebody ought to take him and beat the living daylights out of him! Why—"

"Well, we don't want to start any of that," Bunting said.

"You don't, huh?" said Longstreet. "How'd you like it if your two little girls were up there at high school and some teacher did that to them? Why, he ought to be sterilized! What are you going to do to him?"

"Send him to the reformatory."

"Yes, and they'll let him out in a year or two and he'll do it again somewhere. Another thing. How did he get away with it all that time? Doesn't Rawle know what goes on in his school? The board ought to fire him."

Bunting looked at Abner, and then back at Maynard Longstreet. "Come on, Maynard!" he said. "It isn't the first time in history a man gave some girls a going-over. Let's get it down to normal. The thing is, what you'd better print about it."

"What I'd better print about it is the facts. And I'm certainly going to ask in an editorial for Rawle's dismissal and a shake-up in the school board What else?"

If Mr. Rawle were dismissed, or forced to resign, the matter of whether Bonnie kept her job or not was settled. A new principal, a man from outside, would want that job for someone he knew. Abner felt an immediate relief—the callousness of feeling relief over what would be a real disaster for Mr. Rawle was apparent to him; but what he felt, he felt—for, if Bonnie lost her position, she lost the basis for the argument. Abner would have to find a way to make his income meet the expenses; and if he had to, it seemed somehow foregone that he could.

Bunting said, "Print anything you like; but I think it can be phrased so as not to be any juicier than necessary. We don't need a lot of city tabloids on our neck. Will you write it and let me see it?"

"Why should I?" said Longstreet.

Bunting said, "For the damned good reason that you wouldn't have known anything about it until tomorrow if I hadn't been decent enough to tell you. The next time something comes up, do you want to know about it, or do you want to have to find it out?"

"Say, if you think you're doing me any favors—" Maynard Longstreet began, his black eyes blazing higher. At that moment, the telephone rang.

Catching it up, Abner said, "District attorney's office."

"Oh, Ab," said Bonnie. "You aren't through yet, are you?"

"I'm afraid, not quite."

"Well, I think I'll go home."

"How are you going to get there?"

"I'm going to walk, naturally. I do it every day during the winter. I guess I can manage it now."

"Wait a few minutes. I'll come up."

"No, don't. I'm leaving now."

"You sound displeased," Abner said.

"No. I'm not. I'm sorry if I do. Are there other people where they can hear you?"

"Yes. But—"

"I'll call you tomorrow. Please, Ab. Thanks for dinner." She hung up.

Putting the telephone down, Abner saw that at some point Maynard Longstreet had begun to laugh. He proved to be saying: ". . . I don't know what there is about you, Marty, that makes a fellow mad. You're so damned dictatorial, I guess. Didn't you ever hear of the freedom of the press? What do you want to act like God Almighty on wheels for?"

"I know, I know," Bunting said. "That's your job, and nobody can cut in on it. Look, Maynard, I'm sorry if I offended you. This Zollicoffer thing dumped on us was bad enough; and now this mess—why don't you co-operate for once in your life?"

"He's asking me!" Longstreet said to Abner. "All right. Let me have that typewriter. I'll run it off now and you can see it, if you'll shut up for half an hour."

Bunting said, "I'll go out. I want something to eat. I didn't get any dinner."

Maynard Longstreet waved a hand at him. "Beat it," he said. "You, too, Ab. I have to concentrate."

"Better lock the safe," Abner said.

Longstreet had noticed the photographs. "Say!" he said, examining them. "So this is how you spend your spare time! Say!"

"Put those back when you get through with them," Bunting said.

"Say, what are these? That's a nice little number."

"Yes," said Bunting. "That's what Field must have thought when he posed her. Now, put them away before we have you sterilized."

Abner went downstairs with him and out onto the sidewalk in the warm night. Bunting said, "There's nothing to hang around for, Ab, if you want to go. I'll send the file over to you in the morning, if you don't mind taking it. I'm going to see Irwin at quarter of eleven. He was out to dinner." He stood still a moment, looking at Abner. His face, though calm and contained, was tired, his expression absent and worried.

Abner's half-formed idea had been to go along with him and tell him, to get it over, about the interview with Jesse. When Marty did find out it would be hard to explain why Abner hadn't told him when he had a perfectly good opportunity to. Abner did not know whether or not he was excusing his own disinclination, his willingness to put off what was bound to be unpleasant, with the argument that Marty had enough on his mind.

"See you in the morning," Bunting said. He turned and walked down past the dark store fronts toward the lighted windows of the Acme Lunch at the corner.

Abner got into his car and searched for his keys. When he had found them and started the engine, he paused. Bonnie might not have reached home yet; and for an instant he thought of driving over. However, like talking to Marty, it meant a problem in what to say—whether to tell her, since it was likely to concern her, about Field; whether to say nothing. One of the things the business of the law had taught Abner was not to tell all he knew; and the temptation, so urgent to most people, to be the first with news, did not trouble him much any more. He could easily enough say nothing; but tomorrow, when Bonnie, along with everyone else, learned the news, she would think it queer that he hadn't told her.

Abner decided to go to bed. He let in the clutch and the car began to move. At the corner the traffic light held him up. Through the bright window of the lunch room he could see Marty, the only person in the place, sitting at the counter. There was a mug of coffee in front of him and he was talking to Walter Fowler, who was making him a sandwich. Abner remembered that Walter was out on probation. Walter had stolen—that is, taken without the owner's consent—an automobile because he thought he needed it to get married. He had a girl, whose name, somehow absurd and pathetic when you saw her, was Regina; and it had been advisable for Walter to marry her at once. His idea had been that, if he could get a car and take her somewhere out of the state, this could be done inconspicuously. He thought they could then say that they had done it long ago, and Regina's condition would be all in order. Unfortunately, going to pick Regina up, he wrecked the car he had "borrowed"; making one of those miserable situations that seem to illustrate the scriptural principle of taking even that which he hath from him who hath not.

Marty found Walter the job at the lunch room, so Walter could tell the Judge that he had a job; and Walter was given a suspended sentence. That was not to say that Walter's troubles were over. Walter had married his Regina (which Abner was fairly sure Walter didn't want to do); and now he had her and a baby and the payments for the smashed car—all charges on what little he was making as he worked nights at the Acme Lunch. Abner was fairly sure that the courts had not seen the last of Walter, that those slow distracted wits that evolved the original marriage scheme would be driven by circumstance into evolving something equally futile and unfortunate; and when it happened, the fact that the district attorney had been so decent to Walter would be just one more thing against him.

The light changed and Abner let in the clutch again. He swung around the block and back up to Court Street. On the courthouse tower lifted above the trees the moonlight was faint, for the sky had covered over with thin clouds; but the clock face could be seen with the hands at ten o'clock; and at once, slow and harsh, the hour struck through the quiet night. Abner drove on home out Court Street.

Judge Coates had just got to bed. A light was placed so that he could read from a book or magazine leaning on a rack before him, and he sat propped up in the vast old bed; an island of radiance in the dusk of the high-ceilinged, heavily furnished room.

The Judge had called out when he heard Abner's steps on the stairs. When he saw Abner, he said, "Didn't expect you yet. Go swimming?"

Abner said, "Marty turned up a mess, and I had to come back. I've just been over there."

"Anything interesting?"

"It's going to interest people around here. We have three A and B indictments against Sam Field for fooling with school girls—you know him? Those were the Fields over at Mill Spring. Sam went to school with me, and then to the State Teachers College."

"I know. His father was a minister. So is an uncle of his, I think."

"Yes, that's right. I guess it isn't Sam's fault; but that will make it worse."

"What happened?"

Abner told him. "It looks as if Rawle were going to be on a spot," he said. "I don't even know who's on the school board any more—except Mrs. Ballinger, and Doc Mosher."

"Alfred Hobbs. Eleanor Carver—and Jesse."

"Jesse Gearhart?" said Abner. "What's he doing there?"

"Opinions differ," Judge Coates said. "Yes, Jesse has been on the board for years."

"I never knew that!"

"Maybe it never interested you much."

"Is he a friend of Rawle's?"

"Yes, I think so. I think he supported Rawle's appointment. I don't know that they were ever close friends. There's been some opposition to Rawle among the faculty, and I know Doctor Mosher thought they ought to make a change." Judge Coates stirred his body in a frustrated, restless movement and Abner said, "Can I get you something, sir?"

"No, no," he said. "It's just—" He lifted one of a pile of paper tissues beside him and dabbed the corner of his mouth. "It's wearing," he said. He made a deprecatory gesture with his good hand. His expression was half angry, half shamefaced. He said, "I don't like things like that happening! I suppose it's because I'm a sick old man. I don't mean that the way it may sound. Sorry for myself."

Judge Coates' voice was controlled; but the need to control it showed that what he said was only partly true. He *was* sorry for himself; not in the usual easy emotional way of disappointed anticipation, but because he suspected that he made a pitiable spectacle, because something, his state, drove him to say things that he remembered despising other men for saying. He said, "I always used to think that it was cowardly not to face facts—young men are great ones for facing facts! Even when they don't like the facts, there's a kind of tonic in them. Dwelling on how all-wrong the world is may help them enjoy more the feeling, even if they don't know they have it, that they're strong, they're well, they'll live forever, they're all right. But when you get older, you can sympathize a little with the rebellious children."

Looking at Abner, he saw that Abner didn't follow; and he added, "I mean, in the Bible. 'Which say to the seers see not; and to the prophets, prophesy not unto us right things, speak unto us smooth things, prophesy deceits.' " He shook his head. "None of you know the Bible any more. Well, why should you? You don't believe in any of it, do you?"

"I wouldn't go as far as that," Abner said, embarrassed, for there seemed to him little point in discussing religion. "I didn't know you believed in it, much."

"I don't know. Old Senator Perkins used to say there's a little something about a drink of whiskey. Well, there may be something about some of those sweet passages in the Book. Sometimes I feel they may be true, not words."

Abner found himself blushing. "Well, sir," he said, "when I've had your experience— Senator Perkins seems to have been quite a sayer."

"I know," Judge Coates said. "It's speaking unto us smooth things, again. Yes, Perkins was a character. They don't have men like that any more. Everybody's more like everybody else—" He sat brooding; and the thought occurred to Abner that, a generation from now, there was a good chance that certain old men (including himself) would be telling young men that old Judge Philander Coates was a character, that they didn't have men like that any more. He said, "I didn't mean to bother you with the Field business. I don't know why I told you. Just wanted to talk to someone, I guess."

"No, no," Judge Coates said. "I hope you won't do that— not tell me things. I didn't say quite what I meant." He drew a breath. "My brain's injured," he said, "that's the size of it. That's natural. I really wouldn't take my own advice. I wouldn't advise you to."

However reluctant to face facts, apparently he had just succeeded in facing something in his own mind. Abner, though he kept his face quiet, looked at him with distress.

"It hasn't had much effect on my memory," Judge Coates said. "That was a surprise to me. It's the thought process. Think of one thing; and then something else comes up, and I can't keep from going off on that. I can't pull up when it's enough; the ideas push right on in. What I mean is, when I hear something like this high school business, I think like any man; well, that's deplorable. But then I don't stop; it goes on and on. I can only say, it makes the heart heavy. But just not knowing it, wouldn't help matters; it would have to not happen." He laughed shortly and wiped his mouth. "Well, if everybody reformed, I suppose you'd be out of a job."

Abner looked at him thoughtfully. "I'm out of a job anyway," he said. "I'd be glad if you wanted to advise me about that. I don't know how well I advised myself. I told Jesse I wouldn't run in the fall."

Judge Coates reached over to get a cigarette and Abner jumped up. "No," said the Judge. "I ought to do everything I can for myself, Mosher says. Sit down."

Putting the cigarette in his mouth, he got a match lit, showing a certain skill, with one hand. "There," he said, "you couldn't do that. Why, I think maybe you're wise not to run. You've had an experience that ought to be useful to you always; but it isn't very pleasant work. On the other hand, it does keep you in the public eye, and in touch with people. If you have an ambition to go on the bench, that's important. I suppose you haven't. I don't know why you should have. It's an idea that appealed to me—three generations of us. But I'd be dead and gone long before then anyway. What did Jesse say?"

"He said he guessed they could get someone else."

"Seem disappointed?"

"I don't know, really. I know I've never liked him, so I suppose he never liked me." Abner shrugged. "I guess he expected me to say yes. He probably figures that the job

241

pays a pretty good salary, and I wouldn't want to miss that. I could use it, all right; but not if I had to owe it to Jesse."

"Did you tell him that?"

Abner laughed. "Pretty nearly," he said.

"Then, if it hadn't been for how you felt about Jesse, you would have run in the fall?"

"I guess I would. I don't like politicians. I've tried to; but I don't."

Judge Coates said, "If you want to get away from them, you'll have to get away from human society. There wouldn't be any society without them. It's attempted every now and then. Some so-called reform movement made up of people who aren't politicians sometimes wins an election. Either they learn how to be politicians pretty quick, or they don't last. I'm not sure we could do without Jesse."

"I know," said Abner. "There seems to be a certain amount of dirty work that has to be done; and somebody has to do it. But I don't have to be the one."

"I've known Jesse to do things I wouldn't care to do," Judge Coates said, "but I've never observed a human activity in which the practice is the same as the theory. Perhaps the laborer is worthy of his hire."

"I don't know about that," Abner said. "I don't know that he ever did anything that you could call criminal. But if a friend of his gets into trouble, Jesse would like to be able to call up and fix it. Not with me."

"Yes," said Judge Coates. "It's a kind of modern benefit of clergy; rich medicines out of poisonous ingredients, a merciful mitigation of the general law—they don't give you Blackstone any more, I suppose. Well, it's your loss! The proposition is that circumstances do alter cases. If a friend wants to borrow five dollars, most men, if they have it, will give it to him; but most men would refuse a stranger. I don't know that taking circumstances into consideration is necessarily the same as selling justice."

"I don't see why it isn't," Abner said. "It may not be done

for money; but a contract of sale can be a contract of sale on the basis of a valuable consideration, can't it?"

Judge Coates said, "And who determines whether the consideration is valuable? Who accepts the value? It isn't the buyer. When a man indicates to you that he wants something you can supply, you decide whether he can have it or not, and on what terms. It takes two to make a bargain. You know what you get and what you give. You remember the story of the judge who was offered twenty-five thousand dollars for an opinion favorable to the plaintiff. He threw the man out and when his colleagues sympathized with him over the insult he'd been offered, he said to them: 'Gentlemen, I didn't worry about the insult; you can't insult integrity. What worried me was that he was getting too damned close to my price.' Speaking of money, how are you going to be fixed, Ab?"

"I don't know exactly. I guess I'll be all right."

"What did you make last year? I mean, in private practice?"

"I'd have to figure it out," Abner said. He spoke with ill-ease, for that was not true. Arlene Starbuck's bookkeeping system was one she got from a handbook on law office management, and it was meant to order the affairs of a firm of the size and importance of Paul Bonbright's Frazier, Graham, and Rogers. In addition to the ledger, there was a cash journal with twenty-six or seven columns covering two loose leaf pages. When Abner's business was displayed this way the effect often seemed comic to Abner; but Arlene was serious about it; and it did serve its intended purpose of showing at a glance (or at a bookkeeper's glance) where you stood. At the end of the year when Arlene closed the books and solemnly carried over the credit balance into what she called the Undivided Profits Account, Abner knew to a penny what he had made.

His father said, "You don't seem very cheerful about it."

"Been a hard day, I guess," Abner said. "I was examining

that Leming fellow—he was scared of Marty. It takes it out of you."

"Where did you have dinner?"

"Oh, we went down to the Black Cat. It's a road house Howard Bessie's running."

"Have a row with Bonnie?"

"No," Abner said. "What made you think that?"

"People do have rows." Judge Coates pressed out the cigarette. "You have many good qualities, Ab; about as many as anyone I know. But you have some that might be a little exasperating, too. It's a good thing to be steady and level-headed; but the defect of the virtue can make you seem a little remote, or apathetic. Phlegmatic, maybe. Women don't like it."

His father's penetration, when it was directed at other people, had often impressed Abner, so it would be right to assume that when directed on him the points offered would be good. Nevertheless, though a gentle one, it was a criticism not easily brooked. Abner said, "Would they like it any better if I went around trying to act like Harry Wurts? I guess that's what's called mercurial, or something. There are some women who don't like him."

"No. I couldn't say I'd want to see you be like Harry," Judge Coates said. The bagged skin under his jaw quivered a little. "You've been a great satisfaction to me, Ab. Children aren't, as a rule, you know. I've seen enough to realize that I'm very fortunate that way. I ought to let well enough alone." He paused and wiped his mouth.

"When you get to be my age," he said, "you have a feeling, and the vainest feeling in the world, that you'd give a lot to have known some of the things you know now when you were young. You wouldn't have. You wouldn't have listened to them. But that doesn't stop you from wanting to tell younger people about them."

"I'd like to hear them," Abner said. He was tired; but if his father wanted to talk, listening to him was one small

244

thing Abner could do; and it was true that he would like to do it.

"No," said Judge Coates. "It's a form of meddling. And, of course, what seems right and good to me seems that way and is that way because my feelings are different. I value different things. I can give you an example. I sit on the porch there and look out and I've seen not so many less than seventy springs. I was sentient. I had eyes—better ones than I have now. Yet I hardly ever saw anything; all kinds of things I might have been observing and enjoying. I think to myself: Ab's doing just what I used to do. If I could only tell him, so he'd start now, he'd have years of the kind of pleasure I missed. It seems so easy. But, of course, it's impossible because it mixes cause and effect. What I'm really doing is busying my mind; and when the mind's busy you're happy. To say you ought to sit in a chair and look at the garden is absurd. You don't have to."

"Still, I might try it," Abner said.

"No, no. I'm afraid you'll come to it sometime, and you can remember I said it. Same way about Bonnie. I don't want to meddle there, either. You know I'd like to see you marry her. And why? Because she's a remarkable girl. She'd make you a wonderful wife. It takes a lot of experience to judge about such things, and I say to myself: The damned young fool! Like the base Indian, threw a pearl away, richer than all his tribe—"

"Sounds like Shakespeare," Abner said.

"It is Shakespeare! Didn't you ever read Othello? 'And say, besides, that in Aleppo once, where a malignant and a turban'd Turk—' " His formidable voice was weakened and obscured; he mouthed the words loosely: " 'Beat a Venetian and traduc'd the state, I took by the throat the circumcised dog, and smote him—thus . . .' "

"Gosh!" said Abner.

"Yes," said Judge Coates. "Hasn't much to do with the

case, has it? Well, you'll have to do what you want to, Ab."

"If you think I don't appreciate Bonnie, you're wrong, sir," he said.

"Well, I hope you do," the Judge said. "You'd better go to bed. You look tired."

Six

Abner's office was a small white-painted wooden temple behind the Centennial Block. The little pediment with fan-slatted ventilator, the ornate wooden entablature on four Doric columns, faced Derry Street; an alley paved in cobblestones and barred to vehicles by iron posts planted in its entrances on Court and Broad streets. The building stood behind, and belonged to, the Childerstown Savings Bank, whose janitor mowed the strips of lawn around it in summer; and whose steam pipes had been extended to heat it in winter. It had been the office of a Lawyer Coates for more than sixty years.

The peculiar form was due to the fact that it stood originally not behind the bank in the Centennial Block, but as an appendage to the Derry house, a big temple built under the influence of the Greek revival of the 1830s. Abner's grandfather, that Judge Coates who came back from the Civil War and hanged men without loss of appetite, held a mortgage on the Derry place; and after the main house burned, about 1870, he acquired the land and the little building, which had been used as a consulting room and pharmacy by old Doctor Derry. The land was sold to the savings bank when the block was put up in 1876; but Abner's grandfather retained a ninety-nine year lease on the building.

Though not in every respect convenient, changed values made this lease very advantageous. One nuisance: that the rooms had to be heated in winter by Franklin stoves, Abner's father had taken care of with the extension of the steam pipes. Another: that there were no washroom facilities and when Arlene had need of them, it was necessary for her to shut the place up and go over to the bank, Abner planned to do something about that the first time he got a little ahead. This was a change of attitude; for, when Abner began to practice, the old office struck him as absurd and a little embarrassing; and he was resolved to move as soon as possible. He would not have occupied it at all, except that his father seemed to expect him to; and, until Abner made more money, it was of course silly to give up quarters which, after all, did serve his purpose; and which, even with an extra charge for the steam heat, cost him only about a third of what he would have to pay for rooms in a modern building.

Abner's change of attitude began when, as time passed, a number of country people came to him with small businesses because they or their fathers had come to that same office to see Abner's father, or even his grandfather. They did not know where else to go when they needed legal advice. At the other end of the scale of sophistication, a lawyer named Menken, up to consult with Abner about local holdings of an estate that his firm represented, exclaimed with pleasure when he saw the temple. Far from finding the arrangement ridiculous or pitiable, he said that he found it entrancing. By commenting on them, Mr. Menken pointed out details to Abner that Abner had not particularly noticed before—the proportions of the building, the paneling of the rooms, the fine iron work and brass of the Franklin stoves. Abner thought Menken somewhat effeminate in his interests and affected in his speech; but when he was gone, Abner could not help viewing in a new light the things that had been pointed out. Noticing these things, Abner began to see that the visitor was right; that he had something here that he would be foolish to give up.

Sometime during the night, those thin clouds that veiled the moon above the courthouse tower had thickened. When

Abner awoke in the gray morning, he could hear steady rain on the long slate roofs and the gush of water in the spouts. Rain fell straight and quiet from a low misty sky. In the open windows of Abner's bedroom the unstirred air was warm and moist.

At ten minutes of eight Abner put his car in Hollis's Garage, beyond the bank; and, buttoned in a slicker that was too warm, went past the shining iron posts and down the wet cobbles between the windows of the bank building and the blank brick wall of Wister's store. The oblong of clipped grass about his office was a beautiful refreshed green. He went up the worn stone steps and found the door already open. Arlene, in a transparent pink rain cape with a hood that covered her hat, was just putting down the telephone. "Oh, Mr. Coates," she said, "that was Mr. Gearhart. Do you want me to call him back?"

"No," said Abner, "not now. I'm in a jam this morning. I've got a guilty plea at ten o'clock. You just get in?"

"Just this minute. I could have come earlier; but I didn't think—"

"No, that's all right. I was expecting some stuff from Mr. Bunting. I guess I'd better call—"

"There's Mr. Costigan now," Arlene said. "Maybe he has it." She slipped out of her flimsy cape and hung it on a rack in the corner.

John Costigan came up the steps between the pillars and rapped on the frame of the screen door. "Morning, Ab," he said. "'Lo, Arlene. Marty asked me to bring this over. It's the Field stuff. You're going to want me to testify, aren't you?"

"I haven't talked to Marty this morning yet; but I guess you'd better. You made the arrest, didn't you?"

"Yes. Somebody busted into a shop in Milltown again last night. Kids, I think. I'd like to get over there later; but I guess this won't take long. Well, everything's here, Marty said. Oh. The carbon is for the *Examiner;* what he and Maynard wrote up last night. Be seeing you, then."

"Thanks," Abner said. He drew the file folder out of the damp Manila envelope and went into the small room behind where he had his desk. On top of the pile, and the packet of photographs with a plain paper wrapped chastely around them, was a yellow sheet with several typed paragraphs beginning: "Samuel Field, 30, member of the Childerstown High School faculty for the past four years today began serving a [there was a blank] sentence at [another blank]. Field was arraigned this morning in Quarter Sessions before President Judge Horace Irwin who accepted guilty pleas on indictments presented by District Attorney Martin M. Bunting. Two charges were for assault and battery and a third for simple assault. They named the defendant as having made improper advances toward school girls. District Attorney Bunting said the offenses consisted of Field's conduct in summoning girls to his private office and under various pretexts of authority asking them personal questions and caressing them. 'No girl has been violated beyond this extent,' the district attorney reported.

"The Childerstown Board of Education in a special meeting this morning accepted Field's resignation as a member of the high school faculty, where he was listed as a teacher of English, and director of audio-visual education. Field was placed under arrest last night by County Detective John Costigan and taken before Justice of the Peace Ralph Emerson Delp. Field pleaded guilty to the three specific charges based on complaints signed by parents of the girls involved and waived submission of his case to the grand jury. He was held in Childerstown jail overnight and brought before Judge Irwin by Assistant District Attorney Abner Coates at ten A.M. this morning"—underneath had been scrawled in Maynard Longstreet's large hand: *to kom.*

"Mr. Coates," Arlene said, her forefinger to her lip,

poised in the door. "That Blessington stuff. We'll just have to—"

"Yes," said Abner. "We will. Let's have it. And take this," he said, extending the sheet. "You might as well know about it now. That's the start of a story going in the *Examiner* today."

The telephone rang. "I'm not in unless it's Mr. Bunting," Abner said.

"One moment, please," Arlene said. She put her hand over the mouthpiece. "It's Mr. Gearhart again," she said.

"I don't want to talk to him."

"Well, it's really Hazel Finch, Mr. Coates. She mentioned she just saw you come in from their window—" Twisting her mouth up, Arlene paused significantly. "Had I better say you're out?"

"No," said Abner. "Switch it on to this phone." He dropped into the carved swivel chair covered with cracked leather that had belonged to his grandfather, tilted back, and put his feet on the desk. With the telephone balanced on his chest, he said, "Hello."

"Hello, Abner," Jesse said gravely. "Good morning. Marty tells me you're taking the Field case this morning."

"Yes," said Abner.

"Well, Ab, the board is having a special meeting later. I thought I'd better see the papers in the case. Marty says you have them. If I came over right away, could you let me see them before you go to court?"

Abner closed his mouth tight. Opening it, he said, "They're a public record, Jesse. When they're filed, anybody can see them. But while they're in my custody, it isn't up to me to show them to anyone. Marty will give out as much as he thinks ought to be given out. He knows much more about it than I do, anyway."

Jesse said, "That's kind of foolish, Ab. Marty would have no objection to my seeing them."

Abner said, "If he wants them for anything, he can send

for them; and what he does with them then is up to him. I'm sorry, Jesse; but that's how it is. I—"

But Jesse had hung up. Abner hung up himself, took his feet off the desk, and began to turn over some letters. He had looked at several before he realized that he was not taking in what he read.

There was a tap on the door, and Arlene carried in the yellow sheet and put it down beside him. "Oh, isn't that awful!" she said, coloring. "I don't see how he could do it! I mean, with girls he was teaching—"

"But otherwise you think it would be all right," Abner said.

"No, I don't," she said, coloring more and laughing, "but it wouldn't be so bad."

That was about the size of it, Abner reflected; and as to how Sam Field could do it, how he dared to do it, you had to conclude that the repeated arguments of desire somehow vacated common sense. Abner could remember one or two cases of assault by homosexuals, in which the defendant, though not unaware of the danger, nor careless of it; and not deranged, nor giving way to any impulse that he could not govern when he chose, took the risk of accosting complete strangers, or even the boys who lived next door. As far as Abner could determine it was not audacity nor deliberate recklessness, but just poor judgment. The accoster had convinced himself that he saw signs of his own bent in the stranger; or that the boys, because he was nice to them and gave them little presents, would never tell on him. In Sam Field's case, success with some girls and their silence in a few nervous preliminary ventures would be taken by Sam as proof that he was reasonably safe. Moreover, he probably imagined (like many people without experience in such matters) that as long as he didn't go too far, he could easily deny everything. He had never faced practiced investigators like Bunting and John Costigan. He did not realize that his own nerves, strained by the sudden awful danger and shaking with consciousness of guilt, would betray him. Until this mental anguish was actually suffered, he had no way of knowing how soon (hadn't Marty said about ten minutes?) it would break him down. You needed hard experience, the complete knowledge of the police system enjoyed by men like Leming and Howell to be able to stand your ground and lie with any hope of success.

The telephone rang again.

Abner looked at it a moment without taking it up. He knew that if Jesse went to Marty about the papers, Marty would never refuse him. Jesse's position on the school board would make his interest legitimate enough for Marty. Since this was so, Abner could see that Jesse had been right; his own refusal was foolish. In honesty, Abner had to admit that spite more than duty made him refuse. Ashamed of himself, and yet not repentant, he lifted the receiver.

The mild, high, quick voice was Judge Irwin's. "Ab," he said, "if I'm correct in understanding that you will be the one to take the Commonwealth's case before me this morning, I wanted to ask you to see me first. I'll be in chambers. There are one or two details I think it would be wise to settle."

"Yes, sir," Abner said. "About what time?"

"Well, quarter to ten ought to be time enough, if that's convenient."

"Yes, sir."

"I understand the defendant has no counsel. I don't suppose it is necessary; but I would like you to make sure that he knows that he is free to have counsel if he wishes."

"I'll call the district attorney."

"Yes. Do. Since the matter seriously affects defendant's reputation, he ought perhaps to have advice about—well, character witnesses, say."

"Oh, Lord!" thought Abner. "The impression I got, Judge," he said, "was that he considered it to his own advantage to get it over as quickly as possible. Unless you feel that it would be a help to you in determining the sentence."

"No. It seems fairly clear—I mean, of course, what has been told me seems clear. I would not come to any definite conclusion until I had heard the evidence. As you know, I have a certain scruple about these more or less summary processes—well, I won't detain you now. I'll expect you at quarter to ten."

The line hummed in Abner's ear, and he broke the connection, held it a moment, and said, "Four two, four two."

Theda Heidweiler, Bunting's secretary, said, answering, "District attorney's office. Oh, hello, Ab. Yes, he is. Did you get those papers from Mr. Costigan?" She called him Ab, when she addressed him, just as she called John Costigan, John; but, by the etiquette of local business usage, to any third person they were Mr. Costigan and Mr. Coates. Speaking to Bunting, she said, "It's Mr. Coates, Mr. Bunting."

Abner said, "Marty, I got the stuff all·right. Judge Irwin asked me to come up and see him first. He wanted me to ask you to be sure that Field knows he can have counsel if he wants."

"He knows. I've just had a talk with him. His uncle, and his sister and her husband will be there, by the way. Do you know them?"

"I know Beatrice. Married a man named Wright, didn't she?"

"Yes. That's it. The uncle is a minister. Won't make it any easier; but we can't keep them out; and, as a matter of fact, it seemed to me decent of them to want to stand by. They're seeing him now. Warren Lyall will bring him up to number two at ten o'clock. When you get through, come right down. I want to put on Smalley; and then Lieutenant Dunglison and Mr. Kinsolving."

"Anything I can do now?"

"No. Mr. Kinsolving's here. I think all you need to do upstairs is put on Costigan and the three girls. Oh. Don't let anything come out about the photographs. The Judge has seen them. I spoke to the girls and told them not to mention that unless directly questioned. So don't question them. There are some newspaper men from town around—they'll be downstairs; but I don't want them to get wind of anything."

"Did Jesse call you?"

"No. Why?"

"He wanted to see the papers."

"Well, he can. He'll probably be there. I forgot. The board's meeting to act on Field's resignation. Mrs. Ballinger told me she was asking Jesse to attend and get the facts for them. All right, Ab. See you later."

"Mr. Coates," Arlene said, tapping on the open door. "You aren't going to forget the Blessington—"

"No," said Abner, looking at the immense old banjo clock between the window moldings. The brass pendulum, as big as a dinner plate, depended on four gleaming rods, winked majestically back and forth. "Is that right?" he said. "Well, let's have it—"

The telephone rang.

"Unless it's Mr. Bunting again, tell them I've gone up to court," Abner said.

At the phone in the outer room, Arlene said, "I'm so sorry; he's on his way to court. Could he reach you anywhere later? I could get a message to him. Yes."

Coming in with the Blessington folder, she said, "That was Janet Drummond, Mr. Coates."

"Did she say where she'd be?"

"She said she had to go over to school." Arlene spoke primly; and Abner could guess that she was thinking that when you practiced to deceive, even through your secretary, any unwished-for results served you right. "Everything is here. Yes. There's Senator Little's last letter; and the one from Mr. Fuller—" She laid it before him on the desk and went out.

Abner looked at the folder with distaste. Last night, when he said to his father that there was a certain amount of dirty

255

work that had to be done, but he did not have to do it, he was perhaps speaking too confidently. Abner could say in his own defense that he had refused cases—he remembered specifically a man who wanted to plead the statute of limitations against a debt. The plea was undoubtedly good; but the man had the money to pay if he wanted to, and Abner didn't like his attitude and told him he would have nothing to do with the case. It was not always as easy as that.

Abner had never known Herbert Blessington, a copy of whose last will and testament was among the papers under his hand, personally; but Abner felt as if he knew him, for twenty years ago Blessington owned an ice cream plant in Childerstown, and Abner could remember very well the red and white signs standing in front of most drug stores and confectionery parlors. They were lettered: "Blessington's Dairy-Made Ice Cream. A Treat to Eat"; and certainly he used to find it so. The pleasure and promise associated with the name made him feel as though he were litigating the last will and testament of Santa Claus.

Like Santa Claus, old Blessington meant to use his position as a gift-giver to reward those who were good and to punish, by leaving them nothing, those he considered bad. In life Herbert Blessington had often been described as an eccentric; a short way of saying that he was a stubborn, vindictive, selfish, and unreasonable old bastard. He had never married, and his heirs were four sisters. Each of them had at one time or another served as his housekeeper, the service ending in a violent quarrel; so that at the time of his death, Herbert Blessington was not speaking to three of them; and to the fourth, who was then caring for him, he spoke as little as he could. Probably he would have quarreled with her as soon as he got better, if he had got better.

However, in the legal meaning, Herbert Blessington was of sound mind; and the will, drawn up by Bill Fuller, the Childerstown Trust Company's attorney, was, naturally, in order. It provided that the estate be held in trust for the fourth sister, Elvira, on condition that she never live with the others, and never make them any gifts. That was the old man expressing his own malicious intent; but, next, Bill Fuller had plainly taken a hand, and told Herbert Blessington that he was running a legal risk; for a clause followed providing that, in event of the court holding the condition invalid, his estate was to go to Peck College, a small denominational school that Abner, for one, had never heard of.

Abner heard about Peck College, and also about Blessington's death and his will for the first time, when he got a letter from former Senator Enoch Little, a friend of Abner's father. The Senator wrote that it would give him great pleasure to retain his old friend's son in a matter which interested him as Chairman of the Board of Trustees of his former college. The trustees had been notified by Mr. Fuller that they were mentioned in a will about to be offered for probate, a copy of which the Senator was enclosing for Abner's consideration. In the Senator's opinion, the condition of the first bequest was clearly one in terrorem; and ought to be held contra bonos mores, and so void; bringing the alternative into effect, and giving the money to Peck College. What was Abner's opinion?

Senator Little, besides being his father's friend, was a man of importance with a long listing in the Directory of Directors. Abner looked up the point about conditions in terrorem in Corpus Juris; and though he discovered there that a condition providing that a wife's sister should not reside with or dwell in the house or place of residence of the wife had been held good, he thought that Blessington's provision about gifts would not be good, as involving or tending to encourage the violation of the duty which one member of a family owes another. At least, it would make a moot point on which the Supreme Court might be asked to rule. Arguing before the Supreme Court was always to the advantage of a young lawyer. Abner wrote the Senator that he was entering an appearance with the Register and would be happy to represent the Trustees. He was, in fact, pleased; and when he showed his father Senator Little's letter, it was plain that Judge Coates was even more pleased.

Abner went over to see Bill Fuller. Bill, a short fat man with a few strands of gray hair on his square head, was an old hand at such matters, and didn't mind being frank. He said that Blessington was a louse if ever there was one; that the sisters, who had done everything they could for him, were poor as dirt and desperately needed the money; and, of course, it was to the Trust Company's interest to maintain the original bequest. He said, "Ab, I wish I'd let the old fool alone. In equity, I don't have to tell you, if the condition is void, the bequest's still good. Elvira would get the money and go right ahead and provide for her sisters; and that's the way it ought to be. They're old ladies, and they need that money. Two of them never married—Elvira, and what's her name, Julia. Thing was, he wouldn't let them; they had to work for him. One of the others is a widow; and the other has a husband who's an invalid, or something. I don't know what they live on."

Bill got redder, incensed by the picture; and perhaps also by a recollected disregard of his admonitions. "Well, sir," he said, "when Herb told me what he was planning to do, I had a good mind to let him. Then I said to myself, 'Now, Bill, my friend,' I said, 'evil communications are kind of corrupting you! This rat in pants here's come for legal advice; and to the best of your knowledge you've got to give it to him straight.' I said, 'Herb, you don't want that condition. The court would throw it out, ten to one.' He says, 'And what then?' I said, I had to, 'Elvira gets it unconditionally.' That brought him up. He says, 'Not if I know it!' He used to do a lot of praying (and, boy, he needed it!) with some Christer who went to this jerkwater college. Well, I did my

duty, Ab; though it damn near killed me. If you file exceptions to our account as executors, I'll fight you, of course;
but I'm afraid you're going to win."

Abner said, "From what you tell me, Bill, I don't like it.
I never knew anything about Mr. Blessington except he
used to make swell ice cream. But there's this friend of
father's who asked me if I'd take it. Withdrawing would
be—"

Bill said, "Hell, Ab, if it wasn't you, it'd be someone else!
Go to it. The public policy point needs a ruling anyway. Make
it clear just how far you can go with a condition subsequent.
I know you can't require a person not to marry, that is, if
the person hasn't been married; and I know you can't require a change of religion. Those are void as against public
policy. Well, we'll see what the Orphans Court thinks. Are
you willing to submit on briefs?"

"Sure," said Abner.

Submitting on briefs suited him better than having to
stand up and argue; probably before Judge Irwin, who had
a sharp eye for actual as well as legal equity. The cause Abner
was representing might not offend right and justice; but it
did do a certain violence to one's sense of fairness or human
decency. Abner sat for some time looking out at the heavy
fall of rain on the brick backs of the bank and the Gearhart
Building beyond it. He saw then that it was twenty minutes
of ten; so he quickly signed in the spaces awaiting his signature, brought the folder out to Arlene, and said, while he put
on his hat and raincoat, "All right. Shoot it in."

Entering the courthouse by the door under the passage
to the jail, Abner found the gloomy, damp-smelling back
hall already stirring with people. Nick Dowdy, who had
been leaning against the radiator with his cigar, shuffled up

to him and murmured, "Ab, two fellows there; reporters. Asked to see you or Marty. You want—"

"Not now. I have to see the Judge."

Around the bend of the hall, the door to the courtroom was open. Malcolm Levering with little pulls and pushes was aligning the jury's chairs neatly. Abner opened the door of the Attorneys Room. It was hazed with tobacco smoke. Old John Clark and George Stacey and Mark Irwin sat with sections of the morning paper; but they were not reading, for Harry Wurts standing against the fireplace, bright and clean-shaven, was saying, ". . . at the age of fifteen she was ruined by a traveling salesman. 'What do you mean, ruined?' says Mike. 'Put the boots to her last night, and she worked swell.' "

John Clark's dignified "Heh, heh" rang out. George and Mark laughed; and Mark said, "Reminds me of the one about—"

Harry said, "Well, well, greetings, Mr. Commonwealth! How are all the little Commonwealths this morning? None the worse for their harrowing experience yesterday, I trust?"

"Nuts to you," Abner said, hanging up his coat and hat. "I have to see the Judge—"

"Now, wait, wait!" said Harry. "What's all this about that Field, Sam Field, over at school? Hey, Mark, don't let him out! We have to get to the bottom of it."

"Sounds like you could tell me," Abner said. "What?"

"Mark, here, says that Marty was over to see his father last night."

"I wasn't there."

"Rumor hath it that a couple of high school girls were suddenly taken enceinte—means, ungirdled, George—and that—"

"Well, that's definitely not true," Abner said, "so you'd better get a new Rumorer. Who told you about it?"

"Don't you wish you knew?" said Harry.

"Not much," Abner said. "So long." He went out into

the hall and made his way past the loitering groups to the door of Judge Irwin's chambers.

The inner room, where Judge Irwin sat, corresponded in shape and position to the Attorneys Room on the other side. It had the same Gothic fireplace and ogee-arched door-frames to the courtroom, to the hall, to the lavatory in the corner, and to the law library. Here the two windows were on the sunny side of the building and they had been equipped with awnings, now dank and taut with rain. The darkness of the day and the lowered awnings made it necessary for the lights, in a bowl of white china hanging on bronze chains, to be on. In this wan mingling of daylight and electric light, Judge Irwin, slight and neat, wearing a suit of blue serge, a stiff linen collar, and black knitted tie with a pearl pin in it, sat restlessly looking at the latest paper-bound supplement to the *Atlantic Reporter*.

Seeing Abner in the door beyond, Judge Irwin took off his glasses. "Well," he said, "it's a wet morning. Come in, Ab." Joining his long-boned hands, he wrung them together gently. His acute, anxious gaze fixed itself on Abner. With a little preparatory grimace showing discomfort or distaste, he said, nodding at the folder in Abner's hand, "This is a repellent thing; and it's for that reason that I think we ought to be careful to see that it's kept impersonal. It is natural to feel an indignation; but we should not be biased into forgetting that the offense was not worse than it was, if I may put it that way."

Taking up his glasses, Judge Irwin produced a fresh handkerchief and began to polish the lenses. He said with active distress, "I do not mean to minimize the element of betrayal of trust. We have a right to expect that a man will be alive to his duty and responsibility; and when he goes clean contrary to them, when, instead of helping those in his charge to self-control and the formation of wise and wholesome habits, he sets them an example of license, and introduces them to, or at least, assists them in, debasing practices, the offense is heinous." He cleared his throat and put the glasses carefully in their case.

"Doctor Janvier came in earlier," he said, "and I had a talk with him. He doesn't find any outright abnormalities in the defendant; but he thinks that psychologically he is not quite normal—whatever that may be. I mean, I have, as you must have, often wondered what is normal; and who is. I think we all recognize in ourselves occasional impulses or ideas which, if put in practice or disclosed to the world, would cast the gravest doubts on our own normality. In short, what is abnormal is not perhaps the impulse, whatever it may be; but the giving-way to it, when it is one that most men's reason, or conscience, or even mere fear of the police, restrains. No man can be excused from conforming to the requirements of the social order; and it is right to penalize him when he fails to conform; but I think we should bear in mind that what is none to us, may be to him a great temptation. I don't know whether I make myself clear?"

"Yes, you do, Judge," Abner said. When Irwin went into one of his monologues, sign always that he was greatly upset, he talked less to the person he addressed than to himself. With his great resources of knowledge and experience he assayed new explanations of the inexplicable; patiently, unwilling to despair, he argued the world around him back to some degree of reason.

"Then, I think we can go up," Judge Irwin said.

The lavatory door opened and Judge Vredenburgh came out. "Morning, Abner," he said. He took his robe from the hook in the corner and thrust his arms through the wide silk sleeves. His full face was drawn down a little around the firm mouth, the second chin just showing solidly above his collar. His blue eyes were shrewd and thoughtful. "Horace," he said, "I was racking my brain about that Field boy. Ask Mat Rhea, when he has time, to go through the docket around 1880. I think you'll find that Field's grandfather had some trouble in connection with molesting girls. His mother's father, that was. I think the name was Ireland, or Irish."

Judge Irwin bit his lip. "That would be a curious coincidence," he said. "I don't know that we should consider it germane to—visit the sins of the fathers upon the children." He grimaced.

Judge Vredenburgh said, "I understand there's a respectable precedent for doing that; but I'm not urging it. I just thought it might interest you. Afraid it's going to be a bad thing for Oliver Rawle."

"Yes. Jesse Gearhart called me about it, though; and I think Oliver will have some support on the board."

"Well, I must go in and get on with this," Judge Vredenburgh said. "I hope we can finish today. I don't think there's much doubt about what the jury will find. Those men ought to be electrocuted; and I'm only sorry we'll have to stall around with an appeal. What with motions in arrest of judgment, and for a new trial, it may be a month before we can even sentence them."

"If it were my life," Judge Irwin said, "I don't know that I would regard the delay as inordinate." He arose and got his robe from the other hook. "One must put one's self in the other person's place." He smiled, took up two green bound volumes of statutes and a yellow pad.

"Yes," said Judge Vredenburgh, "and let them put themselves in this Zolly, this Frederick Zollicoffer's place. They didn't wait around while someone like Harry Wurts filed motions and printed records and took appeals."

Judge Irwin smiled again. "I'll say this, Tom. I have heard nothing about them to make me think that they are persons on whose conduct we should model our own. I may come down for a little while later."

"Wish you would," Judge Vredenburgh said. He opened the courtroom door, and Abner could see, sidelong, the cavernous gloom, the partly filled benches rising to the gray windows. Nick Dowdy's mallet hit the block; and with a

263

ripple and stir everyone stood up as the door softly closed. High in the haze of rain above the roof, the tower clock began to bang out ten.

The number two courtroom upstairs measured about twenty by thirty feet. Half this space was taken by the jury box—three rows of empty chairs ascending on shallow steps. The bench, witness stand, and railed clerk's desk formed a small unit at the end. To get to it, one had to move, with little room to spare, past counsels' tables; like the jury box, too big for the room. At the back, next to the door, were two long benches, each accommodating a dozen people. Bunting had managed to keep the affair this morning so quiet that the benches were not filled when Abner came in with Judge Irwin. Sam Field and Warren Lyall, the deputy sheriff, sat at the end of the first table. Behind them sat Sam Field's uncle, the minister; and Beatrice Wright (Abner knew her to speak to, but no more) and her husband, a beefy, solemn-looking young man.

Judge Irwin went briskly past to the bench, and Abner, following him, laid his folder on the first table. Judge Irwin said good morning to Maynard Longstreet, who had made himself at home at one side of the clerk's desk; but there was no clerk. The Judge said, "Where is Mr. Bosenbury? Wasn't he told?"

Everitt Weitzel, who had been whispering to Norman Creveling, broke off and said, "I'll see, sir. He knows," and limped out the door. "Well, we won't stand on formality," Judge Irwin said. "The court of Quarter Sessions of the Peace is now open. You may proceed, Mr. Coates."

Abner slipped out the three bills of indictment. "Samuel Pierce Field?" he said.

The girls and their parents were in the second bench; and beyond them, in the corner, sat Adelaide Maurer looking at her pencils. The door opened, and Theodore Bosenbury, the deputy clerk of Quarter Sessions, a stout aging man with a white mustache, entered in a hurry. John Costigan, who followed him, strolled up and sat down at Abner's table. The door opened again and admitted Jesse Gearhart, carrying a wet umbrella. He glanced around, tiptoed past the minister and the Wrights, and seated himself at the far end of the front bench.

When his name was called, Field had arisen, and Abner walked over to him. Field looked haggard and ill. Beside him, Warren Lyall cast his eyes down, examining his own muscular hands with a decorous professional indifference. He was the instrument of the law, with his duty to do, which was to have ready the body of his (or Hugh Erskine's) prisoner. Warren did not let the rest of it concern him; partly because everything that could be said or done was now an old story to him; and partly because an impersonal, disinterested manner saved trouble. A prisoner could not help seeing that to argue with disinterestedness would be absurd, and to appeal to impersonality, useless.

"Sam," said Abner as gently as he could, "I have here indictments charging you with assault and battery on Mary Beach, Nina Friedman, and—er—Helen Hartshorn. How do you plead to them, guilty or not guilty?"

"Guilty," said Field in a very low voice.

"All right; if you'll just sit down, please."

Turning, Abner said, "I'll call John Costigan, your Honor." Bending over his own table, Abner took a pen and began to endorse the pleas on the back of the three bills. Theodore Bosenbury said, "John Costigan sworn," closed his Bible and sat down under the bench. "Mr. Costigan," Abner said, still writing, "what is your occupation?"

"County detective."

"And do you know the defendant, Samuel Field?"

"Yes, sir, I do."

"Well, will you just tell us what part you played in this case?"

"Yes, sir. Last evening at"—he looked at his notebook—"six-forty-five o'clock I received a call—"

Jesse Gearhart, down in the corner of the front row, and half hidden from Abner by the empty chairs of the jury box, held his chin in his hand, leaning forward slightly. His pallid immobile face seemed even tireder than last night, as though sleep did not rest him. Abner looked on to the girls and their parents. Mary Beach he recognized at once from the photographs. The girl seated between Leon Friedman and the dark woman was obviously Nina. The other, the Hartshorn girl, it seemed to Abner he had seen somewhere, though without knowing her name. Her father, next to her, was, by his appearance, a farmer. He had a strong, blunt, determined face. His little worn anxious wife in a shabby hat sat on the other side. Abner's gaze encountered Adelaide Maurer's, and she lifted one eyebrow and smiled faintly.

To Costigan, Abner said, "And after that you were present at the hearing at the justice of the peace's office?"

"Yes, sir."

"All right. I think that's all. Unless your Honor has some questions?"

"I don't think that Mr. Costigan explained what the purpose of the search in Mr. Field's office at the school was."

"Why, we—" Costigan began.

"I think, sir," Abner interposed, "it was thought that some evidence of Mr. Field's activities might be found."

"Oh," said Judge Irwin. "Yes. Yes. That will be all, Mr. Costigan."

"Mary Beach," said Abner. "Will you take the stand, please?"

She came down with composure, perhaps to be expected in a girl who had made no objection, or none that wasn't eventually overcome, to posing as Sam directed. She was a hefty girl, bold-faced but pretty in a thick blonde way, and well-made—Abner could see Maynard Longstreet looking her up and down as she pressed her hand on Mr. Bosenbury's Bible. She went up on the witness stand with a little self-possessed flick of her skirt, and sat down, swinging one leg over the other.

"How old are you, Mary?" Abner said.

"I'm sixteen."

"Now, Mary, you testified before Squire Delp last night that on the afternoon of March fifteenth or sixteenth, last, Mr. Field requested you to report to his office for a conference. I want you to tell his Honor, Judge Irwin, in your own words what took place there after you had reported."

"Well," she said, lifting her shoulders a little, "he began by asking things about my work; and then he said he would have to ask me some personal questions, and I must not mind answering them, because it was just like talking to a doctor—" She paused and said to Judge Irwin, "Do I have to say everything he asked me?"

"No," said Judge Irwin. "That will probably not be necessary, if you will just indicate the general nature."

"About, well, whether I was, well, mature or not—"

In spite of her mannerisms, she was a good witness; better, probably, than if she had been hampered by maidenly innocence. Abner recognized the type. A girl who had her reputation was almost always either an outright moron, or, like Mary Beach, entirely adult in her point of view—much more than a match for boys her own age; and often no less than a match for men as much older as Sam Field. Her testimony seemed to Abner straight and plausible; but of course she didn't, and had no reason to want to, and perhaps anyway couldn't, report along with what he said and she said, her by-play of look and tone. She did not say, as probably the case was, that at previous conferences her precocious senses had apprised her of the teacher's involuntary interest in her; and for the fun of it, and because she enjoyed her power, and because she was experienced enough not to be afraid, she

267

kept signaling little invitations, making them, if Sam pretended to ignore them (as he very likely did at first) bolder each time and more alluring.

Abner could see that actually Mary Beach might be to blame for the whole business—the dates of the other charges were all later. She had excited his imagination, and shown him how easy it was, and he had profited by her instructions. Abner looked at Sam a moment, wondering if by any chance Sam realized this—the fact, so well known to the district attorney's office, that, unless the man were insane, or very drunk, the woman was always to blame for what happened to her. She could end it any time by an honestly meant flat refusal.

Abner said, "On these, or other occasions, Mr. Field never went further than that, did he? I mean, just putting his hands on you—" But his indirection, he saw, was ridiculous. "In short, he never at any time had, or attempted to have, sexual intercourse with you, did he?"

"No, he never did."

"Your Honor? That's all, then, Mary. You may step down. Nina Friedman, please."

The Reverend Mr. Field, looking sadly at his nephew's back, shifted and swallowed, like a man who has borne up in a period of prolonged strain, and at last reaches the end; only to find that he is not through, for another one, a fresh one just like it, awaits him.

Nina Friedman came down and faced Mr. Bosenbury. She was much slighter and looked much younger than Mary Beach; but she, too, answered that she was sixteen. On the witness stand Nina was tense and jerky, her smooth head and small warm colored face in ceaseless movement while she looked at her finger nails, sidelong at the ceiling, out the window into the dripping green summits of the trees. At each question of Abner's, she went through a high-strung pantomime—obedient attention, quick comprehension, careful reflection, ready response. Invited to tell what had happened

268

to her in her own words, she began with vivacity, then stumbled and went scarlet at her own words. Her eyes filled with tears, and she gave a light laugh. She said, "He never did any more than that. He really didn't—"

To accept Mary Beach's standing invitation was one thing; but to fool with a kid like this—Sam ought to have better sense! Abner exchanged a glance with Judge Irwin and checked her. He said, "Thank you. That will be all, Nina. Helen Hartshorn."

Mr. Hartshorn turned to his daughter and said audibly, "Go on up there!"

By the note of brusque authority, Abner could guess that Mr. Hartshorn was an old-fashioned disciplinarian. He expected justice to be done and Field to be punished; but that was not his only concern. One of his duties, and he was the man to do it, was to see that his daughter behaved herself. Common sense must have taught him that truth about where the blame lay that the district attorney's office knew so well. Once Mr. Hartshorn was certain that Helen had not been forced to allow the familiarities by superior strength or fear of injuries, he probably came to the rough and ready conclusion that the teacher wasn't the only one who needed correction. Abner suspected that Helen, when she got home last night, had been given a good licking. She was cowed and mournful, and when she sat down in the witness chair, she did it with such care that Abner was obliged to bite his lip.

"How old are you, Helen?" he said.

"Fifteen."

"And you're a student at Childerstown High School?"

"I was. My father says I can't go back."

Abner could see a change in Jesse Gearhart's expression. Mr. Hartshorn might be—he looked as if he would be—a member of his township sending board, the body that arranged for sending children in to the central high school. It was easy to guess that he was going to demand changes— Mr. Rawle's head; and if he felt that way, other men like him on other sending boards were bound to feel the same. Jesse was going to have bad news for the meeting.

"Well, that's too bad," Abner said, "but—"

Mr. Hartshorn stood up and said, "You needn't be worrying your head about things too bad, Mr. Coates. We're looking into this school business; and it's going to be too bad for some people I could name in Childerstown, if that is what you mean. Yes, I—"

"Mr. Hartshorn!" said Judge Irwin.

"Things haven't been going right here, and—"

Judge Irwin had no gavel, but he rapped his knuckles violently on the desk. A delicate pink flush came up his cheeks and he said, "If you do not sit down at once and be quiet, I shall hold you in contempt! This is a court of law, Mr. Hartshorn, not a public forum."

Reddening, Mr. Hartshorn sat down. "Proceed, Mr. District Attorney," Judge Irwin said.

Abner said, "Well, Helen, you were a student at the high school during last May, weren't you? And you testified that on May third—"

Sam Field had bent his head down further. The only thing Sam could have to hope for in all this was that it would soon be over, and fairly soon forgotten; and Mr. Hartshorn's contentious words perhaps reminded him that this hope was unwarranted. Four years' service had given him his place in the squabbles and schemings and jealousies and long-holding of grudges that made up so much of the life and world of the school office and the faculty room. Though no longer present, Sam Field would not be quietly released from their talk and thought. In the struggle about to be joined, the coming together in opposition about who was to blame and who would have to pay, they would expose Sam Field anew at every meeting, and retry the case every day for weeks, while his friends hated him for putting them at the disadvantage of having been his friends, and his enemies gloated quietly together, telling each other again and again that they had told each other so.

When Abner called his name, Sam Field jumped, starting erect. This made it necessary for him to stand a moment, drawing back stiffly, while Helen Hartshorn returned to her place. She slipped past him and sat by her father; and Field came down with constrained steps to where Mr. Bosenbury held the book. When he was in the stand, Abner said to him, "Mr. Field, you have heard the evidence that has been offered"—the truth was, Abner thought, he had probably heard little of it—"and I will not ask you anything about it in detail, unless there are details that you feel should be corrected. You have a right to question any of the witnesses if you want to."

"No," said Field.

"Mr. Field, can you give his Honor any explanation for these actions of yours? Can you say anything about why you were led to act this way?"

Field said, "I don't know why."

"That will be all, then," Abner said with relief. "Unless your Honor—"

"No. That is all. I have no questions." Judge Irwin cleared his throat, took a last look at the page of the open volume of the statutes under his hand. "Samuel Pierce Field," he said, "come before the Court."

"Right here," Mr. Bosenbury whispered, indicating the space by the rail in front of him. When Field stood there, Judge Irwin went on, "You have pleaded guilty to charges that are very serious. However, because you have pleaded guilty, because you have co-operated with the Commonwealth, I will not pain you, or others, by dwelling on the detestable nature of what you allowed yourself to do. I think you regret your acts. You are a young man of education and intelligence and though it is necessary for me to sentence you as I am about to, the Court feels every confidence that what you have been guilty of is merely a misstep, and that you will in the future—er—be a useful and honorable member of society."

Judge Irwin shifted in his chair, clearing his throat again, and went on: "The sentence of the Court is, first—this is the first indictment, Mr. Bosenbury; number sixty-three. First, that you pay the costs of prosecution." He paused and looked at Field. "And that you undergo a term of imprisonment at the Blue Hills Reformatory of not less than one year, nor more than—"

Muffling an exclamation, Beatrice Wright put a hand over her face and began to cry.

To Abner, John Costigan murmured, "Got a break. Didn't send him to the pen, at any rate."

Coming behind Abner, Warren Lyall whispered, "Were those to run concurrently?"

"Yes," said Costigan. Lyall squeezed his shoulder, stepped by him, and made a gesture to Field. Maynard Longstreet, folding his copy paper, stood up, put his elbows on the front of the bench, addressing Judge Irwin, who bent forward to hear. Everitt Weitzel said to the witnesses, "That's all. You can go now."

Standing up, Abner found himself facing the Reverend Mr. Field, who said agitatedly, "I just wished to ask you whether it's proper for us to speak to him; whether we can see him a few minutes—"

"Certainly," Abner said. "This courtroom won't be in use now. I think Mr. Lyall will be willing to let you talk to him here for a few minutes." He glanced at Field, who stood white and silent under the high window through which the falling rain could be seen. Abner walked up to him, put out his hand, and said, "Good luck, Sam."

Field took the hand weakly; but he did not try to say anything. Abner saw that, like most impulsive gestures, it had only served to distress them both. He nodded, took up his file folder from the table, and started toward the door.

Jesse Gearhart was still sitting in the corner, his hands

balanced on his umbrella handle; and Abner went over to him. "Marty says he's willing for you to have this," he said. He lifted the folder, not sure whether Jesse would take it or not.

Jesse said, "All right, Ab. Thanks."

Abner turned and went out the door and downstairs. In the hall below he caught up with Everitt Weitzel. "Bad thing, that, Ab," Everitt said, seeing who it was.

Finding that he remained somewhat shaken, Abner said, "Yes, it is." He lit a cigarette, took a couple of puffs, drawing the smoke deep into his lungs. Coming to the courtroom door, he dropped the cigarette, trod it out, and let himself in quietly.

A gloom like that of dusk filled the great cavern of the main courtroom. Outside the morning had darkened and the fall of rain was so heavy and loud that the sound of it passed in drumming echoes across the varnished ceiling boards from slope to slope. Behind the stained glass wheel the thousand candle power electric bulbs were burning. Their diluted light, falling fifty feet on the well of the court, fell on Abner as he approached the Commonwealth's table.

Bunting, a paper in his hand, stood by the rail beside Joe Jackman's desk. Kinsolving, the Federal Bureau of Investigation Agent, was on the stand. Big waisted, big shouldered, bull necked, he sat in the poor light like a rock. Abner saw his face, hard and reposed in profile, against the glow from Judge Vredenburgh's green-shaded reading lamp. When Kinsolving spoke, it was with the economy and precision of an expert witness. He might seem easy and negligent to the uninstructed; but a lawyer who knew the rules of evidence soon saw that Kinsolving knew them, too.

Bunting said to him, "How frequently did you see Stanley Howell?"

"Oh, approximately every hour," Kinsolving answered. By the jury's close attention Abner knew that Kinsolving was not the first witness. This was a continued story. Lieutenant Dunglison, who sat at the Commonwealth's table, must already have been examined and cross-examined. Abner took the chair beside him. Dunglison moved to give him more room, and whispered, "Morning, Mr. Coates."

Abner whispered back, "Good morning, Lieutenant. How are we coming?"

"All right." He directed a short hostile stare at Harry Wurts. "Our friend there's making trouble; but it don't do him any good."

"Smalley been on?"

"Yeah. Corroborative, mostly. They didn't cross. Couldn't get much out of that butt peddler." Dunglison looked at her with disgust.

Taking them up from Joe Jackman's desk, Bunting said to Kinsolving, "I show you a number of sheets of paper that are fastened together and marked Commonwealth's Exhibit number eighteen, and ask you whether you have seen those before?"

Bunting handed them up, and Kinsolving looked at them calmly, turning the pages over, and said, "Yes, sir, I have. I signed them as a subscribing witness at the same time stated before, in our office."

Bunting said, "And you were present, Mr. Kinsolving, when Stanley Howell made a statement to a stenographer in that office?"

"Yes, sir."

"And was that statement subsequently transcribed and reduced to typewriting?"

"It was."

"Is that the statement which you hold in your hand; Commonwealth's Exhibit number eighteen?"

"Yes. It is marked C.X. eighteen."

"Cross-examine."

From his seat beside Basso, George Stacey arose, fiddled a moment with the papers spread on the table, and came down before the jury. It seemed to Abner that the jurors' faces showed disappointment. Harry Wurts' performance on Lieutenant Dunglison must have been a good and exciting one, and they had been hoping for more. Abner was surprised, and looking at Marty, he saw that Marty was surprised, too, that Harry would leave so tough a witness— and, moreover, a witness whose testimony dealt entirely with Harry's client—to George.

Slight and uneasy, looking worried but resolute, George said, "Now, do I understand, Mr. Kinsolving, that you first saw Stanley Howell on May third?"

That was also, Abner remembered, the date on which Sam Field had "seen" Helen Hartshorn. The two actions, moving toward the same place, had been paralleling each other; Sam "seeing" the girls in his office on the same spring days that Bailey and Howell and Basso and Leming plotted the kidnapping of Frederick Zollicoffer, captured him, killed him, scattered for safety, and were overtaken.

"That is correct," Kinsolving said kindly.

"And between May third and the morning of May sixth, you were with him practically all the time?"

"I was in the room, in and out, Counselor." Though spoken gravely, without a trace of derision, the title was wildly derisive when you looked at George pecking nervously at this bulwark of ease and experience; and suddenly Abner saw why Harry was not doing his own cross-examining. There was little chance that Harry or anyone else could shake Kinsolving; and in a flash, Harry's acute and foxy mind must have seen how to turn Kinsolving's impregnability at least a little to the Commonwealth's disadvantage. Give him to George, who would have trouble taking candy from a baby, and let the jury feel sorry for poor George, so unfairly matched.

George said, "Now, did you talk to Howell about making a statement?"

"Oh, yes. Several times."

"And what was his response?"

"Why," said Kinsolving amiably, "he seemed undecided, Counselor. He was considering what he ought to do, he told me."

"And what, if anything, was done by the men in your department to help him decide?"

"Why, we told him what we already knew; the confession by Bailey implicating him."

"You didn't inflict any punishment on Howell, did you?"

"I did not."

"You don't remember twisting his thumbs back, do you?"

"No, I do not."

Slumped in his chair, his chin on his chest, Judge Vredenburgh said, "Did you do it, or didn't you?"

"No, sir," said Kinsolving, inclining his head toward him, "I did not."

Bunting said to Abner, "What did he get?"

"One to three."

"Make out all right?"

Abner nodded.

George Stacey said, "Now, while you were talking to Howell, where was he—I mean, in what position was he?"

"He was on the table with an Oregon boot on him, a leg boot."

"What is that?" said George. "An instrument of torture?"

"Why, no, Counselor," Kinsolving said, smiling. "It's a short length of chain that prevents a man from running."

"He also had handcuffs on?"

"Most of the time."

"And you don't think being loaded with chains helped him decide what he ought to do?"

"It may have," Kinsolving said equably. "He must have seen that he had no chance to escape this time. His record showed that he had made several escapes from various authorities who neglected to take proper precautions."

"And where did he sleep?"

"On the table."

"I suppose this wasn't an upholstered table?"

"Just a plain wooden table. I think he had his coat; and we put some other coats under him."

"And that is how he had to sleep from May third to the morning of May sixth?"

"That is correct."

"Isn't it a fact that he was not permitted to sleep at all?"

"I think that is incorrect. I know it is not correct."

Abner could see the jurors asking themselves how much sleep a man would get with his hands and feet chained, lying on a wooden table, even if he wasn't otherwise disturbed. On the faces of some of them was a faint uneasiness, an imaginative discomfort; and George, noticing it, too, showed that he thought he had an advantage to press. He said, "Did you ever see him when he was asleep?"

"Yes; on two different occasions."

"And when you caught him sleeping, you woke him up, of course?"

"Why, no, Counselor. I had a good deal on my hands just then. I just looked in occasionally to see that he was all right. When I saw that he was asleep, I caught up with my other work."

"How about the rest of the men? There were other men working on him, weren't there?"

"I couldn't answer for other men, Counselor. Yes, there was Special Agent Shannon, Special Agent Klapper—three or four others." He nodded courteously.

It was, Abner told himself, like a checker game in which George, clutching his pieces, made impulsive, immediately obvious moves, jumped at certain small chances and took them; while Kinsolving, a professional player with the pattern of the whole game in his head, good-humoredly watched

George imagine that he was winning. Kinsolving kept his eye not on the jury, which knew nothing about the realities of this business, anyway; and if the jury were swayed by sympathy for Howell in chains sleeping on a table, it would as readily be swayed back when the district attorney summed up the things that Howell had done. Kinsolving watched the rules of evidence, had regard for the charge of the Court, considered the record that would go up for appeal. Abner did not doubt that Kinsolving would unhesitatingly perjure himself, a risk he was prepared to take in the line of duty, to protect all really important parts of his legal position. If George thought that anything Kinsolving had assented to so far would stand in the legal meaning as coercion, it could only be because George knew less law than Kinsolving did.

George said, "And these special agents, they were also trying to get a statement?"

"To obtain information is the duty of a special agent of the department, Counselor."

"And to get that information by any means at all?"

"No; that is not the policy of our department, Counselor."

"I don't care anything about the policy of your department," George said. You could hear the echo of Harry Wurts; George was trying to copy that harsh backlash; but since he lacked Harry's confident, insolent gaze, and Harry's bold, overbearing voice, the effect was only querulous. Everyone looked at him, surprised; and, blushing, George said, "I want to know what was done in this instance."

"I have related that," Kinsolving said mildly.

"Well, I mean what means do you take to get this information?"

"I find kindness as good means as any, Counselor; if by 'you,' you mean me personally."

"May we have an example of your kindness?"

"Getting him a glass of water," Kinsolving said. "Giving him cigarettes. Talking heart to heart with him."

"And these other agents you mentioned, were they kind to him, too—are they here in court?"

"I can't answer for them, of course. They are experienced men, however; and I should think they would agree with me that that is the best method—no, to the extent of my knowledge, they aren't here. I have not seen them."

"Your Honor," said George, "I think those men ought to be here."

Judge Vredenburgh stirred. "Do you mean that the Commonwealth should have called them, Mr. Stacey? In that event I'm afraid the district attorney must be allowed to judge. Do you mean that you should have called them yourself?" Though Judge Vredenburgh smiled, he sounded testy; and after a good deal of pleading before him, Abner could recognize Judge Vredenburgh in conflict with himself. Judge Vredenburgh was displeased not with George, but with Kinsolving; yet, since Kinsolving's behavior and answers were scrupulously correct, and Judge Vredenburgh could find no fault of a cognizable sort in him, he made himself retain his displeasure until someone, by any little error or silly remark or hint of impertinence, tripped the trigger and opened an outlet. The Judge did not like Kinsolving's expertness, the cool choosing of what he would tell and what he wouldn't; so George was rapped for lack of expertness, for failing by some masterpiece of cross-examination, to bring out what Kinsolving had the presumption to withhold.

Red with embarrassment, both because of the reproof, and because he saw now that he had impulsively put his foot in it, George none the less managed to stand his ground, and Abner silently applauded him. George said, "Well, sir, I am not satisfied that this witness is telling all he could if he wanted to."

As that was probably the Judge's own opinion, he was mollified; but he said remotely, "He will be required to answer any questions you wish to ask him, Mr. Stacey."

"I don't think I want any more of the kind of answers the witness gives, sir. No further questions."

Bunting stood up beside Abner and said, "One moment, Mr. Kinsolving. I will ask you a question that Mr. Stacey has not asked you. Did Stanley Howell, before making this statement, complain to you of any physical abuse?"

"He did not."

Judge Vredenburgh said, "Did he complain of any part of his treatment?"

"No, sir."

Judge Vredenburgh pursed his lips, his sharp gaze fixed on Kinsolving's calm face. "Did you see any sign of injuries or anything of that nature?"

"None at all."

Judge Vredenburgh nodded, looking away. George Stacey said bitterly, "You didn't look for them, did you?"

Turning his head with an air of surprise, Kinsolving said, "I didn't see any on him, Counselor."

"I mean you didn't make any examination of him, you didn't examine his body—did he have his clothes on?"

"Why, yes. He was sitting there with his clothes on. There was no outward sign of anything on his face or what parts of his body I could see."

"That's all."

"That's all," Bunting said. "I desire to offer in evidence Commonwealth's Exhibit number eighteen."

Harry Wurts held up his hand, and Judge Vredenburgh said, "Are you objecting, Mr. Wurts?"

"Well, yes, your Honor; I will object, of course. But right now, I wish to ask for a recess. On account of Mr. Kinsolving's kindness, again."

Judge Vredenburgh drew his mouth down. "You will have an opportunity to advance what theories you may have when the defense opens, Mr. Wurts. Keep them until then. There will be a five minute recess."

While Howell was taken out, Bunting sat down again. "You through with us?" Lieutenant Dunglison asked.

"Yes, thanks. I'm just going to have the confession read into the record."

Dunglison nodded and went over and sat down in the ring of seats along the outer rail by Kinsolving. Abner said, "They don't see much, do they?"

"They're pretty careful. They know they're going to be witnesses to the signature and will have to testify. The Judge didn't like it." Bunting sat back stretching and yawning. "I don't like it either. But they had the goods on Howell. There was never a doubt in the world; and they know the kind of evidence they have to present—Kinsolving, there, has a law degree. He told me this morning. A lot of the Federal men do. There's no sense, or no use, in handing over to us a case that won't stick." Bunting shrugged. "Of course they have no right to take it on themselves to decide whether the goods they have on a man are really good. But I'd trust them. They know when a man is guilty. You know yourself how that is. We've had cases when we knew who did it, but we didn't have the proof. Well, Field was a good case. We had to work on him. We say he confessed of his own free will. It isn't true. We broke him down. Of course, all we had to do was just talk to Field and keep after him; but how far would you get just talking to Howell? In principle there isn't a nickel's worth of difference."

Abner said, "Well, were you going to beat Field up, if talking didn't work?"

"No. Certainly not."

"You mean, because it would have made such a stink?"

"I mean, because I would have felt a reasonable doubt about his being guilty," Bunting said. His smile was dry. He struck a light emphatic fillip against Abner's arm. "Don't work so hard at it, Ab. There is always theory and there is always practice. If you think you're going to change that,

281

you're wrong. Theory is where you want to go; practice is how you're going to get there."

"Yes," said Abner, "or else, theory is what you tell people you're going to do; and practice is what they catch you really doing. Get anything out of Susie?"

"Not much. Harry asked for an offer of proof and so I made it, and he objected. Immaterial, of course. Vredenburgh said it would show they were associated, and continued to be associated—stealing the other car, the one they wanted to use when they got rid of the one they used for Zolly." Bunting shook his head. "Matter of fact, Harry fooled me. I didn't expect that, because I thought he'd like to cross-examine to try to mix her up in it more. The way it came out, I couldn't risk asking her a lot of questions I might have, because I wanted to keep it narrowed down so he'd have to take a few points I'd laid for him. Harry did the smart thing by just saying no questions. The jury was disappointed, I think. They were expecting some hot stuff." He looked toward the hall door. "There's Howell. Now, we'll have a brawl over the objections. I want you to read the statement, if and when." He pushed it over to Abner and stood up.

Judge Vredenburgh said, "You were making an offer in evidence, Mr. Bunting."

"Yes, sir," Bunting said.

George Stacey said, "I object to the admission of any confession so far as it concerns the defendant Robert Basso."

"Yes," Judge Vredenburgh said. "That objection is well taken." He leaned back and lifted off his glasses. "I think I shall caution the jury that the statement or confession will be admitted, if it is, only as against the defendant Howell. I will so instruct in the general charge; but in order that the jury may not get a wrong impression, we will state to you at this time that this alleged confession will not be considered as in any way affecting Basso."

Standing up, Harry Wurts said, "And now, if your Honor

please, I object to the introduction of the confession in the circumstances under which it was obtained. The testimony shows that this confession was obtained by—"

Judge Vredenburgh said, "You need not review it, Mr. Wurts. You are overruled."

"Very good, sir. I enter a further objection on the ground that only the last sheet of this alleged confession bears the signatures of the attesting witnesses."

"That objection is also overruled."

"And the further objection that the confession is in no way fastened together, but consists merely of five or six loose sheets. Will your Honor rule upon that?"

"Overruled. We will grant you exceptions, Mr. Wurts."

"If you please!" said Harry. He sat down, satisfied, Abner could see, that he had tried everything—more things than most people would think of.

Abner went around the table to face the jury. In the poor light he was obliged to hold the typed pages close to see them. He read: "I, Stanley Howell, do make the following statement of my free will and accord, without threats or promises of immunity and with full knowledge that the same may be used against me in court. On or about April sixth—"

The dark courtroom sank in silence. For a moment no one stirred, no one coughed or murmured or moved his feet. Just over the top of held-up sheets, Abner could see in the front row of jurors Louis Blandy's pop-eyes strained with attention. To the side, against the curve of the rail, Mrs. Zollicoffer's haggard face was white in the gloom. In the rising rows of benches most of the spectators had leaned forward, and Abner raised his voice: "—we, that was Robert Basso, Bailey, Roy Leming and me, we left this bungalow we had been at and drove along some roads I don't know and we got out to Zollicoffer's house at around ten-thirty at night. It was early yet and in about twenty-five minutes Zolly pulled up in his machine; and when he pulled up and put it in the garage, Basso and me and Bailey, we had been in the garage. Bailey was standing here and I was in the corner. When he came in and got out of the machine, he did not see us; and Bailey hit him with the butt of a gun. When we carry him out, Zolly, he thought it was the law shaking him down for dope. He got hit again; and the stuff dropped out of his hand; and I was picking it up. He said, 'Let me do away with this junk and I'll pay.' He went in our machine and I got in front. Bailey hit Zolly twice. Bailey said, 'You bastard, many a poor soul you destroyed. I never killed anybody.' There was no more conversation until we got to the bungalow."

Abner paused for breath. It was surprising when you thought of it, that however little they feared God or regarded man, they still wanted to make out a case for themselves. The many poor souls presumably referred to were Zollicoffer's customers; Zollicoffer's business gave Bailey a chance to feel that he was the moral superior of his victim. That Bailey had never killed anyone was not, perhaps, quite true; but perhaps he never had sold narcotics. The truth, surprising to Abner when he first observed it, was that men like Bailey were often letter-perfect in any number of ethical and moral platitudes. They were usually reformatory boys; and that meant that without wishing to, with hatred and rebellion in their hearts, they had just the same absorbed certain principles. Outwardly, they might despise and deride those principles, and never think of putting them in practice; but when the need came to make moral judgments, to strike an attitude in defense of themselves or condemnation of others, they opened their mouths and outspoke the warden and the chaplain. They had not respected these men or their talk; but it was talk that perhaps corroborated the warnings of a poor old mother; and, in turn, was corroborated by laborious reading (there was so much time to kill in such a life; the days in hiding, the months in prison) of pulp paper magazines and Sunday supplement feature articles. Narcotics destroyed both body and soul; all his authorities said that; and Bailey must, in fact, have seen the destruction himself in men he knew.

Abner read, "They took him in and put him upstairs in this room, and it was cold and I throw the coat over his feet. We stayed there talking the four of us, and he said, 'I know who is in back of this.' He said Roy Leming was. He said, 'What did you have to do this for?' Bob Basso told him that many a person—" (The elegant phrase, so often repeated, was probably Bailey's—the warden and the chaplain, again; and Basso, impressed, echoed it; and Howell, admiring, remembered it) "—he had killed. So he said to Roy Leming, 'You sat in my office many a day. If you wanted anything you were welcome to it.' Roy said, 'If I went up in your office you know I'd be out on some road now.' Bailey said, 'Is your life worth one hundred thousand dollars?' Zolly laughed at him. He said, 'They had that money one time; but no more.' "

Abner cleared his throat. Though hardly begun, the statement already seemed to him long, and he began to read more rapidly, "I went downstairs and came back in about an hour; and they left me with him. Zolly said, 'Have you got anything I can smoke with?' He says, 'Haven't you got an outfit?' I said, 'I don't use it.' I said, 'I never smoked,' and he said, 'I have been smoking eight or ten pills a day. The same way as you like liquor, I like this.' I told him I only like beer. I told him I take it or I leave it alone; and he said, 'I crave this just like you crave beer.' When Bailey came in, he said, 'How are you going?' He said, 'You do not like me, do you?' and Bailey said, 'No.' They started arguing; and I said, 'What is the use of arguing now; the people in the next house will hear us.' He said, 'All right. I won't say nothing more.' He wanted a smoke; and I said, 'I will give you a shot of booze.' "

Frederick Zollicoffer must have been having a bad time. When Abner read the account before, he did not notice that point about the people next door. Abner had seen the houses and it would not be hard to make oneself heard from one to another; but Zollicoffer didn't dare. The neighbors might hear and call the police, and the police would come and release him; but that took time. In time the police might come; but Bailey and those who obeyed him were here now. Meanwhile they had been arranging meetings with Walter Cohen, a tedious and delicate negotiation. Abner read, "We waited, myself, Bailey and Basso in the machine until three o'clock; and they didn't show up. Basso said, 'I know how he is.' We got back to the house; and then Zolly said, 'What is the matter?' and we said we didn't see Cohen. Zolly said Cohen was afraid to go out on a lonely road; that there was some clique after him. He said he had been shot at around February. Zolly said, 'You can't blame him for not coming out.' So Bailey got him to write another letter to the office. We are back in the house; and Dewey has the breakfast cooked; and Basso says to me, 'I am sorry I went into this God damn thing.' I said, 'I feel the same way.' I laid on the bed and went to sleep and woke up around ten; and Bailey said, 'You go down and eat and tell the others to come up.' I ate and Roy Leming went up. That is the way it went on from day to day. The meet we made where we got the money, I don't know the time, a Saturday. I went to get it with Basso; but I didn't like the look; and so Basso gets it from a car. When we come back, I says, 'Now we can turn him loose.' Leming said to me, 'He is not going to be turned loose. He is going to be killed.' I said, 'Well, that is murder.' Basso was worried that Zolly knew him and Bailey. He did not think it would be so good for them if Zolly was let loose. He would say one minute, 'Kill him'; and the next minute, 'Let him go.' Bailey says, 'We will vote on that. What do you say?' I and Leming, we said, 'No.' "

Abner thought that very likely. Though the account did not tally at all points with Leming's statements, and neither version was necessarily the true one, Howell tacitly allowed Leming's minor part by mentioning him so seldom. They were both scared, in short; and the dangers of murder scared them more. Abner read on: "Bailey said, 'We will kill him. We will put him in the car and take him up the road and kill him.' It was then agreed that he would be killed on account of him knowing them, and letting him go was not safe.

"I went upstairs and said, 'Where do you want to be turned loose?' and Zolly said, 'Where is Walter's machine at?' I said, 'You will see; but we will not go there first. We will drive you around so you do not know where this is.' He said, 'Can I get dressed?' and I got the pants for him to put on. He said, 'Give me my vest,' and I did. After a while I went downstairs and Basso and Bailey comes up. He said, 'All right. I am ready to go home.' I put his coat and overcoat on him, and Bailey said, 'Do not forget I am going to put something on his face.' He put a piece of blanket over his face and tied it. We took him down and put him in the machine. Bailey says I am to drive; so Bailey and Basso and Zolly are in back.

"After we had driven some, all of a sudden I hear two shots. Bailey said, 'That's another God damn monkey gone.' And then I got pretty leery. Bob looked at me and I am getting pretty leery. Bailey said, 'We will stop here and put some weights on him.' The weights are in the car. Bailey took care of the weights. I don't know where they came from. Then I drove up the road to the creek bridge; and Bailey said, 'Here it is deep. Stop.' With the weights, they couldn't one of them lift him. He fell in the road; and Bailey said, 'Put out those lights, are you crazy. We do not know when some car is coming.' So the three of us got him on the rail. He fell in. It was about half way across the bridge we threw the body, the left side going up. We went back to the bungalow and Susie and Leming were there; and Leming says, 'Where is he?' and Bailey says, 'Where you will be if you ask them questions.' So we left the bungalow and did not come back there. I hereby certify that the foregoing statement is true and correct to the best of my knowledge and belief. Signed: Stanley Howell. Witnesses: P. T. Kinsolving, Special Agent; Merrill Klapper, Special Agent; J. J. Shannon, Special Agent.'"

Lowering the paper, Abner turned and walked in silence around the table and sat down. Bunting said, "If the Court please, I desire to offer in evidence the criminal record of Stanley Howell and the criminal record of Robert Basso, for the purpose of giving the jury information on which they may base the penalty in the event that they find the defendants guilty of murder in the first degree."

Judge Vredenburgh said, "Any objection?"

"Yes, sir," said Harry Wurts. "We object, sir, to the introduction of evidence of prior convictions as being prejudicial to the defendants' interests."

"All evidence may be that, Mr. Wurts."

"I respectfully submit, sir, that there is no authority in law for introducing the previous convictions. The Act of 1911 not only prevents the question being asked, but prohibits an answer."

"You cannot be unaware, Mr. Wurts, that that act has been several times the subject of interpretation. The Supreme Court has frequently held the material admissible; though, of course, only for the purpose for which the district attorney says he is offering it."

Harry said, "Well, I submit to your Honor that when a given result is inevitable, that result may be assumed to be the real purpose of an action, all high-sounding declarations to the contrary notwithstanding. The inevitable result here is to prejudice the jury. Therefore—"

"That is an ingenious argument, Mr. Wurts; but to hear it is not within the purview of this Court. You are overruled and you may have an exception."

Bunting, who had been standing patiently, slipped a paper from the open file folder in front of him and said, "Members of the jury, at this time I am going to place on the record in your hearing the convictions of each of these defendants. The Commonwealth's purpose is to aid you in fixing a penalty, in the event that you find these defendants guilty of first degree murder."

George Stacey said, "Mr. Bunting, I understand this is just to be convictions?"

"That is right," Bunting said. "The defendant Stanley Howell, as Stanley Howell, sentenced to the Boys Reformatory at Enfield to an indeterminate term, January twenty-sixth—"

The door to the chambers was opened just far enough for Judge Irwin to slip around it. He walked softly to the steps and went up to the bench, seating himself in the high backed chair next to Judge Vredenburgh. Judge Vredenburgh swiveled about; asked him a question. By their expressions as they bent whispering, their heads together, Abner could see that they were discussing Field—Irwin, anxious and still visibly upset; Vredenburgh with the brusque down-in-the-mouth look that he put on when he considered matters he disapproved of. Vredenburgh grimly nodded his head several times; Irwin gave his head a faint, sad little shake; and they drew apart and turned together to listen to Bunting, who was adding in his matter-of-fact voice item after monotonous item.

Howell's present age was twenty-eight, and during the last ten years he had six recorded convictions. In addition to Stanley Howell, his name had been John Howell, and Stanley Howe and Frank Stanley; and it was plain that his occupation was robbery. Those indictments that did not charge it charged offenses that Abner knew to be the ones used when by bad luck or a legal technicality, robbery could not be made to stick—conspiring, entering, assaulting with the intent, carrying concealed deadly weapons.

Bunting paused; and then said, "As to the defendant Robert Basso, I desire to read in your hearing and have entered upon the record, the following—"

Judge Irwin listened with his usual acute attention, his narrow lips pressed tight together, a look in his eyes that was almost chagrin; as though on behalf of the law, he took to himself great blame for the proved failure of those other judges who had pronounced sentence after sentence, punishing but not correcting, until today Robert Basso stood insolently mute on the verge of his grave; and it only remained for one more judge to crown the law's achievement by pushing him in.

Bunting laid his paper on the table and said to the bench, "The Commonwealth rests."

Judge Vredenburgh looked at the clock and said, "We have almost half an hour before noon. I do not want to waste time; so I think I will ask the defense to open. If necessary, we can delay recessing. Is the defense ready?"

George Stacey leaned across in front of Basso and spoke to Harry. "Yes, sir," Harry said. "Mr. Stacey will try not to prolong our fast beyond twelve-thirty."

George got to his feet, gathering up his notes. He lifted his hand to adjust his necktie; but since it had been straight before, the tug he gave it moved the knot well over to one side. He moistened his lips and marched tensely up to face the jury.

Abner knew how George felt because he remembered feeling the same way himself. There was no reason to feel that way, for speaking to people who were ready to listen was the easiest thing in the world—you just went ahead and spoke. To tell George this truth was as useless as telling a person who did not know how to swim that all he had to do was jump in and go ahead. George was trying to remember to keep his voice up, to speak slowly, to look directly at the twelve staring faces of his principal hearers; not to depend too much on his notes, not to talk too long, not to forget that one especially good point that came to him just as he spoke to Harry—

George said earnestly, "Ladies and gentlemen, you have

heard Mr. Bunting and his colleague present a case for the Commonwealth. I venture to assert—"

Abner whispered to Bunting, "Marty, I have a phone call I want to make if we're going to be late recessing. Mind if I duck out a few minutes?"

"No. There's nothing to this. Go ahead. Oh, Ab. That Willis fellow from Warwick. F and B case Pete Van Zant has. You know about it?"

"Yes. Arlene said they came around to my office yesterday. She told them to see you."

"See the plaintiff?"

"Yes. She's a little slut."

"They think they can prove he isn't the father. I asked Miss Wheeler to see her and find out what she could. She called me this morning and said it was pretty bad. What do you think?"

"I suppose we'd better drop it."

"Yes. I just wanted to see whether you had any other angle."

"Nope; except John Costigan told me Willis had been tom-catting around there for years, and it was time somebody hooked him."

"Well, we can't enforce morals; we have trouble enough enforcing law. I think Van Zant may be outside. He said he was coming up today. If you see him, tell him we aren't going on with it. The county'll have to support her brat."

Abner left the table and went down along the rail under the bench toward the far door so that he wouldn't add to George's troubles. At the last desk, Hermann Mapes, the clerk of the Orphans Court, winked at him. Half lifting a hand in response, Abner remembered that he had said last night that he was going to get an application form for a marriage license from Hermann today. He went around through the high deserted back hall and entered the Attorneys Room. This was deserted, too. Abner dropped a nickel in the telephone. At the high school office an unfamiliar voice answered; and he said, "Is Miss Drummond there?"

"Yes, she is. Bonnie! It's for you."

Bonnie said, "Hello."

Leaning back against the wall, Abner said, "I am going to get an application from Hermann."

"Oh," she said. "No. Don't."

"I think I will. Look, why don't you come out and have lunch? I'll stop by for you."

"I can't. They're having a board meeting. Why didn't you tell me last night?"

"I didn't know until I saw Marty. I'll come over."

"I can't leave."

"You won't have to." Abner hung up and went to the courtroom door. Opening it a crack, he heard George saying, "—what we are going to show you, ladies and gentlemen, will change this entire picture; and I have the utmost confidence that when you have heard—" Abner let the door close. The other door opened and Pete Van Zant walked in.

Van Zant was a man of middle age with an odd, duck-legged fussy walk. He carried his gross friendly red face cocked back, his prominent light gray eyes bulging with, or as though with, a mingling of sensuality, surprise, and sardonicism. His cropped blonde hair had a ripple in it. "Well, well," he said. He snapped on the electric light switch, which someone had economically turned off when the room emptied. He was much shorter than Abner, but by putting his head far back he managed to look down his nose at him. "How's tricks, Ab?" he said. He came up and punched Abner in the arm. "Getting much?"

"Anyhow," Abner said, "I hear this client of yours, Willis, gets plenty. Marty wanted me to tell you we'll drop it."

"Now, wait a minute!" Van Zant slid his big rump onto the table edge and half-sat, swinging his foot. He produced two cigars. "Don't want one, do you?" he said. Abner shook his head, and Van Zant put the first back and stuck the second, unlighted, in his mouth. "What do you mean, drop it," he said, working the dry cigar up and down. "You mean, nolle pros?"

"Isn't that what you want?"

"No, sir!" Van Zant said, rolling up his eyes. "That is not what I want. Now, Ab, why don't you fellows be decent? Now, here's the situation. Hank's no criminal, for God's sake! He's a substantial and respected citizen of Warwick. That girl hasn't any idea of who the father of that child is. Hank gave her a lay, sure; but that was more than a year before the child was born. We can prove it. She names him because he's a generous guy and a good sport. But, hell, everyone in Warwick had been there—if you want to know, I have myself. She worked at a house, and if you weren't in Marty's office I'd tell you where. Now, you nolle pros, and what is it? Why, it's nothing but a damned kind of stay! No, sir! I want him vindicated!"

"Well, it's not up to me," Abner said. "I think you're out of luck, Pete. How about that motion to quash I heard you were planning? You wouldn't be any better off."

"Now, Ab; what do you want to be technical for? Sure, if the Commonwealth was going to bring it to trial, I might move to quash; and I could make the motion lie, too. But Marty admits there's no case. As good as admits it. Now, why can't we have it tried before a judge without a jury, and give him an acquittal? On the weight of the evidence, you know he'd get it; and I think he ought to have it. Why, I'll tell you how bum your evidence is! I'm even ready to plead nolo contendere; because when the judge has heard it, he'll direct the verdict, direct an acquittal."

"That may be what you think. But if you put that up to Marty, I can tell you what he's going to think. If you want to know."

"What?"

"What anyone with any sense would think. He'd think there must be something in this. Why would you care, unless you knew the real story was liable to come out sometime;

and if it did come out, the only way your man could beat it would be pleading autrefois acquit? I don't say that's how it is. I just say that's how it looks."

"Why, that's the most unreasonable, unjustified,—why, I'm going to see Marty!"

"Suit yourself. He ought to be through pretty soon."

They looked at each other while Van Zant produced a match slowly, struck it on the stretched seat of his pants, and held the little liquid burst of flame suspended. He began to grin then. "You don't do so bad for a young fellow," he said. He applied the flame to his cigar end. "You're all right, Ab. Don't know it's to my best interest, but I hate to see a sap in the D.A.'s office. Hank's my client, and I do what I can; but between you and me, he's a son of a bitch. If he can't keep his nose clean, I'm not going to wipe it for him." He blew a long plume of smoke across the table. "You going to run in the fall?"

Disconcerted, Abner said, "I don't know who's running. You'd have to ask Jesse."

"O.K., if it's a secret. I don't want to know Jesse's secrets. He's another son of a bitch. That's why, if Marty's quitting and I hear he is, I'd like to see you in there. Government of checks and balances. When you get ready to come out with it, anything I can do for your campaign, let me know. I mean that. We don't want Art Wenn." There was a muffled, rising murmur behind the closed courtroom door, and Van Zant went and opened it a crack. "Recess to one-thirty," he said. "Say, those defendants are mean looking bastards! Going to burn them?"

"If we possibly can," Abner said. He took his hat and raincoat. "So long, Pete. I've got to run."

Empty and gleaming in the rain, a line of automobiles stretched along the curve of the graystone gravel drive up to the main door of the high school building. Abner, who had not bothered to get his own car, walked past them. In the Board Room, to the right of the principal's office, the lights were bright against the white ceiling. Abner went up the steps and came under the arch of the wide doorway. Affixed below the label was a stone shield bearing a seal on which was represented a lampadedromy.

Nine people out of ten wouldn't know the meaning of that word; but anyone who went to Childerstown High School could tell you at once that it meant a race with a torch held in ancient Greece. On the seal were the runners running, and the torch being handed over (for it appeared to be a kind of relay race); and a line of Scripture: "So run that ye may obtain the prize." Abner could remember thinking resentfully that that was just what a teacher would say. The prize could be obtained only by one person, so the others were, when you got right down to it, bound to be running for nothing; and so were being what was then called gypped by their designing elders. It had always seemed to Abner a lot like (another phrase of those days) scrambling a nickel; for five cents, the thrower of the coin got more action than he had any right to expect. In Abner's hand the big worn, slightly loose knob turned and he came into the hall.

A telephone was ringing in the office; and, stepping in, Abner was in time to meet Bonnie who rushed out the opposite door, which led to the principal's room. She gave Abner a distracted glance, lifted the telephone from the desk and stood resting one knee on the seat of the chair while she answered. Abner closed the hall door behind him and dropped his wet hat on the bench along the wall under a big framed print that displayed the signing of the Declaration of Independence. It was a bench he could remember occupying once or twice in considerable anxiety, waiting to see the principal, a Mr. Metzger, now many years gone. The desk beside which Bonnie stood with the telephone belonged in those days to a Miss O'Brien. She was probably little older than Bonnie; but Abner used to think of her scornfully as an old maid. When he looked back on it, most details about school seemed to Abner depressing or distasteful—like that characteristic smell, neither very strong nor very unpleasant, but definite; whose source was the simple circumstance that most of the children could not or did not take as many baths as they needed.

Frowning, Bonnie said to the lifted telephone, "No, I can't. No. Never mind about me." She wore a plain white blouse and a short flaring black skirt. She looked pale and tense; and Abner, feeling an inarticulate concern for her, came across the room and sat on the edge of the desk. He took her free hand between his.

Turning her mouth from the telephone, Bonnie murmured, "Don't sit there. You're all wet." She tried to draw her hand away, and then let him hold it. She moved her head wearily and closed her eyes. "Oh, Mother, no!" she said. "I can't tell you now. I don't know. I have to go back. I'll call you when I can." She hung up.

Through the door, left open a little, Abner could look across Mr. Rawle's office and through a second half-open door into the lighted Board Room. Leaning forward, he could see Mrs. Ballinger, her stout bosom hung with a fussy cascade of black ruffles, sitting as chairman at the head of the oval table. Her face was sunk in lines of vexation and discouragement. She slumped dejectedly, opening and closing on the table her hand, whose fingers bore a number of old-fashioned diamond rings. From the general movement in there, it seemed plain that the meeting was over; and it could not have ended to Mrs. Ballinger's satisfaction. The view of her was cut off by Alfred Hobbs whose gray hair was disordered above his stern face. He bent, balanced like a stork on one leg, and Abner could see that he was angrily pulling on one of a pair of rubbers.

Still holding Bonnie's hand, Abner said, "It's over, isn't it? What happened?"

"Yes," said Bonnie. She took the hand away. "I can't leave, though. I'll have to help Mr. Rawle with a statement he's preparing. I don't really know what's going to happen. Mr. Hobbs tried to force a resolution censuring him."

"Don't worry about it," Abner said.

"How can I help worrying about it?" she said impatiently. "I'll lose my job. I haven't any tenure." She bit her lip. "I'm just as bad as the rest of them. All I worry about is what's going to happen to me."

"We fixed up what was going to happen to you last night," Abner said. "I'm sorry about Mr. Rawle; but if you want to know, I hope you will lose your job. That would be fine. We won't have to argue any more. Now, I'm going to get an application when I get back to the courthouse. You can just tell your mother you're getting married."

"And I can just tell you I'm not!" Bonnie said. She jerked her chin up bitterly. "Ab, haven't you any sense? I told you not to come over here now. You just have a genius for picking a time when—"

"You don't have to do anything now," Abner said. "I'll bring the application form over tonight; and all you have to do is fill in your part of it. By the new law, you also have to go down to Doc Mosher for a serologic test for syphilis, because we have to file the reports with the application. If I don't get it started, we'll still be fooling around—"

"Ab," she said, "I won't have you treating me this way! You seem to think I haven't anything to say about it—"

"You do nothing but say," Abner said. He had meant to speak placatingly; but what she said, sinking in, began to sting; and in an eruption of anger he could not help pointing out to himself that, as a matter of fact, it was *she* who seemed to think that *he* hadn't anything to say about it. She seemed to think she was the only one with any worries.

She seemed to think he had no right to open his mouth until, at her good pleasure, she told him he might.

Abner opened his mouth; but Bonnie had already turned to walk away with a movement for which the hostile word was flouncing. She could not have been looking where she was going, for at the door she nearly collided with Jesse Gearhart who had been coming out through Mr. Rawle's office. "Oh, beg pardon, Bonnie," he said.

She said with difficulty, "I'm sorry." She stepped aside and went by him; and Jesse came slowly and heavily into the room. "Here's your stuff, Ab," he said, holding the folder out. "Much obliged."

"That's all right," Abner said, swallowing.

It was not the moment Abner would have chosen for a talk with Jesse; but because he did not know what if anything Jesse had heard, he felt like a fool; and in order not to appear like one, it seemed necessary to say something more. He said, "I didn't mean to make a fuss about it this morning, Jesse. It wasn't an ordinary case; and it seemed better to try to keep it as quiet as we could—" Abner found himself remembering what his father said last night about people having rows; and he had just had a row with Bonnie; but you couldn't say that he brought it on by being a little remote, or apathetic, or—he searched for the last word, the one he liked least—phlegmatic! He didn't like it any better now. It was a word that seemed to him somewhat fancy, not a word he would be apt to use himself; but if he had to use it, he would probably apply it to someone like Jesse—the flat lifeless hair, the gray lumpish face, the pale fishy eyes.

Jesse, standing still, by a motion of the head acknowledged the apology, or at least, the excuse, taking his due; but at the same time and by the same motion, he thanked Abner for offering it; and then, still in the same motion, he disembarrassed them both of the whole matter, implying that they need think no more about it. Since none of this could be expressed in words, Abner was astonished both by the feat, whatever it was, of unmistakably conveying it; and by the delicacy of perception that told Jesse when to hold his tongue.

Abner saw with confusion that he knew nothing at all about Jesse. He knew the face that he had just thought of as phlegmatic; and he knew a half a dozen stories or parts of stories—or even, mere epithets: Van Zant saying in passing, but positively, "He's another son of a bitch." They were all more or less defamatory, the relations of Jesse's enemies; but out of them Abner manufactured his idea. He had not even troubled to see whether the idea squared with the evidence of his senses, whether his picture of Jesse corresponded with what he could see. The picture was that of the politician of popular legend, tough, cynical, and corrupt; yet if Abner asked himself when he had noted those qualities in Jesse, he could not answer. He had certainly never seen Jesse in that well-known room, little and smoke-filled, trafficking in offices, dividing booty, making deals with similar scoundrels at the cost of the just and the upright. Indeed, when you considered this familiar figure, a difficulty presented itself. How did such a man, who must by definition be disliked on sight and distrusted by everyone, win himself a position of power?

Jesse said, "Ab, what do you think about this?"

"I think it's too bad it happened," Abner said. Granted that the wicked man in the little smoke-filled room—like Lucius' "gangsters"; perhaps, like a good many other everyday fantasies to which nothing had yet happened to attract Abner's critical attention—was at variance with plain facts, Abner still found it difficult to be easy with Jesse. At Jesse's question he was filled with uncontrollable suspicions; something balked in him again at the note of consultation, which must be meant for flattery, and must mean that Jesse wanted something. Abner realized that his tone bristled. To cover it up, he said, "What's the board think?"

"I don't know that we're really thinking as a board yet," Jesse said. "We're thinking as individuals; so, of course, we don't agree. Going home to lunch?"

"I haven't time," Abner said. "We resume at one-thirty." He looked at his watch. "I'll run down to the Acme and get a sandwich, I guess."

"Can I give you a lift? I'm going that way."

Abner was sorry that he had not brought his car. "All right, thanks," he said. He took up his hat from the bench and Jesse opened the door.

"Yes," Jesse said, when they were out in the rain, "we haven't reached any agreement yet. One attitude is that Mr. Rawle is personally responsible, and we'd better clean house. I don't know how fair that is."

They got into the car and Jesse started it. He had the old man's driving habit of doing dangerous things calmly and ill-considered things with great care. He came out the drive into Academy Street without looking for oncoming cars; but when he got himself in a position where such a car, if there were one, would have the most trouble to avoid hitting him, he stopped and peered around. Slowly starting again, he then observed a car turning in half a block ahead. He was well-out toward the middle ·of the street, so when he put his brakes on with no warning and no apparent reason, a laundry truck that left the curb and came up close behind had to swing away, missing him by a miracle. The shaken driver yelled through the rain, "Whyn't you stick your hand out, stupid!" but Jesse was not perturbed. He said to Abner, "Strike you Rawle's to blame?"

"I don't know," Abner said, somewhat shaken, too. "I suppose you have to trust someone. I should think the point would be what was best for the school system. Whether this shows Rawle isn't able to run things—"

"You like him?"

"Why, yes," Abner said. "I hardly know him." He felt himself stiffening again; for it crossed his mind that Jesse, who knew all about Bonnie's position, might think—Abner didn't know what, exactly.

"Would you be interested in helping him?" Jesse said. He had been driving faster; and, passing a car, he cut in in front and carefully slowed down. Abner instinctively looked over his shoulder. Collecting himself, for the other driver had fortunately been paying attention and was able to get his brakes on in time, Abner said, "Well, sure. But I don't see exactly what I could do."

"There's one thing," Jesse said. "If we have a hearing, it would be more or less formal; a lot of testimony and so on. Would you care to act as his counsel?" Turning his attention soberly from where he was going, he looked at Abner. "I don't think you'd be expected to do it for nothing," he said. "It would take time and be a good deal of trouble. We couldn't afford much; but—"

"I don't mind about that part of it," Abner said, rubbed the wrong way again, "but I'm not up on the law in the case. It would be all new to me; and I don't see how I'd be much use to him." He paused, trying to keep still; but Jesse continued to drive without looking where he was going, so Abner said hastily, "Car coming out there, Jesse."

"Oh. Thanks. Didn't see it." Jesse avoided the car by a few inches. "Well, what I was thinking, Ab, was that, after all, you were the one who prosecuted Field. It wouldn't really be a matter of law, I think. It's knowing how to question witnesses and so on. I think you could do him a great service. Mrs. Ballinger and I are pretty much alone at the moment; but I don't think we'll be helpless by any means. The Department of Public Instruction can be brought in on it; and I know Ed Holstrom, the County Superintendent, thinks Rawle's a good man. Well, would you think it over and let me know, Ab? We're meeting again this evening, and Holstrom will be there then." He slowed down in the thickest traffic of Broad Street; and Abner said, "This will do me fine, thanks, Jesse. Why, I don't know that I need to think it over. I'll do what I can."

Jesse said, "Well, I certainly appreciate that, Ab; and I know Rawle will. I'll tell them, if it's all right with you." He stopped, holding up a long line of cars, and Abner jumped out.

"I'll call you later, then," Jesse said.

One or two of the drivers behind began to blow their horns indignantly; and Abner waved a hand, and crossed the pavement to the Acme Lunch. With the immediate pressure of Jesse's presence removed, he could not understand why he had said he would—except that it was hard to know what else to say when you were asked to help a man who was in trouble.

In the Acme Lunch there was one vacant place at the end of the counter. Going to it, Abner found that Everitt Weitzel sat next to him. Everitt was finishing a bowl of cornflakes and milk. Peering up sideways, he said, "Well, Ab, coming down in the world?"

In court, in his neat tipstaff's jacket, Everitt had an air of authority and importance; but when he put the jacket in his locker, he put the air away with it. He was an obliging and gentle old man. The minor court-attendant jobs were dealt out to the deserving and necessitous. It was policy, since the purpose was vote-getting, to select a member of some lodge or association who was well-liked and who, through illness or misfortune, badly needed the small salary. As a likeable person, as the recipient of political favor, as a sufferer from considerable troubles, the selected man tended to be affable but anxious, to be free with little jokes and slow to contradict, to be philosophic and yet melancholy because of his life's ups and downs.

Everitt said, "That Jesse you were with? I noticed him

302

there upstairs this morning. I guess Field's making a lot of trouble for the School Board. Well, if a fellow wants some of that, he ought to take them a little older; that's what I say. Get a superior article, too. They ought to be properly developed for best results." His amiable coarseness had the sad overtone of age, the half-heartedness of a discussion now purely academic, in which he obligingly catered more to what he knew was the normal interest of other men than to his own. "They going to fire Mr. Rawle?" he asked.

"I don't know," Abner said. "How about some service here?"

"Willard's sick today," Everitt said. "There's more than one man can do. Hey, Al, you got company!"

The boy in the dirty chef's apron who was pressing half a dozen hissing pats of meat on the hot griddle with a spatula turned his sweating face and smiled. "Be right there, Mr. Coates."

Abner said, "A ham and egg sandwich and some coffee."

"It's mainly a matter of politics," Everitt said. "Perhaps it shouldn't be; but it is. Somebody has an eye on Rawle's job. That's the size of it. I don't think Mr. Hobbs gets along very well with Jesse." The workings of the system which had found him his own job were familiar to Everitt, and he was cautious about criticizing them; but a man had a right to speak his mind. As long as he didn't get too positive (as though he were trying to run things), and didn't make remarks that, if repeated, would offend and anger those to whom he should be grateful, he was free enough.

Abner watched the progress of his ham and eggs in a skillet over the gas flame. He said, "I don't know, Everitt." Everitt's art of being meek, but with dignity, was a good art, and took skill and judgment; but, supposing he had any skill and judgment, Abner wondered if he wanted to use it that way—to get and keep a job. His situation there, he saw, had points in common with the situation he had got himself into with Bonnie. In both cases he wanted what he wanted, but on his own terms. When you were as old as Everitt, you probably found that what you wanted could never be got that way. The only things you could have just the way you wanted them were those things you could give yourself.

Everitt coughed and said, "Got to be getting back up there. Can't start without me! Think it will go to the jury this afternoon?"

"I hope so." A plate bearing the sandwich rattled down on the counter in front of Abner. "What's your hurry?" he said, feeling that he had not been very cordial to Everitt, whom he liked. Everitt patted his back gently, turning away. "Don't move as fast as you do," he said. He made a gesture with the old umbrella that had been leaning against his stool. Peering out the wide window, he said, "Looks to me like it's easing up."

Following him five minutes later, Abner found that the rain had stopped. The warm air was gray and still, almost as wet as rain. Water ran in the gutters of Broad Street, and Abner looked at the weathervane, an elaborate little iron banner, on the cupola of the county office building. It remained pointing southeast, so the rain was probably not over. Abner crossed behind the courthouse and walked up under the silent, dripping trees to the door at the arch.

In the depressing gloom of the hall, Hugh Erskine methodically chewing a tooth pick, waited by the bars of the passage to the jail. "Ab," he said, "that Field business was a rotten thing! I never would have thought it of him! Warren says he only got a year—"

Hugh wheeled around, hearing steps in the passage. Unconsciously he touched a hand to his left armpit; and by the mechanical gesture he showed that there under his coat was strapped a holster with an automatic pistol. Hugh did not ordinarily bother to go armed; but it might have occurred to him that these prisoners of his, whom he was about to acknowledge taking into his own hand, were in as desperate a case as men can be. The grill opened and the warden came out carrying his book. He and Hugh bent over the open page on the radiator top while Hugh signed.

Abner went up the passage to the door of the Attorneys Room. It was crowded. Joe Jackman sat in the corner with Bob Fuller, thumbing over the pages of a thick brief. Pete Van Zant was still there, talking to John Clark. Abner saw George Stacey and Mark; and Jake Riordan, telling them something. Mr. Servadei was speaking to Bunting by the fireplace. At the telephone by the lavatory door were two city reporters. A hubbub of conversation arose.

"Suppose you had to bring five or six separate suits—"

"I ought to go over to the office, but if I do my girl will have something—"

"That on for argument? I thought I saw—"

"I always found him a very fair fellow to deal with. Can't control his client, I guess—"

"Yeah, but won't equity leave them where it found them—"

"If that's constitutional, I give up—"

"John, you're the attorney for Saratoga Township, aren't you? Well—"

"You don't know how they're going to construe the crazy thing—"

"Listen, that's setting up a new statute of limitations—"

Mr. Servadei in his soft somewhat accented voice was saying to Bunting, "Mr. Bunting, I want to tell you how much I appreciate—" The reporter at the telephone, the receiver pressed to one ear, his hand covering the other, proved to be expostulating loudly, "No! This is Duffy; Duffy, at Childerstown courthouse! Now, give me the city desk—"

In the lavatory Abner found himself face to face with Harry Wurts who was drying his hands on a paper towel.

"Ah!" Harry said, "don't think nobody saw you! Making peace?"

Abner said, "I don't know what you're talking about."

"And how was Mr. Gearhart this fine morning? His usual candid upright self? God damn, boy, you must want to be the county's chief hired assassin bad!" He threw the crumpled towel in the waste basket. "Or, now you're getting to know him, I suppose you find he's been cruelly misjudged? Yet seen too oft, familiar with her face, we first endure, then pity, then embrace? Well, has the hugging started?"

The morning had been a trying one; and Abner could feel, like bruises in his mind, numerous sore points at which the touch of a thought made him wince. Harry's taunting tone, provocative both because Harry meant it to be, and because, in ways Harry probably never dreamed of—that trick of quoting verse or something made you tired—stirred anger. Abner thought a moment of giving him a short hard jab in the mouth; but to do that he would have to let his temper go and, as his sore and subdued mind could tell him, bruise himself further and make himself more trouble. With a great effort, Abner said indifferently, "Not yet."

Abner had seen how impossible it was to start a brawl here, with the next room full of people, and with court about to resume. He saw now from Harry's expression that Harry had thought of it, too; that Harry, for reasons best known to his secretive, sensitive self, hoped Abner would start something. Harry was ready to take a sudden punch in the jaw as the price of getting Abner into an absurd and humiliating position.

Since they were looking each other in the eye, Harry probably realized that Abner had grasped his intention. He looked sheepish; and Abner, baffled a moment, knew then from the sensation of his own face that he himself was looking the same way. In fact, it was no more Harry's nature to pick a quarrel than Abner's; and if Harry felt like quarreling, there was a reason; and the reason could only be that Abner was

306

himself provoking—no doubt because of those qualities, or some tricks of manner or attitude derived from them, which Judge Coates had mentioned last night.

Harry said in a not-quite-natural voice, "Kidding aside, Ab, you going to run for D.A.?"

"I honestly don't know who's running," Abner said.

"If Jesse knows what's good for him, he'll run you. Hell, Ab, don't let the racket get you down! Onward, Christian soldiers!" He turned to the door.

"Thanks for the kind words," Abner said, conscious of a considerable triumph, if not over Harry, over himself. "But if you're marching as to war, you'd better button your fly, hadn't you?"

"Oyez," said Nick Dowdy, "oyez, oyez—"

He crouched, bent forward over his desk, supporting himself by the gavel with which he had just struck the block, blinking up at all the people on their feet. "The several courts this day holden are open in their entirety!" He let himself plump the short distance into his seat and smiled contentedly at Abner.

Judge Vredenburgh who had been standing, too, straight and stiff, now held up his glasses, polishing them, and said, his chins down, his eyes up, addressing Joe Jackman, "Note that the defendants and their counsel are in court."

To Everitt Weitzel, he said, "You may call the jury." He put the glasses on and sat down, looking about the well of the court, where in renewed movement everyone else was sitting down. "Mr. Wurts!" he said, and beckoned to Harry, who came up to side bar where they whispered to each other a moment.

Turning, Harry said, "Stanley Howell, take the stand."

During the recess Howell had slicked his hair with water. His cheap and badly fitting brown suit seemed to have been brushed or somehow made a little neater. With a qualm at the futility of it, Abner supposed Howell had done what he could according to a reformatory boy's forlorn idea of recommending himself. Above the buttoned coat, under the plastered hair, Howell's furtive, unfirm little mouth and wild sick-looking eyes made the effort repulsive and unconvincing.

Harry, waiting while the jury was seated, compressed his lips with ironic resignation. Harry meant (and perhaps he was right) that, given anything like an even break, he could get his man off; but who could get Howell, a person like Howell, off? Harry fingered the cropped hairs of his smudge of reddish mustache. He looked at the jury with an appraising eye, marshaling his faculties for an engagement that he was too wise to expect to win. Whoever had advised Howell to get Harry—Abner suspected that it was Mr. Servadei's firm—had not advised Howell badly. Howell had to fight. There was nothing to be gained by throwing himself on the mercy of the court; for that chance was open only until Leming had taken it. There was nothing the Commonwealth wanted from Howell but his life; and Howell's choice was between pleading guilty (a plea which would not be accepted) and throwing his life away at once; or pleading not guilty and forcing them to come and take it. They were coming; and Harry had found no way to stop them; but Howell for his last money had bought the only chance; and if, in the long run, it did him no good, in the long run money saved would be no good to a dead man, either.

Harry turned a cool reprehensive gaze on his client. Raising his voice so that the sounds fell strong and clear, struck out like the round opening notes of a solemn composition, he said, "What is your full name?"

The jury had settled itself and grown as quiet as it is possible for twelve human beings to be. For them, the name might be Cain; and since they could feel no reasonable doubt that they looked at a participant in murder, Harry's distant, level manner was the right one. To pretend to be defending an innocent man only invited scorn, if the jurors believed him sincere, because he was such a fool; and if they believed him insincere, he invited their anger, because he showed in that case that he thought he was smarter than they were. Harry's tactic was to put it to the jurors that he was a shrewd man, and they were shrewd, too; and they all disliked Howell; but more than they disliked Howell, they loved justice, he and they. Harry phrased his formal questions—where Howell had been born and raised; where he lived; how long he had known Leming and Basso and Bailey; just when he moved to the Rock Creek bungalow; and who was there.

These monotonous facts, the bare names and dates, bored the jury. In most cases they could not or did not carry any exact earlier statements in their heads, so whether Howell gave answers agreeing with what Leming or someone else said mattered little to them. They already knew that Howell was acquainted with these people. They knew about the bungalow and who was there. They began to cross and un-cross their legs, to scratch their noses and ears. A boy like George Stacey might have seen these symptoms with dismay; but Harry bored them calmly, with ease and assurance; figur-ing, Abner supposed, that when he got ready to interest them they would welcome it, less alert to contend.

Harry said, "Now, Howell, before we go any further, the Commonwealth has introduced in evidence, C.X. eighteen—" He extended his hand to Joe Jackman, who searched his desk a moment, found the right papers, and gave them to Harry. "Thank you," Harry said. "This purports to be a statement made by you on May sixth, last. Will you look at it?"

Howell said, "Yes; I guess you would have made a state-ment, too, if you—" Here was the chance he had been wait-ing for; and he snatched it with a convulsion of face and mind, his words tumbling over each other in his hurry to take his own part.

Harry said sharply, for he had to keep Howell from assuming the ridiculous role of injured innocence, "Just answer the question!"

"That is the statement," Howell said sulkily. Abner could see that he hated and feared Harry; and it was a hard thing when you hated and feared the man you had to cling to.

Harry said, still dissociating himself from Howell's wrong attitude, "Don't you think you'd better read it?"

Howell took the sheets held up to him, his hand shaking, and made a pretense, moving his eyes over the first page or two. "Well," said Harry, "you heard it read here in court this morning?"

"Yes."

"And that was the statement you signed?"

"I signed it. They made me. They kept me there, the Federals—"

"Just a moment! How long were you in their custody?"

"Until, I think, the seventh."

"The day after you signed this paper?"

"I think so. My mind was a blank—"

Harry frowned, for the phrase, as Howell offered it, would not be acceptable to anyone in his right senses. That was something he had read somewhere; and so he naturally spoke it like a liar. Harry cut in, "Do you recall the time of day or night when you signed?"

"I guess I do!" Howell said. "It was around one o'clock in the morning."

"One o'clock in the morning. Now, Mr. Kinsolving expressed the opinion that you signed at one o'clock that morning of the fourth day because of the constant kindness shown you by him and his associates—"

Beside Abner, Bunting said, "Your Honor, I think before Mr. Wurts goes on, he should ask the witness directly about the truth or falsity of his statement. I submit—"

"I am happy to ask him," Harry said. "You are familiar with the statement that was read here this morning by Mr. Coates?"

"I am, yes."

"Are the facts contained in that statement true or untrue?"

"Not all the facts is true."

"You mean that part of it is true, and part of it is false."

"Part is truth; and part of it is just to keep them off my ear." Howell turned an appealing glance to the jury. He twisted his mean little mouth to a sort of smile, as though asking them to appreciate this wry joke. They looked at him coldly; and Abner found himself uncomfortable; not, certainly, sympathetic; but exercised by the shame that the heart feels to see any human being caught in a weak and sickly trick, and that the head resents as a clumsy insult to all human intelligence.

Bunting said, "I'm sorry to interrupt again; but I think the witness should be asked which parts are true and which parts are false."

"If you please, Mr. Bunting!" said Harry. "We will get to that. Now, Howell, what did they do to you when they brought you up there?"

"Well, they put shackles on me."

"You mean, on your wrists?"

"No, on my legs; and then they put handcuffs on me; and then they got to working around. Bust me on the chin; twist my ears; twist my arms. Then they took my overcoat off and then they got to working on me with hoses they had." He spoke jerkily, expelling the phrases with bitter little grunts. It had the ring of truth to Abner. The pain and panic Howell must have felt burned those moments into his mind. He spoke what he knew. Harry, seeing that he had at last evoked something effective, said gently, "Yes. What then?"

"They put me on the table after they took my coat off, put me on the table, like the table you got there." Howell brought his knuckle up and scraped it with his teeth. For nerves in as bad shape as his, the memory was agitating; but Abner could see that the jury was not responding. They saw his suffering; but it disgusted them. They were moved; but with revulsion, less as though he were a wounded man than as though he were a wounded snake.

"That is the table Mr. Kinsolving described this morning?" Harry said.

"Yes. That is right."

"Go ahead and tell us."

"So they taken the handcuffs off, taken my other coat off, and put my handcuffs on me; and put me on the table. I am lying on my stomach; and one is holding the handcuffs up this way—" He raised his wrists over his head. "They got my hands out this way."

"Just a moment," Harry said kindly, "that won't mean anything in the record. Your arms were stretched over your head?"

"Yes," Howell said. He wiped his mouth on the back of his hand. "They are holding me there, so I cannot move."

"And your coat was off?"

"My coat was off. The only thing I have on is a vest and shirt. Then they beat me over the kidneys with the hoses."

Harry Wurts said, "What do you mean by hoses?"

"It's a little piece of hose, see? About a foot long; about like a garden hose."

"Who are 'they'?"

"Why, two of the men. That wasn't all. After they—"

"Just a minute!" Harry said. "Take your time. You say they were beating you this way. How long did they beat you?"

Howell said, "Well, to my knowledge, it seemed like eight hours; but I guess it was around an hour and a half or something around there. Every bit of clothes on me was wringing wet. I couldn't sit down, couldn't stand up. I was weak—"

Harry cut him off. "As a result of this treatment was your back lacerated?"

"Oh, yes. Then they—"

"What other effects did this treatment have on you?"

312

"Oh, well, it put my kidneys on the bum. My kidneys is on the bum yet—"

"That is the reason that you have to be withdrawn at frequent intervals?"

"That is the reason."

"As a result of this treatment did you pass blood?"

"Yes. When I first got it, for twenty-four hours I urinated blood."

"Did those officers there who had charge of you see that?"

"Yes. They seen it. I asked for a doctor. They said, 'You don't need any doctor.' They said, 'We will doctor you.'"

Harry Wurts nodded. He took a turn down past the jury, looking at the floor, his face morose, making to them the simple appeal of his troubled mind. Leaving Howell aside, and no matter whether Howell repelled them or not, or whether he told the exact truth or not, the suspicion and possibility (and anyone could see it was more than that) put the jury's back up. The law was aspersed. They could joke about the law, and speak of it disrespectfully; and say that there was no justice, or that the rich could get away with murder, or that political influence was what counted; but, in fact, they never believed it. It could not be true because they had the final say. When they swore that they would well and truly try and true deliverance make between the Commonwealth and the prisoner at the bar, they meant it. Their minds shared Harry's trouble. They did not like any of this.

Harry said, "You saw Lieutenant Dunglison on the stand here this morning and heard him testify that when you were turned over to him you had not been injured. You saw Mr. Kinsolving on the stand. Was he in the room at the time this treatment was given to you?"

Howell screwed his eyes up, looking in the gloom of the court along the row of chairs below the rail until he found Mr. Kinsolving sitting there with Lieutenant Dunglison. "The lieutenant may have been there, outside. I don't know.

He was there right away when they called him. That big fellow, huh! He said he didn't do nothing to me! He only twisted my arm pretty near off and my ears."

"That is Mr. Kinsolving?"

"Yes. Kinsolving."

The jury looked, too; and Kinsolving, undisturbed, let the trace of a faint contemptuous smile appear at the corners of his strong mouth. Unselfconscious, he gave his head a slight pitying shake.

Harry said, "Now, this treatment you describe, this show of kindness; just when did it occur, how soon after you were taken into custody?"

"Well, I will tell you the truth," Howell said. "I don't know if it was day or night. I am in a room with glass all around, and on the outside is a big office. I didn't see no daylight, and they had electric lights on all the time, and I don't know if it was daytime or nighttime. I would say I had been there a day or two. They would leave me sleep a few minutes, so I suppose it was night when that was."

"And the rest of the time they beat you?"

"No," said Howell. "They only beat me once with the hose. They only need to beat you once."

"Yes?"

"Then a man come in, you know, and my back was so sore—" Howell bent forward and touched himself gingerly. "My back here. And they come in and press down on it; and then I was getting alcohol baths three times a day to take the marks off."

"Who was giving you alcohol baths?"

"I don't know their names. The chief inspector, I guess it is, come in and says to me, 'How did you get that, Stanley?' I said, 'Fell down the stairs.' He said, 'What do you mean, fell down the stairs?' If I had opened my mouth I would have just got it over again; so he said to me, 'You look like you have hives.' I said, 'Yes. I guess I have got them.'"

"You mean that you would have been beaten over again if you had not agreed?"

"He just asked to see what I was going to say. If I had said anything—well, you know, I would have got it again."

"How often were you asked to make a statement?"

"I was asked all the time. One would stay in twenty minutes, and another would come in, and another one, and another one. I don't know how many."

"And what did you answer?"

"I would answer I don't know nothing."

"Then they would go out?"

"Yes. Then they said, 'I will put that laugh on the back of your face.'"

"Who said that?"

"A couple of them. I don't know them by name."

"And did the punishment which was inflicted on you, which you have described here, have any influence in making you willing to give a statement?"

"I would have told them anything," Howell said. "I couldn't stand no more of that."

"Then the part of the statement in which you say that you are making it of your own free will and accord is not true."

"Not true."

"Not true. Now, I call your attention to another statement you made, about obtaining the ransom money: 'I went to get it with Basso, but I didn't like the look, and so Bob gets it from a car.' Is that correct in all particulars?"

"It says what I did. It don't say why I did it. I have to go with him, because Bailey give me orders; but I—to tell you the truth, I never wanted to be mixed up in this job; so when we are out, I said, 'I will not do this. I don't like the look.'"

"And what did you do?"

"I stayed at a drug store, like, until he is through."

"You told him that you were not taking any part in it. You withdrew before the money was obtained?"

Judge Vredenburgh said, "Mr. Wurts, if I understand what you are driving at, I must remind you that the only time when one of the persons conspiring to commit a crime may repent and withdraw and so avoid liability is before the commission of the act constituting the crime. No person can purge himself of an offense once committed by an act subsequent—at least, not unless he marries the girl." He smiled.

"I simply wished to show, sir, that under the influence of pain and duress the defendant allowed it to appear that he had taken a larger part in the business than in fact he did take."

"Proceed."

"Now, when you returned with Basso and this money that he had obtained, was there a conversation in reference to taking Frederick Zollicoffer home?"

"That is where I thought he was going."

"I say," said Harry, less patiently, "there was a conversation in reference to that?"

"Not just then there wasn't."

Harry weighed this perverse display of scrupulosity—Abner could see Harry asking himself what the hell this half-wit Howell thought he was doing—and threw it out contemptuously. "Well, when was the conversation?"

"I went upstairs," Howell said, sulky again, "and some time later, Bob Basso come up and told me Bailey wanted to do away with him." His air was aggrieved; but fundamentally he was still in good spirits, the next thing to vivacious. Howell rose to the occasion of showing off. He resented Harry's refusal to let him do it his own way, but even his resentment helped to keep his mind busy and excited. He had forgotten the fear of death and the anguish of suspense in the strong conceit of I, I, I.

Harry said, "You were upstairs guarding Zollicoffer?"

"Yes. I was playing pinochle with him. Bob gives me a sign to stop the game; so I go out, and he says about doing away with him. I said, 'Positively no. I do not go in for that,' and me and Bob went on talking, saying we did not want to go in for that; so I go downstairs, and I—"

"Now, just a minute! You went downstairs. Where was Basso?"

"He stayed with Zolly. He says, 'You punk,' he was speaking in fun, 'you want to take me on?' He means the pinochle game, where I had laid the cards down—"

Abner had been over the bungalow and seen this bare upstairs room. He could set the grim little scene, the gross prisoner, disheveled by his captivity, marked by his use of drugs; the cards; the slow game to kill time; Basso's pleasantry while Frederick Zollicoffer's life entered its last half hour. Howell said, "So I went down and I began to reason with Bailey; and he said, 'Oh, all right, all right, all right. Go ahead upstairs; everything will be all right."

"Who said that?"

"Bailey. So I went upstairs again and told Bob; and Bob went down again to make sure; so when he came up, everything is supposed to be O.K."

"What do you mean, everything was supposed to be O.K.?"

"That he was going to be let go home."

"You mean that Bailey had satisfied you that no harm was to come to Frederick Zollicoffer?"

"I was satisfied. I said, 'Should I get the car?' and Bailey says, 'Yes.' He told us, 'You needn't carry no guns; we will let him go.' So I get the car out. Bailey said, 'You haven't got no guns, have you? We do not want any accidents.' I said, 'No, I have not.' I said, 'You told me before.'" Howell gave the jury a bold look, as though he did not believe that he could be failing to impress them with his essential innocence. "Bailey said, 'Are you sure?' I said, 'Yes, I am sure.' He said, 'All right.' So we go and put him in the car."

Harry said, "Now, just tell us how you put him in the car."

"He was on the floor. His back was to the right hand door in the back of the car, with his face facing the left hand door, and his head was like by Bailey's knee. Bob is next to Bailey. So I am driving, and—"

"Were you told to drive any particular place?"

"We agreed so we would drive the other way, we would drive out in the country, so he could not tell where we had kept him at."

"Did you know where you were going? Did you know that you had entered this county?"

"Not then, I never knew. They tell me we did. I never done it intentionally. I drove like at random." It would have saved this court a lot of trouble, Abner reflected, if, in his driving like at random, Howell had just stayed over there. "So I drove quite some time, taking different turns. So I hear Zolly, not very good, he had this blanket over him, say, 'Come on. I want to get home.' So Bailey says, 'Do not worry. Here you go.' So all of a sudden these shots went. I come near running the car off the road. I flinch."

"And why did you—er—flinch?" said Harry.

"I thought I—who wouldn't? Say, when they tell you not to have guns, what do you think would enter your mind?"

"The question," said Harry, "is not what would enter my mind. I wasn't there. What entered your mind?"

"Well," said Howell, spreading his hands for the jury. "I thought maybe I was going to get it, too. I didn't know."

"And after you had finished flinching?"

"I look around. Bailey was saying, 'There is another monkey that will never kill any more.'"

"Did Bailey have his gun in his hand at the time?"

"He had something in his hand. It is dark in the back. I couldn't say for positive it was a gun he had."

"And did Robert Basso have a gun in his hand?"

"No. Bob didn't have no gun. I am sure of that. He got the same orders I got when we left. I know neither of us have guns. That was when it entered my mind. I thought: I and Bob are going next. Bailey says, 'Turn around. Get off the road.'"

"And you did?"

"Yes. And then I pulled off on some kind of a road up there, country road. You know, it was dark. There was no lights on that road; and Bailey says, 'Stop.' "

"And what did you do then?"

"We took out the body, and laid him in this lot, this field, and put the irons, tried to put the irons on him. I said, 'Leave him here; what is the use of putting them around him?' I wanted to get out of there, I am telling you. I did not feel so good; so anyway, I said, 'You are never going to lift him; put those weights in the car.' Bailey said, 'Yes, pile him back again.' "

Howell paused. Now that he was picturing to himself the grisly incidents of that night, some cold sense of what all this meant to him had probably begun to dilute the warmth of so much self-expression. He remembered now how he had felt when the thought 'entered his mind' that he was going next; and suddenly it must have come home to him that danger of death, which he was describing as though it were something past, faced him this very minute. Bailey with his gun and his contorted mind was never so implacable and dangerous, never so far beyond the reach of argument or the influence of pity, as Mr. Bunting and Mr. Coates, sitting silent at the table there regarding him. In their expressionless faces and disinterested eyes he could probably read a good enough equivalent of Bailey's epitaph on Frederick Zollicoffer: *There is another monkey that will never kill any more;* and this time, the monkey was Howell himself, already done for, by due process of law bleeding invisibly to death from wounds which he could not feel, but which would prove as fatal to him as the wounds of Bailey's bullets to Frederick Zollicoffer.

Harry said, "Go on."

Howell wet his lips. "So we all put him back in the car," he said mechanically. "So Bailey ordered Basso in the front seat, so he should drive. So he said to me, 'Come on back here.' So I got in back and figured—well, he told me to get

in back of the car, so I figured: well, what is he going to do?"
He paused again uncertainly, the terror of that moment perhaps a little dim beside the quiet but real terror of this moment, the present. "He said, 'Hold him here—'"

Bunting said, "Just keep your voice up, please. I can't hear you."

"Talk into the microphone there," Harry said. "Nobody can hear you."

Howell said, louder, "So he said, 'Hold him here a minute.' I am holding him. I didn't like to hold that man. I am trying to hold him; and he said, 'Come on and hold him; we will see if we can get the weights around him.' So then Basso drives out on the road, and we come down toward this bridge."

"You got the weights on?"

"Not me, I didn't do none of it. Bailey did. So we come to the bridge."

"The state road bridge over Fosher's Creek?"

"Yes. In the middle of it we stop. We take him out."

"Who?"

"Zolly, his body—"

"I mean, who took him out? Who is 'we'?"

"The whole three of us. So we heave him in. So we go along and down the road, and Bailey says, 'If any of this ever leaks out, you know the consequences.'"

"He said that to you?"

"To me and Bob Basso, both."

"All right," said Harry. He turned abruptly to Bunting and said, "Cross-examine."

Bunting tore off a sheet of his yellow pad on the table before him and looked a moment at his notes, but he did not bother to take them with him. He got up and went over to Joe Jackman, who gave him the confession. Lifting it,

Bunting said to Howell with a note of good-humored long-suffering, "Now, Stanley, I show you your statement, Commonwealth's Exhibit number eighteen. What part of that statement, if any, is untrue?"

Howell considered the question with visible caution. He said, "There is some true, there is some isn't true."

Bunting said, "I will ask you what part, if any, is untrue?"

Howell took his time. He said guardedly, "I would have to read the whole thing, and then tell you after I read it."

Bunting said, "Can't you, just off-hand, think of anything in it that is not true?"

Howell said, "Well, the first part; that isn't."

"You mean," said Bunting, "the part that says you are making it of your own free will, and without any threats or promises having been made you?"

"That is positively untrue."

Bunting looked off to the high corner of the sloping ceiling. "What else is not true?"

"Well, I would have to read the whole statement."

"Can't you think of anything else, if you know of anything that is not true?"

"No," said Howell doggedly, "not just at the present time."

"You can't think of a thing in it that is not true. Isn't that because it's all true?"

"Some," said Howell, "is true, and there is some is not true."

"I want to know which part is not true."

Harry Wurts said, "If your Honor please, this statement is several pages of typewriting, and if the witness is given a chance to read the statement—"

Bunting turned to him and said, "If I have to take the time, I will permit him to read it, if you would prefer to have it done that way."

Harry said, "I don't see why not."

"Well, I do, Mr. Wurts," Judge Vredenburgh said. "In my opinion, it is unnecessary to take all that time."

"If I may say so, sir," Harry said, "when the district attorney keeps repeating a question which, he is well aware, cannot be answered off-hand, there is a certain loss of time. too."

"And I think you are aggravating it, Mr. Wurts."

Harry sat down, and Bunting said, "You signed this statement, Stanley?"

"Yes."

"And you read it before you signed it?"

"Yes."

Harry said, "I object to the district attorney going on with this statement unless he lets the witness take it as he requested, sentence by sentence—"

Judge Vredenburgh said, "He is not asking anything about its contents just now."

"He probably will."

Judge Vredenburgh pouted. "There is no question asked at this time. You will have to wait."

"Has your Honor ruled on my objection?"

Judge Vredenburgh laid down his pencil and took off his glasses, rubbing his eyes. "I suggest to the district attorney that he shall not press that line of examination if it involves having the witness read us the whole statement. However, he has a right to, if he wants to."

Bunting said, "I don't want to, your Honor. I'm not going to do it."

"Well," said Harry, shrugging, "if he is not going to comment on it, I will withdraw my objection."

"So that counsel will understand," Bunting said, "what I mean is, that I am not going to ask again what part is true and what part is not true."

"But you are going to take up the different sentences?" Harry said.

322

"When necessary, I purpose to read them to him, just as you did."

"Then I ask that the witness be permitted to read out the statement," Harry said to Judge Vredenburgh. "This is simply beating around the bush."

Judge Vredenburgh shook his head. "The district attorney is the judge of how he is going to do it. Objection overruled."

To himself, Abner thought, "My God!" It could not be said to have taken many minutes; but when you heard them waste time and waste more time complaining about whether they were wasting time or not, what could you say, except that the law was an ass? They acted as though all eternity were at their disposal. If it did not get through this afternoon, there was always tomorrow, and the next day; and next week, and for that matter, next month, and even next year.

Below the bench Abner could observe the faces of those paid to wait it out, and by practice prepared to: Mat Rhea and Theodore Bosenbury side by side, their eyes fixed in space; Gifford Hughes, who was asleep, and Hermann Mapes, who had as usual brought down some work and was inconspicuously doing it; Nick Dowdy, also asleep; Joe Jackman, his alert face and half bald head turning a little from sound to sound while with steady precision he marked up column after column and sheet after sheet of his ruled paper. Above them, in the glow of his desk lamp, Judge Vredenburgh had now begun again to write steadily, too; and though he darted occasional sharp glances at the witness, or at Bunting questioning him, he was probably working on the draft of his charge with the hope that he would have a chance to use it before the afternoon was over.

Leaning back, Abner looked at the wheel of stained glass, bright with light, above him and thought, "Maybe I am in the wrong business." Reviewing his career, it seemed to him that he had never shown much aptitude for law. They had expected him to go into it, and he had gone—but had he ever taken to law the way Harry Wurts took to it? To Harry, all was as natural as breathing. Harry did not put to himself (Abner surely would have) needless questions when he was asked to assume Howell's defense. Harry estimated the hard work in the almost hopeless case, found out how much could be paid, decided it was enough, and accepted—partly because he did not mind hard cases, partly no doubt because he did not mind obliging Servadei, or his firm. Having taken it on, Harry flung himself into it, working furiously and well, though not through a sense of duty or obligation to his client. Tuesday in the Attorneys Room he had made no bones about his client being guilty; and the way he treated Howell showed the contempt he felt for him. That it would profit Harry to oblige or impress Servadei was problematic; and Howell's last few hundred dollars (they must have come from the division of Walter Cohen's payment) were poor pickings; so Harry was really defending Howell for the fun of it. He enjoyed the intellectual tussle with Bunting. It was a pleasure to obstruct the Commonwealth; and if, in fact, the ends of justice could be defeated, that was justice's tough luck. It did not seem to Abner that he himself had ever managed to feel quite that way, or to litigate for the sheer love of litigating.

On the stand Howell was in difficulties. Abner had been paying no attention. There could be nothing new after five weeks of turning over and over this complicated yet meager material, and Abner was fed up with the detail; but he could see the virtue of Bunting's unwearied pertinacity, the steady plodding and pressing. Like a man doing a jigsaw puzzle, Bunting searched and searched for the piece he wanted; and in the end, sure enough, he found it, fitted it into place, and looked for the next piece. He must just have found one, and Howell was apprehensive.

Bunting said to him, "Stanley, I never got on your ear, did I?"

His voice was mild and dry; he smiled. Bunting was

capable of subtleties, too; and it occurred to Abner that leaving Leming to him had served a double purpose and that Marty had planned it to serve the double purpose. Not only would Leming do better with Abner, but Marty would be left freer to make a personal approach to Howell. Howell was not silly enough to trust anyone; yet he might not distrust Bunting quite so much as he would distrust a person who let it be seen that he had the traitor, Leming's, confidence.

With an answering uncertain smile, Howell said, "On my ear?"

"Yes."

"You only asked me down there, 'Do you want to talk to me?'"

"Did you get the impression that if you refused to talk to me that I would beat you up?"

"Oh, no. I never said you, down here, made threats or done anything."

"So what you told me, anything you said to me was not said in fear?"

"Not in fear, no."

"Do you remember telling me how Zolly was killed?"

Howell said, "You spoke to me how Zolly was killed; and I said, 'Put in the machine,' didn't I?"

"Well, now, Stanley," Bunting said, "I can't very well testify. I'm not a witness. I'm asking you."

"Yes."

"And at that time, when you were not in fear of being beaten up, you told me, didn't you—"

Harry Wurts said, "Now, if the Court please, I am going to enter an objection here to these questions of Mr. Bunting's in reference to any conversations he had with the defendant, unless Mr. Bunting is going to take the stand and be cross-examined."

"No," said Judge Vredenburgh. "I don't know of any rule that requires that."

"Well, sir," said Harry, "he is asking Howell about a conversation he had with him."

"And the defendant is answering," Judge Vredenburgh said. "If it is not contradicted, it is acceptable."

"Well, I enter an objection."

"Overruled. You may except."

Bunting said, "Stanley, you remember talking to me when they brought you up here, don't you?"

"Yes," said Howell, "I said, 'I will see you when I get a lawyer,' didn't I?"

"And this gentleman was there, wasn't he?" Bunting turned and indicated Abner.

"I don't know whether he was then. I seen so many people."

Abner had been there. He remembered Howell producing a slip of paper and explaining that this was his lawyer. Somebody had written down Harry Wurts' name. Afterward, Bunting said, "It would be Harry!"

Bunting had a job to do; and he knew Harry well enough to be sure that Harry would make things no easier. Though good at them, Bunting did not enjoy contests of wits. Abner had seen him faced with a smart trick often enough to remember as characteristic that change that came over him; Marty's dry expression getting drier. He did not lose his temper, for it was no inconvenience to him to have to think fast; and he could usually meet tricks with a trick of his own worth two of those; but he was disgusted. The truth was, Marty had no sense of humor. Seriously absorbed in a serious and absorbing piece of work, he saw himself interrupted by some idle buffoon's attempt to play a pointless practical joke on him. He might see it in time to stop it, and even to put it in reverse; but he still did not like being interrupted, and he stared with astonished contempt at the person who would seize such a moment to do such a thing. Though a sense of humor was generally spoken of with approval, and a man was pitied for lacking one, Abner supposed that he must lack

326

one himself. When he saw a sense of humor in action, it always seemed to Abner a lucky thing, since somebody had to do the work of an unappreciative world, that a certain number of people could be relied on to lack it.

Bunting said, "Now, Stanley, whether you remember that, or not, you do remember telling me—"

The door of the Attorneys Room opened to let out Malcolm Levering. He had been in the tipstaff's chair at the far end where he must have been able to hear the telephone ring through the closed door. He passed quietly along behind the jury, skirted Harry and Basso and George Stacey in their seats at the second table, and came across on tiptoe to Abner. He bent and said hoarsely in Abner's ear, "Ab, a Sergeant LaBarre, I think his name is, State Police, Newmarket sub-station, wants to talk to Marty as soon as he can. Very important."

"Is he on the phone?"

"No. I told him Marty was in court."

"Ring him back and ask if I can do anything. Tell him Marty has a witness on the stand. Oh, never mind; I'll do it." On his pad Abner wrote: *State Police, Newmarket,* drew a circle around it, and laid it where Marty would see it if he looked. He crossed over after Malcolm, who climbed into his chair, and Abner passed him and went into the Attorneys Room.

Both of the wide screened windows had been left open to air out the tobacco smoke; and the entering dampness of the day filled the shadows with mustiness from the shelves of leather-backed books and the old plaster and wood. It had been raining; but now the rain had stopped again. The big trees, extending down to the corner where High Street intersected North Broad Street, hung wet and heavy with a kind of haze around them. Abner dialed the operator.

At the Newmarket sub-station the man on the switchboard said, "State Police."

Abner said, "This is Abner Coates of the district attorney's

327

office, Childerstown. The sergeant was calling the district attorney a moment ago. He said it was important."

"O.K.," said the operator. "Here it is." There was a click, and a voice said, "LaBarre speaking. Mr. Coates? Look, I've been off since Tuesday night. I just came on. That Mason case, the manslaughter, the motor vehicle thing. You know which one I mean?"

"Yes."

"I don't know what you're doing about it; but it seems there's a misunderstanding, or something. Now, let me tell you the facts. I was there myself two or three minutes after it happened—it was right down beyond here; you could see it from here. Private Lynd, he's the arresting officer, actually saw the cars hit. He was just going to his car—I mean, the patrol car in front of the station."

"I think Mr. Bunting has the report," Abner said. "The inquest is set for tomorrow. Wasn't your man notified?"

"Yes, he was. Now, here's the thing. Somebody was squawking about us holding this Mason for manslaughter."

"What do you mean, squawking?" Abner said. With a start of cold annoyance the thought came to him that Jesse, leaving no stone unturned in his anxiety to serve and please George Guthrie Mason, had approached the police as well as the district attorney. "Who is somebody?"

Sergeant LaBarre said, "Well, if you want to know, we heard it was you, Mr. Coates. We heard you said he ought to have been just charged with being involved in a fatal accident; and you were going to make a complaint higher up."

Disconcerted, Abner said, "I don't know who told you that. It isn't what I said." Jake Riordan wouldn't be likely to go down and gossip at the sub-station; but what he could do and probably had done was make a remark to somebody who told somebody else, who told somebody else. "What I said was that I would have to see the report and talk to the arresting officer. The J.P., Wiener, told me he didn't think it was Mason's fault. Mason told me the same

328

thing; and said you, or some other officer, said the tire marks showed the other fellow ran into him. What I said was, if there were no specific grounds for charging him with manslaughter the J.P. should have been allowed to set bail, and there was no reason to jail Mason. If it wasn't Mason's fault, if the other driver caused the accident, your man, your Private Lynd, ought to know better than to charge Mason with manslaughter. I don't know what they do other places; but in this county we're certainly going to squawk."

"Now, look it," Sergeant LaBarre said. "The reason we charged Mason with manslaughter was reckless driving. I can't help what he told you. I mean, reckless in the language of the statute. Means negligently; the absence of care under the circumstances. Right?"

"Yes."

"While doing that, he accidentally kills a man. That's manslaughter, as far as I know; and that's what we charged him with."

"Then it was his fault?"

"Sure! Lynd sees this car going a pretty good rate, but not more than fifty, come up the road and take this other car, it's going the same way, just off the left rear corner. Like he's come up to it, and then he saw it too late, and tried to pass, and didn't get by. See? The other car drives into the guard rail on its right and folds up on this other driver, a colored man, this victim. It was just an old pile of junk; and Mason has this big car, and they can take it; so Mason only bangs his head on the dashboard a little."

"Sounds to me as if the other driver put his brakes on," Abner said, remembering the laundry truck when he was driving down town with Jesse.

"No, there were no marks; but Mason's brakes, you could see he slammed them on. First thing Lynd thought was he, Mason, was drunk. But I saw him myself, and he wasn't. So what I am pretty sure of is, he went to sleep; he just nodded off, and woke up too late. That's too bad, but it's his job to stay awake."

"Did he admit it?"

"No. He said he didn't see the other car until he hit it. Well, now the other car had a reflector on its tail light; and here he is, a clear night, with headlights like they have on a big car, coming up behind on a straight highway—no. Either he dozed off, or he wasn't looking where he was going. Either way, we charge him with manslaughter. Right?"

"If that's how it was, yes."

"Well, Mr. Coates, I didn't want a misunderstanding about us making an improper charge."

"If it was that way, it sounds proper to me. I think we'd like to have you come up yourself, tomorrow. I think you'd better be ready to testify."

"O.K. See you then."

Abner hung up and looked out at the damp afternoon. Jake Riordan must have told Mason what to say, or what not to say—admit nothing until you saw what the case against you was. That was certainly his right, and good practical advice, too; but Abner could feel a sort of weariness, a distaste of mind—what did the kid mean, the other car ran into him? If the police told him anything about the tire marks, they told him that they showed that the accident was his, not the unfortunate Negro's, fault.

Getting to the bottom of things like that was impossible. You just had to take the practical view that a man always lied on his own behalf, and paid his lawyer, who was an expert, a professional liar, to show him new and better ways of lying. Abner remembered a passage his father was fond of quoting from a life of Chief Justice Parsons, or someone like that, about the plaintiff who brought action against a neighbor for borrowing and breaking a cooking pot. Advice of counsel was that the defendant should plead that he never borrowed the pot; and that he used it carefully and returned it whole;

also, that the pot was broken and useless when he borrowed it; also, that he borrowed the pot from someone not the plaintiff; also, that the pot in question was defendant's own pot; also, that plaintiff never owned a pot, cooking or other; also, that—and so on, and so on.

Beyond the screened windows, the afternoon seemed to be brightening a little, as though the rain were over; and Abner, rousing himself, went back to the courtroom and resumed his seat. Harry glanced at him casually and winked. Bunting was still cross-examining Howell; and the jury, tired of sitting still, and tired of hearing the same thing, looked restless.

Restless, too, in the rising semi-circle of gloomy benches, singly or in groups of three or four, sat eighty or ninety spectators. There was plenty of room lower down, but many of them were content to sit well back. Abner knew a few by name, and a good many more by sight—there was old John Hughes, generally called Grandpa, who always attended court, hardly missing a day in the last five or six years. He received a small pension of some kind, and had nothing else to do. At Harry Wurts' urging, Grandpa had been elected an honorary member of the Bar Association; but if the intention was to have some fun with him, it failed. He came to the yearly dinners, and though he ate everything offered to him, and even got quite drunk, he could not be persuaded to make a speech. Grandpa was very deaf and did not try to hear when spoken to. He simply nodded a little, smiled a little, grunted a little, and watched brightly—at first glance, you might think with the detachment of a philosopher; but it was soon apparent that the gleam in his seventy-year-old eyes was only the aimless curiosity of a baby. Even Harry ended by letting him alone. Grandpa probably had little or no idea of what was going on this afternoon; but the strange faces kept his eyes busy, and the activities down in the well of the court beguiled him; and when he went home to supper he would probably feel that he had passed a pleasant afternoon.

331

What the others felt was harder to guess. Abner supposed they felt that same devouring curiosity that brought people, often in crowds, to stand staring at the scene of an accident or a crime hours or even days after it happened. (What did they hope to see? What did they want?) Many of those present now had been present since the opening of the trial. The oak benches were as hard as iron to their buttocks; they did not know these people who were on trial; they could hardly hear what was being said; they did not understand the procedure of the court well enough to follow the drama if it could be called one; but still they sat. They looked thirstily, drinking it in, slaking their indescribable but obstinate and obscene thirst. They looked, but never quite their fill, at Howell and Basso who were probably (terrible and titillating thought!) going to die; at Leming, who took his drugs before breakfast; at the widow of a murdered man, the whilom sharer of his bed; at Susie Smalley, the lewd object of what lewd passions; at Judge Vredenburgh in his robe whose word was law; at the clerks serving some purpose they did not know under the bench; at the jury, whose word was life and death; at the attorneys making their assured gestures, familiars of the solemn mystery in which, all jumbled together, the just entered into judgment with the unjust.

Bunting said, "Now, then, Stanley, you knew Zolly was to be killed when you took him out that night, didn't you?"

Howell said, "I never knew." He was feeling the strain. His water-slicked hair had long ago dried and some strands of it toppled forward, so he kept pushing them back.

"You told me you knew, didn't you?"

"You are wrong there."

"You told me in the presence of Mr. Coates and Mr. Costigan that you knew Zolly was to be killed when you took him out that night, didn't you?"

"No," said Howell. "You are wrong. No."

As a matter of fact, Bunting was right. Abner had heard Howell say it. Bunting said, "That isn't true?"

332

"That positively isn't true."

"You didn't say it?"

"No."

The jury, obliged to choose between Howell and Bunting, chose Bunting, of course. When they were charged to disregard Howell's confession if they thought it had been obtained by force they would understand why Bunting had been so careful to let them know that Howell had told him much the same story, and by Howell's own admission, told it freely. This was a nice piece of work. The jury might not realize it; but Bunting was now testifying, yet in a way that those who did realize what he was doing could not challenge. Calmly, disarmingly, calling him by his first name, Bunting was sewing Howell up so tight he would never get out. Abner looked at Kinsolving, grave and reflective beyond the sheriff. An F.B.I. man must feel relief when he found a country district attorney who knew his business. Abner saw George Stacey bend to the side and speak to Harry; but Harry rolled his eyes, shrugging silently.

Bunting said, "Now, Stanley, after Zolly was killed, did you ever go out on any job with Bailey and Basso?"

Jerking himself forward, throwing off his resignation, Harry half-arose. He said, "I object to any questioning of this defendant as to any offenses other than the one for which he stands trial."

Bunting turned patiently, and Judge Vredenburgh said, "That would be the general rule. This witness has testified, however, that he was afraid of Bailey." He turned back the pages of his notes, the lamp light brightening on his bent face. "Yes. While he did not definitely say so, he implied that the reason that he accompanied them was that."

"Exactly, sir," said Harry with alacrity. "There can be no doubt that he acted only through fear."

"The doubt, or lack of doubt, belongs to the jury, Mr. Wurts," Judge Vredenburgh said. "We will agree that the witness may have feared Bailey, that he may have thought,

333

if he refused to go with them, that his own life would be in danger."

"It seems to me a strong presumption, your Honor."

"It is one that the Commonwealth is entitled to attack. I think it would be greatly weakened if the Commonwealth showed that Howell continued to associate with Bailey. I take it that such evidence would be admissible for that purpose, at least."

Bunting said, "It is also offered for the purpose of showing the jury what kind of men these were."

Judge Vredenburgh nodded. "Showing their character; on the question of punishment, if that should arise. Yes."

Harry Wurts said, "Well, sir, I object."

"Overruled."

Bunting said, "Didn't you go with Bailey and Basso a few nights after the killing of Frederick Zollicoffer, before Bailey went away to hide, and attempt to steal a car—"

"If your Honor please," George Stacey said, "I desire to make an objection to that question on behalf of the defendant Basso, for the reason that Mr. Wurts assigned for the previous objection; and for the further reason, that though there may be exceptions to the other rule, this is a misuse of that exception by the Commonwealth to throw something into the jury box that has no right there. Therefore, I object."

"I think I understand you, Mr. Stacey," Judge Vredenburgh said, "but suppose this defendant testified that he was afraid for his life while he was with Bailey; and then suppose that the Commonwealth were to show that he continued with him in other affairs. Wouldn't that throw doubt on the genuineness of his fear, very serious doubt?"

George Stacey blushed. "My objection, sir, on that point is this," he said. He paused a moment, collecting himself with a doggedness Abner admired. Abner could remember such painful moments of his own during his first years of practice, when, on his feet, every eye bent on him, and the Court

334

waiting, confusion scattered his thoughts in all directions and he could not catch the one he wanted.

"The reason was," George said, "the reason he was in fear that night, was because they were involved in the disposal of Zollicoffer, who was in their custody and alive. They were now returning him. The testimony of the witness was that he was under the impression that Zollicoffer was to be released."

Judge Vredenburgh resumed the minute movements of shaking his head. "That would be a matter of argument, but not a matter of law."

"That is true, sir," George Stacey said, "but I will make my objection."

"No. You may have an exception."

Abner guessed that George's point, unfortunately left out, was that Howell and Basso feared Bailey under the particular circumstances of that evening; and the fact that they did not fear him so much under different circumstances did not mean that their fear had not been genuine. George, back in his seat beside Basso, sat tense, undoubtedly going over— how well Abner remembered!—what he had said, trying to show himself that it could have meant what he intended to say. Abner felt like standing up and straightening it out for him.

Bunting said, "You and Basso went on this attempted robbery, this garage job, with Bailey, didn't you?"

"No," said Howell.

He produced the word with furtive suddenness. It made Abner think of a poor card player boggling an instant, so that his desperation was betrayed; then making an asinine lead and fatuously pluming himself on the general surprise.

"You didn't?" said Bunting.

"No."

"You didn't tell me and Mr. Coates, and Lieutenant Dunglison, that you took part in it?"

"No."

Bunting said, "Is Lieutenant Dunglison in court?"

Where he sat over by Kinsolving, Dunglison raised his hand and said, "Yes, Mr. District Attorney."

"Oh. All right, thanks, Lieutenant." Bunting came back to the table. Abner said, "Want to put Dunglison on?"

"No," said Bunting. "Just give Harry a chance to drag out some cross-examination. Let him go." He looked at Howell and said, "That is all."

Judge Vredenburgh said, "Will you want to offer anything in rebuttal, Mr. Bunting?"

"No, your Honor."

"The defense rests as to Howell," Harry said.

"Mr. Stacey?" said Judge Vredenburgh.

"Yes, sir, I rest, too. Defense rests as to Basso."

On the stand, Howell said, "Could I be excused a minute, Judge?"

"Yes. You may. Sheriff, take out the defendant. If you have points to submit for charge, Mr. Wurts, you may submit them now. The jury will be withdrawn. Mr. Bunting, come to side bar, please."

Abner looked across at Harry Wurts who was snapping the loose leaf binder on the sheets of his trial brief. George Stacey's blonde head was bent, asking Harry some long anxious question. Hugh Erskine, down from his seat, came over to Basso, touched him on the shoulder and spoke to him. Basso shook his head. Howell, with Max Eich, seemed to be waiting to speak to Harry; and Harry, now on his way to join Bunting at the end of the bench, stopped, facing Howell. Abner could not hear what Howell said; but Harry answered, "No. We've closed. It's all over. I'll see you in a minute."

Harry walked on, and Howell convulsively made a movement. Max Eich tapped his arm, and Howell turned, as though to back away. Right behind him he found Warren Lyall, who had come along the front of the now empty jury box. Warren stood stock still, and said, "Take it easy, Bud!" He was so close to Howell that Howell could not move without touching him; and, crowded together, they stood an instant, nothing spoken, nothing done. Howell let himself relax then, swinging his pinched face from side to side. Max closed a hand on Howell's left coat sleeve, deftly, neatly, so it was hardly noticeable, snapping on the handcuff. Abner saw the instant's wink of the bright steel and heard the little click.

They moved off then, and Abner found that he had been holding his breath. He shifted in his chair uncomfortably. It was one of those moments, fortunately rare, in which you saw, under the forms, the human facts; the terrified prisoner; the stout burly guard with the ready manacles; the young tough impassive deputy-sheriff. Warren spoke his hard, but not harsh or brutal, word to the wise; with a delicacy, with a consideration almost incredible when you saw Max's beefy face, Max understood and mitigated all he could the shame of the steel chain, the guerdon of a dog. In Howell's heart, even despair must have died, and they marched the man out to relieve himself.

Bunting made his way clear of the empty seats of Nick Dowdy and Joe Jackman and came back to Abner. "Well," he said, "that could have been worse. In fact, it was a damn good case. I'd like to get more like that."

"Nice going," said Abner. "Surprised when he lied to you?"

"The first time. When he said he hadn't told us about knowing they were going to kill Zolly. Not the second time." Bunting smiled. "The Judge had just finished telling him to lie. I was watching him while the Judge explained to Harry and George what it would mean. Right then Stanley changed his mind. Well, I hope we cooked his goose. I think we did."

"I think you did," Abner said. "They got it, all right, when you asked if Dunglison was there."

Bunting said, "It's not the kind of thing I like; but, if you don't know it already, take a tip. Never give anyone like Harry any opening of any kind. The way those smart alecks get to a jury is just on some foolish side issue. Let's grab a cigarette."

Seven

Joe Jackman said, "Well, Marty, another day, another dollar!" He held up his right hand, flexing the fingers. "I wish it was! I suppose we'll be here all night with the arguments." He looked at the end of his middle finger. "I was cutting some roses for my wife this morning before I came over, and damned if I didn't run a little bit of a thorn in there. It's exactly where it catches the stylo. Boy, is that sore!"

Bunting said, "Why don't you just take a knife and cut the finger off?"

"Huh!" said Jackman. "Feeling good, are you? You'd better wait till you find out what the jury says. You never should have let Genevieve Shute on that jury. She likes to be a mother to bad boys. How about you, Nick? You think they ought to have another chance, don't you?"

"You fellows!" Nick Dowdy said. "This Basso doesn't care, I guess. Stanley Howell, he'd like to have another chance; he'd like to do something to this Leming, I guess. We going to get through tonight, Marty?"

"I don't see why not. I don't see how they can argue very long. They haven't anything to argue. The charge may take some time, though."

Nick Dowdy said, "Judge Vredenburgh was in the library here last night working on it, dictating to his daughter."

"Annette?" said Joe Jackman. "My God, does she know how to do anything?"

Bunting said to Abner, "What was it at Newmarket?"

"LaBarre," Abner said. He suppressed a feeling, not, cer-

339

tainly of satisfaction, for he would have preferred to find that Mason's story was true; but, perhaps, of self-justification. His suspicions, of which Marty had made him feel ashamed, would seem to have been well founded. He went on, "It seems that Mason didn't get it quite straight. LaBarre was there at the time, and one of his officers saw the accident happen. What did the report say?"

Bunting said, "It came up after I left this morning. I haven't had time to go back to the office. I haven't seen it. I thought Pete Wiener told you it was the other fellow's fault."

"He did. I don't know why, unless LaBarre and his man didn't get over to Pete's office right away. They may have sent Mason over with someone else. They had the dead man to take care of, and I suppose it was a fine mess. Pete may have called me without waiting for them, as soon as he talked to Mason."

"Well, we'd better see the report—"

Malcolm Levering pushed the door open and said, "Judge wants you, Mr. Bunting."

"All right," Bunting said. "Ab, phone Theda, will you, and ask her to bring that report up. We'd better see how we stand."

Malcolm, who had withdrawn his head, now put it in again. "Mr. Jackman, he wants you, too. Jury's coming back, Nick."

Left alone, Abner called Bunting's office. When he had finished, he dropped in another nickel. At the high school there was no answer and the operator gave him his nickel back. Probably Bonnie had gone home; and he hesitated, not particularly wanting to talk to Cousin Mary; but if he didn't call now, he might not get another chance.

It was Jared, junior, who answered, his voice sharp and impudent. "You got the wrong number," he said.

"Come on!" said Abner. "Hurry up."

"What do you want her for?"

340

"None of your business," Abner said.

"Oh, so you won't talk, huh? G'by—"

The telephone was taken away from him, and Bonnie said, "Jared, if you don't stop trying to be funny—"

Jared said faintly, "It's just your boy friend. He wants you to come over and pitch some woo—"

"Jared, when mother comes home, I'll—"

"Bonnie's mad," yelled Jared more faintly, evidently leaving the room, "and I'm glad—"

Bonnie said, "Hello. Are you through?"

"No," said Abner, "and I don't know when we will be. But I want to see you tonight."

"I don't know whether I have to go back to school or not. They're having another meeting at eight."

"Well, will you do something?"

"What?"

"If we aren't through, or if we are, and it's gone to the jury, we'll recess by six. Will you come over here and wait?"

"Where can I wait?"

"In the courtroom. Just sit up by the door, and when we break, I'll be able to go out and eat with you."

"All right. I'm sorry I lost my temper at noon."

Taken by surprise, Abner said, "You look good that way. You'll come?"

"All right. Oh, damn it, Jared, go away!"

Before she hung up Jared could be heard yelling, "Oh, Bonnie's swearing, Bonnie's swearing—"

Abner went into the courtroom and took his seat by Bunting. He thought of Jared with loathing.

Harry Wurts said, "Ladies and gentlemen—"

He arose, it was plain, not to exhort or harangue the jury, but to counsel with them in a friendly way and to ask them to

341

consider with him some problems which, by the grave, even worried, expression of his face, troubled him.

Abner was not sure that you could call it guile. Harry was cynical about other men's motives, and quick to spot the pretense or the assumed role; but his own motives were so urgent, the importance to him of persuading or wheedling or winning so profound, that Harry always spoke when arguing for what he wanted with complete sincerity. It could not be said that his troubled frown was faked; this was a tough assignment; he frowned at its difficulties. He was troubled by the problem of how to phrase and arrange the few things he could say to give himself every chance, no matter how remote or small, of getting at just one juror, of giving just one man or woman some scruple or sentiment that, catching in the simple or the over-complicated mind, would stay there, resisting the consensus, immune to sense or reason, only hardened in obstinacy by the arguments or expostulations of the others.

Harry said, "I think we have all been watching with something like amazement the work of the Commonwealth over the last few days. Mr. Bunting will shortly sum it up for you; and I look forward to hearing him. I think you will find that the case follows with an almost mathematical precision the lines laid down by Mr. Coates in his able opening— I refer, of course, to his remarkably detailed outline of what the prosecution was determined to prove, not to his rather impressionistic and imaginative history of the case. There, I think we all recognized a flight of fancy and took it with several grains of salt."

Harry smiled good-humoredly and one or two jurors in automatic reaction smiled too. "They should be congratulated," Harry said. "Because it is part of my business, I am a student, you might say, an amateur, of legal tactics; and nothing interests me more than to see a skillful hand taking material in itself of little weight or substance and shaping it so that the result appears as a solid and imposing structure.

Of course, it is a false front; it is like stage scenery, and you must look at it from one angle only, or the sham will be apparent." He smiled again, drew a deep breath, and shook his head.

"However," he said, "before we demolish the make-believe, I think we may learn something by looking at it just the way they want us to. Let us pretend that its foundations are real evidence; let us pretend that it is what it purports to be—a damning case. Actually we may see through it, but at least we must acknowledge the cunning that put it together. Here is no plain blunt tale. Every piece fits according to specifications. No sooner does the want of this or that detail appear than, like magic, it is produced. Perhaps a rubber hose or a little pressure on a drug-destroyed mind was needed to produce it; but there it is! The hat is perfectly empty; yet out pops the appropriate rabbit; in fact, a whole warren of rabbits. In the district attorney's coattails there must be many pockets—

"Briefly, members of the jury, what strikes us about this concoction is that it is too good. Things aren't like that in life. What we lawyers learn from experience with witnesses on the stand is exactly what you have learned yourself from your experience in meeting the everyday problems of sizing people up. Your natural common sense makes you distrust the man who knows all the answers. If I may venture a criticism, I think the prosecution would have served its purpose better if they had left just a few contingencies unprovided for; if, once in a while, one of their witnesses had seemed less than letter-perfect—"

A little edgy, Bunting said to Abner, "And if I were to venture a criticism, I'd say he'd better cut that before somebody wakes up to the fact that when it comes to fooling people, he has a lot of ideas on the subject." He took up a pencil and began to draw a dog on the margin of his pad.

Harry said, "The purposes thus to be served are, I think, fairly plain. Mr. Coates, you may remember, asked you to

343

find the defendants guilty of first degree murder with such penalty as you believed deserved. He avoided asking you outright for the death penalty, and this was an astute move. He did not want to fix in your minds the thought of the electric chair; for, as the case developed, you would then be constantly weighing what these men had actually done against what you were being asked to do to them. By now, you would almost certainly have reached the firm conviction that the crime and the demanded punishment did not balance, that here was no cool-headed and disinterested justice, but a vindictive hounding to death. It would be time enough to ask you to crown the district attorney's career with such a triumph when actual evidence and testimony were past, well-buried in words; and when an adroit summing up might manipulate them somewhat for your persuasion—though, of course, within the limits of propriety. I am sure the prosecution would not risk a censure from the Court."

"I am not sure, Mr. Wurts," Judge Vredenburgh said, "that you have not been risking one yourself. I do not need to tell you that as a general rule counsel in argument must confine themselves to the facts brought out in evidence. Reasonable freedom of debate and illustration, yes. Gratuitous impugning of methods and motives, no. Proceed with that in mind."

Harry said, "Thank you for correcting any false impression I may have given, your Honor. I did not mean that the prosecution's methods and motives are those of malice. I meant simply to comment on what seemed to me an extraordinary zeal to convict, so that the jury might weigh the arguments with an open mind. Ladies and gentlemen, Mr. Stacey, for whose client I am also arguing, and I do not ask the acquittal of these men. That would not be justice. Their records show that they cannot be trusted; and while, in spite of the district attorney's efforts to make them appear to be, they are not on trial for their records, it is right for you to take into consideration the kind of men they are.

"What they are on trial for is murder. You may ask how this can be, when even the prosecution has not insisted that they actually killed anybody. Murder is killing. How can you be guilty of murder if you don't kill? The answer is in a technicality, a provision of statute. In its wisdom the legislature has seen fit to declare, as it has the power and right to, that murder shall be a good many things besides that crime of killing with deliberate intent which is what you and I mean by it; and which I think we may with all reverence assume was Almighty God's meaning in the commandment: Thou shalt do no murder."

Bunting looked at Abner. "Something for old Daniels," he said. Abner could see him studying under his lowered eyelids the faces of the jurors; and no doubt wondering, as one always had to, if this or that choice from the panel had been good. Mr. Daniels was probably all right. He was a leading Baptist of one of the small severe sects. God's work, as such men saw it, usually included making the transgressor's way as hard as possible. For that very reason Abner remembered being surprised when the defense accepted Daniels; and so now it was necessary to wonder whose estimate of Daniels was correct.

Harry said, "The legislature, let us hope, would not lightly have undertaken the presumptuous job of rewriting and giving new-fangled meanings to the Sixth Commandment; and we can follow part of their line of reasoning. It is reasonable to hold that a group of people, if they agree together to go and murder a man, and the first one who hits the victim kills him so that the others do not have to, and do not, take any part at all, just the same they are guilty of murder Of course, that is not the case here. There was no agreement to murder Frederick Zollicoffer. Quite the contrary! Howell and Basso went along because they believed that he was to be taken home. They were unarmed; and, surprised, facing a vicious and desperate man with a gun, they could not prevent the crime. Bailey, the murderer, kept them in fear; and I don't think any of us, offered the choice they were offered—that is, keeping still, or dying— would have chosen differently. So much for that."

Harry took a short thoughtful turn down past the box, his head bent, his hands clasped behind him. On the way back, he said, "We come now to the legislature's further extension or invention by which the punishment deemed proper for the foul crime of murder may be inflicted for a number of other offenses. This is new, in the sense that it has only recently been thought up and added to the law; but in another sense it is old, it is what we have so long and painfully struggled to get away from. It is a step back to those dark days of the eighteenth century when literally scores of crimes were punished by death. Those barbarous laws, as futile in practice as they were disgraceful in theory, were eventually abolished; not a little because the conscience and love of justice of members of juries made them refuse to bring in verdicts of guilty. Jurors might not be able to make the law; but they had something to say about justice, and they said it until even cruel judges and despotic kings had to listen.

"Well, neither can we make the law. We are supposed to abide by it. The law is that those who take part in one crime, kidnapping in this case, shall also be held to have taken part in another crime, murder, if, before the kidnapping is over, someone kills the kidnapped person. All the kidnappers do not have to join in the killing. As in this case, some may object and protest; but the law doesn't care about that. The essence of every other crime is intention; that is how you tell when it constitutes a crime. But not here. Here you may become a murderer without doing anything at all. You may be as innocent of any intent to kill as the engineer of a train that runs over a man who jumps in front of it."

Harry shook his head. "It isn't right. Instinctively we recoil from so gross an affront to wisdom and reason; yet that is the law. The legislators tell us what they have de-

346

cided will be law and it goes into the books. Law is law; and if we say we don't like it, they simply laugh at us. They are the all-wise statesmen; and who are we? Why, we're a bunch of ignorant hicks who don't understand these things. We can shut up and sit down.

"Well, maybe we can; and maybe we are just ignorant hicks; but you at least, ladies and gentlemen, are more than that. You are duly selected and sworn jurors, free men and women; and if they laugh at you, that's their mistake, because you are the ones and the only ones who can by your verdict deliver over to them subjects or victims for the caprices of their law-making. It is your conscience, and not their vindictive or vainglorious vaporings, that are decisive. There is no power on earth that can force you to send to death men whose offenses do not warrant death."

Harry spoke with great earnestness, hammering home the successive sentences, not by raising his voice like an orator, but by putting force behind each moderately spoken word. Except for lifting or lowering his head, or bending his shoulders forward a little and then straightening up, he made no gestures. He did not show the consciousness, which few glib speakers can conceal, of handing it out, of going good. The jury listened, not spell-bound (a state that flattered a speaker on his manner and proved that he could give good entertainment; yet meant in fact that what he said hardly mattered); but disturbed, stirring with the discomfort of not knowing what to think.

Bunting said, "Ab. That's Theda, up there at the door. Will you—"

Abner looked up. The door opened, awakening Everitt Weitzel. Everitt got stiffly to his feet, took the paper, and came limping down.

Harry said, "The nature of these men's offenses ought to appear from the evidence. Let us consider what the Commonwealth has offered us—"

Everitt came furtively across the well of the court and

347

laid the papers he carried beside Bunting, who pushed them over where he and Abner could both read. "Well," Bunting whispered at last, "that's clear enough. What did the kid do, deny it?"

"No," said Abner, "not exactly. Naturally, I wasn't holding a hearing. Jake was there. He made some remarks. I didn't pay much attention."

"Well, what was LaBarre's trouble?"

"Somebody told him I said the state police shouldn't have made the charge manslaughter. Jake did say something like that. As far as I remember, all I said was that we would have to see the report. I may have told Mason that if it wasn't his fault, he needn't worry. He was sort of shaky, and I felt sorry for him."

Bunting said, "I don't know that I'd ever do that, Ab. Even if it's not his fault. Even if he's completely innocent, it's homicide. He's killed somebody, and if that's a little inconvenient for him, all right. I guess you could say being killed was not exactly convenient for the other fellow. You have to remember that you represent the Commonwealth, and that means the other fellow, the Negro who died."

"I know that," Abner said, flushing. "I didn't mean—"

"I know you didn't. There's no harm done. Whether Mason says he's guilty or innocent doesn't matter—manslaughter's bailable. All we want is for him to put up two thousand dollars for his appearance at the inquest, and he can go home. I just mean, I wouldn't in a case like that let him talk to me about it; or express sympathy, if you did; or anything of that kind. If he's shaky, well, he ought to be shaky. He'll have a chance to tell his story in due course; and meanwhile, let him worry about what he's done. It usually does him good."

Abner said, "You told me to go out and see him. I didn't want to. Jake did most of the talking. I don't think he knew just what the evidence was—"

Judge Vredenburgh tapped the metal shaft of his desk

lamp with his gold pencil. Harry had paused and turned to look at them. The Judge said, "I think your conversation is disturbing counsel, Mr. District Attorney. If it is necessary for you to confer, confer in lower tones."

"I beg your pardon, sir," Bunting said. "Sorry, Mr. Wurts." To Abner, he murmured, "If Jake doesn't know, I think we'd better show him this. Probably he's at his office. Take it down, will you." He pushed the report over to Abner, settled back in his chair, and turned his attention to Harry.

Harry said, "The witness on whom the Commonwealth chiefly relied is Roy Leming. It won't be very pleasant for you, but I must ask you to look at him again, sitting over there beside the sheriff. There is said to be an honor among thieves, and that must be a low sort of honor; but even so it is too high for Leming. He is the sniveling coward who, to save his worthless skin, sells out his friends. Look at him! He is actually smiling. He is proud of his double-cross. He is happy thinking of his miserable life that the Commonwealth is going to let him keep as a reward for the story he cooked up. What word can you apply to such a man? One comes to my mind. With apologies to a common musteline mammal, known to zoologists as mephitis mephitis—in English, that means stink-stink, Leming is a plain skunk. This is what the Commonwealth expects us to trust and believe! This is—"

Abner went along below the bench and out the door by the Judge's chambers with Harry's voice pursuing him. Harry would stir them up a little, looking now for some sluggish juror who needed violence to move him. It was still not guile, or at least, not after the first word or two following the deliberate change of tone and appeal. His own tone affected Harry as much as it affected anyone else; he himself heard and heeded his own appeal. When he looked at Leming, Leming looked like a skunk to him, and he would rant on in full sincerity until some instinct told him that that was

349

enough of that. Even after the door closed an echo of the tirade came through the dull stained glass transom. Abner went down the back steps and out under the arch.

The point he might have made if Judge Vredenburgh had not interrupted them preoccupied Abner, though it was hard to phrase it clearly. He could say that because Marty had chided him for being tough about Mason, he had taken care not to be—after all, Marty was right. It wasn't up to Abner to try Mason and find him guilty of having a father who knew Jesse. Accordingly he was careful to give Mason a break; and as a result, Marty now read him a lecture about his duties as counsel for a dead citizen—as though Abner were the one who tried to help Jesse try to help Jesse's consequential friend. Now, though presumably still representing the dead citizen, he was sent down to let Jake see the report so Jake would not be (if he were actually in any danger of being) taken by surprise when the police testified. The Commonwealth was under no obligation to show Jake its case and so give him a chance to do what he could to defeat it; but that was Marty for you! There was a characteristic open temperance about his actions—not that he couldn't be made to lose his temper, nor that he never did anything short-sighted. Abner has seen Marty make mistakes; yet the point probably was that he never saw Marty make a mistake without being astonished—in short, you recognized that it wasn't "like" Marty. The things that were like him were wisdom and foresight, patience and temperateness.

Abner thought suddenly that if he had chosen to run for district attorney, and if he had been elected, he might not have found the job quite so simple as he seemed all along to have assumed. Just being familiar with the work might not have qualified him completely to take Marty's place. When he said, as he so often had to, "Well, that's up to Marty," he sometimes meant only that he could not act without Marty's consent; but often he meant, too, that he

would not want to act without consulting Marty's experienced judgment. It was not easy to imagine anyone saying
with so much confidence, "That's up to Ab." Making the
effort, Abner thought of George Stacey. He might have offered George the job of assistant district attorney. George
would probably have jumped at the chance; and Abner, with
an amusement in some respects wry, could at least conceive
of George asking what to do, and of George listening while
Abner told him.

Jacob Riordan's office was a little red brick house next to
the county administration building. It was older even than
Abner's temple behind the bank. One in a one-time row of
old lawyers' offices, it now stood alone, for the rest had been
torn down and the county building occupied their sites.
The changed level of the paving when Court Street had
been first paved made it necessary to descend three steps to
enter the door which opened directly on a large front room
with a fireplace. Every inch of wall space was packed frame
to frame, from the delicately molded but dirty plaster ceiling to the yellowing paint of the low-paneled wainscoting,
with an extraordinary collection of prints, pictures, and old
notices.

Jake had fitted in framed clerks' certificates showing that
he was entitled to plead before the Orphans Courts of several counties, the Superior Court, and the United States Supreme Court; but almost everything else was left from the
days when it had been Webster Binns' office. There were
Currier & Ives prints of presidents and presidential candidates of a hundred years ago; not, however, like most such
prints, collected for their quaintness within the last decade,
but put up when they were published and never since moved
(nor even, you might think, dusted). There were daguerreotypes of people nobody could any longer identify. There was

a framed pair of faded tickets, signed by Mr. Binns' grandfather as president of the company, entitling the purchaser to pass one gate on the Childerstown & Western Turnpike with the amounts in shillings and pence. There were several broadside advertisements, brown as dead leaves, offering a reward to the recoverer of runaway slaves. There was a black-edged announcement of the schedule of President Lincoln's funeral train. There was the lithograph called Gentlemen of the Jury which in the '70s must have been sold to half the law offices in America. There was a framed letter with a two foot column of signatures dated 1890 and inviting Mr. Binns to a testimonial dinner to celebrate the fiftieth anniversary of his admission to the bar.

Abner could remember Mr. Binns, who was ninety-eight years old when he died. His birthdays had become civic celebrations, and everyone anticipated with confident excitement that he would live to be over a hundred. To the day of his death Mr. Binns came each morning to the office here—the firm was Binns & Riordan then—and at ninety-five he argued a case before Judge Coates in Common Pleas. Abner had heard his father say that the argument was one of the ablest he ever listened to.

To a child, Mr. Binns with his mop of white hair down over his coat collar, his huge rugged face and vast dignified belly, was more of a monster than a man, and when Abner read about ogres in children's books, he thought of them as looking like Mr. Binns. Much later, he began to value the memory. It came to seem something of a personal accomplishment to have looked with his own eyes at a man who had been named Webster because Mr. Binns' father's friend, Daniel Webster, on his way to Washington to argue the later celebrated Dartmouth College Case, was a guest in the house that day in 1818 when Webster Binns was born. This had been a law office, then as now, so the odds were that Daniel Webster had stood in this room, and perhaps for a few minutes, or even longer, rested his godlike fundament in one of the heavy windsor chairs that still stood here.

Abner let the door slam and since nobody was in the outer room called, "Jake!"

The white paneled sliding doors were parted at the back, and Jake showed himself, leaning forward from the window ledge on which he seemed to have been sitting. "Oh, Ab," he said. "Come on in. Gone to the jury?"

"No," Abner said. "They're arguing. Look, Jake. Marty's just got the police report in the Mason case. He thought you'd better see it."

Jacob Riordan's seamed, yet oddly young-looking face came to attention. Abner had hoped to find out whether Jake knew all along; but the changed expression gave nothing away. It simply accepted what Abner said as of interest, and waited, prepared for him to continue.

"Want to see it?" said Abner.

"Be glad to, thanks. Come in."

Stepping into the room, Abner held the folded sheets out. He saw then that Jake was not alone. Hunched in a padded leather chair in the corner sat Jesse Gearhart. "Oh. Sorry," Abner said. "Didn't mean to interrupt you."

"You don't," Jake said. "As a matter of fact, we—" He took the report, seating himself on the window ledge again, and held it up to read.

Jesse said, "Stopped raining, Ab?"

Abner nodded. Jake's eyes shifted quickly over the lines of typewriting and after a moment's silence he said, "Uh-huh."

"Did you know that?" said Abner.

"I didn't know exactly what their story was going to be."

"It doesn't look so good," Abner said.

"No. Well, thanks for letting me see it."

"O.K.," said Abner. He did what he could to cover the fact that he was taken aback. He held his hand out for the report; and Jesse cleared his throat. "Got a minute, Ab?" he said.

"Sure," said Abner.

Jesse said, "Jake and I were talking over various members of the bar." He paused and Abner could hear from the barred back windows of the county building the punctuated key strokes and light banging shift of an adding machine. "This matter of district attorney is going to take a lot of consideration." His pale, steady, tired eyes looked up at Abner from the corner. "You don't have any idea of reconsidering, do you?"

The adding machine began again. Along the pavement in front somebody walked scuffling his feet and whistling. Abner said, "Reconsider what? You thought you'd better get somebody else, Jesse. There's nothing I can very well reconsider."

Jesse said, "We'll have to get somebody else, if you won't run. If you will, we'd rather have you."

Jake, humped in silhouette against the window, said, "What's the trouble, Ab? Not enough money?"

Abner said, "There's enough for me. I told Jesse last night what the trouble was."

Jesse said, "Well, Ab, it didn't seem very clear. Except you didn't like politics. You didn't say why. If you mean that you don't want to go out campaigning, asking people for votes—well, we would have to get somebody else. And, as I think I said last night, if you won't go to that much trouble, it must mean you don't want the job much; and if you don't want the job—"

Abner said, "I'm perfectly willing to speak for the ticket."

Jake said, "Well, what *is* biting you, Ab?" He spoke good-humoredly, though his tone made it clear that he thought Abner was unreasonable in answering always beside the point. Abner didn't deny it. Deviousness seemed unreasonable to him, too; but his profession had taught him to curb the impulse to blurt out what was on his mind. He certainly wasn't afraid of displeasing Jesse; but a man who let himself say what he couldn't back up with acceptable

354

proof wasted everybody's time and showed that he had no judgment.

Abner could say, plain and blunt, that what bit him, for one thing, was Jesse's virtual control of public monies. The county placed every year scores of separate orders for supplies and services, and the general fund expenditures ran to about five hundred thousand dollars; and if anything were certain, it was that little or none went to people of whom Jesse disapproved. This was an observable fact; but simply stating it was not good enough. What was Abner trying to imply? The orders were filled by sealed bids to the county commissioners in answer to public advertisements and the comptroller's scrutiny ruled out all the easy or shocking grafts of forty or fifty years ago. There was no reason to doubt that everything the county bought, from a gross of typewriter ribbons to a tractor, was the best available at the price. Abner could say, if he wanted to, that it was very strange how enemies of Jesse's either did not have the required materials, or if they did, were always underbid on them; but that was all he could say.

Then there was the matter of jobs. As good as at his disposal, Jesse had hundreds, even thousands, of little presents in the form of road maintenance work. Nobody opposed to Jesse ever got one of them. So what? Somebody had to keep up the roads. Abner might know that certain men were on the payroll because they could get Jesse votes; and that such jobs were calculatingly distributed through the upper, middle, and lower county so that party workers everywhere would be encouraged and see that their own turn might come. Jesse was using the public payroll to maintain his personal power.

But what did you mean, get Jesse votes? When Abner said a thing like that he ought to give specific examples. If he could show Jesse accepting a bundle of bought votes and exchanging a job for them, that was one thing. If he merely *knew* it came down to that, it was something else, and no good for his purpose. People had a right to vote for those whose election seemed to them to their advantage. What else was voting for?

If, on these or any other grounds, Abner wanted to question the budget, he was given every opportunity to. Annually the *Examiner* published the whole thing, certified by the auditors, accounted for in detail enough to fill seven or eight double columns. If Abner thought that some of it went into Jesse's pocket, all he had to do was challenge the item, and, at a hearing where every facility would be given him, show that was where it went. Jesse might have influence, but he did not have enough to keep himself out of jail if he were found diverting public funds.

Abner said, "That isn't what I meant by politics. I told Jesse what I meant. I'll say it to you both, because you both know about it. This Mason business. I don't care whose son he is—" Abner was aware, as he said it, that it was a silly thing to say, or at least a silly way of saying what he meant. He sounded self-righteous.

Jesse said, "Well, Ab, you wouldn't say he wasn't entitled to a defense, would you?"

"He's entitled to just what everyone else is entitled to. No more. No less."

"What's he getting?" said Jake. "More or less?"

"I don't know yet. That's what I may find out."

"If you mean what I'm going to do for him," Jake said, "why, I'll tell you now, if you want. We haven't any evidence, except his own statements. If it seems at the inquest tomorrow that it was his fault, I'll advise him to plead guilty. When it comes up, I'd plan to introduce character witnesses; and I'd ask the judge not to send him to jail. I don't think he ought to go; and I don't think the judge will think he ought to go. Do you think he should?"

"No," said Abner, "there'd be no point in that."

"Well," said Jake, "suppose instead of being a rich man's kid, a college boy with enough money to pay a stiff fine, the

356

son of a prominent man, he was a tough little nut with no friends and no money. Would he go to jail then?"

"That's up to the judge."

"The rich boy goes home; the poor boy goes to jail. That the way you see it?"

"O.K.," said Abner. "Money's a useful thing to have. When you pick your father, pick a man who amounts to something. If the judge fines Mason, and he can pay, and does, he's free as far as the law's concerned. And that's as far as I'm concerned."

The momentary light of amusement in Jake's eyes faded to boredom. Strictly speaking, it was not his affair. His good nature made him willing to lend a hand in putting right something that seemed to him easily fixed; but he was not going to argue about it. Jesse, who had been sitting in patience, waiting for Jake and Abner to finish their exchange, said, "Do you want to think it over, Ab?"

"I've thought it over," Abner said. "I'll run, on condition that—" He paused; for it would be inane to say "on condition that I have a free hand." Who was refusing it? He could not say, "on condition that you don't butt in"—it was too childishly offensive. He said, "On condition that I make my own appointments."

Jesse said, "The statutes give you the authority to do that, Ab. You have to have the approval of the Court in the case of any county detective you appoint—"

Jake said, "You don't want to get rid of Costigan, do you?"

"No," said Abner. "We can work together all right. I don't want to change anything there. But I'll have to have an assistant, and—"

Jake said, "Got someone in mind?"

"Yes. I have George Stacey in mind."

"I think he might be all right," Jake said. "He's got a good head. But doesn't he have to have been a member of the bar for a certain number of years? Five?"

Jesse said, "That's only the district attorney himself. About John Costigan, you may have to replace him. I'm not sure he won't be running for sheriff on this ticket. Wish Hugh could succeed himself; but since he can't—that's in confidence, for the moment."

"How about Warren Lyall?" Jake said. "Isn't he going to feel that he—"

"He's too young," Jesse said. "He wouldn't be good at all. He hasn't any claim on it."

"He's got a lot of friends in Warwick—"

"No," said Jesse. "I know about his friends."

Abner said, "Well, I've got to get back to court."

"Yes," said Jesse. He got up. "I've got to go, too, Jake. See you tomorrow." He went through the outer room with Abner and they came up the steps to the street together. The afternoon had grown brighter with a haze of sunlight close behind the gray clouds. On Abner's face a light warm west wind blew and the pavements were beginning to dry.

Jesse said, "I spoke to Rawle. You don't think you could get over there tonight, do you?"

"Well, Jesse, I don't know. I can't do much about anything until this case is over, until the verdict's in."

"No. Well, I think we have a good chance of stopping the whole business. There's no sense in it, really. Eleanor Carver ought to know better." He paused a moment, and Abner could see that he was spending it in a quick, silent review of his mind's full dossier on Miss Carver. Miss Carver, the now-elderly daughter of a former president of the Childerstown National Bank, had the leisure and the money and the officiousness to take a hand in local politics; and Abner supposed that she often made a nuisance of herself. Jesse said, "Doc Mosher's just stubborn. I think Alfred Hobbs' idea was that Rawle could be embarrassed into resigning. You see the *Examiner?*"

Abner said, "I saw Maynard's draft of the story."

Jesse took a folded copy of the paper from his pocket,

half opened it, and tapped a boxed column on the front page. It was headed: "Why Did No One Know?" "You might read it when you get time," Jesse said, handing it over. "That's going to make a lot of trouble. Maynard shouldn't have done it. He isn't helping anything; he's just fanning up a factional row. You heard Hartshorn this morning when he made Judge Irwin mad. What does that sort of thing get you? Maynard ought to think a little."

Though nothing was expressed in Jesse's voice but regret, a weary reasoning against a course that his experience disapproved, it was possible to read into it more than that. The *Examiner's* was not the only shop where the county printing could be done; and unless Maynard wanted to lose seven or eight thousand dollars worth of business, perhaps he ought to be careful. Touched on the sore spot again, Abner did not say anything. They were in front of the courthouse, and Abner nodded to Jesse and ran up the steps. Not so settled in his mind as it seemed to Abner that he ought to be, he stood still in the hall.

Out the door of the office of the clerk of the Orphans Court came Miss Hulsizer, Hermann Mapes' deputy. She nodded to Abner and went upstairs, entering the register's office. Since Hermann was in court, Abner realized that there would now be no one in the office she had left. He walked directly over. As he foresaw, the big room was empty. He passed around the counter under the ranks of japanned tin filing boxes and the shelves in which the buckram bound docket folios lay on their sides. A series of drawers was set into the back of the counter; and Abner opened them quickly one after another until he found a stack of "Application for Marriage License" forms. Flipping the top one off, he folded it, shoved it in his pocket, and shut the drawer. Miss Hulsizer's steps could be heard on the stairs, returning, but he was able to slip out, not yet in her line of vision, push the swinging door of the courtroom vestibule silently open, and disappear.

The well-managed purloining cheered him, for Abner had not been looking forward much to the barrage of leers and witticisms which Hermann, considering it a perquisite of his office, laid down on any personal acquaintance who came in to get a form. This way, Hermann would not find out about it until the application was returned.

Through the oval lights in the second pair of swinging doors Abner could see the body of the court below the curving rows of the numerous but scattered spectators, set like a calm hushed stage with the silent orderly arrangement of people in their appointed places. More time had passed than Abner thought, for Harry was back in his seat and it was now Marty who was talking to the jury. Abner let himself in, went quietly down the sloping aisle, crossed over to the Commonwealth's table, and sat down.

Bunting was not an eloquent speaker. His thoughts were clear and logical, and he put them plainly; but unlike Harry who could speak in many manners, and in all of them give the impression of naturalness and simplicity, Bunting had only one manner, and he unselfconsciously was natural and simple. Along with the virtue, he had the vice of unselfconsciousness. Absorbed in what he wished to say, he never thought of standing off and looking at himself to see how he was doing, or of asking himself if this were the way he would like to be talked to. His custom was to instruct juries. He assumed (and not incorrectly) that when their duty was made plain they would do it without being coaxed or urged.

Bunting told them, with no effort to arrange his material to any advantage except that of orderliness, what the evidence was and what facts proceeded from it. He did not argue; he made statements. Though he respected the letter of his obligation in ethics not to assert outright his personal belief in the guilt of those he prosecuted, his whole presence and manner asserted it for him. Of course they were guilty! No rational person could doubt that the man against whom a grand jury found a true bill had committed the offense charged. The trial determined not whether he had done it, but whether he was going to be punished for it.

A miscarriage of justice, with some good, brave man in the interesting and dramatic plight of standing trial for what he never did, might get by in a book or a play where anything could be made plausible. In practice, in real life, it could be made plausible only to those ignorant of how a prisoner at the bar arrived there. He was not arrested on some random arbitrary suspicion, dragged in without ceremony, and arraigned out of hand. Experienced investigators found such overwhelming evidence against him that they knew he was the one, he must have done it, and then they arrested him. A justice of the peace heard his explanations, if he cared to make any, and noted them down for him. The district attorney's office checked all this over, saw the prisoner, saw the other witnesses, and satisfied that it could not be otherwise, charged him in a bill of indictment. When the Grand Jury found that bill a true bill, it meant that at least twelve and often twenty-three disinterested persons of generally admitted prudence and common sense agreed that the evidence showed that the prisoner must have done it. The prisoner could be innocent still, just as a bet on a thousand to one chance could pay off. It was not practical to take so remote a possibility into serious account.

In the case against Howell and Basso there was not even the one chance in a thousand. Abner could see that this, the incontestable, the uncontested, certainty that they were guilty as charged made Marty even drier and more matter of fact. He answered Harry by ignoring him; and here perhaps a lack of all art served as well as art could have. The singleness of purpose that was too busy to bother with what Harry said must surprise and then impress every listener. They were surprised because Bunting, obliged to sit still while

Harry derided him and his case, did not take the opportunity to respond in kind. They were impressed because, though they would have enjoyed a joined contest, they after all respected the man who would not stoop to it.

The jury might be—and looking at them, Abner saw that they, or several of them, were cruelly bored; but Bunting's moral ascendency of fixed purpose and unsmiling resolve compelled their attention. Whether they liked it or not, they listened while he told them that there were no facts in conflict and no issue in doubt. The point for them was (a) nobody denied that Frederick Zollicoffer had been kidnapped, and while still in the custody of his kidnappers, killed; (b) nobody denied that Howell and Basso assisted in the kidnapping. That was all there was to it. If the jury believed that the evidence established this point (and what alternative was there?), let them bring in a verdict of first degree murder and assign the death penalty as by law provided.

Bunting, his lips coming together firmly as he stopped speaking, looked at the jurors in a sharp, detached way to see if anybody did not understand. Because he never built his arguments to a high point, he was never in any danger of anticlimax; there was no effect to spoil. Bunting had concluded; but seeing some movement of mouth or expression of eye that did not satisfy him, he went drily on to conclude again.

He said, "In conclusion, Members of the Jury, I will remind you of what this evidence shows, at the same time, about the character of the defendants. In law, Basso's refusal to plead and testify isn't a sign of guilt; but it is a good indication that he is non-co-operative, that he feels contempt for the law and for society. Howell says now that he didn't want to see Zollicoffer killed; but his character as a criminal is such that we may reasonably doubt it. He did not want to get caught, yes; I am sure of that; and at the time, the surest way not to get caught must have seemed to dispose of Zollicoffer and hide his body where it could never be found. I think he assented for that reason. I think the effect of leniency on such characters would be to prove to them, and incidentally to the criminal circles of several large cities, that you can get away with murder. I don't think you would want to give notice to a lot of city criminals that if they come across the county line here and commit their crimes they will get off easy. For this reason, too, the Commonwealth asks you for a verdict that will leave no doubt that here the law is fully enforced."

He nodded briefly, nodded again to Judge Vredenburgh, and came over and sat down by Abner. He looked at his watch and said, "Twenty-five minutes. That's not bad. See Jake?"

Judge Vredenburgh said, "We will now take a recess for five minutes; after which I will charge the jury."

Abner said, "Jake and Jesse were there."

Harry Wurts got up and came over to the Commonwealth's table. "Well, gents," he said, "want to bet? Too late! Offer withdrawn in toto." George Stacey came over, too; and Harry said to him, "Go on, George; give him the works. Ask him what he meant by trying to prejudice the jury against your client."

Bunting said, "I'd like to know what you meant by vindictive."

"I meant you," Harry said. "What else is it? What's the difference between you and them? I'll tell you. They never meant to kill anyone; but you set out with malice prepense to burn them. Say, if I wrote the laws, I'd require the prosecutor who asked the death penalty and the jury that voted it to attend the execution. Then you might know what you were talking about."

"I thought you did write the laws," Bunting said. "It certainly sounded like it, when you were giving them that stuff—there comes your man back; you'd better go hold his hand."

George had been standing with an indecisive smile, probably waiting for Harry to indicate what they ought to do next. Abner said, "George, there's something I want to see you about. Going to have any time tomorrow?"

"All day, I guess," George said. "I haven't got anything on."

Harry had started back to the defense's table. He stopped now and said, "He wants to see you about being assistant district attorney and dog-robber in chief. Just say no. Why should you do all the dirty work?"

George blushed. He looked away in confusion, showing that he might not be averse to the idea, if by any chance he were going to be offered the job; but Harry and Harry's kidding had taught him useful lessons in wariness. He said stiffly, "Any time you like, Ab." Basso had come in with Hugh Erskine, and George went over and seated himself.

Bunting looked at Abner and said, "Are you going to run?"

"Unless Jesse changes his mind."

"He doesn't change his mind," Bunting said. "Why didn't you tell me?"

"I didn't know until just now. We didn't settle it last night. And what do you mean, he doesn't change his mind? He changed something; because Jake said he was ready to plead Mason guilty. They weren't ready yesterday."

"Look, Ab," Bunting said, "Jesse very likely would do what he could for Mason; but he won't do what he can't. I suppose he asked Jake not to make a fuss." He picked up a pencil and began to bounce it lightly on its rubber eraser. "There's such a thing as give and take," he said. "Did you mention Mason to him last night?"

"I may have said—"

"Yes. Well, don't get cocky about it; but he made up his mind long ago that he wanted you on the primary ballot. It's not the easiest thing in the world to get up a ticket. He didn't change his mind. He just decided that if you were worrying yourself about some idea you had about Mason, well, that could be fixed. That's give."

"Yes," said Abner, "and what's take?"

"Take's when you tell him you'll run." Bunting paused and held the pencil poised. "If he does something for you, you do something for him." He gave Abner his faint, tight-lipped smile. "Only, I wouldn't try to stick him on the deal, if I were you. A lot of people have tried to stick Jesse. Nobody I ever heard of ever did, except maybe Jared Wacker, and that wasn't politics."

"This isn't any deal," said Abner. He knew that his tone was huffy and he tried to modify it by laughing. "He doesn't have to give me anything."

"That's right. He doesn't. Just keep that in mind. But I guess you want him to."

"What do you mean, I want him to?"

"For crying out loud!" Bunting said. "Nobody's making you be district attorney. If you run, it must be because you want to. If you went into the primaries and tried to get the nomination on your own, do you know what you'd get? About twenty write-ins. If you ran as an independent, do you know what you'd get? You'd get the pants licked off you. Now, why don't you act your age? This isn't the college debating society election where you vote for the other fellow to show how modest you are. You may be the best man for the job, and I think you are; but nobody's going to bring it to you on a platter."

"I know," said Abner, "but do you mind very much if I still don't like the way it's run? What right has Jesse to decide who's going to be what? Does he own the county?"

Bunting said, "Standing off and saying you don't like the way things are run is kid stuff—any kid can work out a program of more ice cream and less school and free movies and him telling people what to do instead of people always telling him—"

Abner said, "I don't want any more ice cream, thanks."

"Maybe you don't; but what you're saying is the same damn thing. If things were run according to your ideas instead of the way they are run, it would be much better. Who says so? Why you say so! That's what the dopes, the Communists and so on, all the boys who never grew up, say. Who's going to be better for it? Their fellow-men? Horse feathers! I don't say some of them don't hope so; but the only thing they can be sure of is that it would be better for them."

In Cambridge Abner had seen a few people who said they were Communists. Naturally they had not bothered to explain their ideas to Abner. If they had, he would not have known what to say; they seemed queer and set apart, like poets, or homosexuals, so that it was hard to think of them as real people. He did not pretend to understand them, and he would admit that they all seemed to have something wrong with them; but on the other hand, Marty had probably never seen a Communist, so how did he come to know so much about them? Abner said, "So you say."

"What I say is," Bunting said, "until you have some responsibility, do something besides kick, or try to heave in a few monkey wrenches, you aren't going to know what you're talking about. Sure, one way to get rid of the rats is burn down the barn! That's brilliant. Wait until it's been up to you for a few years, until you've had to decide, until you've seen how a few of those brilliant ideas turn out. Wait until you have to do the work instead of the talking. Then you may begin to know something, not just think you know." He pulled open the table drawer before him and tossed the pencil into it.

"I never claimed to know much of anything," Abner said.

Bunting looked past him to the door of the Judge's chambers. Judge Irwin was coming out, drawing his robe together over his blue serge suit. He carried his bald head and distinguished thin face bent forward, moving in nervous haste; but he was soon brought to a halt by two state policemen.

366

They had left their seats at the end of the row and stood talking together in such a position that they blocked Judge Irwin's route to the bench steps. Judge Irwin pulled up, hesitating with the quaint but pleasant delicacy of a shy man.

One of the troopers, hearing or sensing a movement behind him, glanced over his shoulder. His companion looked, too; and they stepped away in confusion, apologizing. Judge Irwin smiled in gentle embarrassment. Abner could hear him say, "Thank you—" as though it were their courtroom, not his. "I thought I would come in and hear the charge."

Still more confused, one of the troopers said, "Yes, sir. Sorry, sir."

"Well, you'll learn!" Bunting said, looking back to Abner. "God, how you'll learn!"

Judge Irwin passed along the bench quickly and took his seat. Bunting said, "We'd better shut up. I guess Vredenburgh's ready."

Judge Vredenburgh said, "Members of the Jury: in this bill of indictment the two defendants on trial before you are charged, together with Roy Leming, with murder. It is averred that they did kill and murder within this county one Frederick Zollicoffer."

He paused, tilting his head to rest a moment against the high carved back of the chair, his eyes focusing on something far off which he seemed to look at with a stoical severity. He said, "Two only of the defendants named in the bill are on trial before you, because there has been a severance or separation of the defendants for the purposes of this trial. Therefore, your duties in this case relate only to Stanley Howell and Robert Basso."

He cleared his throat, looked at the desk before him, and then directly at the jurors. "You have listened patiently and closely to the testimony for three days. You have indicated

367

by your attention that you know the seriousness of your task. You were picked after a painstaking examination of many members of the panel in order that both sides might be satisfied that each of you was intelligent and unprejudiced. You have noticed, no doubt, how you have been guarded and perhaps restricted. This surveillance was not at the whim of the Court. The law requires it. The law is solicitous that the defendants shall have a fair trial, and also that the Commonwealth's case shall be fairly and impartially heard and tried."

Abner tipped his chair, easing himself to a more comfortable angle. He looked past the defense's table to Warren Lyall who sat in the tipstaff's seat behind. Next to Warren was Mrs. O'Hara, and next to her sat Susie Smalley, one thin leg thrown over the other under the skimpy skirt. She seemed to be staring blankly at the back of Howell's head. John Clark sat next to her. His air was calm and pompous. Dewey Smith was next to him, and Dewey was thoughtfully picking his nose. With an expression so like John Clark's that it could be seen to be what it was—the professional expression—Mr. Servadei looked at the Judge, polite and reflective. Between him and Hugh Erskine sat Leming. Leming was uneasy; and Abner supposed that he would go on being uneasy as long as Howell and Basso lived.

Judge Vredenburgh said, "The distinguishing mark of murder is malice aforethought. This is not malice in its ordinary meaning alone, a particular ill-will, a spite or grudge. Malice is a legal term implying much more. It means wickedness of disposition, hardness of heart, cruelty, carelessness of consequence, and a mind without regard for social duty. Of possible kinds of murder, the Act of Assembly provides as follows: 'Murder which shall be perpetrated by means of poison, or by lying in wait, or by any other kind of willful, deliberate and premeditated killing, or which shall be committed in the perpetration of, or in attempting to perpetrate, any arson, rape, robbery, burglary, or kidnapping, shall be deemed murder in the first degree; and all other kinds of murder shall be deemed murder in the second degree.' "

Judge Vredenburgh looked up from his desk. "You will notice that under this Act, murder in the first degree may be by poison or lying in wait. There is no evidence of such means in this case. Or it may be any willful, deliberate, premeditated killing. It may equally well be any and all killing, whether premeditated or not, done in the perpetration of those felonies named.

"In the kind of murder described as willful, deliberate and premeditated the intention to kill is the essence of the offense. Therefore, if an intention to kill exists, it is willful. If the circumstances evince a mind fully conscious of its own purpose, it is deliberate. If sufficient time is afforded for the mind to formulate a plan of action, it is premeditated. No particular period of time is fixed by law as sufficient. It may be very short. It must be long enough for the intent to form, for the means or instrument to be selected, and for the design to be carried into execution."

Bunting murmured to Abner, "Hope he doesn't get too highfalutin for them. Know what evince means?"

"And so do they," said Abner. Judge Vredenburgh's style, especially when he had worked on it, was better than the legal average. The Judge talked the way he looked—severe, somewhat curt, short with liars and people who wasted his time; his even-handed sense of justice sometimes overborne, or nearly overborne, by his well-known little crotchets; his sharp observation and good sense supplying him material from which he occasionally (he was no joking judge) struck out a flash of quick, rather grumpy, humor. Abner preferred Vredenburgh's charges to Judge Irwin's.

Just the same, the charge was to the jury, and Judge Irwin, whose habit was to ramble along, repeating himself, saying it the long way, impressed on the jury the things they should know. The circumlocutions gave his hearers

369

time to take in a point, mull over it a moment so that it left an impression; and then, without the worried feeling that they had meanwhile missed something, they found the next point before them. Judge Irwin, though talking all the time, contrived not to say anything until they were ready and waiting.

Judge Vredenburgh said, "All felonious homicides and intentional killings are presumed by the law to be murder in the second degree. This is a presumption apart from and not to be confused with the invariable presumption that all defendants are innocent. The Court instructs you so to presume, here as in every criminal case. The burden of proving guilt is and remains on the Commonwealth throughout the trial. In the case of murder, the Commonwealth must also prove that the murder amounts to more than murder in the second degree. For the purpose of so proving, the Commonwealth has offered testimony along two lines: first, that the killing was willful, deliberate, and premeditated on the part of the person or persons alleged to have shot Frederick Zollicoffer, which is to say also on the part of those who were present, knowingly helping, aiding and abetting the act. Second, that the felonious killing of Frederick Zollicoffer was perpetrated in the course of committing a kidnapping in which the defendants are alleged to have taken part. If the Commonwealth has established these contentions, or either of them, beyond your reasonable doubt, then these defendants, or either of them, would be guilty of murder in the first degree."

Judge Vredenburgh took a sip of water from the paper cup standing in a holder on his desk. He turned a sheet of his manuscript. In the courtroom there was a corresponding little stir and pause. At the defense's table Stanley Howell put his head toward Harry and made an anxious inquiry. Basso's head was bent, his eyes closed. He was either asleep or giving a good imitation of sleep. Behind them, Susie still stared, her mouth open a little.

Judge Vredenburgh drew a breath and leaned forward, his elbow on the desk, his chin on his hand. He said: "Most of you are probably familiar with the term; but the Court will now define reasonable doubt as it is understood in the law. Reasonable doubt is a doubt that arises out of the evidence or lack of evidence. It is such a doubt as would make a reasonable man in the conduct of his own affairs and in a matter of importance to him, pull up, hesitate, and seriously consider whether the thing he thinks of doing is right and wise. It must, however, be a real and substantial doubt; not, for instance, the idle reflection that nothing is perfectly certain in this life. It is a doubt that bases itself on serious gaps or loopholes in the evidence; that persists actively and positively. It is the doubt of a man who has heard and considered all the contentions of the prosecution, and yet who is not satisfied that the defendant must have done what he is charged with doing.

"If you feel such a doubt about the guilt of these defendants it is your duty to give them the benefit of your doubt and to acquit them, or that one of them that the doubt touches. If, on the other hand, you find no good ground for doubt, if what you have heard results in your abiding conviction of their guilt, it is equally your duty to convict both or either of them."

Judge Vredenburgh looked at the defense's table where Basso still sat with his head bent and eyes closed. Judge Vredenburgh compressed his lips; and George, watching him, moved an elbow, jogging Basso's arm. Basso's eyes came open and Judge Vredenburgh said, "Before referring to the testimony and your duties toward it, the Court deems it proper to instruct you on the status of the defendant, Robert Basso—"

Basso closed his eyes again and it was plain that Judge Vredenburgh observed his impudence. Judge Vredenburgh said, "When he was arraigned before us, Robert Basso elected to stand mute. That is, he refused to enter a plea. The prisoner's plea is the answer he makes to the clerk when the clerk after reading the bill of indictment to him in open court, asks him whether he pleads guilty or not guilty.

"In a capital case, where life is or may be at stake, the law is tender of the prisoner." Judge Vredenburgh paused; and Basso could not have been quite so indifferent as he seemed, for he must have felt the terrible silence and his eyes opened. Judge Vredenburgh said, "If he does not know his rights, the law will inform him of them and sustain him in them. If the prisoner cannot or will not safeguard his own interests, the law will safeguard them for him. It will not allow him, by any act that the Court can nullify or neutralize, to put himself, his rights, or his interests in jeopardy greater than the jeopardy that a man who pleads properly and is tried by God and his country submits to. Therefore we directed that a plea of not guilty be entered for Robert Basso. That became his plea; and it was, and it is, in no way prejudiced by his refusal to plead for himself. He has the benefit of the presumption that he is an innocent man. You may infer nothing from his refusal to plead, or his failure to testify; and in making up your minds about his guilt or innocence you will ignore everything but the actual evidence presented to you."

The color of repressed annoyance faded off Judge Vredenburgh's forehead. Glad to get back to an impersonal topic, he said, "We will now consider the testimony. First of all, I wish to point out that it is your duty to remember it. You will not accept—"

Abner, who could feel little interest in hearing that story all over again, looked at the jurors. He did not believe that Basso would get the benefit of being considered innocent. The habit of innocence, unjustly accused, is not to keep still. In its alarm and indignation, innocence cannot wait to answer. Silence showed a wish to conceal something, and no juror was going to suppose that the "something" was innocence. Even the law, trying to maintain that fiction was perhaps tender not so much of the prisoner as of the record that might go up on appeal.

Behind Abner, in the seats along the curving rail, there was a sound of smothered disturbance, and Abner, recovering the Judge's unattended last words, realized that they had been about Frederick Zollicoffer's body. Mrs. Zollicoffer, whose presence Abner had almost forgotten, sat beyond the center aisle next to Mrs. Meade in her tipstaff's jacket and frilled collar. She had begun to cry and Mrs. Meade bent toward her to see whether she was going to require attention. Next to her, on the other side, William Zollicoffer gave her an awkward, heavy-handed pat.

Judge Vredenburgh said, "We come now to the testimony of Roy Leming. Leming was an accomplice of these men, and the testimony of an accomplice is not looked on in law as evidence of a high type. He is, to an extent, an impeached witness by reason of his own participation in the crime; and anything he says should be received with caution. If you are satisfied that some or all of his statements are truthful, you should, of course, accept them, even if they are uncorroborated. However, we will particularize only statements of his that did receive corroboration."

Leming, sitting below Hugh Erskine, shifted with embarrassment; and Abner was obliged to smile. No doubt Leming was genuinely hurt to hear his honor aspersed; and you could learn from Leming's look of protest the farcical nature of the ideas a man could entertain about himself.

Judge Vredenburgh was saying, "—it was testified that Frederick Zollicoffer was made to sit on the floor of the car in back, his back against the left hand door, his face toward the right hand door—"

Harry Wurts lifted his eyes from the pad in front of him, held up his hand, and said, "That is twisted, your Honor."

Judge Vredenburgh said, "I would be glad to have you correct me."

"His back was against the right hand door and he faced the left hand door."

"That is right," said Judge Vredenburgh. "I recall now. Just the reverse of what we stated. The iron weights were in the car, and—"

Bunting said to Abner, "Remind me to speak to Washburn, will you?" He had been looking over his shoulder. Looking too, Abner saw that several members of the bar were sitting at the long table with Adelaide Maurer and Maynard Longstreet and two city reporters. Evan Washburn, slight and gray headed, saw Abner looking at him and nodded. He was a lawyer who did not often appear in court. Abner said, "Is he going to handle the lottery thing?"

"I think so. That's what I want to see him about. With this out of the way, we can get on with that."

Judge Vredenburgh lifted off his glasses and set them on the desk before him. He turned his chair a little, looking more directly at the jury, and said, "That is the testimony in general outline. If it is accepted as truthful, it would amount to proof of guilt, and of the grade or degree of guilt. According to statements made here in the stand, the defendants helped to kidnap Frederick Zollicoffer, they helped to keep him prisoner, they, together, took him out in the car and were there with him at the moment he was killed. If you believe the sum of these statements—that Frederick Zollicoffer was murdered by their fellow kidnapper, Bailey, while still in their power, then I say to you that you would be justified in returning, and the opinion of the Court is that you ought to return, a verdict of murder in the first degree."

Though it must long have been obvious to every listener that in applying the law to the facts this was bound to be the advice of the Court, the sound of it in words fell, too quiet to be the crack, like the hush of doom. The instant's silence was ended by a general light stir. Several members of the jury let their faces turn, looking at Basso's closed eyes

374

and at Howell who sat rigid gazing at the bench. Judge Irwin lifted a hand and began to pinch the skin beneath his chin. In the light of his lamp, Joe Jackman cocked his head, the last word transcribed, his stylo poised awaiting the next one.

Judge Vredenburgh said, "It is necessary for us to call your attention to the matter of Howell's confession. Against one of the defendants, Stanley Howell, the Commonwealth offers an alleged written confession. This confession states that Howell made and signed it of his own free will, and without force, coercion, or inducement being used to secure it. The defendant Howell admits that he signed this confession, but testified on the stand that it was not voluntary, but extorted from him by beating and abuse. Therefore you are posed with a query: was this confession free, as the Commonwealth's testimony maintained; or was it forced, as the defense claims? That the defendant may have been questioned closely and frequently—"

Looking straight across at them, Abner considered the faces of the jurors as, presumably, they attempted to form that opinion now required of them—Louis Blandy, Genevieve Shute, Old Man Daniels (and his friend, God). The truth was, it would never cross your mind to ask the opinion of any one of them on a matter of importance. Old Man Daniels was a plain fool. Blandy, since his bakery business was a going concern, must have practical sense; but would you ask his advice about anything, except perhaps how to adulterate breadstuffs to the nice point at which the product would be not so bad that nobody would buy, yet not so foolishly good that money was thrown away on it? Genevieve Shute had the face of a silly middle-aged woman, and one look was enough to warn you that, though a great talker, she had learned in forty odd years of life nothing about anything. Perry Vandermost, in the back row, was a house painter. All Abner knew about him was that he was not one of the "good" painters in Childerstown, the ones people who insisted on a first class job waited to get. Except by looking at the slips on Marty's card, Abner could not even be sure what the rest of the names were—there was a farmer or two; a younger woman; and one man, probably the fat one, had said he was a salesman—

Judge Vredenburgh's voice sank into silence, and rousing himself, Abner looked at him. The Judge pushed aside his manuscript, snapped out the reading light and leaned back, resting his hands flat on the desk. He said, "I will recapitulate. This is the application of the law. You have two theories to consider in reaching your conclusion about the possible guilt of the defendants. First, whether the killing of Frederick Zollicoffer was willful, deliberate, and premeditated. Second, whether the murder was committed in perpetration of the felony of kidnapping. If you find, on either one of these theories, that they are guilty, it is sufficient to convict them of murder in the first degree. We say to you that in the opinion of the Court, if you find these defendants or either of them guilty of murder in the first degree, then the death penalty would be the just and proper punishment. However, by the Act of Assembly, you will determine that point, and you are not bound by the opinion of the Court."

Looking down at the defense's table, Judge Vredenburgh said, "Before we take up points submitted for charge, do counsel wish any further instructions on any of the aforesaid matters?"

Harry Wurts said, "No, sir."

"Mr. District Attorney?"

"Nothing further, sir."

Judge Vredenburgh said, "The defendants have submitted several points for charge to the jury." He snapped on his reading light and leaned forward. "The first of which is refused; and therefore not read. The second"—he paused, pursing his lips—"is refused; and therefore not read. The third was fully covered in the general charge, and is therefore not read."

A copy of Harry's points lay on the table before him and Abner looked at them. The third was that Howell's confession was evidence only against Howell. The fourth was: "If the jury find from the evidence that Frederick Zollicoffer was not killed in the perpetration of a kidnapping, they cannot return a verdict of murder in the first degree." Most of the ten items were innocuous and could be dismissed as unnecessary; but Judge Vredenburgh was prepared to find one or two of them less innocuous than they looked, being in fact framed as artfully as possible with the hope of catching him in a moment's oversight or inattention so that he would refuse what technically must be affirmed and give Harry the lucky break of a reversible error.

Judge Vredenburgh said slowly, "The fourth point is refused and therefore not read. The fifth point is covered in the general charge and would be mere repetition. The sixth point"—Judge Vredenburgh smiled and looked at Harry, letting Harry see that he was not blind to dangerous ground; but he wanted Harry to wonder a moment—"is as follows," he continued. "If the jury believe that the defendants were unarmed at the time of the killing of Frederick Zollicoffer, and had such a fear of Bailey that they were unable to form a deliberate intent, the verdict cannot be first degree murder." He paused and added, "Affirmed as stated. But of course if the jury find that the defendants took part in the kidnapping, the Act of Assembly holds that deliberate intent in the killing does not have to be shown. Seventh point; refused as stated. Eighth and ninth points were fully covered in the general charge. Tenth point"—the corners of his mouth drew down—"is refused and therefore not read."

Looking at the carbon copy, Abner saw that the tenth point was: "Under all the evidence the verdict must be not guilty."

Judge Vredenburgh snapped out the light again. He said, "Members of the Jury, we will say a word more as to the form of your verdict. Your verdict in this case may be not guilty as to both defendants, or it may be not guilty as to one defendant. Your verdict may be guilty of murder in the first degree as to both defendants, or it may be guilty of murder in the first degree as to one defendant, and a different verdict as to the other defendant. Your verdict may be guilty of murder in the second degree as to both defendants, or as to one defendant, with a different verdict as to the other.

"In short, you will render for each defendant an independent verdict. Both may be the same; but you will, in arriving at them, consider them separately and independently. We have already told you that, in case either one or both verdicts is murder in the first degree, you are required also to fix the penalty, which may be either life imprisonment or death. If your verdict is murder in the second degree, the penalty will be imposed by the Court, and does not concern you.

"You will take this case, Members of the Jury, and give it your very careful consideration, all the consideration that the gravity of the crime merits, all the consideration that the length of the testimony requires. You will render your verdict unaffected by any bias or prejudice, or hatred or sympathy. Such feelings have no place in the deliberations and conclusions of a jury. We suggest to you that you look upon this task as a problem to be solved by a co-operative effort, to which each of you must devote his judgment and understanding; and not as a contest or debate in which sides may be taken and arguments advanced for the sake of arguing. It is a cold question of fact for you. You will render that verdict that your reason and your consciences approve."

He looked down at Mat Rhea and said, "Swear the officers."

Harry Wurts said, "If the Court please, and before the jury retires, and in their presence, I want to ask a general exception to your Honor's charge; also an exception to the defendants' points for charge that were refused; also that portion of your Honor's charge wherein you stated that the kidnapping enterprise did not end until the victim was returned."

Judge Vredenburgh said, "Exceptions allowed as requested. How about you, Mr. Stacey?"

"Yes, sir. The same, if the Court please."

"Allowed also for the defendant Robert Basso."

Malcolm Levering and Albert Unruh came up to the bar, their bald heads and blue jackets close together as they put their hands on the Bible Nick Dowdy held open for them.

Standing up, Mat Rhea said, "You do swear that you will well and truly keep this jury in some private and convenient place, until they have agreed upon their verdict; and that you will not suffer any person to speak to them, nor speak to them yourselves, without the leave of the Court, except it be to ask them if they have agreed on their verdict. So help you God."

Judge Vredenburgh and Judge Irwin arose on the bench. Nick Dowdy closed the Bible and taking up his mallet hit the block. "The Court of Oyer and Terminer and General Jail Delivery here in this day holden stands adjourned until eight o'clock P.M."

Bunting leaned back, clasping his hands behind his head and stretching. He looked at the clock and said, "Ten of six. You going home? I guess I will."

"Want me for anything?"

"No."

"How about Washburn? There he goes."

Bunting came to his feet. "O.K. See you later."

The aisle leading up to the main doors was filled with moving people. Abner saw Bonnie sitting in the shadowed top row beside Everitt Weitzel who was talking to her. He went over and stood with the group at the foot of the aisle waiting to go up. Just ahead of him was Adelaide Maurer looking at her folded sheets of copy paper. She smiled in a

379

worried way, waiting an instant so that Abner came beside her.

She said, "Ab, how long do you think it will take? I want to send my story in. When it gets late, they always find some reason to cut it, darn them!"

Abner said, "They oughtn't to be very long. I doubt if they have to argue much about these foreigners. You write out what you have, and we'll get the rest of it for you by nine o'clock. How's that?"

Adelaide said, "If you don't, I'll sue you."

She went ahead, and Abner, now almost the last in the long procession, reached the top bench. Everitt Weitzel had gone, and he sat down by Bonnie. "Want to go eat?" he said.

"Do you have to eat a lot?"

"Why?"

"Come down to the house and I'll fix you something. Jared's in some scout show, or I don't know what, and Mother has to go to it. She'll be back by eight, but she didn't want to leave the twins alone all that time."

"Why not?"

"Harold isn't feeling well. He was over at the Simpson's, and one of the kids bought a lot of cream puffs, or says he did—I think, as a matter of fact, they probably swiped them from Blandy's delivery truck. Harold must have had a good many and they made him pretty sick."

"Even one of those would make you pretty sick," Abner said. "Blandy's foreman of this jury. I guess he'd better go home and take care of his business."

"Aren't you through yet?"

"I wish we were. The jury just went out." He looked down at the well of the court, now almost empty. Bunting was talking to Evan Washburn over by the big table. Hugh Erskine came through the door from the back hall and made his way around the jury's empty chairs and started up the aisle. Reaching the top, he said, "Hello, Bonnie. What do

380

you want to hang around here for? I wouldn't, if they didn't pay me."

"Get them off your hands?" Abner said.

"And glad to! No fooling, Ab; every time, I'm glad to! I don't like that Basso boy. He's a mean one. I'll feel a lot better when they take those boys away. Look. Do you think I have to bring them back here until the jury comes in? I didn't get a chance to ask the Judge."

"I don't think so, Hugh. I don't see why. I don't think there's any reason for them to be present until the verdict is read."

"I didn't know, exactly."

Hugh's broad, good-natured smile went to Bonnie. "Trouble is, we don't have enough murders around here," he said to her. "Don't know the rules. Well, I'll get me some supper." He went on out the doors.

"Let's get us some," Abner said. "We'll have to go by my office and pick up the car. I left it in the garage down there this morning. You going over to school tonight?"

"The meeting's at half past eight; yes. I'm so worried about Mr. Rawle. He's so upset."

"I wouldn't worry about him," Abner said. "Jesse's got that pretty well under control."

"Well, Mr. Gearhart doesn't run the school board."

"That's what you think," said Abner.

At seven o'clock the low clouds broke over the western hills and showed behind them, far higher, and far off against the deep blue of fair weather, alto-cumulus patterns shadowed gray below, brightly white edged. Through gaps and chinks the broad sun streamed in splendor. Childerstown, washed and shining, was flooded with golden light. The wind fell and there was a great chatter of birds.

Sunlight came in the open door and poured across the

table in Cousin Mary's kitchen where Abner sat eating scrambled eggs and chicken livers. Looking at him across the shaft of sun, Bonnie said, "That's nice. It will be nice tomorrow."

"Who cares?" said Abner. "I'll be in court." He pushed his plate away. "No. I don't want any more."

"Well, you might say it was good."

"I never said you couldn't cook. You ought to make some man a wonderful wife. That reminds me—" He got up and went into the dining room where he had laid his coat on the table. Coming back, he stood behind her and said, "Do you know how to write?"

"You're certainly feeling flip," Bonnie said. She drank the rest of her coffee.

Looking down at her head, on which the slight disorder of the brown hair was lighted golden in the sun, Abner could see a tinge of color come up her cheeks. He said, "You know damn well what I've got here. 'We, the undersigned in accordance with the statements hereinafter contained, the facts set forth wherein we and each of us do solemnly swear are true and correct to the best of our knowledge and belief, do hereby make application to the Clerk of the Orphans Court'— I swiped it from Hermann's office this afternoon. He doesn't know I've got it. Now, here's what you do. Full name and surname—you know that. Color—what color are you, anyway? You look pink to me."

"Ab," she said, "I told you—"

"You picked the wrong person. In Marty's office we don't let you talk yourself out of something." Reaching down, he pushed aside the cup and plate, clearing a space on the table to spread out the printed form. Opening a fountain pen he put it in her hand. "Statement of Female. See?" he said. "Write your name. Janet. J-a-n—"

From upstairs a voice, plaintive, not urgent, screamed, "Bonnie!"

"All right, darling," Bonnie called.

"Darling, hell!" said Abner. "Let him wait. He just thinks it's time he had a little attention."

"Well, I know what that feels like," Bonnie said. She laid down the fountain pen and stood up.

"So do I," said Abner. "I think it's time I had a little attention. Sit down."

"No. I have to see what he wants."

"No. You have to see what I want."

"I know what you want. You want your own way. Well, you could have had it once. But not now. So why don't we just call it off?" She stood straight and tense, her hands raised and clasped together.

"Well," said Abner, "I can't make you do anything, of course—"

"That's where you're wrong," Bonnie said. "You could make me do anything. If you knew how. If you wanted to. I was a fool to tell you what I told you last night. I thought I could tell you—Inez or anyone would say I was crazy, that I ought to keep you guessing, that I ought to get someone else interested in me and try to make you jealous. If I could. Only I don't want you to be guessing. I don't want you to be jealous. If I had to do it by a lot of little tricks—"

"Well, what do you want?" Abner sat on the edge of the table. "Maybe we can get it for you."

"Don't sit there. You spilled honey all over that. I have to go upstairs now."

"No, you don't. Your patient's coming down. I can hear him. What is it you want?"

Bonnie turned. In the wide door of the dining room Harold appeared. He was clad in a faded pair of pajamas, half off his thin tanned body. His light hair was on end and his feet were bare. "Bonnie," he said.

"Darling, you must go right back to bed!"

"I'm hungry."

"You must be awful sick," Abner said. "That's a bad sign, being hungry. I guess you need some more castor oil."

Harold gave him an offended look and said, "Bonnie, can I have something to eat?"

"You can't have anything much, Harold. Do you want some milk toast?"

"All right."

"Then you go back to bed, and I'll bring it up to you. Now, hurry. Right upstairs!"

"Will you stay while I eat it?"

"If I have time. Mother will be home pretty soon."

"Where's Philip?"

"He's out playing. Upstairs now!"

Harold had been moving closer. He put out a hand and took hold of Bonnie's wrist, clinging to it. He said, "Why doesn't he have to come in?"; but it was plain that he was little interested in the answer. He wanted to touch her because of the comfort or pleasure it gave him.

"He will have to, in a moment," Bonnie said. Harold took her by the hips and pressed his forehead against her thigh. Bonnie laid her hand on his head a moment, and said, "Go on, dear; or there won't be time to bring you anything."

"All right." Reluctantly he let her go, turned and padded quickly through the dining room.

Abner said, "No. Let's not call it off. What is it you want?"

Bonnie crossed over to the ice box and took out a bottle of milk. She unhooked a sauce pan from the row hanging above the electric stove, snapped on a switch, and poured milk into the sauce pan. She said, "I guess I want somebody who will trust me—about everything. Mother made a mess of her life because of that."

"I don't see that much of it was her fault."

"No. She doesn't see that any of it was her fault. She was crazy about Wacker. I'm not going to live that kind of a life." She dropped a slice of bread into the electric toaster.

Abner said, "There have been lawyers who never absconded with any trust funds."

384

"I don't mean just that. I mean I'm not going to be any man's dear little woman and not worry about anything until he runs off with his stenographer. Get me a bowl out of there, will you?"

Abner took a bowl from the cabinet and put it on the table.

Bonnie said, "She had no business not to know. I mean, how could anyone married to a man not know that he was in trouble about money? How could she not know he didn't want her any more, and that there was this stenographer? How could she not know that he was the kind of person who would steal and then run? Mother could. It never crossed her mind. She never really knew a thing about him; and I suppose he didn't know much about her—except maybe that she was a fool who wanted a man."

That was a good description of Cousin Mary; and Bonnie would always have known it; but Abner doubted if she had ever said it before. He did not know how much anyone ever really learned about anyone else; but he was aware of a knowledge of Bonnie that let him be sure that she would be sorry she had said that. Abner said, "In my line of work you find out a good deal about how people happen to get into trouble. They don't look where they're going. It's like a man driving a car. If everyone kept his eyes on the road there wouldn't be any accidents; but nobody keeps his eyes on the road all the time. You still haven't told me what you want."

She said, "I want you to trust me."

"You'll have to say what you mean."

"Well, here's one thing. You argue about my job. I'm probably going to lose this one; but if we got married we'd have to take care of Mother. I'm sorry; but I'd have to; and what I have to do, we have to do. If we can get by without my working, then I won't work if you don't want me to. Give me that bowl."

"That isn't what you said last time."

"I didn't know I needed to say it." She took the bowl and

put a piece of toast in it. "Can't you see that I'd never, just because I wanted to, do what you didn't want me to? You'd only have to tell me. And everything you did want me to do, I'd do with all my heart." She took up the sauce pan, her hand shaking a little, and poured the scalding milk over the toast.

"We can get by," Abner said. "Do you mind living up at the house for a while—well, what I mean is, we might have to do it as long as Father lived."

"I wouldn't mind living with you anywhere, if—"

"No. Wait. Listen. I think there is a pretty good chance I'll be elected district attorney next November. It's a chance. We haven't lost an election in eighteen years; but that doesn't mean we couldn't lose this one. If we win it, I'll be pretty well fixed. Now, do we have to wait to find out whether I do or not?"

"We don't have to wait for anything."

"Well, then, sit down and fill the paper out. That's too hot for him to eat."

"All right."

She sat on the edge of the metal framed chair and picked the pen up. Abner stood leaning against the sink, looking at her. He found that he held an unlighted cigarette that he had sometime taken out. He drew a booklet of matches from his pocket. The fancy black script on the orange front said *Childerstown Inn.* On the back was a street plan showing where the inn stood in relation to the through routes.

Abner turned it over, taking in the inconsequential detail, which his mind, brought to a nervous pause, made use of as something to think about. He was, in fact, a little frightened by the irrevocable step he had now taken, and had now made Bonnie take. He did not doubt that it was a good step, and the right step; but just as when, in Jake Riordan's office, he had committed himself to Jesse, he was now obliged to wonder whether he was embarking on more than he had the abilities to manage. This was a large order, too. The commitments were not only similar, but linked to each other. He committed himself to Jesse, and so gained a free hand to commit himself here; and the two together must break up the pattern of life which he was used to and knew how to manage.

Living it, the life had seemed to Abner vaguely unsatisfactory; but when he put an end to it there were obvious good points to be remembered. For one simple and artless item, it never mattered when he got home; and though there was rarely or never anything to keep him out and the freedom was useless, he could feel himself being shut in; one after another the ways out closing. Until this afternoon he had also been free to say what he thought about Jesse; but he was not free any longer. As Marty said, he could not stand off and talk in his new position. If he did not like the way things were, he could no longer merely make a complaint; he himself was part of how things were; and he himself would have to work a plan out, implement it, and take the responsibility if it failed.

The sunset light shafted across the table and Bonnie moved the pen from blank space to blank space. Her clear script, wet and shining as the pen point traced it, was already dry on the first lines. Without looking up, she read aloud, "Is applicant an imbecile, epileptic, of unsound mind, or under guardianship as a person of unsound mind, or under the influence of any intoxicating liquor or narcotic drug—" She gave a short nervous laugh.

"Write, no," Abner said. He lit the cigarette. "You can sign it there, and on the second line above. I'll have Arlene notarize it tomorrow. And don't forget you'll have to go down to Doctor Mosher's."

"All right."

"You don't sound very sure," Abner said. He spoke awkwardly, aware in the absurdity of the moment that she felt no surer than he did.

She put the cap on the fountain pen. "I am," she said,

"but I—" She looked at him. "Well, I never did this before." She held the pen out politely.

Taking it, Abner balanced his cigarette on the edge of the drain board. With the hand thus freed, he caught her hand.

"Ab," she said, "do you really—"

"Yes," he said, "I really."

Tightening his grip on her hand, he drew her out of the chair. "It's not as bad as all that," he said. The taut, scared-to-death look on her face made him laugh, even as it filled him with compunction; and suddenly he remembered what he had forgotten—that if he suffered losses, he would have inestimable gains, the charms of her mind and body so joined that there was no distinguishing them. Both troubled his senses and both exalted his heart. Answering the re-pressed, the unformed, query that must all along have been in his mind, Abner thought: I would take any damn job. It seemed to him right that he should. He bent and kissed her.

"Ah, Ab," she said, "you won't be sorry, will you—"

From upstairs Harold yelled faintly, "Bonnie!"

"Oh, Lord!" she said, laughing. "Yes, darling! I'm coming!" She pushed Abner away and took the bowl of milk toast.

"Well, hurry up," said Abner, somewhat shaken. "I have to get to court. I'll drive you over to school."

"No," said Bonnie. "I'll have to stay until Mother comes. I don't need to be at school until half past eight. You go, will you. I'll have to tell Mother."

"Want some help?"

"No. I don't want you to be here."

Eight

O N THE quiet evening air the tolling of the bell broke
out from the courthouse tower. It was not quite
dusk. Abner could see gleams of light through the
Gothic windows of the main courtroom. Lights were on in
the Judge's chambers, and upstairs in the jury room. Abner
came under the arch of the passage to the jail. In the window
of the warden's sitting room Mrs. O'Hara held a red tin pot
with which she was watering, the spout thrust out between
the bars, young petunias in the window box. There was a
smell of fried onions from the kitchen; and Abner wondered
how much Howell and Basso had been able to eat.

At the rear door a man stood with his hand on the knob,
ready to enter. Hearing Abner's steps, he turned his head,
and Abner saw that it was Art Wenn. "Hello," he said.

Art said, "Greetings, Ab!" He held out his hand and
Abner took it. "Long time no see!" Art said. He was snub-
nosed and somewhat dish-faced. He beamed. "Well, sir!" he
said, "I hear I got to beat you this fall."

"Where did you hear that?"

"Why, Jesse told me. Had to see him about a little matter,
connection this school board trouble. We got to talking. I
told him I was going to run. He said you were entering
the primaries unopposed, so it looked like you and me." He
laughed uproariously. "Going in?" he said. "Thought I'd
like to hear the verdict. Commonwealth ask for death?"

Abner nodded.

"Going to get it?"

Abner said, "I don't see why not." He opened the door

and Art Wenn clapped him on the back to make him go first. "By the way," he said, "Pete Van Zant been around?"

"He was here this afternoon."

"What did he want?"

"He wanted to see Marty about something."

"Got to see him. Pete pulled a fast one on me. Let me tell you about it. There's this Mrs. Cooley, see, in Warwick; widow. She and her father, fellow named McGovern, make this promissory note, see, payable to Mrs. McGovern, see, his wife, Cooley woman's mother. All right, it's been discounted by the Farmers Bank and Trust, Warwick, and they pledge it as collateral security along with a lot of others on a Federal loan. All right. Before the maturity of the note, the co-maker, McGovern, dies, see? At maturity, the note was returned to the bank for presentation, collection, or renewal, and was protested for non-payment, see? Well—"

"Look, Art," Abner said, "tell me about it later, will you? Court's going to start in a minute and I have to see Marty."

Art Wenn, it was plain, was offended. "Well," he said, "didn't mean to bore you. It's a kind of interesting point. Pete's going pretty far, I can tell you. He's going to get into trouble one of these days—"

"You don't bore me," Abner said—that was a lie, all right! —"I'd like to hear about it when I have time."

"Sure, sure," Art said. "See you later."

Since he did not mean it, either, the parting was uneasy. Wenn pushed open the door of the Attorneys Room, letting out a burst of conversation. Everitt Weitzel came up the hall and said, "Ab, Marty's in the Judge's chambers. Want to go in there?"

"And suppose I don't want to?" said Abner, relieved.

"Then go anyway," Everitt said. He poked Abner with his finger. "Albert just came down. Spying on the jury."

"What's he say?"

"Says it's eleven to one for acquittal. No. The Judge had

390

him ask how long they'd be. Scared you." He limped on chuckling and went into the courtroom.

Abner went past the back stairs to the lighted glass sign over the door of the library. Opening the door, he found it blocked by Albert Unruh, about to leave. Albert stepped aside and said, "Mr. Blandy thinks they won't be so much longer, Judge."

Judge Vredenburgh, biting his pipe, nodded. From the easy chair in the corner Maynard Longstreet said, "Well, hurry them up, Albert. I have to get over to school in a couple of minutes. Tell them the Court says to get going."

"No," said Judge Irwin, smiling, "don't do that." He and Bunting were sitting together looking at the contents of a file folder on the table. He nodded to Abner. He said, "Judge Linus Coates, Abner's grandfather, was once reversed on that. Did you know that, Ab? The case you find cited is his. I ought to say that he was very rarely reversed; but he had something of a temper."

"Like Ab," Maynard said.

"No, I never saw any signs of it in Ab," Judge Irwin said seriously. "Oh, you meant that as a pleasantry. Yes; I think Ab has a very good disposition. Not that Linus didn't have a good one, as a rule; but in those days judges were often something of a law unto themselves. He sent word to a jury that had been out a long time on a matter that he thought quite simple, that if they did not bring in a verdict within an hour, they would be excluded from jury service thereafter and he would post their names. It was held, I'm afraid quite properly, to be coercion."

"Yes," Judge Vredenburgh said, "better get up there, Albert, and say nothing." He knocked his pipe out carefully in an ash tray. "Well, Ab," he said. He glanced around to see who was present. Besides Judge Irwin and Bunting and Maynard there was only Hugh Erskine who held a copy of the *Examiner* open to the sports page close up to his eyes.

Judge Vredenburgh went on, "I'm glad to hear you're

going to run. It's bad enough having a new sheriff without having a new district attorney, too. I think you and Marty and Horace and I had better fix some time soon to have a conference. Thought about an assistant?"

Abner said, "I'd like to have George Stacey."

"Well, I think you could do worse. He's all right, when he doesn't try to copy Harry Wurts. Harry's a good lawyer, and I like him; but there's a little too much—well, his speech to the jury. A little too smart. It must be eight o'clock. We'd better go in."

Abner said, "Albert happen to hear anything, sir?"

"About ready to convict, according to him. Of course, he's a little deaf, and the door's thick." Judge Vredenburgh smiled and got to his feet. "Coming in, Horace?"

"Yes, I will," Judge Irwin said. "All right, Marty. I think we can get that in Monday morning. Evan Washburn understands?"

"Yes, sir. It was his idea. I told him that the Commonwealth had no objection to hearing it without a jury. It seems to me fundamentally a matter of law."

"Yes," Judge Irwin said. "A lottery is a scheme for the distribution of prizes by chance. If the facts are admitted, then the only question is whether the facts do amount to such distribution. Thank you for bringing it to my attention. I'll have a chance to look it up tonight, I hope."

Abner said to Bunting, "Want to see me?"

"Yes. Just the list for tomorrow. We can do that while we're waiting."

Bunting sat back in his chair and rocked it slowly on its spring. "Quarter past nine," he said. "I guess Albert was wrong." He clasped his hands behind his head. "I don't know whether it's a good sign or not. Of course, some of them have to shoot their faces off. You couldn't stop old Daniels making a speech. It beats me, what they have to argue about."

Abner swung around in his own chair, looking at the electric lighted cavern of the court. The judges had left the bench. The four state policemen in uniform had gathered by the water-cooler, whispering and yawning. On the tiers of benches a number of spectators sat patiently—Abner glanced at them a moment, making a rough count by twos, and got eighty-four.

Bunting said, "The Judge is going to have cots brought in at ten o'clock and they can just stay, he says. We might get some action when they see those cots. They're some they had over at the armory, made of sticks and canvas."

Abner said, "Let's get out."

"Not the Attorneys Room. Harry's in there; and I don't feel in the mood for Harry. We'll go out front."

"I can get a typewriter in Mat's office. Might as well make some carbons of this." Abner took up the yellow pad on which they had been working out the order of cases for tomorrow.

They went up the aisle together to the swinging doors. Most of the spectators looked at them with discouragement at this fresh indication that nothing was going to happen. Abner saw Grandpa, his head hung, his mustache twitching, as he breathed through his mouth, asleep.

Under a green shaded light in the Clerk of Quarter Sessions' office Mat and Theodore Bosenbury were playing checkers. Mat said, "Marty, this is getting tiresome."

Abner said, "Here's something the clerk ought to do; but I guess I'll do it for him." He sat down before the typewriter in the corner. "Where do you keep the paper?"

"There," said Mat, absent-mindedly. "Bosey here is the damnedest old bastard. He's got me in that end game again. White to play—"

"Want to abandon?" said Bosenbury. "It's going to be a draw."

"Keep your pants on. I got to think."

There were steps on the marble pavement outside the door and Bunting said, "Thought you were at school."

Maynard Longstreet strode in. "To hell with them! It's over."

"What happened?" said Abner, dropping his hands from the typewriter keys.

"Vote of confidence for Rawle. Of all the crooked, stinking —confidence! What do they mean, confidence? You know what Holstrom said? Said the County Superintendent was not empowered to take action unless he saw definite cause for complaint! He ought to have his eyes examined!"

Bunting said, "Was it unanimous?"

"It was not. There's some decency left. Doc Mosher and Hobbs are going to forward a petition to the state board."

"Two of them," Bunting said. "Waste of postage."

Abner began to typewrite again. Mat Rhea said, "Maynard, let me ask you something. Why don't you work on your paper?"

"Ah, you jerks!" Maynard said. "Every damn one of you here is in the public trough. What do I expect?"

"You act like you expected some of the swill," Mat Rhea said. He hunched his round shoulders and turned his face up, grinning in the light of the shaded lamp. "Know what makes more noise than two pigs under a gate?"

"Every damn one of you is so busy sucking up to Jesse!"

"When we ought to be sucking up to you, I suppose," Mat said. "Damn if I don't believe you think you're a molder of public opinion! Why, you ought to get wise to yourself! Maynard, I never met anyone who gave two hoots what the *Examiner* said; and I don't believe you ever did, either. Why, the only reason anyone buys your paper is to see what the stores are advertising—well, no; some of them may buy it to see if you got in that Cousin Mamie visited them over Sunday."

"Ah!" said Maynard. "Heard anything from upstairs, Marty?"

"What's the trouble?" Mat said. "Trying to change the subject? Trying to suck up to the district attorney?'"

Bunting said, "We haven't heard yet. Wait a minute. Is that Everitt? He stepped to the door and looked into the hall. "Want me?" he said.

Everitt, limping up from the courtroom, stopped and said, "Yes, they do, Marty. Mat, too. Right away. The jury's coming down."

Mat Rhea said, "Well, halleluiah! Now, let it stand, Bosey. We aren't done yet. We'll come back afterward." He caught his coat up and pulled it on. "Out of my way!" he said. "Judge gets on the bench before I'm there, and I'll catch it. Clerk? Clerk? Where's the clerk?"

Abner typed the last words and drew the sheets from the machine. "Just the same," Maynard said to Bunting as they went into the hall, "letting that school business go, not doing anything at all about it, is an outrage." He turned his head, looking back at Abner morosely. "So they got you in it, too," he said. "Jesse said you'd represent Rawle, or whatever the hell, if they had a hearing. Did he ask you to?'"

Abner said, "He didn't ask me not to."

"I get it," Maynard said. "I didn't at first, but I do now."

Maynard's derisive, wise look did not make clear just what he got; but it was clear enough that, rummaging in his store of local information, Maynard had put together links for a chain of interest that bound Abner to Mr. Rawle, though on the face of it they hardly knew each other.

Perhaps Maynard remembered suddenly that Mr. Rawle's secretary was Janet Drummond, who was related to the Coateses, and furthermore was supposed to be Abner's girl. Perhaps, because he knew that Jesse was going to run Abner for district attorney, he figured that in exchange, Abner was naturally expected to help bolster up Rawle, and so maintain Jesse's influence on the School Board.

Maynard was right.

Those were the facts—Bonnie was his girl; Jesse was going

395

to run him for district attorney; so Abner could see that he stood convicted in advance of any implications those facts might have. It was not possible to be above the reasonable calumny of a suspicious man's suspicions; and dismayed for a moment, Abner remembered his father saying, "You know whether it's a bargain or not. You know what you take and what you give."

The point, driven unexpectedly home, checked his annoyance and eased his embarrassment. Abner saw that he really did not have to say anything. He said, "Do you?" and went into court.

From his seat Abner watched the hall door open and Albert Unruh dodder in. Albert stepped aside and the jury, a close-grouped walking throng, filled the gap. The moment was one that Abner had often sat through and always with an anxiety, great or small depending on how important the issue seemed to him, but uncontrollable. When, as tonight, the anxiety was great, he could feel it physically, a pressure on the nerves, a constriction of the stomach. Abner's reason might assure him that the jury's finding must be first degree murder; but since that was, after all, what he wanted it to be, he heard reason with distrust. Uncomfortably, with anxious distraction, he looked around him.

Dark all day, the night-bound court now appeared bright, filled with light. Through the round skylight the great lamps poured down a radiance like the daylight of overcast noon. This illusion of being outdoors made a man's height inconsiderable. People sitting and standing appeared to cast no shadows. On the bench and on Joe Jackman's desk the reading lamps burned brightly. The hundred or more watching faces, out of the direct light, sloped wanly up to the shadowed windows.

There were a few last movements.

Hugh Erskine nodded to Warren Lyall and Max Eich, left them, and crossed the carpet with quick heavy steps to his chair. Albert Unruh shut the door to the hall through which the jury had come. The state police officers took up their posts with a creak of belts and boots. At the defense's table Harry Wurts sat glum and tired. Abner observed with surprise that Harry's reddish hair was thinning on top. The pale downpour of light shone distinctly on Harry's scalp.

When everything was quiet, Judge Vredenburgh leaned forward, looking down at Joe Jackman, and said, "You may note that the defendants and their counsel are in court. You may take this verdict."

He sat back; and beside him, Judge Irwin hitched himself back, too, clasping and tightening his hands, composing his bare, bony face.

Under the bench Mat Rhea stood up. He had in his hand a board with a clamp to hold papers. He looked at it and said, "Stanley Howell."

Harry Wurts gave Howell a contemptuous jog with his elbow. Mat Rhea said, "Will you please rise?"

Howell came erect. He balanced himself by pressing the fingertips of one hand to the table top. With the other hand he clutched a fold of the cloth of his trousers and hung onto it. His narrow little mouth was pursed, his half-closed eyes blank.

Mat Rhea said, "Members of the Jury." He peered over at them where they stood together flanked by the blue jackets of Malcolm Levering and Albert Unruh. "This verdict will be as to Stanley Howell only." He cleared his throat. "Jurors, look upon the prisoner; prisoner, look upon the jurors."

Sedately, he stole a glance at the paper clamped on the board. "Members of the Jury, have you agreed upon your verdict in the issue joined between the Commonwealth and Stanley Howell"—he consulted the paper again—"on bill number nineteen, May Sessions, 1939; first count, murder?

397

How say you, do you find this defendant guilty or not guilty?"

Louis Blandy at the head of the group lifted a hand and scratched his neck. He felt the embarrassment of his conspicuous position. His eye, shifting, met Abner's; and he looked away, confused, probably feeling that all these lawyers and people were waiting for him to make some mistake; and feeling, too, that he was very likely to make one in pronouncing a rigamarole not familiar to him.

He said, "We, the jury, find—"

He stopped; for his mind, obsessed with the idea of forgetting, duly and naturally performed the act it thought he wanted. He was silent, struggling through an awful instant; then he broke out, more loudly than he intended, "We find the prisoners at the bar, find them both, guilty of murder in the second degree."

There was a dead silence.

Blandy had spoken so loud that nobody could have failed to hear him. Mysteriously emanated, the mental jarring or repercussion from the scores of separate brains, each hearing, each understanding, each reacting, could be felt like a stir of air across the electric lighted void of the court. Howell's stiff figure gave way and he sat down. The color jumped up Harry Wurts' cheeks; and Harry broke the silence, calling harshly, "I didn't hear that. You what?"

"Find them guilty, second degree," Blandy said.

Bunting pushed back his chair, bumping it against Abner's chair, and stood up. "Your Honor," he said, "if the jury has brought in one verdict for both—"

Judge Vredenburgh's face was congested. He said, "Mr. Blandy, didn't you hear what the clerk said to you?" He drew down his upper lip and held his mouth tight closed a moment. "This verdict is for Stanley Howell. You were instructed to bring in separate verdicts. Why didn't you?"

"Yes, sir," Blandy said, paralyzed. "We got separate verdicts here."

"Do not give them together, then! What is the verdict of the jury as to Stanley Howell?"

"Murder, second degree."

Recovering himself, Blandy put into his voice a note of truculence. To the wounding of his vanity, he had let himself get confused with everyone looking; to the worse wounding of it, he had quailed at Judge Vredenburgh's look and scathing tone. Now he felt his wounds. He never asked to be mixed up in any of this; and if they didn't want to hear what he had to say, they didn't have to ask him. His face grew sulky in lines of coarse and irritable impudence. If Judge Vredenburgh didn't like their verdict, why Judge Vredenburgh could take it and shove it—

Bunting, still on his feet, had turned red. He said, "Your Honor, I ask that the jury be polled."

"Oh, now, wait!" said Harry Wurts, up too. The gleam in his eye offended Abner; and probably it offended Judge Vredenburgh.

The Judge said sharply, "Quiet, please!"

He turned to Judge Irwin and whispered a moment. Looking around again, he said, "The Commonwealth's request is granted. The Court considers it an eminently suitable measure for the Commonwealth to take under these unusual circumstances. Are you objecting, Mr. Wurts?"

"No, sir," said Harry. "But I never happened to have heard of it being done before. It is not usual, certainly."

"The circumstances, I am very glad to say, are not usual. The purpose of polling the jury is to ascertain whether or not the announced verdict is in fact the verdict of each and every juror. The Commonwealth has no less right to this assurance than the defendant. The jury will be polled, Mr. Clerk!"

Mat Rhea fumbled with the papers on his board, transposing them. He said, "Members of the Jury, you may be seated—"

"No!" said Judge Vredenburgh. "Let them stand! As each

399

name is called, that juror will step to the front where we can see him; and in a clear, distinct tone, audible to the Court and counsel, he will answer the question of the clerk. Proceed!"

Mat Rhea coughed and said, "Louis K. Blandy, how say you, do you find the defendant guilty or not guilty?"

"That won't do," Judge Vredenburgh said. "Mr. Blandy, if you find the defendant guilty, you will say what degree of murder you find him guilty of. Let's have this in black and white."

"You want me to say it now?" Blandy asked.

Judge Vredenburgh tightened the corners of his mouth with a swelling of his face that plainly contained an explosion. Abner watched him with alarm, for that was Judge Vredenburgh's expression when his patience was ended, when someone, brought in perhaps on a bench warrant, ventured to mutter at the order of the Court. Judge Vredenburgh was as likely as not to snap, "Well, if you don't comply, the jail's always open!"

This time, however, he remained silent, eyeing Blandy, and Blandy wilted. "Yes," Judge Vredenburgh said then. "The clerk has put the question. You may answer it."

"We—I find him guilty. Murder in the second degree."

Mat Rhea looked sidelong to the bench. Judge Vredenburgh nodded; and Mat called out, "Genevieve Shute, how say you—"

Without waiting for him to finish, and in the voice of a woman glad to speak her mind, she said piercingly, "Murder! Second degree!"

Bunting turned and walked over to Joe Jackman's desk, stepped around behind Joe and Nick Dowdy. Mat, holding his board, made room for him; and Bunting put his elbows on the bar, looking up to speak to the judges. Harry Wurts at once arose, came down past Abner at the Commonwealth's table and went in beside Bunting.

"Samuel B. Daniels, how say you—"

In the rocking instant of surprise Abner had found no time to feel anything more than the shock itself. His eye noted what those around him did, their stunned looks, the mouths opening and closing, the changes of color and the incomplete gestures. With the mechanical progress of the poll, the law again in motion after its jolting stop, along familiar and monotonous ways, Abner had time for other feelings to take form and be recognized. He could recognize the artlessness of hurt indignation—for the jury had absolutely no right, or no moral right, to do that—and at the same time, the smart of ingenuous chagrin with which the angry mind confessed that Harry had the proper appeal, the appeal to vanity and sentimentality, and plain boneheadedness. The slick talker by his contemptible slickness had borne down Bunting's unadorned arguments.

Resenting this unfairness, Abner also felt for Marty, who was not used to being defeated—at least, not as district attorney, where the personal set-back, the loss of a case that he had worked hard on, was only a minor aggravation. Marty was ready enough to take a personal set-back philosophically, like a good sport; but he did not take liberal or sporting attitudes when a debt was owed the Commonwealth. He came here to collect it, and he would not regard the bilking of the Commonwealth by a fast talker and a foolish jury as the occasion to show how good a loser he was. Of course, anger would not mend the breach, so it was clearly better and more becoming not to show anger. This was reason; but Abner's own feelings rejected it. Reason or none, it was good to see men get angry at what they thought was wrong.

Abner regarded the pad in front of him on the table, yet in the corner of his eye he was able to observe George Stacey, and Howell, and Basso at the other table. Animation distorted Howell's face. In an ecstasy of small eloquent gestures, Howell ducked forward and pulled back, pointed his finger, chopped the air with his hand, felt his face, stuck his thumb up his nostril, all the while pouring out in furtive vehement whispers a recital made up, Abner judged, of promiscuous, spur-of-the-moment boasts, complaints, self-congratulations and frenzied plans. George Stacey, looking away toward Bunting and Harry at the bar, sat with a strained smile on his lips, now and then nodding uncomfortably.

Basso's dark face showed no change at all. He looked as sullen as ever, and as contemptuous as ever of the whole proceeding. To go to death without batting an eye is a little more than most men can do; but very little more, since it only needs overweening pride, which everyone comes close to having. Abner assumed that Basso had it; but now he was not sure. It took more than bravery and more than pride to support the good fortune that Basso was now impassively supporting; and so the answer probably was that Basso was neither brave nor proud; he was merely a mental case.

Behind the defense's table, in the line of chairs between Hugh Erskine, serious and reserved, holding his full chin, and Warren Lyall, studying his hands and moving his head with slow disgusted or incredulous shakes, ranged the faces of the other parties to the crime and their counsel. Leming sat as though he had been pole-axed, his eyes glassy, his face loose, while he took in the ironic monstrous trick just played on the law's obliging servant. Leming would have the expert knowledge of penalties that is part of every convict's education. For second degree murder, Howell and Basso would get twenty years, all the Judge could give them. He, Leming, the Commonwealth's trusting friend, would have life imprisonment to reward him for his co-operation in pleading guilty. Susie Smalley seemed to have had a similar thought. Over by Mrs. O'Hara, she was hugging herself, her haggard face turned to look down the line at Leming, rapt with hate and triumph. Between Servadei and John Clark, both smiling, Dewey Smith sat pop-eyed like the moron he was.

Bunting took his seat beside Abner, and Abner said, "What's the Judge going to do?"

"What can he do?" asked Bunting irritably. "Harry's

moving for a new trial as a matter of form. He'll withdraw
the motion in a few days and move for sentence. He wants
some time to think it over; but, my God, he's satisfied! I've
got to hand it to him!"

He looked bitter, and Abner said, "I guess we did all we
could."

"Maybe," Bunting said. He took a pencil and began to
draw a dog on his pad with sharp careless strokes. He did
not look up as Mat Rhea, who had been speaking to the
Judge, faced the courtroom again and said, "Robert Basso,
will you please rise."

Basso moved negligently, shifting his remote, contemptuous gaze, and got to his feet.

Abner was embarrassed for the law, which had to insist
on acting out its charade although everyone already knew the
answers. With a start of surprise he turned to look at everyone—those hundred or less spectators, those bitter-enders;
the sovereign people, the critics of the sad show, all unnoticed
until now.

They still sat there, face after face in scattered pale series
across the curving slopes. The demanding watchers watched
and watched, and in time their patience had been repaid;
and what did they make of it? By way of answer, Abner
could see them stirring, leaning toward each other, asking
each other. They had their grand scene, the drama they came
impertinently to enjoy, the big moment to wow those boobs;
and it was all one to them. Something had happened—but
what? Something was happening—but what?

"Jurors," Mat Rhea said sourly, "look upon the prisoner;
prisoner, look upon the jurors. Members of the Jury, have
you agreed upon your verdict in the issue joined—"

Still working at his dog, Bunting said, "It makes you sore.
They haven't any sense." He tipped his head to the side and
said, "Servadei there goes back now and says it's all right,
the juries up here won't convict. They'll find out!"

Abner did not know what to say. The threat was essentially

a child's threat, declaring to those who crossed him that someday they'd be sorry. It was not a prophecy; it was a wish. As for Servadei, he would need to be a much stupider man than he looked to report any such thing to the prominent shysters in partnership with him. He had seen a willful jury find against law and fact, perhaps helped by Wurts (a good man to keep in touch with), but willful juries were not the kind he and his firm wanted. They would not care to expose all the smart and careful work they put into making a guilty man look innocent to the caprice of a lot of stubborn yokels who could not be counted on to play the game according to the rules. Since Marty knew this at least as well as Abner did, the only meaning of his remark was that, as he said, he was sore. If he meant that criminals, once this good news got around, would pour across the county line to commit their felonies with impunity, he was talking nonsense. All crimes by professional criminals were committed with the presupposition that they could be committed with impunity. Since the criminals were confident that they were not going to be caught, the last thing they worried about was how it would go with them when they were put on trial.

It occurred to Abner that though he could not now, and perhaps never could, match Marty's skill and experience; and though he might not have as much actual intelligence as Marty, he had a temperament better suited to meet difficulties like this. The thought came to him that if he had been district attorney in this case, he would not have summed up in such a take-it-or-leave-it way; and he could easily have brought himself to stoop to Harry's level. He did not claim that he would be as good at it as Harry; but he might have been better for the purpose than Marty; and it was just possible that that would have made all the difference.

He said, "I think the Judge ought to say something to them."

Bunting said, "Irwin's going to. A hot lot of good that will do now!"

404

Mat Rhea said, "Your Honor, the jury has been called individually. They are in agreement. Shall the verdict be recorded?"

Judge Vredenburgh nodded shortly, not looking at him. "It may be so recorded."

Harry Wurts stood up and said, "Now, if the Court please, I desire to make an oral motion for a new trial, also an oral motion for an arrest of judgment; and I ask leave to file reasons in support within ten days."

Judge Vredenburgh nodded, his face grumpily turned down. "And for Mr. Stacey, too, I suppose. The motions may be recorded. You may file formal written motions within —four days is enough. Is that all?"

"Yes, sir."

Judge Vredenburgh closed a book he had been looking at on his desk and took off his glasses. He said, "Before Court adjourns, the President Judge has something to say to the jurors. Everyone will remain where he is."

Judge Irwin moved forward to the edge of his chair and set an elbow on his desk. Clenching his thin, long-fingered hand, he rested his chin a moment on the knuckles, looking down at the jurors. He moistened his lips, and said, "Members of the Jury, you may take your seats in the box. I will be as brief as possible—" He checked himself, remembering his purpose. Unclasping his hand, he plucked his chin several times while the jurors distributed themselves.

When they were quiet, he said again, "Members of the Jury, you anticipate, no doubt, the—ah, tenor of the remarks I now find it incumbent on me to make to you. At the conclusion of a case in which much testimony has been heard and on which a number of days have been spent, the Court often thanks the jurors for their services. In this case I do not feel that it would be appropriate to express such thanks to you; for, frankly, we do not feel that you have properly done the duty for which you were summoned; and, incidentally, for which the county is obliged to pay you."

405

Judge Irwin paused, plucked his chin again, and gave them a distressed look. He said, "The allegation that I am making is a very serious one. I will express it in as mild a way as possible, not because it isn't serious, but because I do not, I cannot bring myself to, believe that you acted with any conscious or deliberate intention to violate your solemn oaths. It may show you how serious the matter is, however, if I say to you that, had I actual grounds for such a belief, I would see no alternative but to constitute myself, as I have the authority vested in me to do, a committing magistrate, and to direct the sheriff to arrest you; and you would be held for the grand jury. I will ask you to remember that."

Judge Irwin was silent while his shy but penetrating gaze moved over their faces. Bunting murmured, "Affirmed as stated." The impossibility of ever proving such intention was something the jury was not likely to know about. For all they did know, the Judge was telling them that in another minute they would go to jail, and they looked at each other with consternation, prepared to believe it.

"However," Judge Irwin said, and he allowed a light, wintry smile to appear on his lips, "in the absence of such proof, the Court has no right to assume that you acted otherwise than in good faith, and it does not so assume. What we must assume, then, is that you do not understand your position and your responsibilities. It is too late, as far as the present case is concerned, to remedy that. The defendants in this case may not be prosecuted further for their offense, for when they were put on trial before a jury sworn they were in jeopardy, and the constitution both of this state and of the United States forbids the courts to put any person in jeopardy twice for the same offense. Moreover, on a charge of murder, a conviction in the second degree works acquittal in the first degree."

Judge Irwin hunched himself up a little more and put both elbows on the desk. His characteristic thin-lipped and nervous but singularly sweet smile appeared an instant on his lips again, as though to show that he had now finished with the scolding he had been obliged to give them and could go on to a pleasanter matter, which was the theory of the law. He said, "I will not go into the history and what could be called the philosophy of the general and acknowledged principle, ad questionem juris non respondent juratores—part of an old maxim; which is to say, the jury does not find on questions of law. Both in this country, and long ago in England where our law comes from, it has been fully discussed and argued by many learned jurists and wise men. The reason that argument persists and discussion continues is not because the principle is in doubt. The facts are for the jury; the law is for the judge. That is the principle. But in practice, the law and the facts do not always constitute separate and distinct things.

"Furthermore, we always say to you when we instruct you in the law, that *if* the facts are so and so, this is the law that applies. Now, if you do not find those facts, you have no grounds for applying that law. We are not allowed to give you a binding instruction; that is, to say that you *must* find a defendant guilty; because we on the bench are not judge of the facts. Not being entitled to decide on what are the facts, we cannot presume to say what you will find. Because of this, there undoubtedly exists a power in you, the jury, to override any law as declared by the Court, and to make your action effective by an acquittal; which, in criminal cases, we, the Court, cannot by any means set aside. That is what you have just done—of course, you did convict the defendants of second degree murder; but, as I said to you previously, that is equivalent to acquitting them of first degree murder. Is that clear to you all?"

Several of the jurors nodded their heads intelligently. Watching them, Abner could see that any resentment they might have felt was gone. Some of them probably found the large words and bookish phrases hard to follow and would have trouble telling anyone what it was the Judge had said;

but they responded to the tone, to the careful anxious look. They melted with simple ingenuousness at the sight and sound of a good man.

Judge Irwin said, "Now, in the present case, the case just past, I ought to say—Judge Vredenburgh explained to you very carefully and clearly what the law was. If these defendants took part in a kidnapping, and if their victim was killed before he came to be released, they were guilty of first degree murder. As jurors, you were not bound to follow his instructions unless they applied to what you found to be the facts. You had a right to find, if that was what the evidence meant to you, that neither of these men took part in any kidnapping. If that was what you found, then the law Judge Vredenburgh told you of would not apply. How could it, if these were not the kidnappers?"

He smiled painfully, as if he waited for an answer. Then he shook his head. "To find that they were not the kidnappers you would have to doubt the evidence of numerous witnesses, even including one of the defendants himself. It is not impossible that you should do this; but I wish to ask you, I wish you to ask yourselves, whether this was what you did, whether you felt a reasonable doubt that Howell and—er— Basso took part in the kidnapping of Frederick Zollicoffer."

Judge Irwin shook his head again. He looked at them with something like compassion. He said, "If you did, well and good; you have done rightly, and nothing I have said can have in it any reproach for any of you. If you did not—well, Members of the Jury, I think if you did not, you have something on your minds and consciences to give you pause. I hope you will reflect on it soberly and searchingly. You were sworn to give a true verdict according to the evidence. I do not see how a verdict can be true if it says that a certain crime described to you by law so that you know exactly what it is, has not been committed, when the evidence never at any time by anyone contradicted, shows that it must have been committed."

Judge Irwin smiled again faintly. "So, Members of the Jury," he said, "you are once more judges of the fact. We must leave the case with you. We hope you will well and truly try it. That will be all. You are discharged. You may present your slips—not, I think, tonight; it is rather late— any time tomorrow, or on following days during office hours to the office of the clerk of Quarter Sessions."

He nodded, looked at Judge Vredenburgh, who looked at Nick Dowdy. Nick hoisted himself up and struck his block. He said, "All persons take notice that the Court now stands adjourned until tomorrow, Friday, morning at ten o'clock, A.M."

Everitt Weitzel stooped and set a metal stop to hold open the door of the Attorneys Room. "Air it out some," he said to Abner, who was accompanying him. He lifted a hand to the side of his mouth, winked, and said, "Needs it bad!" Then he remembered that Abner might not be feeling like a joke and said, "That was awful tough luck! Those men never should have got off like that." He bobbed his head, and went on, "Those are the gentlemen there, wanted to see Marty."

They stood together with their hats on in that bored yet inquisitive stance of young newspaper men still secretly excited by their own romantic picture of themselves, and so making an effort to pretend that the power that they had to admit people to print was really nothing much, and the knowledge of inside stories just a matter of course.

Everitt said, "This is Mr. Coates, the assistant district attorney."

They turned their blank, sagacious faces politely, stepping aside from the press of people. One of them mentioned the names of both their papers. Their manner became more off-hand, showing that this was old stuff to them, and that they supposed that it was old stuff to Abner, who, being from the district attorney's office, might very likely equal them in first hand knowledge of what everything, at least locally, was all about.

Abner said, "Mr. Bunting will be busy for a while." In fact, Marty had walked over to speak to Frederick Zollicoffer's widow and her brother-in-law; and Abner had been glad of a chance to separate himself from that painful little circle. "I think he'll see you if you want to wait."

One of them said, "Don't want to bother him—"

The other said, "What we wondered is; any chance of seeing the prisoners a minute—"

Abner said, "Better ask Mr. Wurts about that."

Harry, with a group of people around him, was lounging on the leather couch across the room. John Clark, sitting beside him, had just given him a cigar; and through a break in the crowd Abner could see Harry's flushed face, the eyes intent a moment on the cigar tip as he brought a match to it. Harry removed the cigar, and laughed out loud in the puff of smoke. Mr. Clark's large, pale, reserved features displayed the smile of a man who has seen forty years of court and law and still finds much to amuse him, but mildly.

The newspaper man said, "We meant the other fellow, Mr. Coates, the Leming fellow—"

"And maybe Smalley—" his companion said.

Abner said, "I think their attorneys could fix it up for you. I don't think Mr. Bunting would feel that he ought to arrange it."

"Who's that? Servadei?"

"Yes."

"I know him." The sagacious look deepened to a contemptuous knowingness. "He's a lulu! What's the girl's lawyer's name?"

"Clark. Over there on the sofa."

"The D.A. won't mind if we try, will he?"

"I don't think so," Abner said.

"Well, much obliged, Mr. Coates," one of them said.

"Glad to meet you." The other said, "Oh, by the way, Mr. Coates, there isn't another telephone we could use anywhere around here, is there?"

Abner looked over to the telephone on the wall by the lavatory door. Maynard Longstreet, the receiver to one ear, his knuckle jammed in the other, his lips against the mouthpiece, was obviously dictating with difficulty to a rewrite man on one of the city papers for which he was the correspondent. "One in a booth out in the main hall," Abner said.

"Thanks a lot!"

Someone had come up behind him and Abner, turning, found that it was Kinsolving, the Federal Bureau of Investigation agent. His weighty calm was undisturbed. "Well, Mr. Coates," he said, "those are the breaks! They fooled me."

"They fooled us, too," Abner said. "I didn't think they had a chance."

Kinsolving tapped him on the arm with two blunt fingers, opened his mouth, and then shut it, looking past Abner. Looking too, Abner saw that George Stacey had drawn near. "Well, Counselor," Kinsolving said to George, "I want to congratulate you. It isn't everybody who could have got those clients of yours off."

George blushed under Kinsolving's amiable stare; but he said, fairly coolly, "Well, Officer, if you insist on beating the boys up, what can you expect?"

Kinsolving chuckled. "Stick to your guns, eh, Counselor? Well, if you want my opinion, that yarn of Howell's wasn't ever at issue. I was just going to say to Mr. Coates here. Best line you and Mr. Wurts had was: Are you people going to burn a man who maybe didn't actually take a gun and shoot anybody? That would be my guess, Counselor. They don't think it out, sometimes. You heard what the Judge, the other Judge, said to the jury. Well, I must get along. If you'll tell Mr. Bunting, Mr. Coates, that I'll ring him up tomorrow, or ring his office up. I think the Bureau may have a little additional stuff you could use on Leming. Good night." He nodded and went out the hall door.

Looking after him, George said, "I know damn well what they did to Howell. That was no joke about his kidneys. They gave him a real going-over."

A hand struck Abner on the back. Art Wenn said, "Too bad, Ab. Too bad!" The effect of his concave profile, the jutting chin below, the bulbous forehead above, was to give his tucked-in smile a secret quality of half-concealed satisfaction. He might not go so far as to be glad that the Commonwealth lost its case; but since Abner had told him that they expected to win, it probably caused him no pain to find that Abner was wrong.

However, Art immediately laughed, bringing the hidden smile out in the open, so it was plain that there was not much malice in him. "George," he said, "looks like we need new blood in law enforcement around here!" He laughed uproariously. From his pocket he drew a pack of oblong cards and held one up. On it was a slightly blurred cut of his own head and shoulders with the words: *"For District Attorney, ART WENN,"* in large letters; and in small letters: "YOUR VOTE AND SUPPORT RESPECTFULLY SOLICITED." "That's the answer," he said. "Here, take some!" The joke of pressing his campaign cards on two men who, it was perfectly certain, wouldn't vote for him made him laugh until the tears came into his eyes.

The group about Harry and John Clark on the sofa was breaking up. Attracted by Art Wenn's noise, several of those leaving stopped. Joe Jackman, who had been busy over his brief case on the window ledge packing up his transcript, said, "Hello, Wenn. What's so funny?"

Art said, "Ab and Stacey here are getting up a Wenn for District Attorney club— Say, Pete!" he said to Van Zant, who was at the door, "got to see you! Say, I just had those papers from the bank! Say—"

"Come on," Van Zant said, "I can't wait."

They went into the hall, and Joe Jackman said, "How'd you like to vote for that? They must be crazy to nominate him!"

Coming up now was Hermann Mapes. "Tough luck, Ab," he said. As clerk of the Orphans Court, Hermann was naturally a good party man, and would have none of Wenn's political reasons to enjoy Bunting's defeat; but Abner guessed that Hermann, too, found something not entirely displeasing in it. There is always a little satisfaction in seeing the professionally just, reformers and clergymen, judges and prosecutors and police officers, set back. Hermann's long inquisitive nose twitched with this satisfaction. He gave Abner a covert glance to see how Abner was taking it, ready to enjoy Abner's embarrassment if he showed any.

Joe Jackman said, "It's tough on Ab and Marty; but I have to say I didn't mind. Won't have to do it up now. That would have printed to eight hundred pages."

Mr. Servadei, who had been talking to Harry and John Clark, stopped, holding his straw hat, and said, "Excuse me, Mr. Coates. My understanding with the district attorney is that Leming's plea is Monday. I'm planning to be here. If that doesn't come out convenient, you have only to let me know. I could arrange to make it almost any other day. Would you mind telling Mr. Bunting?"

The others had fallen silent, looking away from Mr. Servadei with a speculative, essentially hostile, reserve that he was probably used to. Perhaps the small-town impudence of stares at the back, the small-town naïveté of mixing contempt with uncontrollable curiosity, amused Mr. Servadei. He had found some way to answer in his own mind the charge, silently made by such behavior, that he was a dirty little shyster. Perhaps he let himself think, when he saw unspoken disdain, of his money in the bank, of big men in the city glad to be his friends, of cases he had won by his superior brains; and so, perhaps, he could feel almost genial toward these self-righteous rustics with their couple-of-thousand-dollar incomes, their pettifogging over the deeds and debts of farmers and shopkeepers, their half-learned law soon half-forgotten. They could not despise him without showing it; and that was the measure of their capacity. Mr. Servadei could despise them, and did, and never gave them a sign of it; and that was the measure, he might think, of his capacity.

Malcolm Levering, who had taken off his tipstaff's jacket and put his coat and hat on, looked in the hall door. "Ab," he said, "telephone. In the library. Guess this line is busy."

"Thanks!" Abner said. He said to Mr. Servadei, "Mr. Bunting will let you know if any change is necessary."

Mr. Servadei bowed and went out.

Going after him, Abner went past the stairs and the barred passage to the jail. The door under the lighted glass sign was ajar. The telephone lay off its cradle on the desk. Taking it up, he said, "Yes?"

"Ab." It was Bonnie.

"Hello," Abner said. "What did Cousin Mary say?"

"Did you really wonder?" Bonnie said. "Darling, how did it come out?"

"How did what—oh! Not so good. As a matter of fact, it was second degree."

"You lost?"

"Well, we didn't win. The jury wasn't having any."

"Oh. I'm sorry you lost. Do you mind my calling?"

"No, of course not. I wish we'd got it; but—"

"I know you do, darling—where are you? They switched me over to something."

"In the library."

"Who's there?"

"No one."

"Do you love me?"

"Yes," Abner said, "I—"

"All right, my dear. Good night."

Most of the people in the Attorneys Room had left. Maynard Longstreet, all this time talking, now hung up, put his hat on the back of his head, and walked over past the empty fireplace. "Well, jerks," he said, "get enough justice for one day?"

Bunting, who was coming in from the courtroom, said, "And enough journalism, too, professor." Mr. Clark arose from the couch and said, "Where have you been, Marty? Make me wait around here all night! About that guilty plea for Susie. No. We'll stand trial."

"See?" said Maynard. "Once they think they can get away with something! The jury lets them off. The school board lets them off. I hope you stew in it! So long."

"Suits us," Bunting said to Mr. Clark. "We've got you down for Tuesday. I wouldn't count on another break, if I were you."

"I stopped counting on anything with a jury in it thirty-five years ago, son," Mr. Clark said. "Go thou and do likewise."

From the sofa, Harry Wurts said, "What you don't grasp, Marty, is the issue."

Bunting said, "You made your speech."

"Now, I'm going to make another; and you'd better listen, wise guy! I don't say we didn't have luck—"

"You don't, huh?"

"I don't. But the point is, a couple of men's lives are at stake; and you feel bad because you couldn't kill them! Why don't you use your imagination? My God, if you had to kill some kittens you'd probably take them over to the vet! But two of your fellowmen—"

Bunting said, "I never heard of kittens kidnapping a man and murdering him."

The hall door opened, and Judge Vredenburgh walked in. "Still hanging around?" he said. "Annette was coming down for me, but she hasn't showed up."

"Give you a lift, sir?" said Abner.

"No, thanks. I'll wait a few minutes longer." He sat on

the edge of the table and took out his pipe. "Harry," he said, "do you think those men ought to get off?"

Harry said, "When I take a case, sir, my client's cause is my cause. If he thinks he ought to get off, I think he ought to get off. Let the jury adjudicate! Moreover, in a capital case, where life is or may be at stake, the law is tender of the prisoner."

Judge Vredenburgh, recognizing the quotation from his charge, drew his mouth down in acknowledgment of the joke. Harry said, "And so am I, Judge; so am I."

"I just want to know," Judge Vredenburgh said, "whether you honestly think those men ought to get off. Never mind the legal aspects. Just tell me."

"Yes, sir," said Harry, "I do. I don't approve of capital punishment, myself; and any time it can be circumvented by due process of law, I am glad to help circumvent it."

"By due process of law," Judge Vredenburgh said. He smiled his tight, drawn-down smile. "A judicious interpolation! I am glad to know about that."

"I don't think you're quite fair, Judge."

"No, that wasn't quite fair," Judge Vredenburgh said. "We're not speaking for the record now, so I don't mind saying that the action of the jury disgusted me. Now, will you feel hurt if I credit you with taking some part in bringing that action about?"

Harry said, "I'm sorry it disgusted you, sir; but, yes, I would be glad to take the credit if I deserve it." He paused. "Since this is all off the record, I wonder if I might ask you why you think—when, under what circumstances, you think the death penalty ought to be imposed?"

Abner, who after all knew Harry much better than the Judge did, could tell in an instant that Harry was serious, that the question was meant respectfully; but Judge Vredenburgh looked hard at Harry for a moment. Casually, he glanced then at Abner and Bunting and George Stacey. They were more or less Harry's contemporaries and so spoke his language. The Judge was looking to see what they understood Harry to intend. Apparently satisfied, Judge Vredenburgh took out a match and relit his pipe.

"Since I've been on the bench," he said, shaking out the match, "I've had only two cases in which I was obliged to sentence men to death. You remember them, Marty. That Negro, Upson, who killed the woman he was living with because he thought she was putting a spell on him—invultuation, it was called. She made an image and stuck pins in it. We all had to take a course in the theory and practice of witchcraft; then, that Lumpkin boy. They were both some time ago. I've thought about both of them a good deal. You remember about Lumpkin, Marty?"

"Yes, sir," said Bunting. "The issue there was what constituted lying in wait. Waiting, watching, and secrecy must concur. We had a little trouble showing it."

"Well, it was upheld," Judge Vredenburgh said. "I don't know whether you others remember it particularly or not. Ab, you and Harry must have been at college."

"Where were you, George?" Harry said, "in kindergarten?"

Judge Vredenburgh said, "This Lumpkin boy, in Warwick, killed a girl of eighteen who was a waitress in the station restaurant. Her name was Gladys something—"

"Edwards," Bunting said.

"Yes, Edwards. Lumpkin stopped in one evening and asked her to go to the movies with him when she got off. They'd been going together for some time. She refused, because she said she had another date. Her other date was this Krause—a married man; ran the Union Hotel. He was no good at all. The girl used to work for him at the hotel, and he got her into trouble there, but I guess he bought her out of it. Lumpkin knew all about that. He was a good boy, perhaps not too bright; but bright enough to run this garage. It had been his father's, but his father died, and he'd been running it several years, making money, supporting his mother and some brothers. Another thing, and an important one, I think; he had a bad leg. He wasn't really a cripple, but he'd had infantile paralysis. He wasn't much on looks either. Most girls might not think he was a bargain; but this Gladys didn't have a very wide choice, either."

"I don't think he was much of a bargain," Bunting said.

"Perhaps not," Judge Vredenburgh said. "Well, he was angry when she wouldn't go with him. He went to the theater that night—do you remember just how that was, Marty?"

"He went to see who she was there with; and when they put the lights on at the intermission, he saw them—Krause was pawing her over in the back row. They didn't see him. So he went out."

"Yes," said Judge Vredenburgh, "he left. He went by his garage and picked up a little twenty-two caliber revolver he had there, and then went over to the house where she boarded and waited for her, sitting on the porch. I think he thought Krause would be coming home with her. However, as it happened, she came home alone. There was a reason for that."

"What?" said Harry.

Bunting said, "It was testified that she was having her menstrual period."

"Quite right," said Judge Vredenburgh, "there are no secrets from the law. Well, when she found him sitting on the porch, she told him to get out, that she was in love with Krause and didn't want to see any more of him. He got up and pulled out the revolver and shot her twice in the neck. She died a couple of days later."

"Yes," said Bunting, "but you left out one important thing, sir. There were these two fellows, a fellow working for him and a friend of his, at the garage when he stopped to get the gun; and he told them he was going to go over and wait until Gladys came home and kill her. They thought he was kidding."

"If they hadn't had reason to think so, why wouldn't they

either have tried to stop him, or notified the police?" Judge Vredenburgh asked. "I think the truth is he *was* kidding, at least in the sense that he'd made similar wild threats before; and these boys who knew him well knew he never meant them. It's not uncommon in a person with a physical handicap, particularly if he's not a highly intelligent type."

Bunting said, "The event didn't seem to prove that he was kidding."

"It didn't seem to," Judge Vredenburgh said. "The evidence was certainly against him. His actions certainly seemed to constitute laying in wait, and that meant first degree murder. Pete Van Zant was defending him, you remember; and while he did his best, I'm not sure—well, I'm not sure that Pete made his client's cause quite as much his own cause as you say you do, Harry. Lumpkin didn't show up well on the stand, and the jury didn't like his looks. They brought in first degree murder with the death penalty. There were no grounds for a new trial. I had to sentence him, and so I did. The appeal was denied and he was executed."

Judge Vredenburgh tried his pipe. It had gone out, so he emptied it, knocking it gently against the ash tray. "That boy never should have been executed," he said. "I don't mean that it could be called a real miscarriage of justice. He was guilty of killing the girl, all right. There was no possible question of his being put to death for something he hadn't done. But I don't think he did it with design and premeditation. I think he got the gun with the idea of threatening Krause with it—he was a little fellow and Krause was about as big a man as I ever saw. I think the things she said drove him to a kind of frenzy, and without any premeditation whatsoever, he shot her. I don't know how far Marty can accept that, but it's my firm belief."

Bunting said, "I can believe that if she had been nice to him, nothing would have happened. Sure, he was upset; but I don't think it ever has been held that a man can't act deliberately, with design and premeditation, just because he was

419

probably resentful at the time. He really may not act deliberately; maybe he really is temporarily insane; but he isn't entitled to that assumption. The Commonwealth never has to prove that the defendant is sane."

"Wrong," said Harry Wurts.

"What do you mean, wrong? Insanity must be proven by the defendant by a fair preponderance."

"Watch that word 'never.' It snaps back and hits you in the eye. If the defendant in a murder case pleads guilty, it is always on the Commonwealth to show that the defendant was sane at the time of committing the crime. Am I right, sir?"

The corners of Judge Vredenburgh's mouth drew down, his eyes glinting an instant at Bunting. "I would have to look it up if I were to rule," he said, "but for the present purpose, I would say undoubtedly. The burden of proving all essential elements would be on the Commonwealth."

Bunting said, "Well, it certainly couldn't happen often."

"All right," said Harry, "all right. If you're now trying to prove that when you say 'never,' you mean 'not often,' you've proved it. And when you're licked, why can't you just admit it? You're interrupting his Honor."

"No, he's not," Judge Vredenburgh said. "That was all I was going to say. I'm not satisfied that Lumpkin was guilty of first degree murder. I think degrees of murder are made to meet exactly such cases. If the law had left me free, I would have given him twenty years. And in the Upson case, the Negro, I would have done the same. That black man was killing in what he thought was self-defense. Neither of them was vicious; one was foolish and emotional; the other was simple and superstitious. Putting them to death was not the answer."

Harry said, "I just wonder whether it's ever the answer." It occurred to Abner that Harry, like Leming, like Howell, like (according to the testimony) the murderer, Bailey, and no doubt like everyone, had a great hankering for the approval of the just. When they thought that men or circumstances impugned them, they all hastened to show their high ethical considerations, whether in betraying their friends, or killing that destroyer of souls, Frederick Zollicoffer, or cajoling a jury. Ought Harry to be blamed for loving mercy? "Yes," said Harry, "but have we a moral right to—"

"Ah! Don't ask me that! Harry, when I sit in this court, the Sixth Commandment is no part of my cognizance, whatever you may feel inclined to tell a jury. My power to hear and decide comes from the Assembly. My authority for sentencing a man to death is the act made and provided." He smiled sharply. "It has been held that death is not cruel in the meaning of cruel and unusual in the Constitution. That is the end of it as far as my official action is concerned. About my personal feeling, I've tried to answer. I can't discuss the present case. On your motion, it's still sub judice. I'd have to rule on your written submissions, if you ever make them. But I may say—"

There was a tap on the door and it opened enough to show Annette, on tiptoe, her head to one side, an expression of mock or humorous awe on her face. Made pretty by a liveliness Abner had never noticed in her before, Annette went through a pantomime, pointing at her father's back, at herself, and then, presumably, home. Her eyes were on Harry in silent, smiling appeal. Harry's answering smile was so genial that Abner stared at him. While an idea new to Abner, it was not by any means an impossible one.

Judge Vredenburgh said, "Yes, yes, I know you're there. Finally! I've been waiting half an hour."

Annette said, "Mother wanted me to take some things to the Ormsbees'. Well, I'm here now, aren't I?"

"All right, my dear. No; you mustn't come in. This is a kind of male preserve—"

"Oh, goodness!" Annette said. She gave them a general dazzling smile and closed the door.

"Well, gentlemen," Judge Vredenburgh said. He put his

pipe away. "Now, I won't have to say what I may say." He yawned. "Well, it's over; and I'm glad of it. Good night."

"Good night, sir," they said together.

The door closed after him, and Bunting said, "Let's go."

They went in silence through the dark courtroom, and up the aisle to the lights of the hall. Their footsteps sounded suddenly loud, echoing on the marble paving. They came out the front door onto the steps, facing, through the trees, the bright moon, just past full.

George Stacey said, "Don't they lock this place up?"

"Mat and Ted Bosenbury are still playing checkers in there," Bunting said. He stood on the top step, looking at the moon and the fountain of three entwined dolphins soughing up water to patter in the little bowl.

"How sweet the moonlight sleeps on yonder bank!" Harry Wurts said. "Childerstown Bank and Trust Company, in fact; Member of the Federal Reserve System. Well, gents, thanks for a wonderful time."

Bending his face to a spurt of match light, Harry relit the cigar Mr. Clark had given him. "Pleasant dreams!" He walked down the steps and strolled away, flourishing the cigar, his linen clad figure growing dimmer in the dusk of moonlight and street light under the big trees. His voice floated lazily back, singing: "Adieu, adieu, kind friends, adieu; yes, adieu . . ."

Bunting said, "Maybe he feels better now about that friend of yours in New York."

They stood silent a moment. George Stacey said then, "You want to see me tomorrow, Ab?"

"Yes," said Abner. "As a matter of fact, what I wanted to talk to you about was whether you'd be interested in being my assistant, if I were elected district attorney in the fall. You'll want to think it over. I don't have to know right away. If you would, I'd like to have you. We'll leave it at that."

George said, "I certainly will think it over." Even in the moonlight his face was warm and radiant. "Only, gosh, Ab;

to be frank with you, I don't know whether I have enough experience. I mean, whether I'd be any use to you—"

"Well, you think about it," Abner said. He was unexpectedly made aware of the pleasure of patronage. It was, he saw, a fairly pure pleasure. If it made him feel good to be able to give what was plainly so much wanted, the good feeling was at least in part the good feeling of being able to adjust the fallings-out of a too impersonal and regardless chance so that the deserving got some of their deserts. It would be a pleasure that Jesse Gearhart had felt often; the one real pleasure, when all was said and done, of power.

"Thanks, I will," said George. "Well, good night. Good night, Marty." He went down the steps and walked rapidly up Court Street.

Bunting said, looking at the moon, "He's a nice kid. Going home?"

"Yes," said Abner.

"See you in the morning. Better come down to the office." Bunting continued to stand still. "Don't take it to heart, Ab. We'll see what we can do with the rest of them."

"I think we did what we could."

Bunting said, "And don't worry about next fall. I know how it feels. You wonder. You'll be O.K., Ab. You have plenty of what it takes—more than I have. Good night."

"Good night," Abner said.

Abner drove his car into the old stables. The cement floor on which he halted had been laid down more than twenty years ago when Judge Coates decided—an unusual step at the time—to keep two cars. To make room, some disused horse stalls were ripped out, and it was discovered then that the old floor was rotten. When the new cement floor was finished and the workmen gone for the day, Abner put his initials in the still-soft surface with a stick; and for good measure, impressed his bare footprints beside them; and for still better measure, impressed also the bare footprints of Caesar, an Airedale dog they then had.

Time had not obliterated those marks. By the glare of the headlights against the back wall, Abner could still see them, just to the left of the door of what had been the harness room. He remembered all that perfectly; taking off the sneaker he wore; and the cement cool and moist against the sole of his foot; and Caesar, years dead and forgotten, alive and struggling in consternation as Abner pressed down his paw. The exact object, if Abner had any beyond showing interest in a material that could be soft today, yet hard as stone tomorrow, was not clear—perhaps just this; that some day, years after, he might notice the marks and think with satisfaction that he had made them. Snapping off the headlights, Abner got out. He noticed and thought, just as the boy perhaps planned.

Closing the doors, he stood a moment in the broad moonlight looking at the big dark mound of the house. These things, he thought, remained—only for a while, of course; but longer, at any rate, than a man did. His grandfather built the house, and for him it had been new and desirable; a showplace, with its great ornamented bargeboards, its cavernous arched verandas and round shingled tower, in the Childerstown of dirt streets and gas lights in the 'eighties. The Judge, the Old Judge, would not have been surprised— what sentient man could be?—to find that the new became old; and the desirable, undesirable; and the house, once so fine-looking, grotesque. As an exercise in reason this was not hard; but how hard to grasp it, to know that the real today, the seen and felt today, and everything around you, and you, yourself as you stood thinking, would dissolve and pale to a figment of mind, existing, like the future you tried to think of, only in thought!

While Abner stood, the old courthouse clock struck twelve (his grandfather would have noticed that the new courthouse

424

clock carried clearly out here). The faint deep bongs rose over the tree tops and the sleeping hill. Surprised to find that it was so late, Abner walked down the brick path.

Under the moonlit roof of the kitchen wing, in the shadow of the shining slates, a voice said suddenly, "Who's that?"

Starting, Abner looked up. In the window of the bedroom where Lucius and Honey slept, the shape of a head a little darker than the darkness, and the shoulders of a dull white pajama coat, showed. Abner said, "All right, Lucius. Who do you think it is?"

"Mr. Abner? I hear that car. Then, nobody comes down. It might be burglars."

"It's all right. Sorry if I woke you up."

"You didn't wake me, Mr. Abner. I keep an eye on things around here. Judge laid up and you out, somebody's got to. You finish that trial?"

"Yes."

"I guess it's curtains for those gangsters?"

"They'll get twenty years in jail, I think."

There was a silence.

"They not going to electrocute them? They kill that man, and they not going to electrocute them?"

"The jury didn't seem to think they did kill him," Abner said.

"Oh!" said Lucius. "Well, I surely thought it was the chair for them! Well, I guess I'll tell Honey. She thought it was."

"All right," Abner said. "Good night."

"Good night."

There was no light in the lower hall, but a dim glow fell on the head of the stairs, showing that the door of his father's room was open. Abner turned the night latch, found the first step with a practiced foot, and went up quickly and steadily on tiptoe. He was expecting his father to call; but when no call came, he stepped faster, with a tremor of alarm, and stood in the bedroom door. His father rested propped up on pillows, his eyes closed, the paralyzed side of his big face hanging with forlorn helplessness. He breathed roughly, but calm and even; and Abner saw that he was only asleep.

Judge Coates stirred. His face worked a moment; his eyes opened. He brought up his good hand and laid the back of it against his paralyzed cheek, as though to cover while he brought it under what control he could, a spectacle that he knew was distressing. "Well, son," he said with difficulty. "Must have drowsed off! Late?"

"Just struck twelve, sir."

"Jury trouble?"

"And plenty of it," Abner said. "Do you want to go to sleep?"

"No, I don't! Sit down! Sit down!" His voice gained clearness as the muscles limbered. "Tell me about it. Verdict in? Smoke a cigarette." He got one from between the piled books on the table. "Sit down," he said. "Light it myself when I get ready."

"Second degree murder," Abner said, sitting down. "Judge Irwin read the jury a lecture."

"Against the evidence?"

"As square as anything could be. Vredenburgh was fit to be tied."

"Harry make a good speech?"

"That's about the size of it," Abner said. "And plain contrariness. I think Marty may have taken it a little too much for granted—"

Abner broke off. The criticism had been just and judicious when he first formulated it to himself, sitting in chagrin at the Commonwealth's table. There was no disloyalty in the silent recognition of a mistake when Marty made one; and no complacency in noting, warned by the mistake, logical ways to avoid it. When he let himself voice the criticism to someone else, there was a little of both: disloyalty in criticizing when his only object must be the trifling but infamous one of trying to dissociate himself from the failure of an enterprise in which he had shared; complacency, for when he pointed out a mistake, he left it plain that it was not one he himself would have committed. "I mean," he said, "Marty had the case cold. There couldn't be two answers to the facts. He more or less left it at that. Kinsolving, an F.B.I. witness we had, who may be a liar but he is certainly no fool, told me afterward that he thought the jury was jibbing at executing two men for something they argued a third man had really done."

Judge Coates said, "A jury has its uses. That's one of them. It's like a—" he paused. "It's like a cylinder head gasket. Between two things that don't give any, you have to have something that does give a little, something to seal the law to the facts. There isn't any known way to legislate with an allowance for right feeling."

"Well, Vredenburgh told Harry this Court wasn't enforcing the Sixth Commandment."

"From the bench?"

"Oh, no. Afterward, in the Attorneys Room. I guess he thought the jury had given a little more than it needed to. He said he was disgusted with it."

"He won't feel that way tomorrow. Tom's got better sense than that. In his time, he's had trouble with his temper."

"What was that?"

"It was long ago," Judge Coates said. "When he was district attorney, he used to go off the handle now and then. He got over it. It isn't a matter of any interest now. Juries didn't always find what he thought they ought to in those days, either. Justice is an inexact science. As a matter of fact, a judge is so greatly in a jury's debt, he shouldn't begrudge them the little things they help themselves to."

"I don't follow," Abner said.

"The ancient conflict between liberty and authority. The jury protects the Court. It's a question how long any system of courts could last in a free country if judges found the verdicts. It doesn't matter how wise and experienced the

427

judges may be. Resentment would build up every time the findings didn't go with current notions or prejudices. Pretty soon half the community would want to lynch the judge. There's no focal point with a jury; the jury is the public itself. That's why a jury can say when a judge couldn't, 'I don't care what the law is, that isn't right and I won't do it.' It's the greatest prerogative of free men. They have to have a way of saying that and making it stand. They may be wrong, they may refuse to do the things they ought to do; but freedom just to be wise and good isn't any freedom. We pay a price for lay participation in the law; but it's a necessary expense."

"You mean," said Abner, "that in order to show he's free, a man shouldn't obey the laws."

"A free man always has been and always will be the one to decide what he'd better do," Judge Coates said. "Entrapment is perfectly legal. The law lets you arrange an opportunity for a suspected thief to steal so that you can catch him. I don't think right feeling can ever stoop to it. Compounding a felony is an indictable offense; but a man feels, just the same, that he has a right to forgive those who injure him, and no talk about his duty to society will change that feeling. In a case of larceny, it may be no defense in law that the party from whom the goods were stolen, himself stole them; but the feeling of the average man does in part defend it by saying it served him right to lose what didn't belong to him. It is held that drunkenness does not aggravate a common law offense any more than it excuses it."

He shook his head. "Depending on the circumstances, it may do either. Most people would feel that committing perjury drunk was not so bad as committing it cold sober; while committing an involuntary manslaughter drunk would be worse than committing it sober. Well, I'm rambling on. I don't know what makes old men like to talk so much. Maybe they're just talking to themselves, trying to find out what they think. I saw the *Examiner* about the Field thing. That's another case mixed up with what people feel. Judging by Maynard's editorial, I don't know that it makes for justice."

"What it made for," Abner said, "was the Board giving Rawle a vote of confidence tonight. Maynard was pretty sore about it."

Judge Coates reached over and took a cigarette lighter from the table. By pressing the top, he made a flame snap up and lit the cigarette.

"Where did you get that?" Abner said.

"Present. Matter of fact, if I have to smoke, I ought to use matches. I was getting pretty handy with them. Mosher is enthusiastic about these wretched little accomplishments. Yes. Cousin Mary gave it to me. She came in this morning."

"What did she want?"

"That's right; she did," Judge Coates said. "She'd heard about the school board business, and she was worried about what was going to happen to Bonnie. I think she thought I might be able to take a hand in it. Of course, there was nothing I could do."

"So you told her not to worry; if Rawle was kicked out and Bonnie lost her job, you'd get her another."

"In substance, yes. When Cousin Mary worries, it shakes the house. You have to stop that at any cost. She has a hard time, really."

"Well," said Abner, "I don't know whether it will make it any easier; but her daughter and I are getting married. Bonnie gave me some supper down there; and we thought we would. I suppose I ought to ask if you mind if we live here awhile."

"When are you going to get married?"

"Some time this month, probably. There are so many forms and certificates and things, you can't say when." He paused "Don't you like the idea? Last night you were saying I was so damn phlegmatic I hadn't sense enough to get married."

"That was an unfortunate choice of words," Judge Coates

said. "I didn't realize you were going to take it so hard. Yes.
I like the idea." His face contorted a little, and Abner was
stunned to see tears appear in the corner of his eyes. "Are
you all right, sir?" he said, starting up.

"Sit down!" said Judge Coates. He plucked at a pile of
tissues on the table until he got hold of one. He daubed at
his eyes. "You can't tell what I mean by what I do," he said
hoarsely. "It would be a favor to me if you wouldn't give
things I can't help quite so much attention. Damnation, I'm
a sick man!" He dropped the crumpled tissue.

"Well, I didn't mean to upset you," Abner said in distress.

"Phlegmatic wasn't the word; it was obtuse," Judge Coates
said. "What did I say that for? I don't mean it. You'd think
I wanted to make you mad. I don't want to make anyone
mad. I'm not fit to stand up to it. You least of all—"

He brought the cigarette up shakily, cocked it between
his lips, and took a puff. "There, that's over," he said. "It
just hit me a certain way. If I had to explain it I would
only make it sillier. Foolish question, do I mind if you live
here. I might ask you, do you mind if you live here. I'll
have another stroke and die pretty soon; or if I don't, I'll
be a driveling idiot. Don't know whether you want to be in
the same house with it. I wouldn't."

Abner said, "I don't think that follows at all. Jesse Gearhart told me his father had a stroke and practically got
over it."

"Well," said Judge Coates, "that's true; Mike did. I
suppose I might. Just don't want to be such a fool as to
count on it. When did Jesse tell you about his father?"

"The other day."

"Oh. I wondered." He crushed out the cigarette awkwardly. "You're probably well out of that. I never liked
politics myself. I don't mean I thought I was too good for
it. Or if I did, it was when I was very young. Men act
through self-interest; and if they do things you wouldn't
do, you'd better not assume it's because you have a nobler

character. There are noble and disinterested actions done every day; but I think most of them are impulsive. I don't think there's any such thing as a deliberate noble action. Deliberation always has half an eye on how it will look; it wants something, if only admiration, for what it does. Did you ever see a law suit which aimed at disinterested justice?" He took another tissue and wiped his mouth. "Senator Perkins used to say that when a man said he was seeking justice, what he meant, if he was plaintiff, was that he aimed to do someone dirt and the Court ought to help him; and if he was the defendant, that he already had done someone dirt, and the Court ought to protect him."

"That's about it, I guess," Abner said. "I had to get in those Blessington will papers this morning. It's certainly doing the Blessington sisters dirt. Well, I got them in. Intelligent self-interest. I guess what I thought to myself was that I couldn't afford to turn down any business. I don't know."

Judge Coates said heavily, "Woe unto you also, ye lawyers! For ye lade men with burdens grievous to be borne, and ye yourselves touch not the burdens with one of your fingers. Yes. We're vulnerable. A lawyer can't very well do to others as he would be done by. Not in the line of business. I don't know whether you're asking my advice. It's the same conflict we were speaking of before—well, I was speaking of before. You don't get much chance to speak, do you?" He worked himself up a little higher on his pillows.

"Here's your Blessington situation. It's provided by law, primarily by statute, that one of a man's rights which the courts shall protect him in, is the disposal of his property after his death according to his intentions expressed in an attested will. It is a very important right. It is part and parcel of human freedom and dignity. Just as the jury must be free to find against the evidence, we have to hold that a man must be free, if he has the legal capacity to make a will, to make an unequal, unjust, and unreasonable will.

431

"True, we can't let him make it against public policy. Expediency will set bounds to his freedom. You cannot define exactly and forever what the right bounds of expediency may be; but you can say what they must not be. The intention to realize is not the intention of the Court, nor the intention of Abner Coates, Counselor at Law. In ethics and morals their intentions may be demonstrably better and wiser and fairer than the testator's intention. You've been saying, in effect, that you'd like to devise a better and juster disposal of Blessington's goods. You have no right to do it. The Court has no more right. The point for you is not whether you personally think the will just and good, but whether you can dispassionately and disinterestedly submit to the Court reasons in law and equity that bear out what you feel to be the testator's intention to leave the money to the clients you represent."

Judge Coates coughed, holding up his good hand so that Abner would not interrupt him. "Sorry," he said, gasping. "Now, if you don't feel and believe that such was the testator's intention, you should have nothing to do with it. In your case, I think it is obvious that the testator's intention, or his contingent intention, was that Enoch's college should get the money. If that was his intention, and if it is not an illegal intention, it ought to be realized. Granted that Blessington intended an injustice (and remember, that is an opinion; you and most other people may hold it, but it remains an opinion), would you say to me that the law ought to betray its great first principle and pay off one injustice (a matter of opinion) with another injustice (a matter of indisputable fact)? I think not."

"I think not, too," Abner said. "It isn't what the law should do; it's what I should do." He repressed a yawn. The long day had tired him, not physically in a way to make him sleepy, but in the protracted drain of nervous energy. He could not seem to whip his mind up to the heavy labor of manipulating abstractions. He said, "I'd like to do what was right. Who wouldn't? Maybe that's only one of those deliberate noble actions you don't think much of. It has something to do with how things look, what people think of me." He paused. "Jesse told me your Senator Perkins said you wouldn't worry so much about what people were thinking of you if you remembered that most of the time they weren't. I'm not so good on come-backs. It took me until now to see what was wrong with that."

In spite of himself, Abner did yawn. "What's he mean? Does he mean that most of the time there's nobody looking, so you can do what you want? I don't give a damn whether anybody is looking or not. I'm looking. I care whether I look like a louse. Certainly I care what people think of me. They may only do it for ten seconds once in ten years, but I still care."

Judge Coates said, "Well, we all have our pride. It does a good deal to make us fit for human company. But I don't know how far the world at large, or Jesse in particular, is in duty bound to minister to yours. You made your decision. Don't go on arguing it over."

"Well," said Abner, "today I guess I unmade it. Jesse asked me again, and I told him I'd run."

"You did?" Judge Coates said. "Why did you do that?"

"Because it was what I really wanted to do," Abner said somewhat defiantly. "At least, I suppose that's why."

"Well, that's a good enough reason," Judge Coates said. "Why do you think it isn't?"

"I don't know that I do think it isn't," Abner said. His mind in desperation refused him its services. "I'd like to think there was more to it than just my own advantage. I wish I weren't so sure of that part of it. If it cost me something instead of paying me something—"

"It seems to me it costs you a good deal," Judge Coates said. "For the last few weeks you've been running yourself ragged on this case, this Howell-Basso thing. What do you

433

get out of it? It puts you on edge, all right; I can tell you that."

"I get my salary out of it," Abner said. "Why shouldn't I run myself ragged? It's my job."

"Then just go on doing it, and don't worry. You take care of your job and other things will take care of themselves."

"I don't remember that things ever did. Things don't look as if they would. You can see them cooking up another war for us in Europe; and when they do, I guess all bets are off."

"Don't be cynical," Judge Coates said. "A cynic is just a man who found out when he was about ten that there wasn't any Santa Claus, and he's still upset. Yes, there'll be more war; and soon, I don't doubt. There always has been. There'll be deaths and disappointments and failures. When they come, you meet them. Nobody promises you a good time or an easy time. I don't know who it was who said when we think of the past we regret and when we think of the future we fear. And with reason. But no bets are off. There is the present to think of, and as long as you live there always will be. In the present, every day is a miracle. The world gets up in the morning and is fed and goes to work, and in the evening it comes home and is fed again and perhaps has a little amusement and goes to sleep. To make that possible, so much has to be done by so many people that, on the face of it, it is impossible. Well, every day we do it; and every day, come hell, come high water, we're going to have to go on doing it as well as we can."

"So it seems," said Abner.

"Yes, so it seems," said Judge Coates, "and so it is, and so it will be! And that's where you come in. That's all we want of you."

Abner said, "What do you want of me?"

"We just want you to do the impossible," Judge Coates said.

434

Printed in the United States
54622LVS00003B/37-39